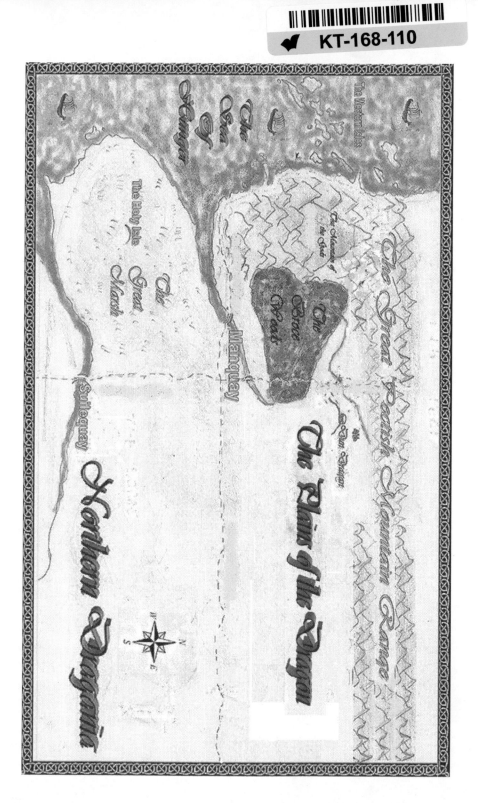

Author's Note

Firstly, a note of caution …

This book was read to my children at bedtimes, nevertheless, this book was not written as a children's story, so please be forewarned. I have noticed strange afflictions in my children since their first exposure to this book. There has been an increased tendency to surliness and a lack of enthusiasm for mornings, as well as bouts of acne and an inability to communicate in more than one syllable. Seeking medical assistance I was assured that, with luck, these symptoms may fade after puberty. I was advised that they could be common during adolescence. I'm not so sure.

The good news is that no animals were harmed in the making of this book … at least, none that I can recall.

*****

And then … a little useful information.

The people and places mentioned in this book are purely fictional, but some influence may be accredited to historical events, folk lore and the legends on which I grew up. These images of the past have always inspired me. The power struggle and social upheaval caused by the invaders in this story could easily have been the Romans in Celtic Britain, or the Danes of Brian Boru's Ireland.

I have used some Gaelic words, such as *'Fear Ban'* and *'An Fiacail Dragan'*, to help distinguish the use of the 'Old Tongue,' of the Pectish Clans, who once reigned over Dragania. I hope that this adds to the texture of the story. I have also used italics to differentiate the use of the 'Old Tongue', as well as for telepathy and 'Dream-catching'.

Maerlin's Storm

The Storm-Bringer Saga: Book One.

By Author: Nav Logan

*****

Published by Nav Logan.

*****

Original Copyright 2003 Nav Logan

Reformatted and re-edited January 2014

*****

ISBN eBook Version: 978-0-9928521-0-8

ISBN Paperback Version: 978-0-9928521-1-5

*****

Learn more on

https://www.facebook.com/StormbringerSaga?ref=hl

Website: - http:navlogan.com

*****

Cover Artwork by Clarissa Yeo Book Cover Art:
http://yocladesigns.com/

*****

Editing and proofreading by: Storywork Editing Services.

www.storywork.co.uk.

*****

Map Illustration by: Nav Logan.

*****

Prologue

They thought I was mad. You could see it in their eyes. They were polite about it, of course, but you could see it just the same. I was a young lecturer then and new to the job. I still had the hunger of youth. I had been sitting in the warm snug of a country pub; sampling the local ales and listening to the villagers spin dark tales of haunting. I smiled politely and took no heed of their well-meant warnings. I had come to this isolated backwater to investigate the ruins of the nearby temple, and not to listen to tall tales.

I was new to the superstitious nature of country folk. I was fresh out of Manquay College, where ideas were wrestled with daily and beaten into submission. The ink of my doctorate was hardly dry on the paper, but there were still so many unanswered questions, and I was convinced that the answers would be found here, at Auldsmead, or rather, at the Temple of Deanna nearby.

I was inflated by the arrogance of youth. Despite the fact that many others had been here before, I was convinced that I would be the one to find something, where so many ot.ers had failed

The following morning, I set out early on my journey, eager to see the mystical 'Island within the Mists' in all its glory. I had only a few miles to hike to reach my destination. I wanted to witness the sun rising over the hill and feel the magic that still seeped from this land.

With a miner's lamp attached to my forehead and a compass in hand, I set off in the pre-dawn darkness and walked briskly westward along the pathway. The mist was thick around me, swallowing all sound. It was not hard to understand the locals' paranoia when walking through the darkness and fog. I walked on, ignoring my own reservations, knowing them as the primordial fears of my culture, I tried to ignore the ghosts I felt around me as flights of fancy. Their ghostly fingers caressed my face and probed into my very soul, but they did not deter me from reaching my destination.

Finally, I climbed the hill and broke free of the mists. I had timed it to perfection. As I paused to catch my breath, I could see the first rays of sun, bursting forth over the horizon. It was even better than I had expected, a truly breathtaking experience, and I sat there and gazed in wonder at the coming dawn. It was enough to breathe a little faith into my atheistic bones. Even a cynic like me could feel the magic within the moment. Is it any wonder that all those centuries ago, the ancient people believed in the power of the gods when they witnessed the rising sun?

I sat bewitched until the sun had burned away the mist, revealing the epic vista of green, lush hills before me. It was easy to imagine this hill as the island it once was and the world around me as a vast marshland. Finally, I shook off my trance-like state and turned around to meet my destiny … and again, I was hypnotised.

The vast marble structure was magnificent, even in its present condition. What a wonder it must have been in its heyday. How had they even transported the huge chunks of marble? They had originated in the mountains of Tir Pect. To get here, they needed to be hauled across the Plains of the Dragon, down the River Man, and finally, be navigated over the Great Swamp. Even using the wonders of modern technology, such a task would be almost insurmountable. That was to say nothing of the artisanship; the years of stonemasonry involved in creating this masterpiece. Arcane knot-work covered every available surface. Immense pictograms told tales of wonder and were surrounded by intricate weavings that captured the eye.

Looking at the immense array of buildings, I was at a loss for where to start. I could be here for a lifetime and still not have searched every square inch of this place. What wonders would I find hidden amongst the brush that had crept in over the centuries and now claimed the temple?

Time passed as I wandered around aimlessly. I was so enraptured by the ruins that I failed to see the warning sign until it was too late. The wind had picked up, becoming blustery, and dark clouds had appeared in the heavens, where once it had been a clear day.

I tried to remember which way I had come within the maze of marble. I had left my pack at the top of the hill, when I had first sat down to watch the sunrise. With it was my waxed jacket. It had been a typical summer's morning, and once the mist had burned off, it had been warm, even muggy. Now, the temperature had plummeted, and as the rain started to fall, the skies darkened further. Thunder rumbled overhead, and the first lightning quickly followed, startling me with its suddenness. The rain grew heavier by the minute, and my clothes were soon drenched, as I looked around for shelter.

Before me, across an overgrown expanse of garden, I saw the dark hollow of an alcove. Seeing nothing more suitable, I hurried over, head down against the now-howling wind.

It was almost dark now. Somehow, the day had been and gone, and I had failed to notice its passing. The locals had given me dire warnings to return before dusk. It was not safe, they had stressed, to be amongst the ruins during the hours of darkness. The ghosts were more dangerous at this time. Lives had been lost, and those who had survived were mere shadows of their former selves, wide-eyed and forever lost in another world.

I stumbled through the fading light, fighting off the undergrowth, which fought me every step of the way. "Nearly there," I panted as I broke through the last of the scrub and came close to my destination. The rain had not abated, and by now, the only light was from the near-constant flashes of streak lightning. Each crash of thunder and flash of light made my heart jump and race faster. My rain-splattered spectacles hampered my vision, distorting what little I could see.

I hurried across the open ground, hoping the alcove beyond was deep enough to offer some meagre shelter from the biting wind and freezing rain. By the time I noticed the steps, it was far too late to stop. My boots slid across the wet marble, seeking purchase, but finding none. I tumbled headlong down the marble steps, rushing towards the intricately carved image of the goddess Deanna. Her outstretched arms greeted me warmly, as I hurtled towards the marble wall on which the image was sculpted.

Death flashed before me as I tumbled, head over heels down the steps, towards the waiting arms of the goddess. Despite the warm welcome on the goddess's face, I could not look. I flinched and closed my eyes, waiting for the inevitable impact.

*****

I woke in darkness and silence. I was still soaked to the skin and bitterly cold. Fumbling around in my pockets, I sat up and flicked the striker on my lighter. I found myself sitting in a thick pile of dust and debris. Before me, I saw the same image of Deanna. No, wait! There was something different about it. I closed my eyes and tried to remember my final moments of consciousness as I fell. Realisation dawned on me. The image before me was an exact replica, but in reverse. It was like seeing it through a mirror.

It was then that I noticed something else, and my heart nearly stopped in fright.

It was my legs. They stopped just below the knees.

There was no blood or pain, but I could not see my feet. They were within the wall.

Slowly, hesitantly, I moved my right leg, raising my knee. The foot appeared, and the image of the goddess shimmered briefly.

I blinked in surprise, before freeing my other foot from the wall.

Standing, I reached out to touch the beautiful face of the goddess. Coldness tingled against my fingertips, and the image rippled. It was like touching a reflection in a pool of water.

Taking a few breaths to steady my racing heart, I thrust my hand directly into the wall. Farther and farther I pushed, until my whole arm had disappeared. I could feel a breeze on my fingertips.

Bracing myself, I pushed my head through the wall.

Lightning flashed … thunder rolled. I was looking up the steps of the alcove, to the Temple beyond.

I looked down and realised that my head must now be sticking out of the wall where the goddess's head should be. It was, perhaps, not an improvement on the original artwork. Withdrawing my head, I turned around and looked into the hidden chamber behind the illusory wall.

"Oh my god!" the devout atheist within me exclaimed, as I raised my lighter higher. I was in an immense, underground vault. It reached back farther than my meagre light could travel. In what little light I had, I could see rows and rows of shelving. My tiny flame was reflecting against a myriad of gems, gold, and silver, crammed without order into the shelves. I had found the hidden treasures of the Order of Deanna. The legends must have been true, after all.

I walked down the nearest row, taking in all before me. I must have walked for a hundred yards before the treasures ended. Before me stood a second set of shelves, reaching high over my head. These were sectioned into tiny compartments, and each box held a piece of dried vellum. Some of the scrolls were carefully wrapped around two rods, making for easier reading. Other, older scrolls were merely rolled up and bound with coloured bindings.

I had found the lost library of the Temple of Deanna. I continued to walk until I reached the far wall. My heart was in my throat the whole time, with excitement. Picking a scroll at random, I started to read. The script was archaic and difficult to decipher in the poor light, but I was able to make out the gist of its content.

It spoke of the early life of the Storm-Bringer.

I must have found the memoirs of the legendary Uiscallan, the Storm-Bringer, and saviour of Dragania!

Chapter One: The Girl from High Peaks

It all started long ago, in a high mountain village in Dragania ...

Maerlin knew all about storms. She could feel them in her bones, especially in her left arm, which she had broken the previous spring. More importantly, she could feel them with her mind. She could feel the power of a storm within her, building up until her head pounded and white light filled her vision.

She was hiding in the small cave above the village, her eyes tightly shut to block out the light. Her head felt like it was on fire, and she could feel the clouds darkening outside. Soon, she knew, the pressure would become unbearable. Maerlin shuddered and wiped away tears, remembering another storm, the storm that had killed her mother.

She vividly remembered the nightmare that precluded that storm and waking up with a jolt to see her mother leaving. Maerlin had pleaded with her not to go. She had warned her about a storm brewing beyond the mountain.

Her mother had laughed lightly. "Don't worry, Little Hawk. I'll be fine. The storm cannot hurt me."

Kissing Maerlin softly on the cheek, she had hurried away to check the cattle in the summer pastures. Maerlin's pleas had been ignored.

In desperation, Maerlin had run to her father's forge, yelling loudly to be heard over the clanging of his anvil. She had begged him to fetch her mother back. She had tried to explain about the storm from her nightmare, the one she could still feel in her head.

He had only laughed, gently scuffed her wild hair and sent her on her way. "Look at the fine day," he had said "There's not a cloud in the sky, Maerlin. There'll be no storm today. Now, be off with you and play. I've got work to do."

Nevertheless, the storm had come. It was one of those freak summer storms that came to the mountains without warning. It darkened the sky in moments and shook the very mountain with its ferocity. Lightning had streaked across the sky as the wind built up to a wail. Day had turned into night.

It was the worst storm ever recalled. Even the village elders agreed on that, and they rarely agreed on anything. Four people had died, including Maerlin's mother. They had found her body later at the bottom of a cliff, just where Maerlin had said it would be.

From that day forward, Maerlin's life had been changed forever. That was the day she became known as 'the Changeling'. That had been the day when she became an outcast in her own village.

Now, she was crouched in the small cave, stomach cramping with anxiety as another storm built. She could feel it growing and knew that this would be a bad one. Fear made her tremble as the thunder rumbled outside and the skies darkened. Her headache was blinding, but she had grown used to the headaches. The cramping, however, was something new, and this, she was worried about it.

Perhaps, she had caught some strange illness. She remembered the miller's youngest boy, the one who had died last year. He had passed away after cramping and vomiting for days. Eventually, he had turned all blotchy and swelled up horrendously. Maerlin was worried that she may have caught the same ailment. The cramps were getting worse, making her back ache. Waves of nausea washed over her as she fought back the tears.

A warm wetness on her thighs caused her to look down. The sight of blood on her suntanned thighs only increased her anxiety. She hugged her knees to her chest as she recalled the events that had caused her to be hiding in the cave.

*****

The day before ...

The day had started well, with Maerlin getting up early to go and milk the cow. Maerlin had slipped out of the hut, barefooted, to do her chores. She loved running in the high meadows and startling the birds that nestled in the course mountain grass. She loved to watch them fly up and hear their shrill protests. She enjoyed this time away from the other villagers, with their snide remarks and suspicious looks.

She was on the mountain before the sun had fully emerged and walked across the mountain to the village herd, buckets in hand. The early mornings were her favourite time, when everything was peaceful and there was no one around to disturb her. The mountain belonged to her at this time of the morning. She felt like the queen of the mountain.

The herd called out to her in greeting. They were used to her dawn milk raids. Greeting them, she walked over to her father's roan cow and stroked the sleepy beast, idly chattering to the docile creature about the weather and her newborn calf. The soft-eyed bull calf shuffled over to greet Maerlin, licking her hand before quenching his thirst noisily upon his mother's teats, shaking with the joys of youth and the sweetness of the milk.

"Hey! Save some for me," Maerlin protested, pushing the calf around to make some room between him and his mother. Slipping the bucket under the cow's side, Maerlin placed her head against the rumbling belly and milked the fore teats. The calf happily slurped on the hind teats as the cow chewed the cud. When her buckets were full, Maerlin rose, ready to leave and face the day.

Maerlin trudged back down the mountain towards the village, careful not to spill any of the milk along the way.

The first signs of life appeared as she crested the last rise and looked down at the neat cluster of huts below. Cooking fires emitted trails of sluggish, white smoke, which climbed into the sky. As she neared the village, she saw the other womenfolk clustered by the village green waiting with buckets in hand, ready for their communal hike up the mountain.

Maerlin slipped quickly away, long since weary of their stares. They treated her with suspicion at best and with open hostility at worst. Using the backs of the huts for cover, she slipped towards her home as stealthily as a cat. Smoke rose from the fire that she had stoked earlier. She was creeping past the old byre, where their cow was wintered, when it happened...

Out of nowhere came a hard clod of dried cow dung, hitting her on the back of the head and landing in her one of her buckets of milk. More followed. Maerlin could hear snickering from within the byre, where the dung-throwers must have lain in wait.

"Hey, Changeling! Are you expecting rain today?" the ringleader jeered. His, was a voice she knew well, even though his face was still hidden in the shadows.

Maerlin ducked more missiles, attempting to protect her precious cargo of milk, as she backed away towards her hut.

"Come back and play!"

Three boys appeared. Their mocking faces filled Maerlin with anger as she stopped to face her tormentors. She was determined that she would not show them her fear. By now, other villagers had been drawn to the commotion like flies to cow pats. Soon, sneering faces filled Maerlin's vision. "You nasty little toe-rag, Duncan Gammit," she cursed "Get out of my yard and take those half-wit cronies with you."

"Or what are you going to do, Changeling? Will you summon a storm to strike us down?" he mocked.

'Changeling': the name she hated above all others. The name she had inherited after her mother's death.

Although her mother had been dark and swarthy, she was striking in appearance. Maerlin, on the other hand, always looked wild and untamed. She had all the beauty of an ugly duckling. The villagers were all tall, fair-skinned people with blonde-haired, while Maerlin was slight of build, with dark swarthy skin, and course black hair.

Since her mother's death, the village children had started to call her a Changeling and accused her of being of fairy blood. She could even see the doubt in her father's eyes, though he refused to speak of it. In fact, he grew angry every time she asked him about it.

"Don't be silly, girl," her father would say "It's all in your mind. Don't listen to such foolish talk."

Looking balefully from the bullies to the rest of the villagers, Maerlin's temper boiled over, and she lashed out in the only way that she could. "I hope a storm does come and that it strikes that stupid grin right off your face, Gammit. That'll teach you."

"OOOOOOOOOooooooooooohhh, I'm soooo scared."

A shadow of doubt crossed his face, however, when thunder rumbled overhead.

Maerlin's hair was, by now, standing up like a halo around her head. She could feel the storm building with every passing moment. The quiet morning had changed, becoming tense, charged, and the rumbling of thunder continued to announce the presence of a building storm.

The boys stopped laughing and looked skyward with horror on their faces, as dark clouds clustered and swirled over the village.

Maerlin looked up, reading the growing storm and sensing the fear of the villagers. Seeing her chance for revenge, she lifted her arms over her head and yelled "Come, storm. Come and strike these imbeciles down." Lust for revenge was burning through her veins.

She felt the storm rising; felt the pressure in her head getting ready to burst. She didn't believe it would actually strike the boys down, but she would be glad if it did. Her inner voice called for calm, but she ignored it as she played her game on the boys. She was glad to have turned the tables on her tormentors, for once. She danced around in a circle, head thrown back as if in a trance and garbling nonsense in a whiny voice. The villagers backed away nervously. Terror filled their eyes as the thunder rumbled overhead and lightning crackled around them.

"You're a witch!" a young girl shouted, hiding behind her mother's skirt. She was only repeating aloud what other villagers muttered behind Maerlin's back. "You're a mad, shrieking witch!"

Maerlin stopped her dance and glared around at the crowd. No one would meet her eye. She could feel the storm coursing through her veins like wildfire, tingling in her nerves.

Suddenly, the door of her hut smashed open and her father's bleary-eyed face poked out. "What in the Nine Hells are you doing, Maerlin? Have you lost your senses?" His temper rose as he took in the faces of the gathered villagers before him. For too long he had endured the snide comments of the villagers. He was at his wit's end "Bugger off, the lot of you. Have you got nothing better to be doing?"

Maerlin glared at her father. He was ruining her chance for vengeance. "Poppa …"

"Get inside, Maerlin. If your poor mother could see you now, wailing about like a demented banshee, she'd weep with shame …" He marched angrily over towards her "Get in the house ... now!"

"But Poppa ..." Maerlin tried to plead her innocence. She tried to explain about the boys throwing dung at her, but he wasn't listening. Instead, he raised his hand and slapped her across the face, hard enough to bring tears to her eyes.

"Enough, I said! Get inside with ya!"

Maerlin reeled in shock. Her father had never raised a hand to her ever before. She looked around at the faces of the villagers; the smug smiles of the small-minded people, and then she fled to her room, slamming the door shut behind her.

Maerlin lay down on her cot, weeping and refused to answer her father's knocks. Finally, he gave up and let her be. She couldn't face him, couldn't let him see how hurt she was. Why didn't he listen to her side of things? Why had he left her alone since her mother's death?

Later, she slept, still curled up in a ball on her bed. Her dreams were filled with storms and the mocking sound of children.

*****

She rose early the next morning, intending to slip silently out of the hut.

"You don't need to be sneaking around like a mouse, girl." Her father's voice scared her half to death. He was never awake this early, anymore. "Come over here and sit down, Maerlin."

She crept closer and settled down beside him. Sniffing the air, she could smell no trace of stale beer. He must be sober for the first time since her mother's death. It had become a habit of his to drown his sorrows each evening. Drunk, he would stagger home in the early hours and cry himself to sleep, not rising until late in the morning.

"I know that I've been a poor excuse for a father this last year."

"No, Poppa. It's not your fault. They just hate me, that's all. They think I'm different."

"And aren't you, girl, with all that sneaking around and that wild hair of yours?" he asked, not expecting an answer "You've never fitted in, even when your mother was alive, bless her soul. This last year, you've become wilder than a mountain cat and about as feral looking!"

"I try, Poppa, honestly I do, but they just don't like me. They blame me for the storms, but I haven't done anything wrong. I hear them blaming me for Momma's death, but it wasn't my fault. I just had a nightmare about it, that's all. I remember waking up to find her heading out the door. I begged her to stay. I told her about that storm, but she wouldn't listen. I pleaded with her, but she just kissed me goodbye and headed off."

Maerlin's voice broke. She couldn't continue, though she wanted to remind her father that she had told him, too. He had shrugged her off and sent her away to play. She still remembered how strong the storm had been, long before it could be seen on the horizon. She shuddered as the dream came back to her: her mother staggering around on the mountain, lost in the near-darkness of the storm, blinded by heavy rain and lightning flashes. She remembered waking up screaming, with the image of her mother slipping over the cliff edge. She could clearly see her mother struggling to grip the ledge, before falling to her death. The feel of the fall was like a blow in her stomach as she woke.

"I know, Maerlin. I hear them in the tavern. They're just superstitious folk, simple mountain folk, who don't understand ... by Dagda, I don't understand. It scares me half to death, which is why I lost my temper."

Maerlin looked over at him, her eyes wet with tears.

"What am I supposed to think? I wake up to the sound of thunder and find you messing around, scaring people with all of that carry on! I just lost my rag ... I'm sorry ... I shouldn't have hit you," he sighed before he continued "Anyway, this has to stop so I've called in a healer."

"A healer...? But I'm not ill!"

"Maerlin ... listen to me. They say that she's really good, and she'll be able to help you to get rid of whatever possesses you."

"I'm not possessed!" Maerlin's voice had gone up an octave in disbelief. "How can you think I'm possessed? I've looked after you this last year.

I've cooked, cleaned, and kept this place together, and you think I'm ... a demon?"

"Now, now, Maerlin, calm yourself down. I didn't mean it that way," he placated, waving his big hands in front of her. He had never been good with words, preferring to express himself through the things he made. "I think she might help sort this mess out, but even if she can't, at least it'll get you away from the villagers for a while and give us all a break."

"What do you mean, 'away for a while'? Are you throwing me out?" Maerlin demanded, struggling to believe her ears. Standing, she looked down at her father with fury in her eyes.

"Maerlin, calm down," he said, desperately trying to make her see reason. It had all sounded so good last night, when he had discussed it with the others. Somehow, it was all coming out wrong. "The healer will have you for a few weeks, a moon or two at the most, while she studies you and figures out what's up. You'll still be able to come home afterwards, when you're feeling better."

"What d'you mean ... better?"

"Look," he said, attempting to deal with the issue calmly "Consider it a working holiday. You'll get to stay over with her in the Broce Woods, take care of her the same as you do me, and learn a few things from her. If all goes well, you can be back here before winter sets in."

"You're getting rid of me, aren't you?" Maerlin accused, her hands on her slim hips "Have you sold me off to some old hag as a housekeeper?"

Maerlin noticed that her father's eyes seemed lost in a painful memory, and knew that he must be thinking about her mother. She had always struck the same pose, whenever she had wanted to intimidate him and it had worked every time.

"No! No! She's just going to help you, that's all," he said, feeling that he was losing the point. "It's just ... I can't afford to pay her, so you'll have to earn your keep."

"I'm not going. Do you hear me! I'll run away and become ... become ..." Maerlin stopped. She was at a loss for words to describe her future self. Nothing came to mind. She had no skills with which to earn a trade, apart from milking cows and cleaning house, and she certainly didn't

14

want to do that. The problem was that all the women she knew were milkmaids and homemakers. In frustration, she stomped her foot and continued "I'm going to be something … something important. Just you wait and see!"

"No, girl, you won't." Standing, he stomped across the room, trying to control his own rising temper. "Get that into your stubborn head, will ya? You aren't special ... at least not in any useful or important way. No one wants a wife who can brew up storms and make lightning bolts blow their house away. These aren't useful skills to make your way in the world. You're going with the healer, and you'll work for her, or … or … or nothing. That's final!"

He was the biggest man in the village and the broadest of shoulder. He glared at her and she was dwarfed by his presence, but her spirit would not be cowered. Instead, she stood before him, chin out, and her face was a mask of determination. Her head was buzzing with rage as she faced him down. She refused to look away, even when her eyes started to shed tears and her vision blurred. She stood toe-to-toe with him and glared, until he gave in and stormed out of the hut. His last words, however, nearly knocked her flat.

"I've had enough of this malarkey! Pack your things, Maerlin. The Healer'll be here by mid-morning. I'll tie you onto her pony's back if I have to."

*****

Maerlin ran from the village. Thunder rumbled in the distance as tears ran freely down her face. She stumbled as the first blast of streak lightning flashed across the darkening sky, got up and staggered on. Half-blind with pain and anger, she headed for her hidey-hole, the small cave where she sheltered from mountain storms. Her cries were lost in the billowing winds and rumbling thunderclaps.

*****

The cramping grew steadily worse, making her moan as she lay down in the dirt. Her stomach had continued to cramp violently all afternoon while she bled. The sphagnum moss she had used to soak up the blood had failed to stop the heavy flow. Eventually the fear of bleeding to death from some unknown ailment overcame her other worries. As the storm abated, she headed down the mountainside to face her father, the healer, and her fate.

The rains still fell as she staggered home, bent double with cramps and fearful for her life. Occasionally, the cramps became so severe that she was forced to stop, waiting for them to ease. By the time she reached the village, she was soaked through and shivering violently. The villagers were huddled fearfully in their huts out of the rain, praying for the storm to blow over. Reaching her father's hut, Maerlin pushed open the door and stood, silhouetted in the doorframe, peering into the dark interior.

He father rushed forward, but stopped dead when he saw her pale features. "What in the Nine Hells …?" he exclaimed, pulling her inside. "You look like a drowned rat. Where've you been?"

"I'm sorry, Poppa, please forgive me." Maerlin staggered forward in a hunched walk. "I don't want to pass on to the Otherworld and leave you hating me."

"What are you blathering on about, Maerlin?" he asked, guiding her towards the fire.

It was warm in the hut, even with a low fire, and the sudden heat made Maerlin shiver more violently. Her teeth began to chatter as she sat on one of the stools near the low flames. Her wet smock dripped onto the earthen floor, and a pool started to form beneath her.

"You'll catch your death, if you stay in those clothes, dear." a voice declared, making Maerlin turn. It had come from the far side of the room. An old woman shuffled forward, carrying one of Maerlin's shifts. As Maerlin studied the healer's wrinkled face, she noticed a gentle kindness in the woman's eyes.

"Go and get yourself a drink, man. Leave me to tend to the wee lass," the healer ordered in a tone that brokered no argument. The blacksmith hesitated for only a moment before relief showed on his face, and he fled.

"Now then, my dear," said the healer "Let's get you out of those wet things and into something warm, or I'll be treating a fever as well as this so-called 'possession'."

"But I'm dying, Ma'am!" Maerlin struggled out of the clingy, wet fabric of her shift. "I'm bleeding inside, and it won't stop. I've got these awful cramps ..."

The healer had been stoking the fire to heat water, when she heard this. She turned around and looked at Maerlin. "Bleeding you say ... cramps?" She shuffled closer. "How old are you, dear?"

She stopped in front of Maerlin and stooped to inspect the blood on her thighs.

"Fifteen, Ma'am," replied Maerlin nervously.

"Fifteen! You look more like twelve. Doesn't that man feed you at all?"

"They say that I'm a Changeling, Ma'am," replied Maerlin as if that explained everything.

"Changeling indeed! You don't even have pointy ears. Don't these folk know anything? You're a bit small and swarthy, that's all. It's probably just a throwback to the Old Blood. You've got the look of a Pect to me. Your mother wasn't born in High Peaks, I'm betting."

Maerlin nodded, though she didn't have a clue what the Old Blood was.

"Well now ..." the healer continued "the good news is that you're not dying. The bleeding is quite normal for a woman of your age. The bad news is that it'll come back again this time next moon, and the moons after that until you get to be as old as me ... or so it'll seem."

Maerlin looked up in confusion, unsure what the healer was telling her.

"You've been blessed by Arianrhod, the moon goddess. You're a woman now, my dear. You're no longer a girl, so you'd better get used to braiding that wild hair of yours. No man in his right mind would court a wee vixen with hair like a deranged hedgehog."

Maerlin listened to the healer, but could barely grasp her meaning. "What about the cramps? It feels like my belly is all upside-down and inside-out."

"They'll go away in a few days. Hopefully, that'll ease after the first couple of cycles, at least a little, but if they don't get any easier, I can give you some herbs to ease the pain," the healer advised. "Now sit still, while I take a good look at you."

Maerlin obeyed, happy to sit down and get warm.

"Are you strong, my dear?"

"Aye, I am." Maerlin was eager to please, now that the panic had subsided. "I can run up the mountain faster than any boy in the village, and I can climb like a goat. I can milk and clean and wash and sweep..."

"I'm sure you can, dear. Now, rest up, and I'll make us both a nice cup of tea," instructed the healer "What do they call you?"

"Maerlin, Ma'am. I'm Maerlin Smith of High Peaks."

"Well, hello Maerlin, it's nice to meet you. I'm Nessa *MacTire* of the Broce Woods. I'm a priestess of Deanna and an Earth-sister ..." the healer greeted warmly "But you can just call me Ness."

Chapter Two: The Coming of Age

Some weeks later, in the city of Manquay ...

Cull staggered down the street, cursing the Watch for the beating he had received. It was not a bad beating as beatings went, but Cull was feeling particularly vexed this morning. "Drunk and disorderly," he mumbled. "The feckers wouldn't know how to spell it, let alone arrest someone for it."

Still, the plan had worked. Scratching the lice from under his armpit, he accosted a young noblewoman, looking for a few shillings. "Hey, Missus! Givuz a few pennies for a bite to eat, will ya? Me poor childer are dying from da hunger, don't ya know." He gripped the woman's cloak with grime-encrusted hands.

Her face was a mask of horror as she struggled to get away from him, and Cull's loud and inventive curses harangued her all the way down the street. He sighed. "Ah, by the Seven!" he cursed "I need a drink. My poor head is throbbing."

Fumbling in the pockets of his many ragged coats, he pulled out a pile of second-hand cigarettes and filled a fresh paper with the cast-offs of other peoples' past-smokes. Deftly rolling it with the skill born of long practice, he lit up and coughed violently. His body folded in two as he choked. Passers-by winced and scurried away as his lungs rasped, and he wrestled with some tarry phlegm. Cull recovered enough to glare around challengingly and cursed "Feck, these things are gonna be the death of me!"

He hawked out the residue from his throat and spat it at the feet of a passing merchant. An aggressive glare from the beggar stopped the merchant from making the comment he was about to make. Cull watched as the merchant scuttled off, fearful of an attack by the offensive and clearly deranged curb-crawler.

Cull straightened up and shambled down the street, searching out any possible 'soft touches'. He checked out the markings on the doorsteps; markings that only a beggar would be able to read. To the rest of the city, there were just scratches in the stone, nothing more. To Cull and his ilk, they were a whole library of information. Finally, he stopped at a baker shop, seeing promise within the hidden writings. Heading for the back door, he knocked and taking a deep breath, prepared himself.

Begging is truly an art form, needing good acting skills and greater understanding of the human mind, and Cull was a maestro in action. He accentuated his stooped posture, hunched his shoulders and his face reflected hunger and cold. When he was fully satisfied, Cull waited. Every nerve was ready as he heard noises from behind the door. Then it opened. The smell of fresh baked bread wafted out to mingle with the fetid street odours coming from the beggar's clothing. Standing in the doorway was the fleshy face of a middle-aged woman. He quickly assessed her before beginning his scam. As if nervous but respectful, he whipped off his greasy, wide-brimmed hat and bowed.

"B-b-beggin' ya pardon, miss …" he pleaded in a wavering voice, knowing full well that she was the baker's wife, from the plump well-fed figure to the flour-stained hands "…b-b-but would ya have a f-f-few f-farthings to spare?"

His eyes watered on cue, and his body emitted the subtlest of shivers. He knew just how to get the best of these signs; knew not to overdo it. It needed to be just enough to be registered within her brain. She needed to know that it was cold outside and that he needed her help.

"A b-b-bit of s-s-stale bread even!" Cull pleaded, now using his trademark look. It was a look that would make a spoilt child gives up its last sweet.

The woman softened like putty in his hand. She whispered nervously "Wait here a moment," and slipped back inside.

As she closed the door, he smiled to himself. He knew that the cold weather and the bruises from the Watch's' handling had made this a good 'blag'. He would not go away empty-handed. Cull's face became a mask of worry and concern again as the door re-opened. A small, cloth-wrapped bundle was placed in his hands.

"I'm sorry, but my husband's home so I couldn't get you much," she mumbled apologetically. Her smile was filled with pity. The silly woman looked genuinely remorseful.

He nodded his gratitude, mumbled an incoherent reply and turned away, before breaking into a scornful smirk. Scuttling away, he paused to mark the kerb with some chalk. The mark was only a tiny slash. It would last a few days and notify other beggars that the house has been 'tapped' recently. The local beggars would stay away until the chalk mark had faded, lest the charity of the baker's wife wear thin.

Cull tucked the package into his many coats, hiding it from prying eyes as he hurried away. When he was safely in an alley, he paused to look and listen. Caution was life in these dark alleys. Satisfied that the coast was clear, he sat down to search the bundle. Inside, he found a small loaf of fresh bread, a warm meat pie, an apple, a religious effigy of no real value, and a small pile of copper coins. With only a cursory glance, the effigy was discarded into the mud. "Hummph!" was his only comment. Cull counted out the copper farthings. There were eight in all. These, he hid in one of the many pockets beneath his grime-encrusted clothing. Only when the money was safely stored away, did he sit back to enjoy his meal. Huddled in a doorway, squatting against the chill breeze, the beggar ate and settled down to doze.

In this position, he blended into the background. Men would walk past him and few would notice his presence. He was just another pile of grimy rags, discarded in a doorway. Those who could see through the camouflage would recognise that a beggar was hiding there. They would be streetwise enough to know not to venture to close to the bundle of rags. Such an action might be hazardous to their health. In a city the size of Manquay, even the beggars knew how to handle a knife. Those who were wiser still, would recognise the greasy broad-brimmed hat and know that beneath this particular heap of rags lurked Cull; one of the most respected beggars in the city. A few might even know that he was heir to the Beggar Throne.

Cull could fight like an alley cat, and he could con the hind teeth out of a camel. Few were foolish enough to steal from him, though in the past a few rash cutpurses had tried. The Watch had later found and disposed of their bodies, dispensing them to the Paupers Graveyard.

Even the Watch tended to give him a wide berth. They knew that behind the drunken mask hid a mind that was sharper and more deadly than the stilettos he concealed about his person.

After a light sleep, for heavy sleepers did not last long on the streets, the bundle of rags moved. Cull had a job to do. He would need to report all that he had gleaned, while lounging in the city's gaol. He shook himself and scratched his armpit in an effort to rid himself of the lice that had crawled under his clothing. It seemed that he had taken on stowaways while lounging in the city's prison. He would need to deal with the pests soon, before they became an annoyance.

First, however, he needed to go and see the Beggar-Lord. The old man would be curious about the comings and goings of the Watch. They had important matters to discuss.

*****

Maerlin sat drinking an infusion of herbal tea. It had a bitter aftertaste, but she had been assured that it would help alleviate the cramps. Nessa asked her question after question, while braiding her hair. Some questions had been about livestock management, while others had been about her family and the other villagers. She had even been asked about the storms. Questions came thick and fast, and in no apparent order, the subject changing constantly.

Maerlin answered as best she could, though at times the answers were difficult. She was fast beginning to like Nessa and to feel comfortable around her. Maerlin's own questions, however, went unanswered. Each time she asked one, Nessa would reply with "All in good time, dear. Now tell me first about ..." Maerlin's question would quickly be forgotten.

Nessa had inspected Maerlin's few shifts with dissatisfaction "These won't do at all," she said, throwing them in a heap on the floor. "They're nothing more than rags and totally unsuited for a young woman to be seen in."

Maerlin felt a glow of pride at being referred to as a woman, and the weight of the braids in her hair attested to her coming of age.

"Stay here and drink your tea," instructed Nessa as she headed for the door "I'll go and fetch you some clothes for our journey." A short while later, she returned with two pleated skirts and two off-white blouses for Maerlin to wear. Where she had obtained these, Maerlin couldn't say, but clearly, she had scoured the village for some more suitable garb.

"Here, try these on for size," Nessa instructed "They aren't great, but with a nip and tuck, I'm sure they'll do for now."

The clothes were big on Maerlin. The skirts fell almost to her ankles, though they had been designed to sit just below the knee, and they were much too wide around the waist. The blouses hung baggily around her slight frame, and the sleeves covered her tiny hands.

"Roll up those sleeves, for now. We haven't the time to turn up the cuffs, at the moment. I think a belt might help you keep that skirt up for now. We can find some things in your size, later. Sadly, they are all big buxom lassies round here."

Maerlin looked down at herself in wonder, dressed up in fine clothes and with her hair plaited up like a woman. Her new clothes felt heavy after the light shifts she had worn since birth, but the symbolism of her newfound status was clear for all to see. She was now a woman! It brought a feeling of pride to her. "I could fix them up, Ness," she said, still slightly uncomfortable with calling the healer by her first name "It wouldn't take me long with a needle and thread."

"Later, dear. I think it'd be best for all concerned if we set off before the day is out, don't you?"

Maerlin looked down, remembering the animosity of the villagers and her recent problems.

"We just have to do one more thing before we leave," Nessa announced, marching into the bedroom of Maerlin's father. Maerlin waited, fiddling nervously with her new braids as rummaging sounds came from within. Nessa reappeared a few moments later with a small pouch. "Ah, I've found it!"

"What is it?" Maerlin asked, accepting the package tentatively.

"Open it up and see," Nessa suggested.

Maerlin untied the bindings.

"They're your mother's things; her dowry and her private possessions. Now that you've come of age, they belong to you."

Maerlin looked into the pouch and gasped in wonder at the jewellery. Inside, there was her mother's favourite pendant; a tiny silver hawk. There were also some silver bracelets that she'd wear on special occasions.

"I can't take these ..." Maerlin protested. Tears were welling up in her eyes.

"Who else is going to wear them? I can't see your father dressing up in silver bangles."

"It's just ..."

Nessa lifted the silver pendant and inspected it. "I think your mother would have wanted you to have this, at least." Walking behind Maerlin, she slipped the delicate chain around her neck.

"How do you know that?"

"She loved this piece, I can tell. It must have been very special to her," said Nessa. Maerlin's eyes fill with tears. "It's a merlin, dear. That's a small hawk. It's the little bird that she named you after. Did you know that?"

Maerlin could not contain her emotions, and soon her tears became long, heavy sobs for her lost mother.

"Yes child, I know. It's all right. Your mother loved you very much" soothed Nessa. She pulled the sobbing girl into her arms and comforted her. They sat like that until the sobbing subsided, and Maerlin regained her composure.

"I'm sorry, but I miss her so much. She was the only one who ever really listened to me, though she didn't listen to me that day. She just smiled, kissed me, and headed up the mountain. I didn't make the storm, did I? I didn't kill her?"

Nessa's eyes met Maerlin's "Listen, dear, and I'll tell you a little secret that only a few know. I've been studying magic for many years now; since I was no bigger than you are, and I can't summon up a storm out of thin air, so I doubt a wee slip of a lass like you can. However, you do seem to have a strong affinity with storms. Maybe you have a gifted that way. You wouldn't be the first to have such a blessing. With hard work and time, you might even be able to bend them to your will and become a Sorceress, but that'll take years of study."

Maerlin listened, her eyes alive with excitement at the word 'Sorceress'.

"I think that the storm was there all along, but you were able to see it better than others," explained Nessa. "Here's your first lesson, so heed it well for it's the key to all knowledge ... 'What we see isn't always there, and what we can't see, still exists'. Remember that, for it will guide you in the years ahead."

"So I'm not possessed?" Maerlin asked, her secret worry coming out.

"You possess a gift; that much is for sure. You're young and don't know your own abilities," assured Nessa. "Tell me, if you got kicked by a frisky colt, would you kill the poor beast, or believe it was controlled by some demon?" She paused a moment, giving Maerlin time to consider the question "No, you wouldn't, would you? He's just young and full of energy. He doesn't realise the harm he can do. He doesn't know his own strength. You need to teach him and harness his energies, put them to good use."

"So, are you going to teach me to be a Sorceress?" Maerlin's eyes were bright with enthusiasm.

"I didn't say that now, did I? Maybe I'll just teach you to keep your feet to ya'self and leave it at that."

Maerlin's face dropped.

"I'm too old to be teaching you more than that, and I fear you're too headstrong to listen to the likes of me. Learning magic is a long, boring process and not all glitter and sparkle. I bet you can't even read your lettering, let alone read the stars or the weather," she saw the look in Maerlin's eyes and chuckled to herself, remembering her own initiation "Let's get you out of this backward hole of a village and we'll take it from there, eh?" Nessa said to reassure Maerlin. "... But I warn you, you're not going to like all the lessons I will teach you. I'll work you harder than your father ever could, and then, I'll give you more to do until you weep with exhaustion and your brain screams with weariness. Once started on the road to knowledge, there is no turning back. Understand?"

Maerlin nodded, nervous but enthusiastic.

"Let's go then, shall we?"

*****

The rain had stopped, and the sun had come out by the time they stepped outside. The villagers had gathered on the village green, having heard that the healer had come to take Maerlin away. Many looked surprised to see Maerlin dressed and braided as a woman, somehow having missed out on that particular piece of gossip. Maerlin held her head high as she followed the healer through the gathered crowd.

Her father stepped forward, leading a small, heavily-laden pony. "We've filled up your supplies, Ma'am," he said, shuffling nervously from foot to foot. Turning to his daughter, he smiled "Are you feeling better now?"

"I'm okay, Poppa," said Maerlin, before her restraint broke, and she rushed forward to hug his broad chest. She clung to him fiercely.

His eyes misted over as he returned her hug. He leaned close to her and whispered in her ear "Go and be ya'self, Maerlin, and make ya mother proud." Wiping a tear away from his eyes, he added "Goodbye, Little Hawk. Come back and visit me sometime when you've found your dream."

Maerlin gritted her teeth, determined not to cry in front of the villagers. "I will, Poppa, I will." Stepping back, they looked at each other one last time.

"Come along, dear," said Nessa "Saying goodbye is like removing a bandage ... best done swiftly."

Maerlin nodded and followed as Nessa took the pony's rope and walked away from the village. She fought the urge to look back. She had no friends in the village, but still, she would miss the cattle and the mountainside. She would also miss her quiet, broken-hearted father. She gripped her mother's amulet as she walked along, tears rolling silently down her cheeks.

They walked quietly for the rest of the afternoon until the sun dipped behind the horizon. Both were lost in thought as they headed down the winding, mountain road.

"We better find a place to camp for the night," Nessa instructed, finally breaking the silence. She pointed to a hazel coppice nearby "That should do us. There'll be water there and shelter from the wind." Her tone became businesslike. "Now, we need to sort a few things out. It's always good to start something well, rather than repair it later."

Maerlin realised why people quickly hastened to do the old woman's bidding. She nodded and listened attentively, wondering where this was leading.

"First things first, the pony needs to be unpacked and hobbled, so he doesn't walk off and leave us to carry all this baggage ourselves. That's your job. In the meantime, I'll put up a shelter for us. Now, when he has rested and cooled down a bit, he'll need brushing down and watering. That's also your job. After that, you can light a fire for us, and I'll cook us some supper."

Maerlin struggled to remember all of the instructions, but the old healer had not finished, yet. She was only pausing for breath, before continuing "You'll need to wash up the plates and pans after supper ... and oh, I nearly forgot. While you're waiting for the pony to rest, we'll need some firewood. Fetch enough to last throughout the night. There are wolves in this part of the mountain, summer, or no summer. Let's not take any chances, shall we? Then, when all that's done, you can take up those clothes. The other set can wait until tomorrow evening, unless you've the time, of course."

Maerlin was exhausted. It had been a long and emotional day for her. She stood open-mouthed, listening to Nessa's ever-growing lists of things to do before she could sleep.

"Well, don't just stand there like a dimwit. Unpack the poor beast before he keels over. I'm sure he's been carrying that bundle for long enough," berated Nessa, her tone spurring Maerlin into action.

Maerlin hurried to obey, her tired muscles complaining as she unhitched the pony. Nessa was sitting against a tree, watching her with shrewd eyes. She could not believe that she was expected to do all the work while the healer sat there. Soon, astonishment grew into resentment and quickly into anger. Biting back the complaint that sprung quickly to her lips, Maerlin turned away and dug through the packs, searching for the hobbles. A fingernail snagged on a buckle, shooting pain up her arm and fuelling her mounting anger. Gritting her teeth, she sucked on the bleeding fingernail and grabbing the hobbles, marched over to the pony and roughly hobbled the weary animal. She felt a momentary twinge of sympathy for the pony, which must have been as tired and achy as she was. When she turned round to continue her chores, she found Nessa relaxing against the tree, gazing intently up at the darkening sky and smoking from a long-necked pipe. To make matters worse, the old woman was blowing smoke rings into the air as if she had no worries in the world. Maerlin stood there in amazement, as Ness blew ring after ring, watching them break apart on the breeze.

"Hurry up, dear. The light is fading and that firewood won't collect itself, you know," instructed Nessa in a calm matter-of-fact voice, which only added fuel to Maerlin's inflamed temper. Turning away, Maerlin stomped off through the undergrowth in search of dry timber.

The day's storm had saturated the area and dry timber was hard to find. Eventually, Maerlin returned as the skies were darkening to evening, with a bundle of semi-dry sticks and a few heavier boughs.

Dumping them noisily in front of Nessa, Maerlin asked "Where do you want the fire?"

"Oh, just there'll be fine. I've found a nice, comfortable spot just here."

Maerlin flexed her stiff shoulders and assembled the smaller twigs into a pyramid, ready to light. That done, she headed back to the baggage. While she had been searching for wood, a small lean-to tent had appeared farther back in the glade though from the look of it, the old healer had not stirred an inch. She was still smoking her pipe. Maerlin considered this as she searched the baggage. "Where's your tinderbox?"

"Oh, I don't use them, dear. They're too much like hard work, but I guess you might need one." Seeing Maerlin's blank expression, she added "You'll find a fire bow in the pack. Use that."

Maerlin growled under her breath. The clouds were becoming heavier and the sky darker, and then, with an ear-splitting crash, the first thunderclap erupted. Maerlin flinched at the volume and nearness of it. She had been too angry to notice the storm brewing.

Maerlin struggled with the fire bow. She knew how the thing worked, at least in principle, but she'd never actually started a fire with one. It seemed simple enough, but the reality was proving to be quite different. She persevered, but to no avail, merely exhausting what little energy she had left. She looked up at Nessa and realised something. Nessa was sitting there, pipe in hand, blowing smoke rings with casual indifference.

"How did you light that pipe?"

"What … this?" Nessa asked, holding up the pipe.

"Yes, that!"

"How d'you think I lit it?"

"I think you used magic," accused Maerlin.

"That's a good guess." Their conversation was seemingly over as Nessa had gone back to blowing smoke rings.

Thunder shook the ground as it rumbled over their heads.

"You really should learn to control that temper of yours, my dear," said Nessa with mild reproach.

Thunder crashed once more overhead, drowning out Maerlin's reply, which was probably for the best.

Taking a deep breath, Maerlin tried another tack. "Why'd you give me this fire bow to light a fire, if you could've done it without any effort?"

Nessa looked pointedly at Maerlin, noting the flushed look on her face and the braids in disarray. Taking another pull on the pipe, she paused before replying "Nothing in life is without effort, least of all magic. The energy has to come from somewhere, whether it's rubbing together two sticks, or using inner energies to draw the flames forth from the wood. Each takes energy. Fire is one of the basic Elementals. It can be useful, but it can also be dangerous and unpredictable. It's a bit like the young colt foal we spoke of earlier. To learn how to use magic, we need to learn to respect it, and to do that, we need to understand it. None of this can be done if you are wandering around with a hornet's nest inside your head. Before I can teach you magic, you'll have to learn something much more important. Can you guess what that is?"

"Is it how to make fire using a fire bow?" Maerlin asked, doubting that it would be that simple.

"No, you dolt! What you need to do is learn *control*."

As if to punctuate this remark, lightning flashed overhead. It was quickly followed by a loud crash of thunder.

"I see that I'm going to have to do the fire this evening, or we'll be drowned in a storm." Nessa got stiffly to her feet and bent over the kindling. "Pay attention!" Nessa stooped forward, her knees creaking as she did so. She raised a bony, arthritic finger towards the pile of sticks. Her eyes focused on the wood, seeming to look within the twigs, seeking out something hidden there, and then she whispered "Fire," barely loud enough to be heard.

Maerlin watched in anticipation, and then in disappointment "It didn't work."

Nessa looked over. "Do you want to do this, or are you going to shut up and watch?"

Maerlin flushed and bit her lip "Sorry."

Nessa took a deep breath, let it out slowly and began the whole process again finishing with the soft whisper of "Fire."

They waited silently, Nessa staring hard into the wood, while Maerlin's eyes shifted from the sticks to Nessa's face. After a moment, Maerlin noticed something. There was a faint smell of burning, then smoke drifted up from the kindling in wispy eddies.

Nessa leaned closer, almost kissing the wood as she breathed encouragement into the sticks. "Burn, my little Salamander, burn!" The smoke thickened and for a moment, Maerlin thought she saw a small face flickering within the pattern of smoke. "That's it, my lovely. Come out and let us feel thy warmth," Nessa cooed, in a soft, seductive voice. The twigs glowed brighter. Suddenly, a tiny flame popped into life and danced within the twigs.

Maerlin leapt up, exclaiming "You did it! You did it!"

Nessa held out her hand. "Give me a hand up and stop all that chattering, will ya?"

Maerlin rushed to obey, her face flushed with excitement. I've seen real magic, she thought.

"You'd better feed our young friend down there. He'll be getting hungry." Nessa pointed at the newborn fire "You'd better put some rocks around him too, or he'll go on a merry dance around the countryside."

Maerlin nodded and fed larger pieces of twig to the delicate flame, encouraging it into greater life. She had never thought of fire as a creature before. It was only a thing, like a pan or a plate, but after seeing Nessa produce fire, she saw it in a new light. "How did you do that?" she asked while she worked, but no reply was forthcoming. Nessa sat silently, smoking her pipe quietly "I asked how you did that?"

"Hold ya whisht, dear. Do your work and leave me in peace. If I explained it to you, you'll be no wiser, so let it be."

Maerlin sulked, but did as she was told. She busied herself with her chores, while her mind replayed the magic she had witnessed. She was so engrossed in thought that even her aches and pains slipped away.

*****

The fire was burning well and protected within a ring of stones, before Nessa spoke again "Did you notice that the storm passed us by while you were working?"

Maerlin looked up at the sky. The stars had come out, and what few clouds were visible in the soft moonlight were light and fluffy. No hint of a storm remained in the heavens.

"Did I make the storm because I was mad at you?"

"I told you, dear, they aren't easily made. Let's just say that you gave it encouragement, the same way that I encouraged the Fire Elemental in the twigs. The difference, of course, is that I controlled the fire, whereas you had no control over the storm. It was drawn to your anger like a moth to the flames."

"Oh, I see … I think I understand now."

"You're a long way from understanding, but you're on the right path," Nessa assured "Go and get the pony some water while I cook us a meal, and then we can get some sleep. It's been a long day and tomorrow is rushing to meet us."

Maerlin led the pony down to the brook before she hobbled him, brushed him down, and wished him goodnight. As she walked back to the fire, she could smell a fragrant stew cooking, and her stomach rumbled, reminding her that she had not eaten all day.

A steaming bowl of broth awaited her as she sat down across from Nessa. She attacked it hungrily. Her second bowl was barely finished when her eyes became heavy. A full belly and a long day had conspired to make her sleepy, even though she had so many questions to ask.

Nessa watched her from across the fire, her face occasionally disappearing in a cloud of smoke "Get some sleep, dear. I'll sort out the dishes for tonight." Nessa pointed towards the lean-to.

Maerlin was too tired to argue and gladly headed to her bed. As she drifted into slumber, she vaguely remembered the healer draping a blanket around her and whispering "Sleep well, Little Hawk."

Chapter Three: An Acorn of Knowledge

The mists dissipated, and Maerlin saw a woman standing on the top of a tall hill. She was looking down onto a plain below, on which two armies amassed. She was dressed in sheer white silk and looked breathtakingly beautiful, her dress billowing in the breeze. Her eyes were fixed on a young man dressed in gilded armour and wearing a white cloak.

He was the leader of one of the two forces. His hair shimmered in the morning sun, flowing like liquid gold behind him as he charged his sturdy horse forward. A gold circlet nestled on his forehead. As Maerlin followed the woman's gaze, she noticed his distinctive eyes. They were sharp blue orbs that could pierce her soul.

The armies met with a thunder-like clash, and men began to die, summoned to Macha, the goddess of death, for their heroic deeds. They would feast in the Hall of Heroes this night, in the Otherworld.

The woman's eyes never left the golden-headed Knight. He was making progress across the battlefield towards a burial mound, where a red tent stood encircled by stone dolmens. A banner depicting a black boar on a bloody field hung outside the tent. Grasping the banner was another warrior. He was garbed in red armour with black trim, and his face was hidden behind his full-faced helmet. He seemed agitated that the battle was turning against his forces. Shaking his head, he marched into the tent behind him.

Like a hawk, Maerlin swooped down and also entered its dark interior.

The air within was filled with the heavy odours of blood and fear, cloying with the scent of incense and death. There, she found a man dressed in black robes, standing before a stone altar at the tent's centre. He was chanting incoherently. In his right hand, he clutched a bloody knife, while in his left was the freshly cut heart of his sacrifice. Upon the stone lay the rest of the victim. The mage lifted the heart and plunged it into the flames of a nearby brazier.

Maerlin moved nearer to see the victim better. She gasped in horror when she realised that it was a small boy lying on the altar in his final death throes. Turning her gaze away from the macabre scene, she glared at the mage. Her eyes locked with the mage's, and she saw the madness within.

The mage raised his bloody hand, and Maerlin could feel his dark power filling the room like static electricity. He muttered a word and gestured towards her.

His magical blow sent her reeling backwards out of the tent. She felt a crushing sensation deep within her chest, as if inhuman hands were grasping her heart. Her vision swam as she struggled away from the tent. She tried desperately to flee from the magical clutching talons of death. Gasping for every breath she fled towards the ridge, where the Lady had stood watching the battle. The pain eased a little with each step she took away from the tent. The talons finally released her heart, allowing it to beat again. Blinking back her tears, Maerlin searched the ridge and found the woman, collapsed on the ground, clutching at her own chest. Her beautiful features were marred with pain as she also fought off the magical attack. Eventually, the woman recovered enough to stand and look again across the battlefield. Her eyes were filled with dread.

Maerlin's eyes turned towards the battle, too. Below, the White Knight was struggling against invisible foes at the centre of the two armies. An eerie grey mist had enveloped the battlefield, and men were dying from wounds, which appeared out of nowhere. Panic swelled in his men, and doubt crept into the eyes of the White Knight as he fought off his ethereal enemies. His men were teetering on the edge of terror, sensing that the battle was slipping away.

The Lady rose to her full height and stood erect and defiant. Her proud features nagged Maerlin with their familiarity. She was sure that she knew this woman, though they had never met. The woman raised her hands high; fingers outstretched, and she drew in her magical energy. Maerlin could feel the power growing, her very being tingled with the magic that was being summoned. The winds built, and where once there had blown a light breeze, now gusts swirled in a vortex around the Lady. Her silken gown clung tightly to her body as Air Elementals caressed her skin. The clouds spiralled overhead, darkening as she invoked the creatures within.

"Come, my children. Come to mine aid, dearest Sylphs for I need thee now!" the Lady pleaded.

The wind on the ridge moaned as the Elementals sang her praise. Wispy humanoid figures, barely visible to the eye, danced around her. The clouds darkened until the sun disappeared from view, leaving the *battlefield in eerie twilight ... and then the storm erupted in all its violent intensity.*

Clashes of thunder shook the ground like earthquakes, knocking men off their feet. The very air reeked of ozone as the storm danced a-frenzy around the Sorceress, but she showed no fear. In fact, as Maerlin looked closer, she noticed a warm, benevolent smile upon the features of the Sorceress.

"I thank thee for thy assistance. You honour me," she murmured as she lowered her arms. When she did this, the Elementals headed where her outstretched fingers pointed, towards the battlefield below.

The winds buffeted past Maerlin, eager to do their mistress's bidding. Rocks rolled down the hill under the powerful surge of air. The winds tore down towards the plain. Men, who had staggered back to their feet after the thunderclaps, collapsed again as the winds crashed over them like waves on a tempest sea. They fell before the raging wind, and it struck the grey ethereal mist like a tsunami. The mists disintegrated before the colossal force of the winds.

"Thunder!" The heavens shook with the cacophony of thunderclaps.

Maerlin clutched her hands tightly against her ears. She screamed as the thunder vibrated inside her head. It blinded her with pain as it echoed across the sky.

"LIGHTNING." The Sorceress had to shout now to be heard over the noise. The world filled with blinding light as sheet lightning filled the sky and streaked down towards the distant tent.

Maerlin strained to watch the battle as bolt after bolt of lightning struck the burial mound.

The armies were in disarray, too intent on survival to care about the war. The White Knight, however, turned to the ridge and bellowed a command to his beleaguered men. Raising his sword high, so that lightning shimmered off the blade, he pointed towards the standard of the black boar. His men rallied to his call, gathered around his Frost Dragon banner, and together, they charged.

The Red Knight moved forward to meet the assault. Many of his men faltered and were swept aside. All could see that the battle was lost, but still the Red Knight prepared to fight, pride forcing him to meet his fate with blade in hand.

Lightning struck the tent, and moments later, the Mage staggered out, his robes smoking. He was clearly shaken, but alive. He looked towards the ridge, and his eyes were filled with madness and rage at the attack. Taking in the scene before him, he noticed the White Knight charging unhindered towards his master, whose army lay in tatters. Mad or not, the battle was lost, and the old mage knew that to stay was to suckle on Macha's sweet breasts. Swirling his cloak around him, he drew upon his powers and cast a spell.

Maerlin flinched, her heart still aching from the previous assault, but the attack did not come.

The black cloak fell to the ground. Where the old mage had once stood there now perched an immense raven. Its black eyes viewed the scene for a brief moment, and then, it spread its wings and took to flight. It flew away, through the buffeting winds of the receding storm. A defiant cawing filled the sky as the Dark Mage cursed the White Knight's army and the Sorceress on the ridge.

As the Red Knight fell under the silver sword, the heavens opened and a torrential downpour fell. The static-filled air shuddered as rainfall washed the blood away from the battlefield in red rivers, striving to clean away the worst of the ghastly sight.

Maerlin swooped down towards the White Knight as he smiled, heady with victory. Gazing into his deep blue eyes, she could feel her soul becoming lost. A shiver ran through her body, and a deep sense of longing filled her.

"Maerlin," she heard him call and blinked in surprise. How did he know her name?

"Maerlin … Maerlin … wake up and breathe!"

Merlin blinked and took a deep ragged gasp of breath, sitting up suddenly as her body shook. Cold sweat covered her, glistening on her skin. Her chest was filled with pain, making her fight back tears. When her eyes finally cleared, she could see Nessa's concerned look in the soft light of dawn.

"Ah, my dear, you gave me an awful fright. You were having a nightmare and I couldn't wake you. I rushed over and found that your heart had stopped. It took all I know to get it started again. Lie back, and let me cover you before you catch a chill."

As Maerlin's senses returned, she gazed around at the small bivouac tent in which she had rested. "Was it just a dream?" she asked "It seemed so real." She touched her chest and winced at the pain there, noticing the colouration in the soft light. "What happened to me?"

"I'm sorry dear, but I had to hit you to get your heart to start beating again. I fear, I've bruised some of your ribs to say nothing of my knuckles, but at least you'll live," replied Nessa, while she flexed her gnarled hand. "Tell me about this dream."

Maerlin sat, wrapped in a blanket, and while her body warmed up she told Nessa about her strange dream. " … But it seemed so real. It was like I was there. I felt I knew the Sorceress and the Knight. He called out my name … or was that you calling me back?"

Nessa sat in silence for a long time. "There was a wild storm here. Whether it brought on the dream, or whether the dream brought on the storm, is hard to say." Pausing a moment, she added "Here, I stitched these for you while you slept. I don't sleep much myself these days. I don't like to think I've missed anything. There's still too much left to learn."

Maerlin took the bundle containing her newly-acquired adult clothes and dressed, shivering in the coolness of the dawn. As she looked outside, she could see the wet grass and dripping hazel trees, testament of the recent heavy rainfall. The fire was smouldering nearby, where it had been banked to protect it from the worst of the storm.

*****

"I'll get the fire going and rustle us up some breakfast," Maerlin offered when she had finished dressing.

The healer was quiet for most of the morning as they headed down the valley. Maerlin was lost in her own world, too. She was reliving as much of the dream as possible and trying to fathom out its meaning. They walked on in silence until the sun reached its peak. The midsummer heat made the day heavy and their pace slowed.

"I think we'll stop here for a while. You need to learn some things, and this seems like a good enough spot to teach them to you."

They had stopped beside a tall oak, which offered cool shade from the midday sun. A small lake glistened a short stroll farther down the valley. The beauty of the mountains surrounded them.

Maerlin released the pony from its burden, while Nessa walked under the boughs of the oak tree and sat down. Laying her head against the coarse bark, the old woman closed her eyes and relaxed.

Maerlin shrugged. She was already becoming accustomed to doing most of the work. Once free from his burden, the pony collapsed onto the ground and rolled, scratching his back as he lay upside down. All the while, he was emitting contented groans of satisfaction. Rising to his feet, the pony shook vigorously, creating a cloud of dust and horsehair, snorted contentedly and began munching on the sweet grass. Pulling out the hobbles, Maerlin quickly hobbled his front legs and left him to graze, before heading for the cool shade of the tree.

Sitting down with a sigh, she took in the magnificent view.

"It's beautiful here. It's so peaceful. This grass is rich and the soil is healthy," her gaze turned to the small, silvery lake below "I bet there's good fishing in that lake, too. Why isn't there anyone living here, Nessa?"

"There's a village on the other side of the lake. We'll stop there later, but this is too isolated for most people. They fear the wolves in wintertime ... and then there are the ghosts."

"Ghosts, what ghosts?"

"There was a famous battle here, many years ago," Nessa explained "That could be the vision you saw in your dream. There was tales of Wild-magic, heroic deeds, and horrors too nasty to utter during the battle, but maybe that's just colour to make the tale juicier, eh?" Nessa joked at the morals of poets and storytellers.

"But there aren't really ghosts here, are there? It seems so pleasant."

"They say that on Samhaine night, the ghosts of the slaughtered walk again. I cannot say whether it is true or not, as I am not foolish enough to tempt Macha's will. Only the foolhardy would walk a battlefield on such a night."

"But those are just fairy tales designed to scare children with at bedtimes."

Nessa sighed and rose to her feet "You didn't heed the first lesson I taught you, did you, dear? Come, let me show you something."

Maerlin followed the healer, trying to remember her lessons "Which lesson was that, Nessa?"

With an exasperated sigh, Nessa answered "Remember Maerlin, 'what we see isn't always there, and what we can't see, still exists.' Do you remember me saying that now?"

Maerlin flushed.

"Either you weren't listening, or you didn't understand. I'll hope and pray to Deanna that it was the latter, or I'm wasting my time and yours."

"But it doesn't make sense, Nessa. It's either there, or it isn't!"

Nessa gently gripped Maerlin's shoulder and turned her to face the tree. "Look there. What do you see?"

"It's just a tree, a big oak tree," Maerlin replied, trying her best to see the catch in the question.

"If I asked you to walk to where the pony is grazing over there and look back, or down by the lake shore, would you still see the same tree?"

"Of course!" Maerlin failed to see where the conversation was heading.

"Would the tree have changed, or moved while you walked?"

"No."

"But from beside the lake, or from the pony's side, the tree would look different. Yes?"

Maerlin thought a moment before replying "Yes, I suppose so, but that's just looking at it from a different angle."

"So, it'd be the same tree, only you'd be seeing it differently," pointed out Nessa, as if that explained everything.

"But it's still there. It's still just an oak tree. It didn't go invisible or anything."

Maerlin could see a flicker of frustration pass across Nessa's face as if she was wondering why she had agreed to teach her.

"Okay. Let us try a different tack. Since we stopped here, the tree has moved. In fact, it's moving right now if you look closely enough."

Maerlin looked until her eyes watered, but could not see the tree move. "Is this some trick?"

"No, it isn't. You see, the tree moves all the time, as do all plants. It follows the sun with its leaves in order to absorb as much sunlight as possible. Its roots constantly move in search of water and sustenance. Sun and water are life to the plants as they are to most things. Just because it moves so slowly that it cannot be seen does not mean it isn't moving. If you watch the sun for long enough, you know, it will head towards the west and disappear. It's constantly moving too, but slowly. 'What we see isn't always there, and what we can't see, still exists'. Are we getting it, yet?" Nessa asked in a hopeful tone of voice.

"Okay, I think I can understand the bit about what we can't see still being there, and the same could be said for what we hear as well, surely?"

"Well done, my dear. I see you aren't a total lost cause," replied Nessa with a warm smile. "Now, if we take your dream as an example. Dreams can be many things from flights of fancy all the way through to prophecy. Our minds use sleep to store the things we learn, but it is also influenced by things that happen while we sleep, such as the storm last night. It is also influenced by things we cannot see with our conscious mind. There are parts of our brain that are wiser, which as we grow older we tend to use less often. We rely on our intellect to sort out reality from the unpleasant things we cannot understand. It makes things disappear out of existence, because it cannot understand how they could exist. A problem arises, however, and it is this. Just because we deny their existence, does not mean to say that they go away. They remain hidden only because we choose to be blind to them."

From the look on Maerlin's face, it was clear that she had become lost somewhere during the conversation. "So, if we choose to refuse to see something, it disappears. Is that it?"

"That's fairly close for a first try, but it only disappears from view, not from existence. Let's head back to the tree and I'll show you something."

Nessa led her to the tree and placed Maerlin's hands on the rough bark. "Now, I want you to close your eyes and relax as if you were sleeping," she instructed "I'm going to have to join my mind with yours to show you this. Please remain calm or you could hurt us both."

Maerlin tried hard to be calm even though her mind was running around in circles, trying to understand all she was being told. Her body quivered with excitement.

"No! No! No! Calm I said. Listen to my breathing and follow it. Concentrate only on breathing and relaxing," instructed Nessa, whispering softly into Maerlin's ear.

"That's it," she murmured after a while "In ..."

"*Out ...*"

"*In ...*"

"*Out ...*" Her words were soft and soothing. They gently brushed against Maerlin's mind as she patiently calmed her to a relaxed state of being.

Moments passed in silence, Nessa's slow breathing calmed her protégé and prepared her for the next step. Maerlin felt light-headed and floaty as if her body was weightless. She was transfixed, listening to the soft gentle rhythm of Nessa's breathing. A voice spoke inside her mind, and it took a moment to realise that she had not heard it with her ears. "*You're learning fast, dear. I didn't think you'd be able to do this yet, even with my help. Now, move your mind gently or you'll dislodge me. When you're ready, focus your mind on the palms of your hands rather than on my breathing.*"

Maerlin's mind rushed towards her hands, eager to be at the next stage, and suddenly, the presence in her mind was gone.

"You moved too quickly, dear. Learn to crawl before you dash off like that!" Nessa reproached, though she had expected just such a thing to happen. "Do you want to try again?"

"Yes please, Nessa. I'm sorry. I guess I'm a bit nervous."

"That's alright dear. Just remember … move your mind slowly at first or I'll lose my grip on you."

Again, Maerlin felt the presence within her mind, and taking a deep breath, she tried to move her mind from her head into her hands. She felt her mind wobble as she moved forward and hesitated, uncomfortable with the sensation.

"It's all right, dear, just a bit of motion sickness. Your brain isn't used to moving around outside of sleep, that's all."

"Is this what your brain does when you sleep?" Maerlin asked, and again the connection broke.

Nessa sighed, trying to recover from the discomfort of being cast out of the mind-meld. "Let's try one more time before we give up for the day," she said, rubbing at her temples "Remember, I can hear your thoughts, so you don't need to speak out loud. When you spoke just then, your brain hopped about looking for your vocal cords."

Taking a deep breath, they tried again. Maerlin concentrated on moving her mind slowly down to her hands, afraid to speak while she moved, until eventually she could feel the texture of the bark against her fingertips.

"How's that?" she asked. This time she remembered to speak with her mind.

"Very good, dear, now let your mind seep into the bark and melt into the wood," instructed Nessa's soothing voice in her mind.

For a moment, nothing happened. Try though she might, Maerlin could not penetrate the thick skin of the bark.

"No, dear, don't attack the tree, embrace it. Become one with it."

Maerlin pulled back, fighting off a wave of apprehension and then tried to go forward again. This time, however, she sought empathy with the bark. She could feel the other presence in her mind trying to help, but for a long time nothing seemed to happen. The hard grainy texture of the bark seemed to resist her every thought while frustration gathered up inside her. *"I can't do it!"*

"You're fighting it, dear. Try absorbing it into your being."

Maerlin thought a moment on Nessa's words and tried a different tack. Instead of trying to push herself into the tree as she had been doing, she wrapped her mind around it instead. The ancient oak was huge, towering far above her head, and it was wide enough that she could have easily hidden behind its broad trunk. As she wrapped her mind around the tree, she could feel her consciousness stretching until her mind touched the topmost branches of the mighty oak. She could feel the wind, rustling through the uppermost leaves and sense them seeking out the sunshine.

"Very good, Maerlin, but don't forget the roots. Half of the tree is below ground."

Maerlin was lost in wonder at her mind's ability to encompass this much of the tree, but she was only halfway there. Turning her mind downwards, she burrowed into the soft soil beneath her bare feet. Deeper and deeper she went, sliding along roots to the feathery tendrils, where the soil and the tree became one. Here, the spirit of the oak and the spirit of the earth became inseparable. She went farther, seeking out the taproot, which ran strong and true into the bowels of the earth. She sensed the changing soil types and delved all the way down to the very bottom of the tree. Only then did she understand the immensity of the tree around which she was wrapped. Her mind fully embraced the tree, sinking deeper into its being. It felt to her like falling through thick molasses as she explored its slow, resilient character. She became aware of the many creatures that dwelt within the tree, from the owl sleeping in its upper branches to the butterfly larvae, cocooned within the leaves. Many tiny insects existed within. To these small creatures, this tree was the world.

Maerlin discovered a completely new universe within the tree. For a brief moment, she even felt something else, lurking deep within the oak's core, but Nessa pulled her back as she started to investigate.

"That'll be enough for one day. Hopefully, you'll understand my lesson better now."

"*But Ness ...*" she protested.

"*... No, you'll be tired enough, as it is. Withdraw your mind from the tree,*" Nessa ordered.

Chapter Four: Mind Games

They rested by the oak tree for the rest of the day. Maerlin spent most of the time drifting in and out of sleep. Thankfully, she did not suffer any further nightmares. Instead, she slept a deep and exhausted sleep. When she woke the following morning, however, it was to the worst headache she had ever had. Even after drinking some willow-leaf tea, her head continued to throb.

"I'm sure it'll ease as the day progresses," assured Nessa. She was smoking her pipe and lounging in the morning sunshine.

Maerlin tried to ignore the constant dull ache as she packed the pony "Does it always hurt like this when you use magic?" She struggled, unaided, to tie a heavy bundle into place.

"No, dear, that's only when we overreach our abilities. It reminds us that we are only human, which is sometimes necessary. Some magicians can be very arrogant, you know."

"Maybe I wasn't doing it right."

"No, dear, you did great. I remember my first time. My poor head throbbed for a week after." She looked at Maerlin's handiwork a moment and commanded "Stop, that won't do at all!" Her tone had gone from soft to harsh, so quickly, that Maerlin flinched back in surprise.

"What's the matter with it?" Maerlin looked at her work. "It was packed the same way yesterday."

"Yes dear, but I think I'll ride today. My old knees are aching. Take off that big, heavy bundle and move the others around. I'll need a makeshift saddle."

"But what are we going to do with all this?" Maerlin asked as she un-strapped the heavy bag. Ironically, it was the one she had such difficulty attaching in the first place. Her head pounded harder as she struggled to undo all of her hard work. She could feel her irritation rising.

"You'll just have to carry it, dear. You're young and strong. I'm sure it won't cause you any difficulty."

The reshuffling took a few moments after which time Nessa nimbly hopped into the makeshift saddle and nudged the pony into a trot. Maerlin could not see anything wrong with the healer's knees. Grabbing the heavy satchel, she hauled it over her shoulders and stumbled after the pony.

"I'm nothing but a skivvy," she complained as she stumbled along the mountain path. Her head was throbbing, and her jaw was clenched tight with anger. She hurried to catch up, but whenever she drew close, Nessa would kick the pony into a trot and leave Maerlin behind in a cloud of dust. This continued for most of the morning, and the clouds gathered and darkened as Maerlin's temper steadily worsened. "Damn her and her stupid pony!" Maerlin grumbled. She tripped over a boulder hidden in the grass and stumbling to her knees. "I don't need this! She can carry her own junk!"

Thunder rumbled loudly across the sky in response.

As if the sound of thunder was the signal she had been waiting for, Nessa halted the pony and dismounted. Looking back up the road, she inspected Maerlin for a moment and opened her mouth to say something, but decided against it. Instead, she turned away and started unpacking the pony.

Maerlin sat in the middle of the road, feeling frustrated, even though she knew she was being unreasonable.

Occasionally, Nessa would glance her way, but Maerlin refused to rise. Instead, she sat glaring at Nessa, head aching and feeling miserable.

When Nessa had finished with the pony, she turned the animal loose and sat down on their luggage. Delving into her coat, she fished out her pipe and filled it. Using a little magic, she lit the pipe and began to blow smoke rings with casual indifference.

Maerlin knew that Nessa could stay that way all day. She contemplated out-waiting the old woman, but she knew such a ploy was useless and that annoyed her even more. She sat there, stewing in her own anger and pondered her predicament. Finally, she rose to her feet and marched over with a determined set in her jaw. She would have this out with Nessa, she decided. She would make her see reason. As she approached Nessa, she considered how to begin the conversation, but nothing seemed appropriate. When the moment finally came to speak, Nessa beat her to it.

"... I was expecting a thunder storm to erupt before you got over your pouting, dear," Nessa commented, matter-of-fact. "That storm's been following you around like a puppy since first light."

Maerlin was lost for words as the reality of the situation dawned on her. Angrily she pointed an accusing finger at the old woman. "You've been goading me, haven't you? You have been doing it ever since we left the village. One moment, you're all sweetness and light, and the next you have me doing useless tasks for no reason."

"Nothing I do is without reason, dear." Nessa assured. "Nevertheless, yes, I have been goading you. How else am I going to see what you're capable of? You do realise that your temper is the key to these storms, don't you?"

Maerlin flushed.

"Well?" Nessa asked.

"Well, what?"

Nessa sighed and took a pull on her pipe, blowing a smoke ring before continuing "Well, if you want to stop bringing storms into the world willy-nilly, you're going to have to get a grip on that temper of yours."

Maerlin sank to the ground. "I can't help it! I get all flustered and mad about things."

Nessa blew another smoke ring, looking calmly at Maerlin. "Do you remember the oak tree yesterday?" She waited for Maerlin's nod before continuing "Do you remember how I got you to clear your mind, so that I could mind-meld with you?"

"Yes."

"When you feel angry or frustrated, or when your headaches come, try to do the same thing to clear your mind. It'll help you to deal with your anger. Is your head hurting now?"

Maerlin nodded, her headache had her close to tears.

"Okay, just lie back on the grass and relax."

Maerlin did so, hoping that it would help.

"Now, close your eyes and picture a blank white screen."

"Why a white screen?" Maerlin asked, her curiosity getting the better of her.

"Do you want to get better, Maerlin, or shall I just bring you back to your village?"

"Okay! Sorry." Maerlin tried to put aside her frustration and could see the vague light seeping through her eyelids. Her headache pounded on mercilessly as she tried to create the white screen. It kept changing colour as her thoughts drifted.

"Have you got it?"

"No! It keeps flickering in and out."

"Don't worry about that, dear. You're probably trying too hard. Just keep practising. You'll get there in the end and when you do, tell me and I'll show you the next step."

"There's a next step! What next step?"

"Don't ask questions, dear. All in good time."

Their journey continued, day after day, becoming a pattern of walking and talking. The conversations often left Maerlin baffled. Occasionally, she would catch sight of Nessa working some magic, but mostly, life proceeded with mundane regularity. At least twice a day, Nessa stopped their journey and asked Maerlin to do her mind-calming exercise. This meant that Maerlin had to try to envisage the white screen within her mind. Maerlin slowly learned to relax, but occasionally, Nessa would goad her into temper tantrums until the storm clouds gathered and thunder rumbled overhead.

The days passed in a blur as they wandered around the mountain range. The only change in routine was the occasional visit to villages and hamlets to heal the sick and restock their supplies. Maerlin wondered when they were ever going to stop travelling and reach Nessa's home. Finally, her curiosity overcame her. "Ness, how long will it be until we reach your home?"

Nessa looked at her in surprise and then with some amusement. "I've many homes, dear, but we're not heading to any of them at the moment."

"Then, where exactly are we going?"

"Nowhere in particular, Maerlin. Why do you ask? Was there somewhere you wanted to go?"

Maerlin thought the answer strange, but much of what Nessa said was strange. Choosing her words carefully, she tried to make sense of it all "We aren't going anywhere … we have to be going somewhere. We were heading south, but we seem to have turned easterly, recently. In fact, yesterday, we even turned north for the while. Just what is the point of all this travelling if we aren't going anywhere?"

"The point is to give me time to work with you without distraction."

Maerlin blinked in surprise. This possibility had never occurred to her. "I thought we were going to the Broce Woods, so that I could look after you while you cured me."

"Do I look that senile that I need to be looked after, Maerlin?" Nessa teased. "As for you … I'm afraid there's no cure for you, at all."

"What do you mean … no cure?"

"Maerlin, my little hawk, you've been blessed with 'Wild-magic'. How you got it, I don't know, but you certainly have it. It's a gift from the goddess, Deanna. How you would get rid of it, I don't know that either. You're just going to have to learn to live with it, like the rest of us. If you were born blind, I couldn't cure you of that, either. Some things are simply beyond my humble skills. You'll just have to deal with your 'disability', the same way I did. Once you can do that, then the choice is up to you. You can smother your gift and over time it will fade, or you can develop it, nurture it, and give it strength. It's up to you."

"You mean I can do magic, but I can't control it?"

"Maerlin, anyone can do magic if they have enough will power and work hard enough. What you have is 'Wild-magic'. That's a different thing entirely."

"I don't understand."

"Let me see if I can explain it to you. Do you know what magic is?"

Maerlin considered the question, but was still unsure of the answer when she guessed "Doing things that can't be explained, things that are impossible."

"No, dear, that's not it. I can teach you how some of the magic in the world works, though I've only studied a few strands of it. As for impossible, it's more likely to be improbable."

"What is magic then, Ness?"

Nessa tried to find an answer that Maerlin would understand. "Let's just say that magic is ..." She paused, seeking the right words. "I remember asking my mentor the very same question, and do you know what she told me? She said ... magic is channelling hidden powers towards a desired goal. Magic is using the mind, and perhaps certain props and aids, to make the improbable, achievable."

Maerlin repeated the phrase a few times, fixing it into her head before asking "So what's Wild-magic then?"

"Ah, now there's a good question! Wild-magic is a gift given to but a few. It comes to those who have an empathy with the Elementals; those are Fire, Air, Water, and Earth. There are many forms of magic which can create fire, but each has its own limitations. Wild-fire, however, knows no bounds. The Fire Elemental is literally in its element. If you can attain true empathy with the chosen Elemental, you can persuade it to do so very, very much more than any other form of magic can ever achieve. The only restraint on Wild-magic is your vision and your control over that particular Elemental. A note of warning, however, if you exert yourself too much, the Elemental can and will consume you. They are not beasts of burden. They have chosen you and will bless you with their powers, but they will not suffer abuse."

Maerlin nodded and considered the warning. "Which of the Elementals have I got ... is it Air?"

"Yes, it appears to be. That's why I test you so much. You must learn self-control before you can master your gift."

"You don't view it as a curse then? They hated me in the village because of the storms."

"There are many views on magic, especially Wild-magic. Some would call you a witch and try to kill you for having the gift, whether from fear or jealousy. Magicians normally learn to be subtle in their magical use. That is, if they want to live long enough to learn more than the basics."

"So that's why you always wait until you think I'm not watching before doing any magic," Maerlin accused.

Now it was Nessa's turn to look abashed. "Sorry, dear. Old habits die hard. I've spent too long being inconspicuous to start changing now. I hadn't planned to become a mentor again or I would've stayed on the Holy Isle. Anyway ..." she said, changing the subject in mid-sentence. She often did this, whenever Maerlin got the upper hand in any conversation. "...I can't teach you very much until you have learned control of your mind. That is the key to all magic, whether 'Wild' or otherwise. Speaking of which, how are you getting along?"

"Not too good I'm afraid. My concentration keeps wandering. I'm getting better though. I can get the white screen now, at least, but I keep getting flashes of colour on it."

"It'll come. Give it time. Why don't you sit back and try it again, now?"

Maerlin did as she was asked, but her mind was much too full of ideas about magic to concentrate on the task. Eventually, after trying for a long time, she gave up for the night and went to bed. "Ness?" she mumbled sleepily "Are we going to wander around in circles until I get this right?"

Nessa did not answer at first. Maerlin was nearly asleep when the reply finally came "No, dear. I think it's time for us to visit the Holy Isle."

Maerlin drifted into sleep with Nessa's words following her into her dreams.

The sound of children stirred Maerlin from her slumber.

Blinking awake, she looked around, surprised at the sound. Had the voyage with Nessa been nothing more than a dream? She lay in the cave again, feeling the chill of the morning on her aching body, but something about her small hidey-hole had changed. She could not put her finger on it at first. Looking out of the cave mouth, she blinked with surprise. Where once had been the wild, rugged mountainside, grazed by the lean, long-horned cattle of her village, now she could see a vast swamp, shrouded in mist.

Stepping out into the milky light, she shivered. It was cooler here than on the mountains and dampness filled the air.

"Ness?" she called out. Her voice echoed back at her through the mist, mingling with the chatter of children at play; the same noise that had woken her.

She could not see the children, so she followed the sound of their laughter. It was coming from over the small hillock into which the cave sat. As she crested the rise, her mind was filled with wonder. A massive, marble structure spread out before her with majestic towers and beautiful gardens, tended by women in pale blue or white robes. Before her, children were playing a game of ball on a well-groomed lawn. They jostled and cheered in wild abandonment. The sun shone clearly as if the mists of the swamp avoided this wonderful haven. It was as if she was standing juxtaposed between two worlds. Behind her was a great swamp, fog-filled and gurgling with unseen terrors, while before her, was a magical land of youth and beauty, emanating peace and tranquillity.

Unsure of herself, Maerlin sat down on the grassy hill, tugging down her worn shift to cover her dirty knees. She yearned to venture forward into this place of wonder, but fear held her back. She did not belong in such a place. She was just a poor mountain girl with no grace.

She opted instead to watch the scene, drawing contentment from the voyeuristic pleasure of watching other people's happiness. It had been too long since Maerlin had played with such wild abandonment, over a year now. She felt ill-equipped to join in with their revelry.

Finally, an elegant woman noticed her and walked over. "Peace to thee, Traveller. Hast thou come to praise our Mistress?"

Maerlin struggled to find an answer. Finally, she blurted out the truth, though it made little sense to her. "I don't know how I got here; I just woke up in that cave back there. I live in the mountain, and I was having a strange dream about wandering around, learning magic. When I woke up, I found myself here." She paused, and then asked "Where exactly am I?"

"Thou art on the Holy Isle, child. It lies within the Great Marsh. Thou art at the Temple of Deanna. Hast thou heard of it?" the Lady asked. "Come, Dream-catcher. Let us offer thee some food and drink, lest the world hears of our tardiness."

"Oh, no, I'd better not disturb your holy place. I know little of gods or worship," Maerlin protested, getting up and backing away.

"Sit, child, and we wilt speak together for a moment." The woman sat on the grass and patted the ground beside her in invitation. "I am the High Priestess, Ceila Ni Madra-Uisce, and this is my domain. No one gains entry to this sacred place without permission, for the Isle is protected by the goddess Deanna. If thou hast managed to pass the sacred wards, then thou must belong here as much as any other. So be at ease, Dream-catcher, for thy place amongst us is assured."

Maerlin sat, more out of politeness than from any reassurance.

"What is thy name, child?"

"They call me Maerlin, Ma'am," replied Maerlin, unsure of the correct address for a High Priestess, but feeling sure that there must be one.

Seeing Maerlin's discomfort, Ceila smiled warmly. "Maerl –een," she teased "... the little thief. So hast thou come to rob us of our wisdom and steal away our magic?"

"No! I'm not a thief, honest I'm not!"

Ceila emitted a soft laugh. "My apologies, Maerlin, I should not tease thee so. I was speaking of thy name. It comes from the small hawk, the merlin. Dost thou not know this? That is what it means in the Old Tongue; in Pectish."

Maerlin blinked, still confused.

"Maerlin, in the Old Tongue, means little thief. Thy namesake is a sharp and wily hawk. Forgive me, I did not mean to offend thee," apologised the High Priestess. "Well, Maerlin. Thou must call me Ceila. Welcome in my home."

"But how did I get here?"

The High Priestess pondered for a moment. "Tell me thy story, child, and I will try to aid thee."

They sat on the bank for some time as Maerlin spoke of her life, her mother's death, and the storms on the mountain. Ceila occasionally asked for clarification, listening carefully to the tale before finally saying "Something is amiss here. Tell me of this dream of learning magic."

Maerlin shifted in her seat, unsure where to begin. "Well, I guess it all started one morning when I was bringing the milk home from the cattle. I tend to wake early and sneak out of the village before the others wake. I like it at that time in the morning ..." She continued the tale of being attacked by the village boys and about her pretending to summon a storm. She spoke of her father's anger and the healer who had come to cure her of her 'possession'. She told of hiding in the cave and of the cramps and staggering through the storm, afraid of bleeding to death.

"That's when I met the healer. She braided my hair and told me that I'd become a woman. She found adult clothes for me to wear and took me away from the village. We wandered around the mountainside for weeks on end, or at least that's how it seemed."

Ceila looked at Maerlin for a moment, and then lifted one of her braids to show it to her. "There is a mystery here, child. Thy hair is braided, and yet thy clothes are those of a mountain girl. Tell me more about this healer?"

Maerlin studied the braid in confusion, before continuing with her story. "She was an old woman, but she was always full of life. In a way, she was like a second mother to me, at least when she wasn't bossing me around. I guess I would've liked her if she'd have been real. She told me I had something called 'Wild-magic'. She showed me how to make fire, and look into the heart of a tree. But that's all just a load of silly nonsense, isn't it?"

"Didst this healer have a name, Maerlin?"

"She called herself Nessa ... Nessa ... damn! I can't remember the last bit, but she told me to call her Ness."

"Nessa MacTire ... was that her name?" Ceila's eyes were wide in anticipation.

Maerlin looked up in surprise. "Yes. That's it. How did you know?"

Ceila laughed; a sweet musical sound. "Oh my ... oh my!" she exclaimed, wiping tears from her eyes as she struggled to control her mirth. "I think our mystery is solved."

Maerlin looked on, confused. "Really. Who is this healer? What does it all mean?"

"Sadly, I cannot answer that, Maerlin, but thou art indeed a special girl to have such powerful dreams. Now listen to me carefully, and do exactly as I say," Ceila instructed "I want thee to lie back, close thine eyes, and relax. Canst thou do that for me?"

Maerlin shrugged her shoulders and slumped down onto the grass.

"I'm going to use a little magic on thee, but it wilt not harm thee, fear not. It'll just make thee sleep for a while. When thou wakes, thou wilt be back where thy belongs. Is that alright?"

Maerlin nodded, still trying to fathom out parts of the conversation. "Can you heal my possession, as well?"

"Nay child, I cannot, but I sense that thy healing has already begun. Canst thou do me a favour while thou art asleep, Maerlin?"

"Yes, I'll try."

"If thou should dream again of this healer, Nessa MacTire, greet her with these words. Tell her that the High Priestess, Ceila, looks forward to their next meeting and wilt search the mists for her presence. She is always welcome in the Holy Isle."

Maerlin nodded, her eyes still closed. "I will," she promised, reciting the words repeatedly to help her remember them.

She felt a soft tingling in her brain as magic was drawn from the air, and then the soft whispered words "Deanna, I beseech thee. Aid me and guide mine hand. Bring this Dream-catcher back to her body."

The power built until Maerlin's ears rang. Her mind was still reciting the message. Realisation came to her then that Nessa had spoken to her of a

Holy Isle. As she blinked and turned, wanting to ask the High Priestess more, a soft command rang in her ears "Sleep."

Her head slumped to the ground, and she was lost in the swirling mists that surrounded the Isle.

She mumbled the words repeatedly, the phrase looping in her brain so that when she awoke, the words were still with her "The High Priestess, Ceila, looks forward to their next meeting and wilt search the mists for her presence. She is always welcome in the Holy Isle." Maerlin rubbed sleep from her eyes and looked around.

"What's that you just said?" Nessa peered at her through the murky light of pre-dawn.

Maerlin's mind did somersaults. "Am I back in this dream again?"

"I don't think so, dear. I think you're awake now," assured Nessa. Her face lit up as she pulled on the long-necked pipe. "Pinch yourself and see."

Maerlin pinched her skin, the slight pain confirming her situation. "I don't suppose I could be dreaming the pain, could I?" she asked, more to herself than to Nessa.

Maerlin sat quietly, listening to the sucking sounds that Nessa made as she smoked her pipe. Her world refused to make sense to her anymore, no matter how hard she tried to understand it. Just when she thought she understood something, her world would turn on its head and all would become a puzzle again. The dream had been so clear. She had been so sure that it was real, but it could not have been. Shaking her head in frustration, she tried to make sense of it all.

"What's the matter, Maerlin? Did you have another nightmare?"

"No. It wasn't a nightmare, as such. It was a dream ... a nice dream. I met a beautiful lady in a magical place, but the whole thing doesn't make any sense."

"Dreams rarely make sense, dear. What's bothering you about this one?"

"She said that she knew you, and she gave me a message to bring into my dream for you, but this isn't a dream, is it? How could she give you a message?"

"Message … what's the message, Maerlin? Tell me." Nessa was suddenly fully alert.

Maerlin sighed and tried to recall the message. "Hang on, I nearly have it," she said. Grasping the slippery message, she dragged it back into the light of day. "Okay, she said … 'the High Priestess, Ceila, looks forward to their next meeting and wilt search the mists for her presence. She is always welcome in the Holy Isle,' whatever that means."

"You were in the Holy Isle?"

"She called it the Holy Isle, or was it the Isle of the Mists?"

"It has many names, dear, but how did you get there? You're such a mystery to me, Maerlin. I really should have taken you there a long time ago. There are others there who are wiser than I am. They would know what to do with you."

Getting quickly to her feet, Nessa commanded "Get dressed, Maerlin. We've a long day's hike ahead of us. You can tell me more about this dream while we walk. I'll start packing. We can grab a bite to eat later."

Their camp was broken in record time, and even before the sun crested the horizon, they had begun the long day of walking. Nessa set a fast pace, intent on covering as much distance as possible. They headed south at a steady pace; hiking steeply down the mountain passes, though sometimes climbing over steep hills to keep on course. The meandering and constant course changes had gone. Now, they had a destination. Along the way, Nessa grilled Maerlin about the dream, going over it repeatedly in case Maerlin had missed out some minor detail. It was almost noon when they stopped to eat.

Their breakfast was quickly over, just some dry rations and water. Even the pony was forced to eat while still carrying its pack. Maerlin had hardly swallowed the dried meat before Nessa climbed to her feet and grabbed the pony's lead rope. Once again, they set off due south, but soon they had to call another halt. Before them they found a broad gully, running east-west across the mountainside. Ten spans farther across the open space, sat the rest of the mountain. Some force of nature, or the hands of a god, had split the mountain in two, leaving the deep ravine before them.

"Which way do we go?" Maerlin asked, looking left and right.

"Damn it! We haven't the time for this. I must've been getting daft in my old age, thinking I could do this alone. Why didn't I see this earlier?"

"What are you talking about, Ness? See what earlier?"

"Nothing, dear, never mind. I'm just kicking myself for being too clever for my own boots. Well, I guess there is nothing left to do but cheat. Can you see anyone around?"

Maerlin looked around. There was no one in sight, only a couple of mountain goats high up on a precipice.

"No, Nessa … why?" Maerlin wondered what had got into the healer.

"Very well then, here goes," muttered Nessa, rolling her sleeves up. She raised her gnarled arms and knelt on the stony ground. Stooping lower still until her head brushed the rugged surface of the rocks, she drew forth her hidden powers.

The hairs on Maerlin's arms tingled as she sensed Nessa's magic building.

"Spirits of the Earth come to my aid," Nessa growled in a harsh gravely tone so unlike the tone used by the White Sorceress within Maerlin's nightmare. Again, Nessa called out "Come, my dear Gnomes, I beseech thy aid for my need is great."

Maerlin's head filled with a buzzing sound, and the earth beneath her feet trembled. Dust clouds rose from the rocky surface as the trembling became a shaking. Maerlin was now sure that what she was witnessing was real and not just her imagination. The very air shrieked in protest as dust eddies swirled about them.

"Move!" Nessa commanded in the same gravely voice and pointed towards the far ridge of the ravine.

Maerlin clamped her hands over her ears as the sound of grinding stone echoed down the ravine. Her eyes watered as the dust swirled around them. Through her watery vision, Maerlin saw lumpy figures of rock and mud, bulky humanoid forms working to stretch and shape the solid rock into a causeway across the gap.

"Well, don't just stand there gaping, Maerlin, hurry! Cover the pony's eyes and lead him across. He won't venture over that bridge without your assistance."

The rumbling, grinding sound had ceased, only its reverberating echo remained. Dust still hung in the air as Maerlin grabbed the lead rope of the wild-eyed beast and covered its head with her shawl. Wrapping the woollen garment firmly round the pony's eyes, she dragged the skittish animal onto the newly-formed rocky outcropping. At first, the pony resisted, but soothing words from a familiar voice calmed the frightened pony, and he allowed himself to be led across the gap.

Maerlin tried not to look down, but the bridge was barely wide enough to walk on. Her stomach lurched every time she peered over the edge, even though she usually had no fear of heights. The ground, far below, seemed to pull her very bones downward. She crept along the thin rocky bridge towards the safety of the far side.

"Hurry!" Nessa urged from behind the pony. "This bridge will not hold long. It defies laws which refuse to be overlooked."

Shuffling backwards along the narrow walkway, coaxing the reluctant pony, seemed to take forever, but eventually her feet touched the far ridge. Sighing with relief, she pulled the pony to safety. Nessa followed a moment later, before collapsing on the rocky soil.

Nessa did not stay on the ground for long, however, no matter how pale and strained her face had become. Turning to look back over the narrow finger of rock, she raised her hands and spoke again "Bless thee, Spirits of the Earth, for thy aid. Thy task was well done."

The rumbling began again and the dust eddies swirled. Boulders within the bridge gave way and fell into the chasm. The noise built, as more and more of the bridge slipped free of its bindings. Within moments, it was no more. Maerlin looked across the ravine in amazement. All that was left of the narrow causeway was the echo of boulders landing below.

She turned to speak to Nessa, excited at the wonder she had just witnessed, but Nessa's pale, haggard face stilled her words. "Ness, are you alright?"

"Don't worry, I'll live. Be a dear, and make up a fire, will you? I could do with a cup of strong tea after that."

Maerlin looked down at the old woman, unsure whether to leave her side.

Nessa smiled weakly and patted her hand "Tea, dear!" she prompted in the hope of shifting Maerlin into action. It worked. Maerlin skipped up the ridge, looking for kindling as if her life depended on it.

She returned a few moments later, relieved to see that some colour had returned to Nessa's face and she began the arduous task of lighting a fire. With no tinderbox to make the task easier, Maerlin was forced to use the fire bow. Even with Nessa's helpful advice, the job took some time, but eventually a small flame appeared. It was carefully nursed into life. Feeding the flames with twigs and dried goat dung, Maerlin created enough of a fire to heat the small teapot and make the herbal infusion. Under Nessa's careful direction, she measured out selected dried herbs into the pot, and soon a pungent aroma rose from the boiling water.

Chapter Five: Dirty Old City

Maerlin repacked the pony while Nessa regained some of her strength. Maerlin was content to stay longer, but Nessa seemed to have an urgent need to be somewhere else. She would hear none of it.

"I'm fine. I'm just a little tired, that's all," Nessa insisted as she made her way to the pony and climbed onto its back. "I'll just ride for a while. We should make good time now. It's all downhill from here."

The trek began again, with Maerlin carrying the heavy satchel and leading the pony down the mountain. As they rounded a bend, Maerlin stopped and stared in wonder at the vista that had opened up before her.

Below her, she could see a vast expanse of grassy hills stretching farther than she had ever seen before. It seemed to go on for leagues and leagues, to a far-distant horizon. Never in her life had she seen such a green fertile land. They had reached the end of the mountains and below stretched the hilly lowlands and fertile plains of Dragania. Two broad rivers cut through the land, converging farther south to create a gigantic wetland. From up on the mountainside, this area looked like a sea of mist, with green hillocks occasionally rising above the deep, foggy sea. Even the late afternoon sun failed to burn away the cloaking mists which covered the marshland.

The view was breathtaking. Even Nessa seemed content to sit and gaze at the scenery for a while. Finally, the healer spoke "The sun's slipping into the west so we should hurry. We need to be down off this mountain before dark."

Maerlin nodded, pulling the weary pony back into motion and turning away from the spectacular view. They headed down the mountain at a brisk pace, meandering along the goat tracks that crisscrossed the rocky terrain. Always, they selected the track that led downhill, zigzagging back and forth as they descended towards the hilly land below. As dusk came nearer, the vegetation changed, becoming greener. Soon they were walking through lush knee-high grass with pollen rising in clouds around them. The pony stooped to snatch clumps of the sweet grass in passing, hungry after the long journey.

"Soon, lad," assured Nessa, patting the pony's thick neck. "We're nearly there now."

"Nearly where, Ness?"

"The city of Manquay. It's a couple of miles farther on. We'll stop there for the night and hire a ship to take us downriver in the morning."

"We'll be sleeping in a city?" Maerlin had never seen a city before and could not keep the excitement out of her voice.

Ness smiled at her protégé. "Cities aren't really all that nice, dear. They're dirty, smelly places, filled with the dregs of humanity. I have no love of cities, or their inhabitants for that matter. Hide that silver pendant beneath your bodice and strap down the baggage. The children here would steal the teeth from out of your mouth, and some of the men are no more than brigands."

The warning failed to dampen Maerlin's excitement; nevertheless, she did as she was bid. Soon, they were looking down at the smoky shamble of the city. The houses were very different from the tidy conformity of the mountain village with its central square and golden thatch. Here, the houses sprang up, seemingly at random. A three-storey dwelling towered over its one-storey neighbour. Thatch mingled with shingle, and occasionally even slate was used as a roofing material. Many of the houses leaned outward, as if straining to reach the other side, leaving the space in-between dark and foreboding.

Dogs ran out to greet them as they neared the city gates. They were barking, mangy creatures with hungry eyes. Children followed, looking as hungry as the dogs. They were dirty-faced and dressed in rags. They tugged on the travellers clothing, eyes vacant and pitiful as they held out their hands in supplication.

Nessa shooed them away with a wave of her hand, her chin determined.

"Let's step up the pace a bit, shall we … or we'll be swamped with beggars," Nessa urged and kicked the weary pony into a reluctant trot. Maerlin groaned as she followed, trying to take in the scenes before her, while hurrying through the cramped streets. Soon, the begging children petered off. The commotion and bustle of the streets, however, only grew worse. Their pace slowed to a crawl as they progressed through the throng.

Hawkers yelled incoherent words and held up choice articles for sale: pig heads, cow hocks, and even some strange-looking fish with razor-sharp teeth. Others sold trinkets, fine goods, beads, and bolts of fine cloth, the likes of which Maerlin had never seen before. Torches hung on rings every few feet, competing with the depleting daylight to fight off the dark shadows. Alleyways cut away from the main thoroughfare, dark and filled with debris.

Looking down one of these alleys as they passed, Maerlin noticed a well-dressed man being held at knife-point by three gangly youths. Another straggly-bearded ruffian was ransacking the merchant's baggage. She stopped in her tracks, watching the struggling merchant pleading with the brigands, until one of the muggers turned and leered at her.

"Maerlin! Stop loitering back there. We haven't got all day, you know."

Maerlin scurried away, hurrying to catch up with Nessa and the pony before they were swallowed up in the mass of people.

"There were thieves back there! They were robbing a merchant … in broad daylight!"

Nessa looked upwards to catch the last of the orange sunlight, gauging the quality of light to determine the time of day. "Mmmmm, they're a bit early," she muttered indifferently. "Still, the early bird catches the worm as the old saying goes. Hurry up, dear. Don't get sidetracked with the more colourful parts of city life."

They hurried on, as fast as the crowded streets would allow, until Maerlin felt well and truly lost in the complex crisscrossing of tiny streets.

"Where're we going?" Maerlin whined, after they had passed what seemed like the fiftieth inn. Her feet ached, and her stomach rumbled with hunger. She longed to be finished with walking for the day and for the comfort of a soft bed.

"We're looking for a decent hostelry, my dear," Nessa explained as they passed one of the many inns on the street.

"What's wrong with the one we just passed?"

"Do you want to wake up full of fleabites and rashes, and probably with the scours from someone's dodgy cooking?"

"It can't be that bad … can it? How would they make a living?"

"I'd imagine they rely on ignorant, mountain folk who don't know any better. The place we want will be off the beaten track somewhere, but not down one of those dark alleys. It'll turn up soon, if we keep going in this general direction."

"You mean to say that you don't know where it is?" Maerlin asked in disbelief. She had been relying on Nessa as her guide.

"Well, no, not exactly … but I'll know the hostel when I see it," Nessa replied, with an air of confidence.

Maerlin had long since given up on understanding all of what Nessa said, so she chose not to argue. They turned into a small side-street, not quite an alley, but barely wide enough for a wagon to drive down, and Maerlin noticed another tavern, up ahead. It was shabby and run-down, so Maerlin expected to pass it by and continue along the street, but as they approached it, Nessa called a halt and inspected the establishment more closely.

"Yes," she said with a smile. "I thought it was. We're here, Maerlin. Take the pony around the back to the stables. I'll go inside and speak to the proprietor."

"Hang on! You cannot be serious. This place is a kip. It's likely to collapse at any moment. There was a much nicer place, back yonder."

"Maerlin," Nessa replied in that sweet old-lady tone, which Maerlin had learned to be wary of. "Have you forgotten the first lesson I taught you?"

"No … but what's that got to do with it?"

Nessa just looked calmly at Maerlin, obviously waiting for something more.

With a sigh, Maerlin repeated the lesson aloud, her tone showing her exasperation. "You said: 'What we see isn't always there, and what we can't see, still exists'."

Nessa smiled. "Exactly, dear. Now hurry along. I don't know about you, but I'm famished."

Maerlin jaw opened, but she was unable to utter any objection as she watched the healer slip down off the pony and hurry inside. She was left with only the pony for company, and it was starting to get dark. Suddenly, Maerlin felt very much alone, even though the streets were still bustling with activity. Nervously, she looked around. Everywhere she looked, she saw the eyes of muggers and thieves. Yanking on the pony's lead rope, she hurried around the side of the tavern and to the stables beyond.

A youth lay snoring noisily on a haystack as she inspected the back of the hostelry. Walking closer, she studied the boy, waiting for him to stir. He was lean and wiry. His face was lightly freckled, and his hair was the golden colour of fresh wheat straw. His snoring was loud and fluty, as if he had swallowed a whistle. He would breathe in with a loud, rattling wheeze, and then exhale slowly in a long whistle-like breath. The sound grated against Maerlin's already frayed nerves. His snoring continued while Maerlin watched, grinding her teeth with vexation. Occasionally he punctuated the snores with a raspy snort, mid-breath. This last sound was even worse than the snoring.

Maerlin cleared her throat to wake the boy, but he only shuffled in his sleep and snored louder.

Looking to the pony, she commented waspishly "... And I thought your snoring was bad enough. It seems we're in the company of Manquay's snoring champion!"

The pony snorted loudly in reply and stretched his neck out to nibble at the hay on which the boy was sleeping. The boy, however, did not stir. He slept as soundly as a gargoyle, if not as quietly.

Maerlin's patience was, by now, seriously wearing thin. It had been a very long day, and she was tired and hungry. Barely holding her temper in check, she cleared her throat again.

The snoring continued unabated.

She cleared her throat as loudly as she could, scraping the larynx raw in her effort to wake the sleeper.

Still, he snored on, oblivious to her efforts. Clouds were gathering overhead, sensing her rising temper.

"Boy!" she called out, her head throbbing. This was a sure sign of trouble, had she been paying attention. The wind had picked up, but in the cosy hollow of the stable area, this too went unnoticed. "Boy!"

There was no response, apart from a raspy snort.

"BOY!" she roared at the top of her lungs. Maerlin stood with her arms tight to her sides and fists clenched, glaring at the sleeping boy. As if to punctuate her shout, thunder echoed loudly overhead. The pony threw its head back at the sound and yanked hard at its rope, only adding to Maerlin's growing temper.

"What? Hmmm!" spluttered the stable boy as he jerked awake.

"You lazy, mange-riddled, goblin-spawned, bag of mule dung!" Maerlin ranted. "I've been trying to wake you for ages …" The rest of her rant was drowned out by a torrent of rumbling thunderclaps above the city.

The boy looked about in confusion at the wild-eyed girl and her skittish pony. Startled, and still half asleep, he slid off the edge of the haystack and hurried across the yard, hoping to put some distance between himself and this clearly deranged madwoman.

"Come back here, right now, you lazy sod. Do you hear me?" Maerlin ranted. "I haven't finished with you yet!"

Lightning flashed overhead as she stormed after the retreating figure, dragging the reluctant pony behind her. She cornered him in the tack room and marched resolutely towards him.

"Maerlin! Stop playing with the stable hand and come inside at once." Nessa's sharp command had come from the back door of the tavern, halting Maerlin just before she could release another verbal tirade on the hapless boy.

"I wasn't playing," Maerlin argued, turning to face Nessa.

Another woman was standing beside Nessa. She was a slightly plump woman of middle years. Both of the women were studying the black, tempestuous clouds, which, as if on cue, rumbled overhead.

Nessa spoke again, looking pointedly at Maerlin. "I think it's time you practised your exercises, dear."

"But …" Maerlin protested, though she never got to finish the sentence.

"… No buts, dear. Leave the boy alone and come inside. There'll be hot food and a bath, soon enough. From the looks of it, I think you're in need of both, don't you?"

A quick flicker of a smile crossed Nessa's face as she stood waiting for Maerlin.

Glaring at the stable boy, she threw the lead rope in his general direction and stormed off, muttering curses under her breath.

*****

Maerlin followed the two women inside, where she was directed to a secluded corner table and told to sit down and do her exercises. At first, she was too tired and frustrated to relax, let alone concentrate on the task; but within a short while, she had calmed down enough to achieve the white screen in her mind. She kept the image there, breathing slowly in and out, until the two women returned. They brought with them a platter of bread and cheese, two bowls of thick beef stew with chunky vegetables, and even some warm milk.

Nessa dished out the meal while continuing her conversation with the other woman. "…So we need to get to the Isle as quickly as possible, where she can get better tutelage. I'm more than able for most of the tasks, but the dreams have me concerned. She needs a Dream-catcher to interpret them properly."

Noticing Maerlin listening, Nessa turned to her protégé. "Maerlin, let me introduce you to Madame Dunne. She's the proprietor of this establishment, and a fine cook." Nessa continued, turning to Madame Dunne. "Ester, this is Maerlin, my apprentice."

"Hello, Ma'am," Maerlin greeted politely. Her mind was doing back-flips at being referred to as Nessa's apprentice.

"Oh, you can call me Ester. You're a woman now, after all," instructed the cheery-faced innkeeper "Small though you are. I see that you've compensated for your size with a feisty temper. You even managed to get Conal flustered. It's taken me a while to get him to stop pouting and fetch some water for your baths. He's normally such a boisterous boy."

"Boisterous!" Maerlin exclaimed "The lazy snot was fast asleep and snoring like an overweight boar-hog in high summer."

"Well, yes, I guess that's true. He does sleep a lot, and heavily at that. I've never seen a boy sleep so much, but believe me, you're better off when he is sleeping. He's a bit of a handful when he's awake, you mark my words."

Maerlin refrained from comment. The boy had got under her skin, and even speaking about him made her blood pulse stronger. Biting back further comment, she went back to eating.

Nessa interrupted at this point. "Do you know a good riverboat that can take us to the Holy Isle?"

"Yes, Ness, I do. As soon as it gets dark, I'll send Conal down to find Captain Bohan for you. The man's trustworthy, and he knows the river like the back of his hand."

"Why wait until then? Isn't it more dangerous for him after dark?" Nessa asked.

"He's as safe as anyone can be," assured the innkeeper. "I swear he must spend the whole night prowling around the rooftops, or down back alleys. I have never known a boy take such an interest in the darker side of the city. He has the nose of a ferret and all the charms of a sewer rat."

"Why do you let him wander, then?"

"What choices have I? I can't have him seen, like I explained earlier."

Maerlin's curiosity was piqued by the conversation, so she sat quietly, eating a second helping of the stew, and listened closely to the women. They talked on, completely ignoring her, which suited Maerlin perfectly.

Madame Dunne continued "He drove me demented at first, of course; though to be fair to him, I can't blame him. I've tried to explain to him, but you know how young people can be, too full of their own importance to listen to reason. Anyway, we argued and argued until eventually we agreed on a compromise. Not that I had much choice mind you, apart from locking him in the cellar, and I don't think that Ceila would approve of that."

"So what did you agree to?" Nessa asked.

"I told him that he could go wherever he wanted after dark, as long as he was careful not to be seen, but he was to stay behind the tavern during daylight. It seemed the only solution. Anyway, since then, we've come to some sort of a truce. He doesn't drive me demented with pranks, and I don't harangue him with nagging. It isn't the best solution, but it works. I'd thought I was onto a good deal minding this old place for the Order until they dropped that little demon into my lap. They might as well have given me a young dragon cub to mind. His blood runs true, that's for sure. I've heard that his father was a wild one, too."

Maerlin was having trouble keeping up with the conversation. It seemed that Madame Dunne spoke as much nonsense as Nessa. Either that or there was something going on that Maerlin was being kept out of. However, she had learned by now that asking questions was a sure way to get her lumped with some horrible chore to do. It never got her any useful answers, so she ate quietly and tried to blend into the background, hoping that they would let something useful slip.

They continued to talk, but the topics soon became dull. Maerlin's eyes started to become heavier and before she knew it, she let out a jaw-cracking yawn.

"I think you should be off to bed, my dear," Nessa suggested.

"No, I'm fine, honest." Maerlin rubbed the sleep from her eyes in an effort to look awake.

"Bed, dear, now." Nessa commanded with a soft smile. "It's the third door on the left, at the top of the stairs. Conal has already put your stuff in there for you. Sleep well. I'll wake you at first light."

With a sigh, Maerlin pulled herself off the bench and headed towards the stairs. "I always miss all the best bits!" she muttered to herself as she stomped up the rickety staircase. In her room, she threw off her clothes, dumped them in a pile and slumped down on the bed. It was lumpy, but clean, smelling of fresh sheets and fragrant herbs, lavender, and rose. Pulling the thin blanket up over her body, she snuggled down and was soon fast asleep.

Exhaustion dragged her deeper into sleep, and soon the dreams came...

She saw the rocks make themselves into a bridge, and then the bridge begin to crumble before she had fully crossed it, forcing her to leap to safety. She found herself falling into an alleyway, and saw the muggers who had accosted the merchant. As the thief turned to look her way, he became the blonde-haired stable boy, leering in her direction.

She tossed and turned, images flashing through her mind in rapid succession, becoming more bizarre with every passing moment.

Suddenly, she found herself in a dark chamber. She could hear water dripping off the roof, falling into small pools beneath her bare feet.

"Hello ... is there anyone there?" Maerlin called out as she groped around. "Hello?"

"It's no use, child. There's no one here to help you." a voice said from behind her, making her flinch and spin around. She noticed a dim light in the distance.

"Where are you?" she asked. "I can't see you."

The reply was a soft, raspy chuckle that filled her with dread. "Maybe that's for the better. Darkness is a mantle I wear well."

Maerlin made her way towards the dim light, stepping carefully through pools of stagnant water.

"Are you hiding?"

"Hiding! Why would I have to hide? I'm the most powerful magician ever born. I've no need to hide. There is none that can defeat me."

"Then why do you lurk in the dark?"

Again, she heard the hollow laughter; a mocking cackle of madness. "You've much to learn, child, and no time to learn it. Give it up now, and let my rats devour you. They'll be quick, if not painless."

She heard the ruffling of feathers in the darkness and sensed power being summoned "Come, servants of the ancient one, I command thy attendance. Come ... do my bidding."

Silence hung briefly in the air, and then she heard a sound that made her tremble. A scratching and soft screeching noise that grew louder as the summoned creatures drew nearer. Soon, her mind was filled with the sound of scraping, gnawing and squealing. A plague of rats was rushing to the summons, and she desperately looked for an escape. None appeared. Tiny, clawed feet touched her flesh, and fur brushed against her naked feet. Feeling the first of the creatures' claws on her leg, she screamed.

Her scream went on and on, until suddenly a light appeared, bright and blinding.

"Hush, dear. It's only a nightmare." Nessa's soothing voice helped to calm her. "It's alright, I'm here now." Her tone changed to one of surprise as she added "What, by sweet Deanna, are they doing in here?"

Maerlin blinked away her tears and turned to look at the writhing forms on her bed. There were three furry creatures staring back at her with sharp, beady eyes. Another was evidently beneath the covers, as a lump was moving up the bed beside Maerlin's legs. Maerlin screamed again, and throwing the blanket aside, she leapt off the bed. Running to Nessa, she clung to her.

"What are they? They're horrible!"

Chapter Six: Conal's Adventures

Earlier that night ...

Conal, the stable hand, was still annoyed. The witch-girl and her pyrotechnical wizardry had really given him a fright, and he was determined to return the favour, with interest.

He had just begun to put his plans into action when the innkeeper collared him, wanting him to fetch water. He hurriedly carried the buckets into the kitchen, hoping to finish the errand quickly. Luck was not with him, however.

"Ah! There you are, Conal." Madame Dunne marched into from the scullery, carrying some pans. "Just the boy I needed."

"What now?"

"I need you to take these bags upstairs to rooms three and four for Nessa and her apprentice. Put Nessa's belongings into the bigger room, and the small leather satchel needs to go into wee Maerlin's room."

"Why me?"

"Who else is going to do it? The scullery maid and the serving girl have their hands full already. All you do all day is sleep. Is it too much to ask for you to give a help out, once in a while?"

Her voice was rising as she spoke, a clear sign of impending trouble, so Conal gave up and with a loud sigh, headed off. The witch-girl was sitting quietly, eyes closed as he slipped through the common room. He clambered noisily up the stairs, weighed down with baggage, and headed for the larger room, where he dumped the bags into a corner. Fishing out the satchel, he headed to the second room and slipped inside. Listening quietly for a moment to make sure he would not be disturbed, he dropped the satchel on a stool and moved towards the window. It looked out onto the stable yard. A small lean-to jutted out below the window's ledge, where guests could tie their horses up out of the rain. Reaching up, he loosened the bolt on the window, leaving it with only a simple clasp to hold it in place. Such a clasp was child's play to any competent thief. Smiling to himself, he hurried away, happy with his newly amended plan.

As he skipped downstairs, heading for the stable, Madame Dunne accosted him again. "Ah, Conal, hang about, I've got another job for you." Her expression broached no arguments.

"What now?" he whined, rolling his eyes. He was never going to get his revenge at this rate.

"I need you to go down to the docks and find Captain Bohan for me. Tell him that I'll require his services in the morning. I want to book passage for a trip down the river. Have you got all that?"

Conal bit back the comment he was about to make, knowing that the innkeeper's patience did not stretch to cheek. He could not, however, hide the look of condescension that passed across his face. Anyone would think he was a brainless dimwit, not to be able to remember a simple message like that. Still, he thought, at least he would have a chance to go out into the city and wander around for a bit, without her asking him where he'd been all night. He might even find a few valuables lying around in need of a good home. The dockside taverns always held a bit of excitement and were a great place to exercise his dexterity.

Conal blinked, wondering why the innkeeper was staring fixedly at him. "What?" he asked.

Ester Dunne sighed and threw her arms in the air, turning away and muttering to herself.

Conal shrugged. "Hey, I didn't ask to live here, you know. Ever since Lord Boare killed my father, I've been mollycoddled by women from the Holy Isle. It took a lot of effort to get Ceila to see sense and let me out of that damned swamp. I would've been happy to make my own way in life, but no, she insisted on me having another babysitter around."

They glared at each other in sullen silence, neither wanting to go over this old argument again.

He was fed up of being constantly watched by this broody spinster who treated him like an imbecile and made him work as if he was some half-wit country bumpkin. He hated being cooped up here, when he could be out avenging his father's death, but in his heart he knew that the Deanna witch's advice made sense. Making sense was one thing, but it did not mean he had to like it.

Conal was finally free of the day's restraints. Darkness had fallen. He scurried to the back of the stables and swept the loose straw away from the floorboards. He quickly found the tiny hole hidden there, just big enough for his finger. Slipping his forefinger inside, he pulled a small section of boards free to reveal the hidden cavity beneath. Below lay the treasures he had acquired over his time in the city. Within, there were jewels, coins, and other small valuables; things that could be easily concealed about the person. There was a tidy fortune within his cache, savings for when Conal came of age. He was a boy with a vision of his future. Reaching down into the cavity, he retrieved a ragged grey tunic and slipped into it. His stable clothes were far too clean and tidy for his night's adventure. He had no intention of become a victim by mistake. Tidy clothes would attract undue attention in the poorer sections of the city. At best, they were liable to earn him a beating. At worst, he could end up floating down the river, come morning; cold, stiff and blue.

A ragged cap completed his disguise, hiding his golden locks and throwing shadows over his distinctive blue eyes. Slipping the planks back into place, he scattered straw over the floorboards and headed to the farthest stall. Here, some cages had been set up in the shadows. Stooping, he scrapped his nail over the wire mesh and pursed his lips together, emitting a soft, screeching noise. From within the cage, a scuffling could be heard. Soon heads appeared, small sharply-pointed heads, covered with brown and white fur. Claws hooked into the caging as they climbed up to greet him.

"Hey there," he greeted, pushing titbits through the cage. Sharp incisors leapt eagerly towards the morsels of meat, and a playful squabble began.

"Settle down. There's enough for everyone!" he admonished as he hurriedly pushed more of the stolen ham through the wire grilling. Sharp teeth nipped at his finger as the big male lunged forward to claim his share.

"Drew!" Conal scolded as he stuck the bleeding finger into his mouth. "Mind my hand, you greedy bugger! Anyone would think I didn't feed you." Conal smiled. It was only a minor nip. He knew that it was more from over-enthusiasm than from any malice.

"I have a job for you, my lovelies," he told the sleek, musky creatures. Small, intelligent eyes watched him as he opened the cage and scooped them into a sack. When they were all secured, he scaled onto the roof of the hay barn. From there to the lean-to beside the tavern was easy for one

75

of his skills. A simple bound across the gap and then a shimmy along the ledge. Creeping silently along the roof tiles, he edged towards the window and peered inside. All was quiet within. He could see the sleeping form of the witch-girl. Now was his time for revenge.

Pulling out his dagger, he slid it between the sash windows and worked it up under the latch. Careful not to make any noise, he prised up the lever and heard it scrape slowly away from its housing. The window was now free to open, but experience had taught him patience. He stood, watching the sleeping girl within, making sure that he had not disturbed her slumber.

She seemed restless, constantly tossing and turning. He smirked, knowing that her sleep would soon be more troubled. It would teach her for ruining his own sleep, he thought, stifling a chuckle.

Slowly, he pried the window open wide enough to allow him access, and slipped into the room. The room was dark enough in the moonlight, so he stepped carefully, lest he knock over a chamber pot or stool. Hardly breathing, he tiptoed over to the bed and looked down at the girl, studying her more closely. She was pretty enough, if a little petite. She had a tiny button nose that suited her face. She frowned as she tossed about on the bed, revealing a naked shoulder in the moonlight. Conal licked his lips nervously and pulled the cover slowly back further until a small, pert breast came into view. He had always wondered why some of the other boys showed such a great interest in them. Gazing down at the small mound, he couldn't see anything special about it. Did something happen to them as they got bigger, he wondered?

"Hello! Is there anyone there?" Maerlin murmured, causing Conal to flinch back, breaking the spell that had held him rooted before her. Cursing himself for daydreaming, he focused on the task at hand. He dug into his pocket and sprinkled morsels of ham onto the bed. Maerlin tossed about, adding to his nervousness as he untied the burlap sack.

"Hello!" she repeated in a frightened voice.

For a moment, he hesitated, doubt briefly touching his mind. He looked down at Maerlin, so delicate and frightened in her sleep. For one brief moment, compassion flickered across his mischievous mind. Such pity was not for little boys, however, especially not this one. Soon, his urge for revenge and his joy of pranks won over his rash moment of pity. With a rueful shake of the head, he tipped the ferrets onto the bed. Pausing only long enough to gather up the sack, he slipped out of the window and into the night.

*****

Sometime later that evening, Conal was on the rooftops, stopping only long enough to smear his exposed skin in a light covering of soot. He headed towards the distant docklands, eyes constantly roving for danger or opportunity. Climbing down from the rooftops and into the myriad alleyways as he neared the docks, he continued his steady downhill progress. It was a good night to be out. The moon hung low in the sky, giving off a poor light, and the earlier storm had passed leaving a clear, starry sky. It was a still night. It was the type of night where mosquitoes lurked, waiting to suck blood from any exposed flesh, but the soot helped to keep them at bay. Conal was content in this dark, exciting world.

He headed down an alley with a confident stride, his feet making little or no noise. He was nearly at his destination when a shadow appeared, silhouetted against the torchlight at the end of the alley. It was a tall man, and he was clearly the worse for drink. Conal slipped deeper into the shadows.

"Come on! Hurry it up, will ya. The girls are getting restless," urged a voice from beyond the alley. It seemed the drunkard was not alone.

"Ach! Stop being such an old woman, Scrett. They won't be in such a rush when they find out we've got good coin to spend," replied the drunk as he staggered farther into the alley, heading towards where Conal now hid. The boy braced himself, knife at ready should he need it. Any moment now, the man would walk right into him, and there would be no way to explain why he was lurking here in the dark. Conal was sure that he could kill the man, whose reflexes would be slowed by drink, but he didn't know how many others waited beyond the alley.

At the last possible moment, the drunkard stopped and turned away. Conal's nerves were humming with the urge for action. Holding his breath, he strained to see what the drunk was doing.

The sound of splashing came to his ears, and his nostrils filled with the pungent odour of second-hand beer, as the man urinated against the far wall.

Calming his pounding heart, Conal waited, ignoring the cloying reek.

"Are ya gonna be all night, Bolcher? We don't have that much time with the girls, ya know. We're supposed to be out searching for the Dragon whelp, remember?"

"Yeah, yeah, yeah, hold ya horses, Scrett!" Bolcher growled. "If I strain any harder, I'll bust me bladder. His Lordship'll just have to wait a while longer."

"That's easy for you to say. I don't wanna be the one to tell 'im that we let the lad slip out of our grasp. Do you?"

"He isn't going anyplace, Scrett, and besides, we've only got a few more taverns to check out. He has to be hiding out in one of 'em. If we don't find him tonight, we'll nab the wee scut tomorrow."

"That's if he doesn't get wind of us first. It's not the first time the lad's escaped from his Lordship's grasp."

"You worry too much, Scrett. Lord Boare's gonna give us a big fat reward when we deliver him the boy's head."

Conal felt a chill run down his spine. He knew, even in this near darkness, what the emblem on the soldier's uniform would be. He would bet his treasure hoard that the drunkard was wearing a black boar on a red tabard. This man and his companion were surely Boarites, and he hated Boarites nearly as much as he hated their master: Lord Boare.

Conal realised that his time as a stable-boy was now over. He had hoped to delay it for a few more moons, but Lord Boare must somehow have learned about his hidey-hole. Conal was getting fed up of running away from the likes of these Boarite scum.

Any thoughts of hiding quickly disappeared as anger flared up in Conal's brain, and he stepped forward on silent feet. The Boarite was busy shaking himself when Conal's knife struck him through his leather armour and into his ribcage. Conal rammed the blade home, forcing it through the tough cowhide and upward, seeking out the soldier's heart. He smothered off the drunkard's cries with his other hand.

The soldier initially froze in shocked surprise, but soon his training kicked in and he writhed about, trying to break free. Conal jumped onto the Boarite's back while the soldier twisted and turned in an effort to dislodge his assailant. All the time, Conal pushed the blade deeper, twisting it to slice through the organs of the upper body. The Boarite gurgled through his punctured lungs, trying to cry out. He slammed Conal into a wall in a desperate attempt to break free. The blow crushed Conal between the wall and the soldier, bashing his head against the brickwork and winding him badly. He was finally forced to release the Boarite.

Stars spun in his head. He strained to keep a grip on the bloody knife as the soldier stumbled away. Conal retched and hacked as he forced air into his lungs. He waited for the killing blow, but badly winded, he was unable to defend himself. The blow, however, never came and as the moments passed, he gasped for breath.

"Have ya gone to sleep in there, Bolcher?" Scrett grumbled from the end of the alley.

No reply came from within the alley, only the wheezing of Conal's ragged breathing.

"Stuff this! I'm gonna catch up with the girls. If you hurry up, I might leave ya one of them." Laughter rang down the alley and into Conal's dazed head, but still no blow came.

After some moments had passed, Conal recovered enough to look down at the body. The man was obviously dead. The blow as he struck the wall, had sent Conal's knife up to the hilt in his back. It must have found the soldier's heart along the way. Conal rummaged the man's body for valuables and stuffed the findings into his tunic. He would inspect them later. Quickly, he pulled his dagger free. Wiping off any excess blood, he sheathed the blade and stood listening.

The night was still, or at least as still as the dockside ever got. Conal considered his options. He could not be sure what he would run into if he continued down the alley, so he opted to take a different route to the dockside. He would need to be extra careful. There may be other Boarites in the city, sent on the same mission.

Eventually, he made it to the dockside inn, 'The Shipwright's Daughter,' and slipped through the rear doors of the ramshackle establishment. The common room was a tempest of chaotic activity: smoky, noisy, and raucous. This suited Conal well. He slipped through the crowd of revellers like an eel through reeds, heading towards the front, where Captain Bohan could usually be found. Three pouches changed hands during Conal's short walk across the room. Quickly and quietly, Conal slipped into the vacant seat opposite the Captain.

He was sitting, sullenly nursing a large tankard and looking morose. "That seat's taken," growled the Captain "Bugger off, ya wee shite!"

"It's me ... Conal!" he hissed, pulling off the battered cap for a moment, and as quickly replacing it.

The Captain squinted, studying the boy's features through drunken eyes. "I don't care. Leave me alone, will ya. You're trouble at the best of times, boy. You nearly got me killed the last time we met, so sling ya hook!"

"I can't! I've got a message for you," Conal protested, leaning close. "What're you so narky about anyway?"

"Never mind why I'm narky. I'm the captain of my own vessel, and I'm entitled to be narky if I want to be. Just bugger off and leave me alone. I've got some serious drinking to do."

"Damn it I can't! I've a message from Ester Dunne," Conal insisted "I nearly got myself killed coming here as it is. I'm not going back empty-handed."

"Madame Dunne, you say?" Captain Bohan grunted "Why didn't you say that in the first place? You, I can happily live without, but Madame Dunne's a good woman, and I'm indebted to the priestesses of Deanna."

Conal sullenly relayed Madame Dunne's message.

"Tell her that my ship'll be ready at first light," Captain Bohan had assured "I'll be happy to be out of this cursed city for a few weeks, anyway. Lady Luck has not been good to me recently, and a good fare will make up for some of my losses. Now, be gone with ya, and leave me in peace." Conal started to get up before the Captain's strong, weatherworn hands jerked him back down "Hey boy, I nearly forgot. Ye'd best be careful. Lord Boare's got men out looking for ya."

"Aye, I know. I had a dance with one of 'em on the way here."

"It looks like your luck is better than mine, boy. Best keep it that way!"

"Aye and my breath is sweeter smelling, too!" Conal sneered.

By the time Conal had returned to the tavern, he was worried. He had come across three more Boarite patrols while crossing the city. This was not another random search. Lord Boare must have been tipped off about his whereabouts. He seriously doubted that the Usurper-king had half his army out looking for some other boy. That meant that trouble was only a few bells or even moments away. He decided not to worry Ester with this news. She would only ship him back to the Isle, and he hated it there. There was absolutely nothing to steal at Deanna's Temple, or at least, nothing he could get away with.

Instead, he would quietly slip away and be out of the city before the rest of the household stirred. He was, he reasoned, old enough and wise enough to make his own way in the world. After all, he was relatively rich, and there were always other cities, if he needed more.

He slipped stealthily into the stables, heading for his secret stash of coins and gems. It would not take him long to gather his belongings and slip away. He would be long gone before the sun came up.

Working in near-darkness, he swept the floor clean of straw and felt around for the finger hole. Pulling up the planks, he retrieved the burlap sack he had used earlier and quickly piled his loot into it. He was feeling around in the corners of the hole to make sure he had left nothing behind, when he heard a small whisper behind him. He froze, not even daring to breathe. His ears strained in the darkness for the slightest sound. When he heard nothing further, he relaxed and continued his search. Satisfied that he had left nothing behind, he laid the planks back into place and stood up, ready to leave. Hefting the bag over his shoulder, he headed towards the stable doors.

"Light!"

Conal was blinded by the sudden brightness. Dropping his booty, he reached for his dagger. The two witches were standing in the doorway, watching him with angry expressions.

"Were you going someplace, Conal *MacDragan?*" Ester asked in a calm tone that failed to hide the threatening undercurrents.

"Erm," murmured Conal, blinking against the harsh light and searching for a way out of his predicament.

"A fine treasure you have there, boy," commented Nessa "How did a stable boy come across such riches?"

Conal looked from the women, to the burlap sack, the contents of which had spilled across the stable floor and were now glittering in the magical light. The light was coming from the tip of the staff in Ester Dunne's hand.

"Pray tell, Conal … what did the good Captain say that has you so jittery and running away without so much as a bye your leave?"

"He said, aye, he'd be ready at dawn," Conal replied.

"And did you want to sail as well, Conal? Is that it? Do you miss the Holy Isle that much?" Ester's question was laced with sarcasm.

Conal couldn't hide his distaste for the Holy Isle. "Not likely! I was going someplace else, that's all."

Ester moved closer. Her face was stormy as she towered over the boy. "Why would you be doing that, then?" she asked in a voice that brokered no lies.

Conal gulped, blinking against the bright light of the magical staff. "Manquay's swarming with Boarites. It isn't safe for me here, anymore."

"I suppose that explains the tunic full of blood. Did one of them have an accident? You can be very stupid at times, Conal, do you know that? One of these days your luck's gonna run out, and then you'll know what real trouble is."

"They killed my father …" Conal protested.

Nessa had joined them, blocking off any possible escape. "...And what about poor Maerlin, eh, did she deserve your little prank, too? The poor girl nearly died of fright."

"She started it. She startled me earlier when I was sleeping. Anyway, she was already having bad dreams before I did anything," he protested. His words only confirmed their suspicions.

"I'll show you scared, young lad," growled Ester, reaching for him.

"No, Ester, wait. I've a better idea. Come here, boy, and let me look at you."

Conal removed his cap and stood nervously before Nessa. He would not cry. He swore to himself, he would not cry.

"Has your nose been broken for long, boy?" Nessa asked.

Conal's nose had been broken three years earlier. It took a moment for him to come to terms with this new and unexpected topic of conversation "A while, why?"

"I'm a healer, Conal, a good one at that. That nose is making you snore badly, making it harder to sleep. That isn't good at all. I bet it gives you headaches, and you get more than your fair share of colds, too. It needs fixing," she stated calmly. "You'll sleep better with it fixed. It ruins your roguish good looks. You could be a real charmer with a straight nose on your face. Those piercing blue eyes will have the girls swooning, if you'd ever learn some manners."

"Will it hurt ... the healing?" he asked, shuffling from foot to foot. He didn't trust witches. He knew from past experience that their minds worked on many levels. He wondered what the catch would be here ... with witches, there was always a catch.

"Oh no, not a bit. I'll use a wee bit of magic to heal it. You won't feel a thing ..." Nessa assured, and then she hit him squarely with a clenched fist. The punch came so fast, he did not even get a chance to flinch, and his head rocked back with the force of the blow. His eyes watered as blood gushed from his newly re-broken nose. He was too shocked even to scream as pain shot through his head. He just stood there, reeling with the impact, dazed and confused.

"Of course ..." she added, matter of fact, "... breaking it first is going to hurt like hell." Both witches cackled loudly.

Blood poured down his now-swelling face to join his already blood-splattered tunic. "Dhatsh noht pare!" Conal protested, glaring at the witches.

"Hold your head back, boy, or you'll get blood everywhere," Ester instructed.

Nessa was already drawing upon her magical powers. When she had ready, she stepped forward "Here … let me see."

Conal backed away warily, blood dripping through his hands.

"Oh, don't be such a baby," Nessa admonished as she grabbed Conal's blood-soaked tunic. Pulling his head back, she inspected his nose. "Ah, that's perfect. A nice clean break if I say so myself. Now, all we need to do is set it. Hold him still, Ester."

Ester gripped Conal shoulders, and Nessa grasped the broken nose between two gnarled fingers and snapped it back into position. Conal screamed as the second bout of pain shot through his brain. His scream was short-lived, however, as he passed out in Ester's arms.

"Heal," Nessa commanded, and warmth filled the unconscious boy's face. The bleeding stopped, and the swelling reduced immediately, leaving only two discolorations below the eyes as evidence of the blow. She absently wiped the blood from Conal's face "How's that?"

"A fine job, very professionally done," Ester complimented as they carried Conal into the tavern. "He'll be a real charmer if he ever gets over being such a complete brat."

"What was all that screaming?" Maerlin asked. She had been told to stay in the kitchen and keep an eye on the captured ferrets. A task she did under duress. Even Nessa's assurances of their harmlessness could not convince her.

"Oh, nothing, dear," replied Nessa. The two priestesses started to giggle again. "We were just fixing Conal's broken nose. After all, we wouldn't want to listen to him snoring all the way to the Holy Isle, would we?"

"What!" Maerlin asked, trying to make sense of the conversation. Then it dawned on her. "We aren't taking *him* with us, are we?"

"Yes dear, I'm afraid we are. Don't worry, though. I'm sure he'll behave much better from now on. Now, why don't you go upstairs and grab our things, there's a dear. We'll need to be leaving shortly, if we're going to set sail at first light."

Maerlin stomped up the stairs, muttering to herself, again.

Chapter Seven: Conal's Many Guises

After some discussion, it was decided that Ester would drive them down to the quayside in her wagon, leaving Nessa's pony in the stable until their return. They could not take the pony to the Isle anyway, so it was as safe here as farther down river. The wagon would also be useful for hiding Conal from prying eyes, being enclosed with a canvas cover. This was essential in the city, not only to protect from poor weather, but also to discourage the light fingers of the city's thieves.

Conal woke as they were bundling him into the back of the wagon, and a short argument erupted.

"Oh, no!" he insisted "I'm not going back to that island. I can make my own way in the world. I've plenty of money now."

"Oh really …" Ester arched her brows "...And where is this wealth that you speak of? Not that heap of stolen trinkets, I hope."

"Yes, those! They're mine. I stole them, so they belong to me."

"Well, I'm afraid you're broke again, boy, and you are going to the Isle. I've stolen your little horde from you, so they're mine now. You can have them back when you come of age, and then, only if you go to the Isle," she added pointedly, and then stuck the knife in to finish the argument. "Otherwise, I think they'll find their way to one of the local charities. There are many hungry children in this city. They'd be eternally grateful to you, Conal, for your generous donation."

"You wouldn't!"

Ester smiled smugly in response, her arms folded across her ample bosom "Try me."

Conal gave up and slumped down in the rear of the wagon. "What about my ferrets?"

"Ah, yes … the ferrets," Ester replied "Maerlin's minding them at the moment, and you'll only get them back when she's satisfied that you are truly remorseful for your behaviour."

"You can't be serious!"

Ester, however, was deadly serious "You don't mind being burdened with this arduous task, do you, Maerlin?"

Maerlin smiled maliciously at Conal's predicament. "Well ..." she said, as if pondering her options "They're very smelly creatures, but I suppose I could look after them; at least until the brat learns some manners ..." she replied sweetly to Ester "Though, he'll have to feed them."

"They'll need handling daily, or they'll go wild," Conal argued, hoping to change the witch-girl's mind. Clearly, she didn't like his ferrets.

"Oh, no. You won't be allowed to handle them," Maerlin insisted, sensing her authority slipping away "They'll have to do without that until you've earned the privilege."

"You can't be serious," he objected, looking from one to the other.

"Well ... there is another option, I suppose," Ester suggested casually.

Conal leapt at the straw of hope "What's that?"

"We could donate them to the starving children, also. I'm sure they'd look after them for you."

"What!" Conal exclaimed. "They'd eat them. Some of those urchins'd eat the shoes off your feet, given half a chance."

"Well, that's all decided then, isn't it?" Nessa pronounced, closing the conversation "Shall we be on our way?"

Conal slumped down, not offering to help as the baggage was stored aboard. The last item stored was his cage of ferrets, which he stared at solemnly as the cart rolled through the streets. He refused to meet Maerlin's eyes, knowing the smug expression that would be covering her face. The two witches sat up front, blocking the contents of the wagon from view.

A few moments later, Nessa hissed "Get under that horse blanket, Conal. There's a patrol up ahead. They've set up a road block."

Conal pulled the course blanket over himself, ears straining for danger as he curled himself into a ball. He hoped to disguise himself as another piece of baggage.

The cart stopped and started a few times as they neared the roadblock. Soon, he heard the gruff command "Halt by the orders of Lord Boare!"

The wagon creaked to a halt.

"What've you got in the wagon, Ma'am?"

"I don't see that that's any of your business, Sergeant," Nessa protested "I need to be on the wharf at dawn, and I don't wish to be delayed. What is it you're after?"

"We're looking for a fugitive, Ma'am. He murdered one of his Lordship's guards. He's a blonde-haired youth with a broken nose. I'll need to check your wagon, Ma'am, on his Lordships orders."

"Well, I've never heard the like of it!" Nessa complained, sounding shocked "Since when does Lord Boare accost decent folk going about their daily business? There is nothing back there but my grand niece and a few belongings. You'll find no vagabonds hiding out in my wagon, good sir. Let me assure you of that!"

"It won't take a moment, Ma'am. Beggin' ya pardon, but I have my orders, and I'm to make no exceptions."

"That's quite alright, officer. We've nothing to hide, though ... I do hope you won't take too long. We've a ship to catch."

Conal could hear the rear curtain of the wagon being drawn back, as a soldier peered inside of the wagon.

He poked randomly at the nearest baggage. "There are a lot of bags and bundles back here, Sarge, and a wee lassie with some ferrets," reported the soldier.

Luckily, Conal was huddling near the front of the wagon, just out of reach of the Boarite soldier.

"What're you carrying, Ma'am?"

"Just a few herbs and such like. I'm a healer by trade, and the girl is apprenticing with me," Nessa explained, continuing in an over-loud whisper "She's an orphan, you know, the poor dear. She's not very bright. Still, what can you do, eh … family ties, an' all. Will there be anything else?"

"No, Ma'am. You may pass. Have a safe trip."

"Thank you and good day to you sir. I hope the murderous scum you seek get his dues," Nessa declared and spat loudly over the side of the wagon at the soldier's feet.

Ester clicked the horses forward, keeping them to a steady walk.

"That was close," murmured Maerlin. "You can come out now. The coast is clear."

Conal flung the covering aside and wriggled his nose. The horsehair had begun to tickle it. "I thought I was gonna sneeze there for a moment. We all nearly ended up in the dungeons."

They looked at each other in silence, concerned by the recent narrow escape. The silence hung heavily in the air before Maerlin spoke "Listen … I'm sorry if I lost my temper yesterday. I was tired and hungry."

"I should think so, too!" grumbled Conal. He was still fuming at the idea of going back to the Isle, and he was determined to be as belligerent as possible.

Maerlin waited, clearly expecting her gesture to be reciprocated, but Conal remained silent. The longer the silence lasted, the more Maerlin expression darkened.

"You're very rude, you know. I've never met a more annoying boy, though I've met some real dirt-bags in my time. I can see this trip's going to be a real bag of laughs with you along."

"Hey! I didn't ask to come, you know, so why don't you just leave me alone …" he snapped "And I'm warning you. You better not let anything happen to my ferrets or I'll gut you like a fish."

"Charmed, I'm sure. You and your smelly rat things can both take a running jump as far as I'm concerned. I hope you both fall overboard and drown, you loud-mouthed, useless thug." Maerlin's temper was now coming to steam.

"Ha! This, from a girl with all the charm of a mangy-coated vixen," Conal retorted "At least I can swim. I bet you mountain folk don't even get washed properly, let alone swim."

"I'll have you know that there's a carne just up the mountain from my village. We swim there all the time. Anyway, I'm cleaner than you are. You smell like a sewer rat, or hadn't you noticed?" Maerlin's face was flushed with rage.

"I bet you're all inbred, up there in the mountains," Conal snapped, determined to have the last word "Tell me, did your father marry his half-sister or something, and spawn you as his whelp? You're too short and runty to be anything other than an inbred, mountain hick."

"Don't you dare insult my mother!" Maerlin yelled, standing up and bunching her fists. Thunder cracked overhead "She was better bred than you, I'll bet. At least she didn't raise me to be a thief and a murderer. What was your father then; some drunken sailor on a one-night-stand? Was she paid well for her trouble? Your mother must've worked night-shift on the streets, hustling for farthings."

Conal leapt to his feet also, as he argued hotly "My mother was a queen amongst women, I'll have you know!"

Maerlin had pulled her fist back, about to give Conal another broken nose when they were interrupted.

"What in the heavens …" Ester's head appeared suddenly. "Sit down, the pair of you, before you bring every Boarite in the city down on our heads. Have you lost what little sense you were born with?"

"He started it," Maerlin accused.

"I did not!" Conal objected. "You did."

"Did too!"

"*Shut up!*" Ester hissed.

The two children glared at each other, but stopped arguing.

"I don't want to hear a peep from back here. Is that understood?"

"I don't envy your job," Ester commented as she turned back to Nessa. "One of them is bad enough, but two's a walking nightmare. I'm sorry to dump him on you, but I can't abandon the tavern. Someone has to make sure that it's safe to return at some point. The *Uisce Beatha* was my first concern … the boy came later."

"Don't worry, Ester. I'm sure it'll all work out fine in the end," Nessa assured. "They'll settle down after a while, and the bruises will heal." Then she added as an afterthought "I might have to take that dagger away from him though. He's a bit too keen with that thing. We don't want any accidents now, do we?"

*****

The rest of the journey to the docks proved uneventful, with the two children glaring at each other in sullen silence. Soon, they heard the noisy sounds of the docks, as stevedores and crewmembers hauled cargo onto various ships along the quayside.

Nessa stuck her head into the back of the wagon soon after they pulled up. "We've got a problem," she announced. "The docks are swarming with Boarites. They're checking out all the passengers." Nessa inspected Conal. "That hair of yours and those eyes are much too distinctive. They'll spot you a mile away."

"What about a disguise? I could wear my cap and pretend I was working on the docks."

"No, that won't work. They're watching much too close for that, but the idea has merit." Nessa considered what her bags contained that might be used to disguise the boy, and an idea came to her. "Maerlin, did you ever get time to fix up those new clothes that Ester gave you?"

"No, sorry Ness, I've been too busy."

"That's okay. Fetch my scissors, will you, dear. I'll get Ester to park the wagon over there, out of the way."

Maerlin dug into the baggage as the wagon made its way through the bustling throng towards the farthest dock, where it was quietest.

"This'll do fine," announced Nessa. "Maerlin, go and snip off the horse's tail, will you. I'll need some hair to braid." She fished in Maerlin's bag for the spare clothes.

Conal, by now, had realised the plan and started to object. "No way! You're not dressing me up as a girl. Forget it. I'll find my own way out of the city."

"We're not going to have an argument about this, are we?" Nessa asked "You're going to shut up and get dressed, or I'll break that nose of yours again, and don't even think I won't. I haven't the time to be arguing with you. We need to get on that ship before the next bell is rung, so shut up and put this on." Ness threw the skirt in his general direction.

"It won't work; I don't look anything like a girl."

"I could always hypnotise you. You'd even think you were a girl, when I'm through," suggested Ness with an evil grin.

"You wouldn't!" Conal exclaimed "You can't do that sort of thing … can you?"

"Oh, I can and worse. In fact, I could go as far as morphing you into a girl, but that can be difficult enough. You might get to like it too much and not want to change back," Nessa teased "Are you going to get that skirt on, or am I going to have to use a little magic?" Nessa flexed her fingers meaningfully.

Conal struggled quickly into the skirt, fighting over the unfamiliar fastenings. "Why don't they put the buttons and ties at the front, like they do with men's clothes?" he asked, twisting his upper body to tie the fastenings.

Nessa giggled as she watched, holding her hand over her face to stifle the noise. "Women tend to spin the skirt around after it's fastened, Conal. It's much easier that way. As to why it is done, it's so it won't interfere with the curves of the body around the stomach and thighs. Men seem to be attracted to such things."

Conal flushed. Their conversation was wandering into dangerous territory. He bit back the next question, nervous as to where it might lead.

"That's no good at all, Conal. You'll have to remove the trousers beforehand. They're sticking out at the bottom."

"Couldn't I just roll them up?" he asked, not liking the idea of undressing in front of her.

"No, you can't. What happens if they start to unravel as you walk? Just do as you're told. Why do young people always feel the need to ask so many stupid questions?"

Conal flushed, cleared his throat and asked "Erm, could you turn around?"

"Don't worry, boy. I've seen it all before, more times than I care to remember actually," Nessa replied, pointedly refusing to turn away. Conal sighed, blushing like a beetroot and struggled out of the skirt and bent over to remove his trousers. Feeling very exposed under the old woman's mocking eyes, he threw his clothes aside and reached for the skirt.

It was at this point that Maerlin's head poked into the back of the wagon. She was carrying a handful of black horsehair. Conal grabbed the skirt, hiding his nakedness as best he could.

Nessa's giggles turned into manic cackling.

"Oh, my!" Maerlin exclaimed "You're not dressing him up as a girl, are you, Ness?"

"Maybe you better help him with those fastenings, dear. He's seems to be struggling there," suggested Ness, between fits of laughter.

"No!" Conal protested. "I can manage."

"Well, hurry up then," commanded Nessa. Seeing him frozen in embarrassment, she softened a little "Maerlin, I think you'd better divert your eyes. The lad's a bit bashful, it seems."

Maerlin quickly spun around, her face flushed almost as red as Conal's.

Conal quickly pulled the skirt back on, his eyes fixed on the witch-girl's back, watching for any peeking. After that, he lifted the blouse and pulled that over his head, stuffing it untidily into the skirt. "What now?"

Nessa looked at him pointedly, before casting her eyes heavenwards. "Why me?" she muttered. After a moment or two of silent inspection, she added "That won't do at all. You're much too tall to be so shapeless. I think we'll need some filling, don't you Maerlin?"

Maerlin turned and inspected Conal, biting her lip to stop herself from giggling.

"He really makes an ugly girl," she managed before turning away, her shoulders shaking with suppressed laughter.

Conal's face would have curdled milk as he stood there, waiting for the humiliation to finish. It only got worse when Ester chose this moment to enter the wagon. A new round of laughter started, leaving him feeling thoroughly picked on. Finally, they got round to practical suggestions on improving his image, but even these didn't ease his embarrassment.

"He needs more around the hips, that's for sure. The boy hardly has any curvature. Even Maerlin has a better hip than that, and she's seriously in need of some filling out. Her father must have kept her half-starved," commented Nessa.

"I'm not half-starved!" Maerlin objected, detracting attention briefly away from Conal.

"You are, too," Ester agreed "But Ness's right. He definitely needs something on the hips. His rump is way too flat."

Conal found himself absently turning to inspect his rear, before flushing even redder.

"Maerlin, I think you need to divert your eyes again, while we fix this," ordered Ness.

"What are you going to do?" Conal asked, fearing magical intervention.

Grabbing the scissors, Nessa cut the legs off the boy's trousers.

"Hey, they're my best pair!" he protested as he watched his clothes being ruined. "I only bought them recently."

"Would you rather I used … other methods?" Nessa asked, wiggling her fingers suggestively. Conal bit back any further protests.

Turning to Ester, she said "Pass me that canvas bag over there, will you? I think we'll use some of the sphagnum moss for filling."

"Good idea," Ester replied, handing over the requested sack.

"Maerlin, why don't you start making braids up with that horsehair? That'll keep you busy, and please ... stop giggling. You're making him fidget," instructed Ness, though she was smirking herself.

Conal stood, arms folded across his chest, fuming.

"Here, try these on," commanded Nessa, handing him the newly-shortened trousers.

Conal pulled them on, wishing they had thought of this before he got naked.

"Your skirt's caught up at the back. You're showing your underwear," Ester pointed out, causing another fit of giggles as Conal spun around, trying to pull out the skirt.

"You look like a dog, chasing its tail," Ness commented, bringing forth another chorus of laughter.

"Are you three enjoying yourselves?" Conal retorted, his temper flaring up with all the giggling and teasing.

"Okay. We'll be serious now. I promise," Nessa assured, only to burst into laughter again.

A few moments later, and after a few coughs and miss-starts, the three women managed to regain control of their humour. Each was clearly struggling with the urge to giggle or make comments, but apart from a few shiny eyes and bitten lips, the situation was under control. Conal absently scratched his hip as he watched them through angry eyes.

"How does that look now?"

Ester walked forward and poked at the rear of Conal's skirt, shifting the emphasis a little to the right. "You were lop-sided."

Conal stood with gritted teeth as the three witches inspected him critically.

"He'll need a bit more upper carriage, too," Ester suggested. "I think we should aim for well-budded … not quite buxom, but with promises of things to come. What d'you think, Ness?"

"Yes, yes, I see where you are going. I suppose one of my old corsets would do the job nicely." Nessa dug into her belongings. Moments later, she pulled out a well-worn, threadbare corset. "Here boy, try this on for size."

Conal looked at the garment, turning it this way and that.

Seeing his predicament, Ester snatched it from him. "Take the blouse off, Conal. I'll help you put this on."

A few moments later, along with two ample handfuls of sphagnum moss, Conal was again ready for inspection. "This isn't going to work," he commented. "Why don't I just slip out of the city and meet you farther downriver?"

"Nonsense, you've already changed into a fine specimen of womanhood," Ester assured "A bit of makeup to cover that bruising and a shawl and you'll be fighting off the sailors."

This brought another burst of giggles from the witches.

"Can we get on with this? I feel stupid enough already, without dragging this out any further."

A few moments later, the group of 'women' climbed down from the wagon and walked along the quayside.

"Which ship is it?" Nessa asked.

"It's that dishevelled-looking one, over there," Ester replied. "Don't worry. It might look like a floating wreck, but it sails like the wind. Captain Bohan doesn't like to draw attention to his activities, so he tends to let appearances deceive."

"Why would he do that?" Maerlin asked. She had been listening in on the conversation, a bad habit that she had picked up recently.

"Let's just say that he doesn't declare all of his cargoes, shall we," Conal explained, as he fought off the urge to scratch.

"Isn't that illegal?" Maerlin asked.

"Really! Is it? I'd never thought of that." His voice was thick with sarcasm.

Maerlin flushed and snapped back "Oh, aren't we being smart for a wolf in girl's clothing."

"Now now, girls, behave, at least until we get on board the ship, then you can scratch each other's eyes out if it'll make you happy," Nessa hissed, cutting off any further argument.

They headed for the ship in sullen silence.

Conal knew that Bohan would torment him about his disguise. The prospect did little to cheer the boy's already surly mood. He could hear the Captain bellowing orders to the rugged bunch of pirates he called his crew. They reached the ship without being disturbed, but as they turned to step onto the gangplank, a voice called out "Hold up there, ladies."

They turned to see a group of Boarite soldiers standing on the dockside. Three of the men, a sergeant and two men-at-arms, marched forward with an officious air. "What business do you have with …" the Sergeant looked up as the side of the ship. "... The Lurching Otter, may I ask?"

Nessa pulled herself up to her full, relatively short height and glared up at the young Sergeant. "Excuse me, sir, but what's that got to do with you?"

The Sergeant paused under the glare of the old healer, nervously tapping on his clipboard as if it was a badge of authority. "Lord Boare's orders …" he started, but never got a chance to finish the sentence.

"This quay doesn't belong to the Boare unless I'm mistaken. In fact, his Lordship's land falls well short of the city of Manquay." Nessa lectured with quiet authority. "So, I'll ask you again … who do you think you are, accosting ladies going about their personal business? Did ya father not teach you any manners, *boyo*?"

"Ma'am …" he interjected, but again Nessa interrupted him.

"Don't you dare 'Ma'am' me. I'm a respectable spinster, I'll have you know! I won't put up with cheek from an upstart like you. You come marching up here as if you own the place, accosting decent women.

That's to say nothing of those two rogues you have beside you. They're liable to molest us in our beds, by the look of them." Nessa's voice was getting louder.

"What's all this then?" Captain Bohan glared down at the Boarites. "What're you doing harassing honest custom away from my ship? I bet it's that bold Captain Sprigg that's paying you to loiter here isn't it. I bet it's his doing." He bellowed to his crew "Men, arm ya'selves. It looks like we'll need to defend these fair and blessed creatures."

Others men gathered across the side of the ship. They were all big, mean-looking individuals, well muscled and stripped to the waist in the summer heat.

"That won't be necessary, Captain. This is no concern of yours. I warn you not to interfere with his Lordship's business," shouted the Sergeant, endeavouring to reassert his authority.

Nessa, however, quickly re-established her tirade on the young officer. She poked him firmly in the chest with a bony finger while ranting "...Marching up here like some weekend militiamen with the top button of your uniforms undone … you didn't even remove your helmets before talking to a lady. Ye do know how to talk to a lady, I hope?"

The Sergeant flustered and quickly whipped off his helmet, glaring at his subordinates to do likewise, as he shied away from the insistent finger-prodding.

"Please, Madame …" he placated.

"... Ms!" Nessa fumed, spittle covering his uniform as she bellowed her lungs out at him. "I'm no one's Madame! Ya must be deaf as well as stupid, boy!"

"I'm sorry, Ms, but I've orders to check all who sail this morning …"

"... Oh, do you now. Is that so?" Nessa retorted, hands on her hips and as immovable as stone. "Well, let me tell you, young man. Check off elsewhere with ya. I'll knock that stupid head off ya shoulders, if you lay a finger on me, or me girls!" Nessa jumped up and danced nimbly in front of the soldiers, her fists held before her like a boxing champion. "Come on! Put them up. I'll beat ya black and blue. I'll teach ya the manners that ya poor mammies never did."

The Sergeant backed farther away from the clearly irrational old crone.

"Now, Nessa!" Ester placated. "Calm yourself down. You don't want to have another of your turns now, do you?" The innkeeper held Nessa's shoulder gently as she endeavoured to steer her towards the gangplank.

"Go ahead, girls. You'd best get on board before she starts frothing at the mouth again. You know what happened the last time she started throwing fisticuffs about." Ester's sharp command broke the spell, and Maerlin grabbed Conal, and propelled him up the gangplank.

"I'm not scared of these wee whelps. I'll take the three of them on, so I will," Nessa yelled, still weaving threateningly before the Sergeant. "I'll whip their sorry asses! Here, I'll even make it fairer! I'll only use my left hand."

"Now, dear, there's no need for that. The Sergeant just made a mistake, that's all. The lad's young and he's new at the job, isn't that so, Sergeant?"

"Y-y-yes, that's right. My apologies, Ma'am," he murmured, before skipping rapidly backwards. Nessa had broken free of Ester's grip and was charging forward, fists swinging wildly.

"Ma'am! I'll give you Ma'am, you cheeky young pup!" Nessa yelled, swinging a fist and missing the Sergeant's nose by a whisker. "Stand still, ya yellow dog, and let me hit ya!"

Ester quickly grabbed Nessa and pulled her away, muttering loudly "Oh dear! I see that you've forgotten to take your elixir again this morning. Settle down now, Ness. The Sergeant didn't mean any offence. He's going to show his remorse by helping unload the baggage for us. Aren't you, Sergeant?" she asked, casting an accusing eye at the soldier, silently reprimanding him for causing Nessa's distress.

He quickly took the hint and bellowed an order to the nearby soldiers. "Men, get those bags out of that wagon, double-time."

"Don't break anything!" Ester warned as she steered the still-dancing Nessa up the gangplank to the waiting sailors, all of who had been happily watching the morning's entertainment. "She'd absolutely burst a blood vessel, if any of her potions got damaged."

Nessa reluctantly allowed herself to be escorted up the gangplank, all the time glaring threateningly at the soldiers. Only when she had been guided into the cabin area, did she let up on her anger and began to laugh.

"You're a very bold woman, Nessa *MacTire*. Do you know that? I thought that poor fellow was going to wet himself when you lunged at him," Ester reproached, trying to stifle her own laughter.

Maerlin burst out of one of the cabins, Conal was right behind her, and both looked concerned. "Is Nessa alright?"

"I'm fine, dear. Never better," assured Nessa.

"But ... the fits?"

"They were just a little illusion to fool the Boarites, Maerlin. Remember, the best form of defence is attack. By being confrontational, we made him think we had nothing to hide, and Conal slipped by, right under his nose."

"You mean there's nothing wrong with you?" Conal asked.

"Not a bit, boy," answered Nessa. "Now get back inside before those soldiers start humping those bags down here."

A short time later, all of their baggage was safely stowed aboard, and Captain Bohan cast off. They slipped free from the quay and headed downriver.

Chapter Eight: The Beggar's Quest

Earlier, in another part of Manquay ...

Cull headed into the depths of the city, checking frequently behind him for any possible pursuit. His route was along paths that would baffle even a master cutpurse. He ambled around without apparent purpose, drifting around the streets. His, was not the stealth of a thief; his was the silent façade of the beggar. He blended, not into the shadows, but into the forefront. All the while, he moved with cautious purpose, heading towards a certain dead-end alley.

As he slipped into the shadows within of the alley, he waited, holding his breath. He could hear the blood coursing in his head as his lungs craved oxygen, but he needed to be sure that no one was following. On an early morning like this, his breathing could easily give him away. It would signal his presence to any spy watching as it billowed out into the cold air.

Satisfied, he felt in the darkness for the hidden latch. With a barely audible click, the secret panel moved aside, letting him squeeze through the gap. Slipping inside, he shut the door and peered through the spy hole. Long moments ticked by as he waited, his legs twitching with the tension. Finally, Cull searched his pockets and struck a match against the stone wall.

In the sudden flare of light, he grinned. Four assassins had been standing silently behind him, patiently waiting. All had bare blades and masked features. So silent were they that he had not even heard their breathing. If it was not for the fact that he had expected them, he might have died of fright. Cull carefully lifted off his broad-brimmed hat, so that his features were clearly visible in the light of the match. Now was not a time for mistaken identity.

"Welcome, Cull," one of the shadowy forms greeted. "You've been expected. They're all waiting for you."

As the match burned down, Cull dropped it, leaving the world in darkness again. The Beggar-Lord, it seemed, had not become slack. He walked down a long passage, following one of the assassins with a lantern. Two more of the shadowy guards greeted them before a set of double doors.

These were not standing to attention as some mercenaries would. They dropped from the rafters in front of Cull and his guide. Again, Cull cautiously removed his hat so that all were satisfied of his identity. He admired the quiet efficiency of the assassins. He was sure that the Order of the Black Dagger were being well paid for their diligence.

Pausing before the door and leaving his hat off, he turned to look at his escorts. One by one, they disappeared into the shadows. When all had gone quiet, Cull waited, holding the lantern high, before the double doors opened, and he was allowed to enter. He stepped through into a small antechamber, and another set of double doors stood closed opposite the first. The room was well lit with sconces, but otherwise, it was bare. Had he bothered to look closely, he would have seen the holes in the walls, holes designed to fire crossbow bolts into the room. He smiled at the irony of it all. It was one of the best security systems in the city, and it guarded a room that held neither gold, nor jewels. Its only wealth was a frail old man waiting on death's door.

The doors behind him clicked shut. This was his signal to proceed into the inner sanctum. As he neared the doors ahead, they opened to admit him into a well-lit room. Eight figures sat silently, waiting.

Cull placed his hat back onto his head as he studied the select group of beggars. He knew each of these men and women, by face as well as name, but that was immaterial. A face could be easily changed, and a name was only a label. He, like these others, had owned many names, many faces. Even on the walk here, he had lost his shamble, lost the wheezy breathing and tendency to double over, coughing. His eyes had lost their dull sheen of indifference. As he walked to his allocated place at the table, he nodded to each in turn. Each of these poorly dressed individuals ruled a section of the city. They ruled not as lords, but in a more subtle way. Yet, each held power, as allocated to them by the Beggar-Lord.

Cull moved to the vacant chair and sat, pausing briefly to smile at the old man who sat on the raised dais at the table's head.

"All praise to the Beggar-Lord," Cull proclaimed. As he was responsible for this meeting, he began the formality.

The others quickly follow suit "All praise to the Beggar-Lord."

Cull sat for a moment, thinking of how to proceed. "Thank you all for coming here today," he began "Something has come up; something that we should all be made aware of. A lot has been happening within Dragania and within the city itself … but first, let us address the issue of Lord Boare and his moves towards claiming the High Kingship." He went on to report all that he had learned, including the reasons and results of his recent excursion into Manquay's gaol. When he had finished his report, the meeting began in earnest.

*****

Later the same day, all had been discussed, and the meeting dispersed. Cull was content to sit in the quiet warmth of the inner sanctum for a while. Here, he was able to shed the many faces and disguises of his profession.

"So, how was Manquay gaol this time, Cuilithe?" The wheezy, but firm question came from upon the dais. Only one man in the city knew Cull's real name, and it was only spoken when the two friends were alone.

"Damp, rat-infested, and with its usual plague of hungry lice. I need a bath, and I'll be lucky if I can rid these clothes of the pests. I hate wasting a good disguise, just because the Watch can't keep its beds clean."

A wheezy chuckle came from above. "I told you not to go. Another could have gained that information for us. You'll have to learn to delegate and spread the burden of leadership, Cuilithe, when you take my place."

Cull shuddered. The throne of the Beggar-Lord was the last thing he wanted, but the old man was right. It was foolish of him to waste time being arrested over a simple matter like this. Others could have done this on his behalf. As for the throne, he hoped to stay off the inevitable for at least a while longer.

As if reading Cull's mind, Broll the Beggar-Lord continued "I'm not going to be here forever, you know. I can feel Macha's fingers stroking my heart with each passing day, and I know my time will be soon. It's time for you to take up my mantle, Cuilithe."

They had known each other a long time, and to speak anything but the truth would have insulted the older man. He was dying. His skin was getting greyer by the day. Although his brain was still as sharp as a stiletto, his body was failing, and he would not survive another winter.

Cull thought back to earlier times, to the wild scams that they had pulled together when the Beggar-Lord had been in charge of the Wharf District and Cull had been his apprentice.

They fell silent for a few moments, both lost in thought. Finally, Broll spoke "I've a task for you, Cuilithe ... one that better suits your talents."

"What is it, Broll?" asked Cull, his head coming up to look into the other's rheumy eyes.

"Come closer. Even these walls have ears."

And so, Cull learned of the task that he was to perform.

*****

The man who left the inner sanctum shortly before dusk would not have been recognised as Cull the Beggar. He was clean-shaven and well-groomed. He was wearing dark but respectable clothing, though the broad-brimmed hat still remained, if somewhat cleaned. He could easily have been mistaken for a minor lord or a wealthy journeyman whose trade was seeing good times. Mounting a roan steed, he rode out of the western gate of the city. When he reached the woodland a mile to the west, he pulled his horse off the road and settled down to wait.

The following morning, Cull crouched, watching the city gates from his hiding place. His horse grazed nearby in one of the clearings. Though Cull was born and raised in the city, he had long grown accustomed to living in a saddle and travelling through the countryside. In fact, to some degree, he even enjoyed the occasional excursion. On such occasions, he was required to venture across the whole of the Dragania, and even beyond, into *Tir Pect*. The tasks he was asked to perform were far more important than anything he might achieve by blending into the streets as yet another beggar. Ironically, though, it was his skill and life as a beggar that had brought him to venture far and wide, disguised as one of the upper echelon.

He smiled at the irony of it all. Many of the ruling class lived in near poverty, in order to keep up their façade of wealth. They struggled to stay ahead of the bills, and the loan sharks that lurked in the shadows ready to claim everything they owned. Life was filled with illusions and sleights of hand, and Cull was a master of trickery. His hands were as dexterous as any pickpocket, and his tongue was quicker than the finest conman. He

104

was wealthier than most of the gentry, and yet he lived in ragged clothing. These clothes were his source of wealth, and so, his wealth remained hidden. His power and the power of the Beggar-Lord were the greatest of all illusions in this world of trickery.

At mid-morning, the riders appeared. The three soldiers wore the sign of the black boar on red tabards, proclaiming them for all to see as Boarites, servants of the Usurper-king.

Cull slipped back into the woods and quickly mounted. Once he had cleared the woods, he kicked the stallion into a gallop, hoping to intercept the riders at the next village.

He smiled at the folly of Lord Boare's spies. They had rushed eagerly towards his trap. The Beggar-Lord had put the word out on the streets that a blonde-haired youth had been spotted in a nearby village and the Boarites had taken the bait.

Heading to the local tavern, Cull slipped inside and waited, knowing that the men would be drawn to the place like wasps to the honey pot. He didn't have long to wait. They had removed their uniforms, and they were now dressed like common mercenaries, but the arrogance remained, marking them as Lord Boare's men as surely as their boar tabards ever had.

Cull watched from the shadows as the Boarites settled near the fire and ordered drinks, while their eyes searched the room for their victim. Cull's professional eye noted the amateurishness of the assassins. Even though they wore their blades well and could probably use them with some amount of skill, these men were soldiers and not skilled in the subtlety of espionage. It seemed that Lord Boare had decided to keep this incident in-house rather than hiring professional help. That was an error that would cost him dearly.

Satisfied with his reconnaissance, Cull slipped through the kitchens towards the rear of the tavern. He was looking for the scullery boy that he had noticed earlier. "Ah, you're just the lad I needed to talk to," he proclaimed "Would you like to earn yourself a gold piece?"

The boy looked nervously at the expensively-dressed man, wondering what he would have to do to earn such a fortune.

"It's alright lad, don't fret. I only need you to play a little trick on some people for me. Can you do that?" Cull showed him the glittering coin as proof of his intent, before continuing "I'll pay you this coin now, and if you do well, I'll give you another one afterwards. Do we have a deal?"

The young boy's eyes lit up with anticipation, hypnotised by the glittering metal "Two gold pieces!"

"Aye, lad, two gold Crowns," Cull confirmed, flipping the first one into the youth's hands. "Here's what I want you to do ..."

Cull moved up the street to watch his plan unfold. The boy was a born actor. He raced around the side of the building and across the front of the tavern, laughing and calling out to some unseen friend as he rushed past each of the tavern's windows in turn. Those within would easily have seen his blonde hair, but his speed would have hampered a closer inspection of his features. The boy ran up the street, still hollering and laughing as he raced into one of the alleyways on the outskirts of the village. In a rush, he shot passed Cull's hiding place and disappeared from view.

Moments later, the men burst out of the tavern, hands already on their blades as they searched the now-empty street. Quickly, they raced after the boy.

He hoped that the boy was as good at hiding as he was in acting. His life might depend on it. Cull waited for a short while. Would they give up and return to the tavern, or would they find the boy and return, dragging the screaming youth behind them? They did not show. So far, Cull's plan had worked. They had failed to locate the boy and had decided to lay an ambush for his return.

Cull crossed the street to the alleyway used first by the boy and then by the Boarites. He paused at the head of the alley, bent down low and peeked around the corner. He smiled. They lurked in the shadows somewhere ahead. He could not see them, but he could sense their presence.

Flexing his shoulder muscles to relieve the tension that had been building there, Cull transformed. He hoped that the bounty-hunters would find this bait too much to resist. It was a gamble he was willing to bet on. An assassin worth his salt would not be so easily conned, but Lord Boare was renowned for his tightfistedness. Cull doubted the Usurper-king would invest on assassins of anything near the quality of the Order of the Black Dagger. Cull's opponents were little more than thugs and murderers, recruited from within his own army.

Concentrating hard on the image he wished to portray, he stepped into the alley on unsteady feet "... And she danced for me then, silk sliding off her skin ..." he sang in a slurred voice as he staggered down the alley.

His skin crawled as he sensed one of the men behind him. "... She danced like a witch, enchanting me with sin. My heart was beating madly ..." Cull staggered on. His eyes scanned the area carefully from under the wide-brimmed hat. His nerves were jumping with anticipation. He wondered whether they would concentrate on the task at hand and let the drunken lord pass unhindered. Slowly, he lurched along, singing loudly out of key.

Cull had nearly given up when he heard the telltale scrape of steel behind him. Had he not been anticipating the noise, he might not have heard the knife being drawn. Fighting the urge to look behind him, he staggered a few steps farther up the alley.

The rush, when it came, was quick, with the tramp of heavy feet rushing towards him. Cull turned, feigning fright as he came face to face with two of the assailants. Staggering against the wall of a house, Cull raised his hands. "Have mercshhy on meee!" he slurred, barely coherently.

One of the two men, a burly man of middle years, sneered. Holding a blackjack in his right hand, he grinned menacingly at the drunken lord. His partner was shorter and wiry by nature and stood slightly behind his partner. This was the one who had drawn the dagger.

"No!" Cull begged feebly, playing his part until the final critical moment.

Everything slowed down as the two assassins came within reach. All pretence of drunkenness left Cull in the blink of an eye, as he tucked under the larger foe's swinging arm, and his clenched fist rammed into the man's groin. His sharp rabbit punch was precise and dealt with considerable force, and he followed it up with another punch. This time it was upwards, into the man's throat.

The scrawny thief recovered quickly from his surprise and thrust his dagger towards Cull's stomach, but he was hampered by his comrade's bulk. Cull skirted around, keeping the larger man between himself and the knife-wielder as he continued his barrage of quick, precise punches. Each blow was aimed with the precision of long practice. Cull attacked the big man's throat and nose, before aiming a nasty kick just below the kneecap.

The larger opponent collapsed to the ground, writhing in pain. Cull stepped back on agile feet and reached into his coat for one of the many blades hidden there. He was ready now to face his second assailant.

Cull could hear the third man's curses as he raced from the far end of the alley. He calmly waited for the knife man to attack, knowing he still had time to deal with the assassin before him. Cull was poised for the knifeman's thrust. His stiletto remained hidden from view. They danced around the alley looking for an opening, each assessing the other, waiting for the right moment. A tentative thrust came and then another with more confidence, and Cull shied away, placing his back to the wall. The knife-wielder smirked, confidence growing, and his third thrust was his downfall.

Rather than dodging away, Cull stepped into the lunge, letting the knife slide along his side and trapping it with his arm. Cull continued the forward movement and his forehead snapped out, connecting soundly with the knife-wielder's face. The sickening crunch of bone as the nose shattered could be heard even over the man's sudden scream of pain. Cull did not pause in his attack. He embedded his stiletto up to the hilt in the scrawny man's chest. A sharp twist of the wrist was enough to still the assassin's cries.

The footsteps were coming closer as the third assailant rushed towards him.

Cull turned to face the final assassin, blood dripping from his stiletto. His face no longer held the mask of a drunken lord. Cull's features had changed into the look of a casual killer. His cold stare caused the final assailant to skid to a halt. Looking at his fallen comrades, one dead and the other writhing in pain, made the Boarite's resolve weaken.

Sensing the other's thoughts, Cull turned to the man who was still writhing on the ground. A quick thrust into the base of the skull was enough to still the moans of the heavyset thug. Silence fell on the alley, an eerie sound after the recent cries of combat. The remaining assassin backed away, seeing the cold eyes of death before him. "I've no argument with you."

Cull's smile was cold and deadly. "Aye, but I've got one with you. Come here and die, Child-slayer."

The alley reeked of fear as the remaining soldier turned and fled. He would head back to the city to report his failure. Cull's mocking laugh followed him.

Wiping the blood from his knife onto the tunic of one of the dead assassins, Cull headed back to his horse. He had not gone far, however, when the blonde-haired boy slipped out of the shadows, looking pale. Cull smiled softly at the boy. "Ah yes, your payment. You did well, boy." He dug into his coat for the other coin.

"You killed them!" the boy exclaimed fearfully.

Cull looked back to the bleeding bodies in the alley, before shrugging. "Aye, it was necessary. They were sent here to kill a boy just like ya'self. I couldn't allow that to happen. Here, take your coin, you've earned it, lad, but if I were you, I'd think about dyeing your hair. Blond-haired boys aren't safe on the street these days."

He flipped the coin to the boy and turned away. Quickly, he left the village, heading west.

*****

The day passed quickly as Cull set a steady pace for the horse, getting the best distance out of the animal. As evening tinged the skies, he passed another village and continued westward in the fading light. Cull was searching for a suitable place to camp. Up ahead, he spotted the warm glow of a fire, set a little back off the road.

Pulling the horse up at the roadside, Cull dismounted and walked slowly towards the campsite. "Hello there!" he called out as he came forward. He kept his hands clearly in view, acknowledging his peaceful intentions.

The campsite had been well chosen within a birch grove. It had a spring near to hand and a plentiful supply of dead wood within easy reach. In the clearing a small fire burned. Sitting beside it was a swarthy little man. He was busy repairing a cooking pot with a lightweight hammer. The man was dressed in the multi-coloured garb of a traveller, *Clann Na Teincheor*. Set farther back in the clearing was a colourfully-decorated wagon.

109

The *Teincheor* had paused in his work and looked up. Seeing only a solitary rider, dusty from travel and finely-dressed, the swarthy man relaxed, and a cautious smile crept into his open face. "A blessin' to ya, Milord," the Tinsmith greeted, laying aside his tools and coming forward. "What can a poor *Teincheor* like me be helping ye with?"

Cull returned the smile as he walked into the camp. "I was looking for a safe place to rest for the night, and I saw your fire. I wonder whether it would be rude of me to ask your permission to stop here," Cull asked respectfully, before adding, matter of fact, "but if I'm interrupting you, I'll travel farther."

"Well, Milord. There's a village back yonder a ways, if you're looking for creature comforts. There's nothing here but the soft dirt of Mother Earth, but you're welcome to a place in my humble camp, if ya want. Sure, I don't own the ground that I'm sleeping on, and good company is always welcome." The *Teincheor* waved a hand around the sparse campsite as if showing off the best room in the house. His eyes twinkled with merriment.

"I passed that flea-pit of a village back there. I think I'd prefer the soft ground of a well-leafed glade than spending my night scratching away the lice in that inn."

"Well put, Milord," replied the *Teincheor* "I'd be honoured to share my fire with you. We could shorten the night with a tale or a song. Though, in truth, my singing is more like the braying of a demented mule."

"Maybe, we might pass on the singing, then," Cull joked, taking a liking to this colourful character.

"I've nothing to offer but a rabbit stew and some *Leithban* mead to wash it down, but you're more than welcome to share my humble fare." The traveller sat down again, inspecting his guest with dark probing eyes. Stooping forward, he placed a cauldron on the coals and stowed away his tools. "So what brings a well-dressed man like ya'self to my campfire, Milord?" he asked "It's not every day that nobility comes a-calling."

"Let's not stand on ceremony, my friend. They call me Cull. It's a simple name, but one I'm fond of. I'd hate to have you spending the evening tugging your forelock. That sort of thing does little to help the digestion, or the enjoyment of the evening."

"Well met then, Cull. They call me *Lon Dubh*, the Blackbird. It's an affection based on my raven locks."

"Could I reimburse you for your kind hospitality, Blackbird?"

"By the gods, no! I'd live in shame if I charge a guest for his supper. Please don't insult me, but I thank you all the same. It's rare to see a finely-dressed man, willing to share the simple fare of *Na Teincheor*. Maybe in the morning, we can do a bit of wheeling and dealing; a lucky trinket, or something perhaps. As for this evening, we'll eat and drink, and not worry a whit about such things."

The evening passed with many a tale, both men well-fed on the fruits of the earth and drinking deep of the strong, sweet mead of *Tir Pect*.

The Blackbird woke early as was his habit and cooked up a filling breakfast for them both. After sharing a fine meal, they began the long and complex ritual of negotiation. The 'haggle' took half the morning to complete, as both men were clearly skilled in the craft and were giving little margin. Both enjoyed the to and fro of the deal, until finally each was satisfied with the barter. When all was settled, the bargain was sealed with palm spitting and a firm shake of the hands.

"For a Lord, you haggle well, Cull," Blackbird complimented, still unsure who had gained the upper hand in the trade.

Cull laughed. "Well, have no fears, your hospitality will be sung long after your death, my friend. May your road be long and prosperous." Again, the two men shook hands before packing up and going their separate ways.

Each gathered up their belongings, some of which had changed hands during the haggle, and set off on their individual journeys. One man, with a bemused smile, headed north on a fine roan steed. He was dressed in all the finery of a lord and carried a heavy pouch of coin. The other was dressed in the many-coloured traditional costume of *Clann Na Teincheor* and sporting a broad-brimmed hat. He headed west at a leisurely walk. His heavyset black stallion was content to plod slowly along, pulling the brightly-painted wagon.

At midday, the wagon stopped, and the stallion was unhitched before his heavy, black tail was cropped short. The colourfully-dressed man gathered up the coarse hair and climbed into the wagon. A short while later, he reappeared, still dressed in the colourful garb of a *Teincheor*. His features were darker, however. His hair was now long, thick, and jet black, and a large, angry-looking boil adorned his nose. Cull finished his lunch and hitched the black stallion back into the wagon before proceeding on his journey.

No one would look twice at a *Teincheor* on the road. He was as invisible as a beggar on a city street.

*****

It hadn't taken Captain Bohan long to find out who his passengers were. His laugh on hearing that Conal had slipped on board, disguised as a girl, could be heard from one side of the ship to the other. He yelled at the top of his considerable lungs, demanding to see the boy, until eventually Conal had feared the calls would be heard from the shore and came on deck. He endured the coarse comments of the Captain and his crew, gritting his teeth as his face turned redder and redder. When he finally fled below deck, he slammed his cabin door and refused to come out for anyone. It had taken all day and much cajoling, before Maerlin persuaded him to open the door and allow her to bring him some food. If it had not been for her pleas that the ferrets needed feeding, she doubted whether he would have opened up, even then.

Taking pity on him, for she herself had been forced to endure more than her fair share of barbed comments, she decided to let him keep his ferrets. Their conversations were muted and strained, however, and she soon left him to his brooding.

That evening, she decided to speak to Captain Bohan about his attitude, in the hope of easing the tension on the ship. It took her a while to catch him on his own, but eventually she saw him standing by the wheel, steering the ship down the river in the half-light of dusk. Grabbing her opportunity and her courage, she stepped forward, hoping he would hear her out.

"Captain?" Maerlin asked tentatively.

The big, gruff man looked down at her, surprise etched into his face. "Yes, lass, what is it?"

"I was just wondering …" she ventured, twirling one of her braids nervously.

"Spit it out, lass. I won't bite ya," he assured, smiling at her with twinkling eyes. "Though don't tell my men that. They'll think I'm going soft," he whispered throatily, before breaking into a raspy chuckle. "What's on ya mind, girl? Ya didn't come up here to fidget now, did ya?"

"No," replied Maerlin, though she was still a little terrified of the big, brooding captain. "It's about Conal. Why do you hate him so much?"

"Conal, you say! I don't hate him, lass, not at all. Why'd ya think that?"

"The way you treat him. I just …" she stopped, unable to express herself.

"Come o'er here and sit down, lass. Let me tell ya a few things." He pointed to a nearby railing.

As she climbed onto the railing as carefully as she could, he asked her "How long have you known the lad, lass?"

"Only a couple of days really, but I think we got off on the wrong foot."

Captain Bohan chuckled. "Aye lass, there are many that could say the same thing 'bout the lad. He has a way of getting folks' goats up, if you take my meaning."

Maerlin nodded.

"You see, lass, he's become a bit of a handful over these last couple of years, though, in truth, I suppose ya can't blame him. He's a feisty one, so he is, 'tis in 'is nature. He doesn't like to be kept still, that's for sure. The fire in his soul hungers to burn."

"But that's no reason to be so offensive, is there? It'll just make him worse," Maerlin protested.

"Ah! I see you've got a big heart, lass, but sometimes a good heart can do no favours. The lad wouldn't like me mollycoddling him, ya see. So it's no use, the likes of me taking it easy on 'im. He'd see through it like a window, and he'd take the hump about it," explained the Captain. "You see, I knew the lad beforehand, when all was well and his father was alive. He was a good lad, back then, not the rogue that he is now, but things changed, and there's no going back."

"But I still don't understand why you give him such a hard time."

"He's young, but he's as brave as they come … and as rash; aye, as rash. He's the luck of the faeries and all, though his past was a shocker. Y'see lass, if he's allowed to keep it up, he'll turn out to be a right wee gutter-snipe. He'd be nothing like his father at all. His head would be as big as that moon up yonder. There'd be no talking to him, then, d'ya see?"

Maerlin was getting lost, feeling again that she was being given half the picture, but she tried to understand. "Do you mean that he'll become too arrogant, if he doesn't get put down once in a while?"

"Aye, that's about the cut of it, lass. He would that, but what I'm saying is this. He's gonna be a big man one day, just like his father was before 'im. His father, however, was as straight as an arrow and as good as they come. I don't want to see the father's name shamed by the son, if ya get my meaning. That's why I do my best to keep the lad from wandering too far from the mark."

"So you don't hate him?"

"Not at all, lass, but keep that to ya'self now, d'ya hear?" he ordered, with a smile. "If the boy ever finds out, I'll get no peace from him. Ya see, lass, I'm honour bound to look out for the wee scut."

"So, how d'you know that he's going to be so important?" Maerlin asked, trying to make sense of the Captain's words.

"Tis in his blood. He was born to greatness. Tis written in the stars and in the colour of his eyes. He's a *Dragan*, and he'll wield the Dragon's fire as his father did before 'im," answered the Captain with fervour in his wild eyes.

Maerlin was getting lost again and had more questions to ask, but at that moment she heard the call from below deck.

"Maerlin, where are you, dear?"

"Coming, Ness." she shouted and turned back to the captain. "I've got to go, but …. Thanks."

"No problem, lass, glad to be of service," he replied, before bellowing to the crew. "Haul the sails and drop the anchor, ya lousy river rats, before I throw ya'll o'rboard!"

The ship came to a halt, ready to sit out the darkness and wait for the dawn.

Chapter Nine: The Great Marsh

As she stepped into the cramped cabin, Maerlin asked "What is it, Nessa?"

"Ah, there you are. I thought you'd fallen overboard. Come and sit down. It's time for your exercises."

Maerlin sighed. She had become accustomed to being asked to meditate at all bells of the day. Sitting on the bed, she closed her eyes and calmed her mind. Within moments, she had the white image firmly fixed in her inner eye and relaxed, letting her mind become completely blank.

"How are you doing, dear? Is your image steady, yet?" Nessa asked softly, trying not to break the spell of calmness.

"Yes, I've been managing it for days now," Maerlin replied, only to have the image flicker for a moment before stabilising again.

"Okay dear, well done. I guess you're ready for the next step. I want you to change the screen from white to red. Take your time and make sure that the transition is completely steady, and the colour is a nice rich red before continuing. Try to avoid melting one colour into the next. You want to avoid having a pink screen at any time. You want to aim for white, then red, with nothing in-between."

"Is that it?" Maerlin asked as she tried to bend her mind to the new image. "That seems easy enough."

Nessa chuckled at the naivety of youth. "Of course that's not it. That's just the first step. You'll need to be able to change the image to each of the colours of the rainbow before you're ready to continue. Then finally you need to turn the image to black. Try it now, and we'll see how you get along."

The exercise proved to be more difficult than Maerlin had originally anticipated. Each colour had a tendency to merge into the next, rather than changing fully. Her mind was swimming like a kaleidoscope. For the next bell, she tried and failed.

"You'll get a headache again, if you try too hard," Nessa advised. "Go back to the beginning and calm your mind. You can try it again, later. Don't rush it, Maerlin. It'll come to you in its own good time."

The journey continued in similar fashion. They made slow, but steady progress down the river towards the Great Marsh. Maerlin persisted in asking questions about the Holy Isle, but Nessa either found a job to occupy her idle mind, or simply informed her that it was time for her exercise again.

*****

Maerlin sat down, breathed deeply and relaxed. Slowly, the imagery became clearer in her mind, as colour by colour, she passed each stage of the exercise. Finally she managed the black screen. This was the most difficult of all the images to hold firmly in her mind, and now she had achieved it. As she returned to the white screen and relaxed, Maerlin grinned with the thrill of success.

"Ness, Ness, I've done it!" she exclaimed as she raced towards the prow of the ship, where Nessa stood watching the river. Her achievement was quickly forgotten when she caught her first glimpse of the Great Marsh. The river had been widening steadily, but now the left bank of it disappeared altogether into the myriad channels of the vast swamp. Maerlin strained to take in the expanse of bog and waterways before exclaiming "By the gods, it's huge!"

Nessa had been lost in quiet reverie, but turned to smile at Maerlin. "They don't call it the Great Marsh for nothing, Maerlin. It stretches for over eighty leagues, in every direction. It sits between here and the river Suile to the south."

At that moment, they heard Captain Bohan's bellowed command "Drop the anchor, ya mangy river-rats. Make ready a boat."

"We'd better go below and pack our things, dear," Nessa instructed. "Our journey is nearly over. Now, what were you so excited about?"

"Oh, I've managed to complete the exercise." Maerlin replied absently. Her eyes were drawn to the rugged marshland before them. She reluctantly allowed herself to be drawn away and went to tell Conal the good news.

"We've arrived!" Maerlin enthused when he allowed her into his cabin. "We've made it to the Great Swamp. Nessa says we'll soon be at the Holy Isle."

"Yeah, I know, just great, isn't it?" Conal replied darkly. "I just can't wait."

"What's the matter, Conal? It's a wonderful place. Why don't you want to go there?"

"Maerlin, you don't know what it's like!" he complained. "Everyone's so damned happy there, it makes me sick. There's no hustle and bustle, no barter or banter. The place is as dead as a morgue. It's just not real. It has no life!"

"But it looked full of happy people when I saw it in my dream."

"Just you wait until you've been trapped there for a couple of years. I'd rather be in prison," he argued glumly. "Give me the thriving life of a city ghetto, any day. Now that's excitement; so much danger and adventure."

"People are getting killed all the time in the city. I saw it with my own eyes, in broad daylight," Maerlin protested. "Children are begging there for food, starving and in rags. Do you think they'd rather live on the Isle, or in the gutter? Sorry, but I really don't see what's so special about the city, Conal."

Conal glared at her in disgust. Clearly she couldn't see what he meant. "I think you'll fit right in on the Isle, and I wish you well there. They're going to teach you magic, so I guess it won't be so boring for you, but for me, the place was a living hell. Thanks a lot but no thanks. The first chance I get, I'll be out of there and you won't see me again."

Maerlin frowned, but she knew she wasn't going to change his mind. "Well anyway, Ness says we need to get packed. They're lowering the boat for us to go ashore. There's a village ahead. We can hire a punt there to take us into the marshes."

"Yes, I know. I've been here before, remember," Conal replied sullenly.

Maerlin gave up and left to pack her own meagre belongings. A short while later she was back on the deck, hauling the last of Nessa's bags up with her.

"Stick it in the pile over there, lass," instructed Captain Bohan, pointing to the side of the ship. "The lads'll load it into the boat for ya, and then ye can be off."

Maerlin did as she was bid, and then came back to wish the captain farewell "Goodbye, Captain."

Captain Bohan stooped down and smiled at Maerlin, before taking her tiny hand into his calloused one. "I've a feeling we'll meet again, lass, you mark my words. In the meantime, pay heed to the good ladies of the Isle. They are as wise as the stars above. Give my blessing to the High Priestess when you get there. Tell her, it's always an honour to serve her and ask her to remember me in her prayers to the goddess."

"I will," Maerlin promised. She had come to like the gruff captain during the journey.

"Okay, lass, you'd best be goin' now. The boat's ready for ya," he instructed, standing up again. As Maerlin looked around, she saw Nessa disappearing over the side of the ship into the small rowing boat. Conal was waiting to descend after her. Maerlin hurried over, eager to see more of the Great Marsh.

The ship soon disappeared as they were rowed through the outer reaches of the marsh and into the first of the many channels. The sailors strained at the oars while the First Mate steered the rudder, navigating through the narrow waterways.

"The village will be coming up in a moment, Ma'am," he announced to Nessa, respectfully. "I'm sorry that we can't take you any farther, but this boat is only suited for the fringes of the marsh."

"That's all right. Tell your Captain that he's done well to get us this far. We're indebted to him for the service," replied Nessa.

"Yes Ma'am."

"We're here!" Maerlin pointed out as a small village appeared out of the mists. It was rough and unkempt-looking, with lichen clinging to the walls of the huts, but otherwise it could easily have been one of the neighbouring villages of Maerlin's childhood.

Villagers came out to greet the boat and secure it to the jetty posts that thrust out of the murky waters.

Maerlin was rising from the boat even before it was secured, but the First Mate's warning stopped her "Careful, lass! If you fall into that soup, you'll regret it. There are leeches in that muck as big as me forearm and as hungry as wolves. That's to say nothing of the eels which lurk 'ere about."

Merlin looked down into the black water. She could see vague shapes moving down there. "Are they really that bad?"

"Worse!" Conal explained morosely "He didn't even mention the gnats and mosquitoes that gather with the dusk. You'll wake up covered in spots, and itching from head to foot if you're not careful. Welcome to the Great Marsh," he added sardonically.

Once the boat was secured, the villagers helped them onto the jetty. Soon, the baggage was unloaded, and the men began their journey back to the Lurching Otter. Maerlin waved to them as they rowed away.

"Come along, dear, don't hang about. It's almost dark, and there's still plenty to be done," Nessa commanded.

Maerlin found herself and Conal busy hauling bags to the guest quarters while Nessa spoke to the village elders.

*****

It was the next morning before they set out into the marshland, as the villagers refused to venture out so late in the day. Conal had explained to Maerlin that the channels moved constantly as the ground silted up and was washed away by the river currents, and when evenings fell, the mists enveloped the land and become so thick that you couldn't see your own hand before your face. She asked him many questions about the marshes. Although reluctant at first to answer, he soon came out of his shell and told her stories of his time in the marsh and some of its dangers.

They set off in the still of early morning, and Maerlin could soon see what Conal meant about mosquitoes. She was constantly swatting at every bit of exposed flesh in an effort to stop the bloodsuckers from biting her "Damn them all! My head's itching!" she complained as she scratched beneath her braids vigorously.

Conal was also suffering from the gnats, constantly slapping at his neck and forearms, though the cap he wore covered his scalp.

"Here, spread some of this on, the pair of you," instructed Nessa, handing over a bottle of pungent salve. "It's my own special recipe; works a treat."

Conal sniffed at the bottle and wrinkled up his nose. "It reeks like a whorehouse carpet. What's in it?"

"This and that," replied Nessa vaguely, ignoring his expression. "I don't think you really want to know. Put it on or scratch away. The choice is yours."

Conal shrugged and smothered his skin in the thin brown liquid, before passing the bottle to Maerlin.

"Don't worry, dear. After a while, you won't notice the smell."

*****

The marshland deadened all noise, making it seem haunted and forbidden. The only sound as they travelled through the boggy swamp was of the water dripping off the raised paddles; that and the constant whine of insects seeking to suck blood from any unprotected skin. Occasionally, a frog or a rat would splash into the water as they passed by. The villagers who navigated them through the reeds and bulrushes were as silent as the world around them. Maerlin longed for the sound of laughter or song as the morning slowly passed into afternoon. The oppressive silence was getting on her nerves. Even the bird-calls seemed muted. Only the occasional raucous cry of a jackdaw could be heard, and this did little to break the sombre ambience.

Finally, they heard sounds ahead, and Maerlin's hopes rose in expectation of arrival. Conal, seeing her eyes light up, shook his head. "We've a ways to go yet. Sound tends to travel in the marshes and wander about. Don't be fooled by the direction of it either. It can bounce off things and change direction. That's why people fear the Great Marsh. It appears haunted at times. It probably is. Many people have died here, lost in the fog or eaten by the leeches. That's to say nothing of the will-o-the-wisps."

"It's been giving me the creeps all day. It looks so wonderful from the outside, but after a while it just gets you down," Maerlin said.

"I did warn you," Conal replied. "Another half bell by my guess and we'll be there."

The arrival, when it came, was so quick that Maerlin was caught by surprise. One moment, she was sitting in a half-daze, listening to the drone of insects around her head as the marsh floated slowly by, and the next, the Holy Isle was before them. Standing at the docks, waiting, was the High Priestess herself and many others, dressed in the white robes of the Order. Other younger girls stood behind, dressed in pale blue, and children played and laughed around the fringes of the assembled group.

As they docked, Ceila stepped forward with a warm smile and embraced Nessa. "Dearest Sister, Ness, my mentor. Thou art always welcome here. My heart is filled with joy to see thee again."

"It's good to see ye too, Ceila. You've come far since first I found you, and you've brought great honour to the goddess." Nessa gripped the taller woman in a bear hug.

Then the High Priestess turned and greeted the sullen Conal "Greetings to thee, son of the Dragon-lord. My house is again yours, though I know it acheth thy heart to be amongst us." She dragged the reluctant boy into an embrace before kissing him on the cheek.

Conal pulled a face, but smiled at the High Priestess. "Let's just hope that my imprisonment is shorter this time. I see no reason for me to remain here. I'm well able to look after myself now."

"Have no fear, Dragonson. I've foreseen thy coming in my dreams and made arrangements that will suit thy restless spirit. It would grieve the goddess to see harm come to thee, for thy time has not yet come. Therefore, I have a new guardian coming to guide thee on thy way to thy destiny."

"Oh no!" Conal declared, stepping back towards the boat. "Forget it. I'll have no more mollycoddling from warm-hearted spinsters, thank you very much. The villagers can take me back. I'll find my own way to revenge my father's death."

A dark expression flickered across the beautiful face of the High Priestess before she replied "Thou must not yet seek revenge *MacDragan*. Thy time is not yet at hand. To do so now would mean failure and surely thy death and the death of thy bloodline. Dragania wouldst fall into dark times, once again," Ceila foretold. "I plead with thee, wait for thy coming of age and thy destiny."

"I'll not be babysat anymore!" Conal yelled, ignoring the request of the High Priestess.

"Then heed me, Son of the Dragon, for I understand thy concerns. The guardian I speak of will teach thee all thy needs to know and more. Wait here for just a few days and at least speak with him before dismissing the man from thy service."

"It's a man?" Conal asked with surprise.

"It is, and this one is like no other, or so I've been told. He is unique."

Conal paused, considering.

"Please, Conal, I beg thee. Meet with this guardian before thou thinketh of leaving. If then, thou wishes to depart, we will not hinder thee in the path to thy destiny," assured the High Priestess.

Finally, Conal nodded his acceptance. "Okay, I'll meet with this man. I guess, I owe you that much ..." he answered "... although I'm not promising anything."

The High Priestess nodded her acceptance and turned to Maerlin. "My Little Thief," she teased, opening her arms to embrace Maerlin. "Thou art larger in real life than in my dreams, yet still, thou hast the look of a sprite. Thou art welcome here amongst the Sisterhood of the goddess. Praise her for bringing thee here." Maerlin fell into the warm embrace as if she had found a long-lost sister.

Ceila signalled for one of the acolytes to come forward. She was a girl of Maerlin's age, though slightly taller. The redheaded girl carried a gown of pale blue silk, which she held out to Maerlin.

"This is Cora *Ni Mannaman* of *Clann Na Rón*. She comes from the Western Isles, Maerlin," Ceila instructed "And this is the robe of a novice. While thou art here, this is thy gown. Wear it with pride, for it symbolises the love we have for our goddess, Deanna."

Maerlin accepted the gown with a smile.

"Cora will show thee to thy room and answer thy many questions. It is not every day that a wielder of 'Wild-magic' comes to the Isle."

Raising her voice so that all could hear her, the High Priestess announced "Sisters! Praise the goddess Deanna."

"Praise be to Deanna!" they replied in unison.

"Today we feast in celebration for the goddess has blessed us with a new Sister. Come, priestesses of Deanna, let us greet Maerlin, Wind-sister and Dream-catcher of High Peaks. She has come here as a novice to the legendary Nessa *Mac Tire*, Earth-sister of the Broce Woods."

Chapter Ten: The Feasting

Maerlin felt daunted as she followed the High Priestess and the girl, Cora, through the throng. She was surprised by the genuine warmth and friendship in the many greetings she received. She realised that she had lost all sight of Nessa and Conal, and she looked around in concern.

"What's the matter?" Cora asked timidly.

"I've lost my companions," Maerlin explained.

Cora smiled warmly. "Don't worry. They've gone to their rooms to freshen up after the journey. You'll see them again at the feast. Come on, I'll show you to your room. It's right next to mine, so you've nothing to worry about." Cora led her to the Novice Quarters, which turned out to be a simple, but elegant building on the western side of the island.

"Have you been here long, Cora?" Maerlin asked, her eyes taking in all before her.

"Almost a year now, though it seems like a lifetime," Cora replied as they walked through the broad corridor of the dormitory.

Numerous doors lay on either side of the passageway, causing Maerlin to ask "How long did it take for you to find your way around? This place is enormous!"

Cora laughed. "It took a few moons, at least."

While Maerlin bathed and changed into her new gown, she drilled Cora with questions, wanting as much information about the Order as possible. Cora answered as best she could.

By the time they were ready to go to the feast, Maerlin was already bonding with the other novice.

"You're beautiful," Cora announced as they stood before a polished copper mirror.

They were examining Maerlin's new gown. Maerlin was unused to compliments, but looking at her reflection, she had to admit that she was

127

at least striking. Her strong cheekbones and swarthy features stood out well against the pale blue silk, and her freshly-braided hair complimented her facial features. Mirrors were not common in the mountains, at least not full-sized ones like this one. Maerlin blushed. "I wouldn't go as far as that, Cora. The High Priestess now, she is beautiful," Maerlin argued, but still she glowed with warmth at the compliment.

"Come on, we'd better hurry. The feast will have begun already."

The two girls rushed off, laughing and giggling as they raced across the broad plaza towards the sound of celebration. After catching their breaths, they walked arm in arm into the feasting hall. The hall was regal in dimensions, its tall ceiling held up by marble pillars of smooth, white stone, etched with intricate knot-work and pictograms. White marble tables covered the floor-space, with wooden trellises sitting next to them. Over two hundred people filled the room in a swirl of white and blue silks. The tables were laden with various foods such as venison, boar and ox, as well as fruits, and broiled vegetables. Goblets of juice and fruit teas filled any spaces remaining at the tables. The noise was incredible. Laughter and chatter echoed off the walls. Music could be heard occasionally as the sound ebbed and flowed. At the far side of the room was a long table, raised higher on a plinth. At this table sat the High Priestess and the other senior members of the Order.

Maerlin blinked in surprise. Nessa was sitting to the High Priestess's right hand side, dressed in a fine white gown with a green-trimmed border. Looking closer, she noticed that a few others within the room were similarly adorned. Others had a piping of pale blue, red or turquoise. A few, including the High Priestess, wore a border of gold on their ceremonial robes.

"What do the colours on the robes signify, Cora?" Maerlin whispered.

"What? Oh those. They are for the 'Wild-magicians'. The colour on their robes signifies which Elemental they have an affinity for."

"Don't you all use Wild-magic?" Maerlin asked with surprise.

Cora giggled and smiled at Maerlin, causing her to frown. "I'm sorry Maerlin. I forget that you are new to the ways of magic. We are all priestesses of the Order and servants of the goddess. You'll be taught the basics of many types of magic while here, including Healing, Augury, Spirit-speech, and many others, but Wild-magic is unique. It's a gift of the goddess, not something that can be learned. Did the great Earth-sister, Nessa, not speak to you of this?"

Maerlin thought a moment and recalled a conversation with Nessa about Wild-magic. Things that had been said back then were finally beginning to make sense. "So Nessa can do Wild-magic too!" she exclaimed, remembering the rocky bridge that Nessa had created. "She's an Earth-sister. That's what the High Priestess called her. So that means that she can use Earth Elementals in her magic."

Cora's face twisted into a slight frown. "We wouldn't consider it in terms of 'use'. It's more like a gift being bestowed at our request of the Elemental, but yes, your mentor is an Earth-sister. She wears the green of the Earth-sisters on her robe."

"Red is for Fire, am I correct, and the light blue must be ... Water?" Maerlin guessed.

"No, silly ... blue is for Air."

"Oh, I see. That means that the turquoise one must be for Water? Why isn't it blue and Air, white?"

"Have you not seen the oceans, Maerlin? There, Water Elementals are truly free. It's a gigantic unfettered beast and it is perpetually hungry."

"I come from the mountains, Cora. I'd lived there my whole life, at least, until a few short weeks ago," answered Maerlin, feeling she had still so much to learn.

"I'm sure you'll see the magnificence of the ocean at some point. I myself am training to be a Water-sister," announced Cora with pride.

Maerlin smiled and hugged her, silently thanking the High Priestess for her choice of guide. "Are there many other novices gifted with Wild-magic?"

"Only three have come to learn Wild-magic in the last five years. One of these chose to suppress her gift," replied Cora with a hint of sadness.

"Are they all girls then, or do boys come here, too?" Maerlin asked.

"No boy has ever been gifted with Wild-magic, though some have great powers in the other forms of the magic. They do not come here to learn. Only young women at the time of their choosing come here to serve the Order of Deanna."

Maerlin considered this, remembering her dreams of the old magician and the ritual slaughter she had witnessed. A sudden coldness passed through her and she shivered, rubbing the hairs on her arms.

"What about the gold piping? What does that mean?" Maerlin asked, drawing her mind away from the image.

"I thought you'd know that one already," Cora replied in surprise. "They are the Dream-catchers. The High Priestess spoke to us of the dream she had of your coming. She said that you must be a Dream-catcher, too. No one else could break through the wards that protect the Holy Isle. Did you not know that?"

Maerlin frowned. "No, I didn't. Ness wouldn't speak to me of my dreams. She just asked me a lot of questions. Suddenly, we stopped wandering around the mountains and rushed here."

Cora considered what to say "Don't worry, Maerlin. It'll all make sense to you in the moons and years to come. The goddess's will be done. Now come ..." she said, her tone becoming cheerful again. "... I'm starving, and the food's getting cold. I'll introduce you to the other novices."

Maerlin allowed herself to be led down the side of the Feasting Hall, while her eyes took in as much as they could. She spotted Conal, sitting off on his own to one side. He was ignoring the celebrations around him and sullenly feeding one of his ferrets a morsel of meat. He was dressed in a short tunic of pale cream with a Frost Dragon emblazed upon the left shoulder. Maerlin waved to him as she was led past, but he was engrossed in the task at hand.

"Conal," she shouted over the noise. "Hey, Conal, do you like my new dress?"

He looked up, hearing his name called, but remained silent.

"What do you think?" Maerlin asked, twirling around to show off her novice's robe.

Conal shrugged his shoulders with sullen indifference, still petting the ferret. He looked at her with those deep blue eyes of his. "The robe suits you, Maerlin. This whole place suits you. I'm sure you'll be very happy here."

Conal's tone took some of the excitement out of Maerlin. "What's the matter, Conal? Why do you hate this place so much?"

"You wouldn't understand."

"Why don't you try me?" Waving Cora away, she sat down beside Conal and looked earnestly into his eyes. "Tell me why you hate it here so much. Help me to understand."

"You've never had someone watching over you the whole time, have you? I bet that up on that mountain of yours, you could run around all day, as free as a bird. No one would bother you. Am I right?"

Maerlin nodded grudgingly.

"Well for me, it's been a lot different. I've always had someone around: always interfering, protecting, and guarding me against any unknown danger. That's why I hate living here. Ceila and the rest of the witches of the Order are forever watchful, even when they sleep. I can't breathe here. Thankfully, I won't have to stay long this time. According to Ceila, my new guardian will arrive in the next few days. I hate the idea of a guardian, having to spend my whole life being watched over and protected. It irritates me more than anything else, but at least I'll be free of the Holy Isle. This place is ... *surreal*."

He sat quietly for a moment, and Maerlin waited, knowing that there was more. Finally, he broke the silence "I remember a time before the Isle. Once, I lived in *Dun Dragan* ... when my father was still alive. I can't remember my mother. She died when I was only two years old. My father was a good man; a good father even, in his own distracted way. I remember his long golden locks, his well-trimmed beard, and his rare but magnificent smiles. I remember those intense blue eyes of his, like when he was watching me in mock combat. One of my strongest memories of all was his hands. They were always tanned and heavily calloused. The backs of them were covered in a light down of golden hairs and a fine mesh of battle-scars. They were the hands of a *Fear Ban* warrior."

Conal gazed down at his own hands and they fell silent again, in the midst of the bustle of the feast. "He taught me the rudiments of warfare and weaponry, even at an early age. He gave me my first practice sword on my fifth birthday and told me gravely "Life is danger, Conal. There will always be someone who wants to see you dead. You must learn to be adept with a blade, for your life will depend on it." Little did I know that within two years, he'd be dead on a battlefield. I spent my seventh birthday in hiding, fleeing for my life towards the Holy Isle."

"Shortly after that, Lord Boare razed the fortress to the ground in an effort to find me and kill me, but I was already long gone. By then, I was safely hidden within the Great Marsh, where no one, not even Dubhgall the Black could find me. Not even Lord Boare's cursed sorcerer can penetrate the magical mists that cloak this Isle. Since then, others had been my guardians- too many to recall -the latest being Madame Dunne. To give her credit, she lasted much longer than the rest, and she showed some spirit. We might have fought like cats and dogs, but secretly, she earned my respect. Now, they are sending for another guardian, and much though the High Priestess assures me that this one will be different, I have my doubts."

"From the sound of it, they're only trying to protect you, Conal."

"I know that! I'm not a complete idiot, you know! I know that other people are constantly putting themselves at risk for me. Do you think that makes it any easier?" Conal leapt to his feet in frustration. "Oh ... what's the point? I knew you wouldn't understand. Just forget it, all right. Just go back to your new friends and leave me in peace."

"Conal!"

"No! Go on. They're waiting for you ... your giggly friend is already looking over here with those moony sad eyes of hers. You can tell her all about our little heart to heart. I'm sure she's just dying to hear it."

"Hey! That's not fair!" objected Maerlin, but he was already storming off across the hall. Looking over, she saw the concern on Cora's face and put a cheerful smile on her face as she got slowly to her feet. Trying to smother her growing frustration, Maerlin sighed.

"Come on, Maerlin! All the best food'll be gone, if you don't hurry," Cora urged.

Conal and his dark mood were quickly forgotten as she was half-dragged to the novices table, and space was made for them at the feast. Time passed as she ate and answered question after question about herself and her life in the mountains. She hardly got the chance to ask any of her own questions. Before she knew it, it was night time.

Cora led her back to the dormitory, and soon, she was fast asleep. Her brain quickly swirled into a confusing dream.

*****

Maerlin awoke on an isolated roadside. There, she found a strange, colourfully-dressed man sitting by a campfire, preparing a meal.

Carefully, he added ingredients to the stew, pausing often to look eastward. His face was as swarthy as Maerlin's own. His nose was sharp and afflicted with a painful-looking boil. His hair was jet black and tied in a ponytail behind the broad-brimmed hat that he wore.

He paused in his cooking and walked towards the painted wagon, set back from the roadside. Rummaging around in his packs, he drew forth two labelled bottles, each corked with a lead seal. He inspected the bottles carefully before breaking the seal on one of them. This one, he emptied into the stew. Carefully, he opened the second bottle, and with a grimace, he took a long swig from the bottle's contents.

Suddenly, his body doubled over, and the man groaned loudly. He shuddered as he swallowed another gulp of the vile-tasting liquid. Curling into a foetal position, he lay panting, gripping the bottle tightly until the spasms passed. "This had better work," he grunted through gritted teeth as he slowly recovered.

Climbing to his feet, he stowed the bottles away. Heading back to the fire pit, the man stirred the contents of the stew again, sipping frequently from a flagon beside him. His eyes continued to look eastward and concern showed on his dark features. He did not have to wait long; however, for soon a troop of cavalry crested the rise and rode towards him.

The traveller sighed with relief, muttering "About bloody time, too!" He pulled out a clay pipe and reached into the fire for a burning twig. Pulling the twig free from the flames, he held it close to his face and lit the pipe. Pulling a few times on the tobacco, he stood and meandered forward to greet the approaching riders.

"G'day to you Cap'n," he greeted as the troop pulled up before him. "Ya look like ye've travelled far. Ya must be in some sort of hurry, that's for sure."

"Tell me, Teincheor, have you been on this road long?" the captain demanded.

The Teincheor smiled softly. "I've been on the road me whole life, sir. Twas born in a Barrel-top, as was me Da before me, and 'is before 'im."

"No, you fool. I mean here ... this road!"

"Ah! Why didn't ya say that? I've been at this 'ere camp for three days now. I'm waiting for some o' me family, ya see. How can I help ye?"

"We're looking for some fugitives, a blonde-haired youth with a broken nose and blue eyes. We think he might be travelling with a minor nobleman. The man wears a hat similar to your own," informed the troop leader, pointing to the broad-brimmed hat on the traveller's head.

"Ah, those two! It's for sure I've seen 'em both. Didn't I just trade with them earlier today for some food? They seemed like decent enough folks to me. Tis indeed the same hat, for twas part of the bargain we struck. I confess I took a bit of a fancy to the old thing," he said, tilting the hat at a cocky angle."Doesn't it look grand on me?"

"When was this?" the captain demanded, straining his eyes ahead.

"Let me see now, twas a good few bells ago, that's for sure. Ya won't catch 'em tonight, Cap'n, I can tell ya that! If you'll take the advice of an ignorant man such as myself, you'll have a care. Yon road can be dangerous after dark. A man could easily lose his seat in all dem potholes. Alas, it seems his Lordship has other matters on his mind besides maintaining decent highways ... but I'm sure he has his reasons."

The soldier's eyes flicked towards the traveller, but let the comment pass.

"How far is it to the nearest tavern, Teincheor?" he asked. His manner was still abrupt and distracted.

"Ah! That's a good auld ways away, to be sure. Tis a good five leagues farther, at the very least ... I know," he added, as if the idea had just come to him "... Why don't you and ya men camp her for the night, instead? I've a nice fresh stew simmering over yonder fire and a flagon of Leithban mead. T'would be only right that I offer ye this small 'ospitality. After all, aren't you the same boyos that've been keeping the roads safe from brigands and thieves, making it possible for the likes of me to make me livin'?"

The trooper looked ahead, clearly wanting to travel farther before darkness fell.

"Don't even be thinking of going farther up yon road, Cap'n. I tell ya honestly. It will do ye no good at all at all. It's as rocky as a quarry on yonder road for the next few miles. There's not a decent camp 'tween 'ere and yonder tavern. Only a fool'd ride that road at night, and I can see by the stripes on ya arm that you're no man's fool."

"Leithban mead, you say?"

"Aye, Cap'n! Da sweetest mead ever brewed in Tir Pect. Those monks know how to brew da sweet nectar, that'd be sure. I can see ya know ya meads from dat gleam in ya eye."

The troop leader looked back at his weary men and once more at the road ahead before he relented "Corporal, billet the men. We'll camp here tonight," he ordered, before dismounting wearily. "That's a mighty offer, Teincheor. My apologies for my rudeness, it's been a long day," the captain apologised as he stretched his cramped limbs and aching back.

"Think nothing of it, good sir, nothing at all. The food'd only be going to waste. My cousin, Felleck, was supposed to be here tonight, and he has a brood as big as a sow's litter. I've the meal ready and waiting for them all, but it looks like they ain't coming. He's likely found an ale barrel to sleep in somewhere, the stupid fecker. The stew might as well be eaten by someone. T'would be a crying shame to leave it to go to ruination, now wouldn't it?"

The troopers picketed their mounts and made their camp around the wagon. Relief showed on many of the faces. It had been a long, hard ride from the city. The Teincheor built up the fire and busied himself with ladling out platefuls of the piping-hot stew and passing them around. His manner was friendly and diffident as he handed over the food, first to the captain and his corporal, and then to the conscripts. Each time he ladled another batch of plates out; he filled his own bowl and noisily ate a few bites of the stew. "Ah! May the goddess bless me dear auld wife," he remarked. "Twas her mother's own recipe. It still tastes as good today as it did when we first wed."

"Where is your good lady, Teincheor?" the corporal asked between mouthfuls. He was clearly enjoying the savoury meal.

"She passed on to the goddess, bless her, in the plague of '38. Twas an 'orrible thing to watch, so it was, her wasting away like that," the Teincheor replied and looked lost in remorse for a few moments. Then he pulled himself out of it, muttering "Ah well, twas the will of Macha, I guess. Who am I to question the wisdom of the Seven?"

Maerlin watched the meal progress and was amazed when men began dropping to the ground, fast asleep. Some even fell over mid-mouthful. The conversation fell silent and, looking closer, she noticed the glazed eyes of those still awake. One by one, the troopers collapsed, until only the Teincheor remained. He was sitting quietly by the fireside, poking at the embers of the fire. When the last of the troopers collapsed, he stood up and inspected the sleeping soldiers before him.

"Tis a mighty stew indeed, even if the antidote tastes like putrefying slugs," he muttered as he poked the flames. "It's going to be a long night." He drew a long stiletto from within his coat.

Stooping before the first soldier, he stabbed him through the heart. The Teincheor's face changed from the smiling character of earlier into a grim mask, as he patiently slaughtered each of the sleeping men.

Maerlin wept in her sleep as she watched the grisly work. It was made more so by the cold efficiency with which it was carried out.

*****

When the killing was over, Cull systematically searched the dead, taking extra time over the captain's saddlebag and pouches. He loaded all the weapons and saddles into the wagon, and then he tied the mounts together with a long lead rope. This he secured firmly to the wagon. He worked quickly but carefully, making sure to leave nothing behind. When he was finished, he loaded the dead into the wagon, stacking them on top of each other to fit them into the cramped space.

The task completed, he checked the campsite once more, looking for any forgotten evidence of the soldiers' existence. Only when he was completely satisfied, did he harness up the black stallion. Taking a taper from the fire, he lit the oil lamps on the front of the wagon. Their light bathed the area in an eerie glow. He walked over to the embers of the fire and smothered them completely in dirt. He was now ready to leave.

"Hyup, lad!" Cull commanded. The dray horse strained into his collar, and the heavily-laden wagon lurched forward onto the Western Highway. Cull walked beside the steed, keeping it to a steady walk in the darkness. The lamps gave enough light to steer the wagon by, avoiding the many potholes on the road. It was as silent as a graveyard at this time of night, but for the creaking of the wagon springs, the thud of hooves, and the rattle of harness. This suited Cull's mood just fine.

He had not liked killing the soldiers, but it was a necessity. Cull knew that Lord Boare would send troops down each of the main highways, hunting for the boy. Cull had waited half a day for the troop to arrive at his camp, picking his ambush site with great care, gauging the exact distance from the city and the terrain in-between. He smiled at the irony of it all. The military precision of the soldiers had ultimately been their downfall. They had ridden the standard distance for a troop in haste, forty miles per day, thus arriving at his camp within a bell of darkness. Had they paced themselves better and kept to thirty miles a day, they would have survived. Cull could not kill so many men in normal combat. The poison was his only possible solution, and for it to work, he had needed to set up his plan precisely.

It would be days before the troop was reported missing and even longer before Lord Boare sent out additional troops to search for them. This suited Cull's plans perfectly, for he would be far away by then. He smiled. All was going well. The goddess Deanna must indeed be looking down at him. As if to confirm his thoughts, a break appeared in the road ahead, and he slowed the horse down ready for the turn.

After turning off the main thoroughfare onto the disused track, Cull headed up the rocky weed-choked lane. He was looking for a suitable hiding place and he didn't have to travel far. At the top of the hill he found a broad clearing. Set into the back of the clearing was the opening he had been anticipating.

This had once been a mining area. Its hills were once filled with iron, tin, and even a little gold. The track led him to a disused mineshaft. He halted the wagon in front of the dark opening and walked over to inspect it. With relief, he noted that the cavernous entrance was the beginning of a deep

137

bore-hole and not one of the earlier open-cast mines. He had not been looking forward to dragging the bodies along its dark passageway, fearful of the roof caving in while he worked.

"Blessed be the Seven," he mumbled, kicking a stone down into the hole.

A deep shaft was perfect for the disposal, with little hope of the bodies ever being found. He carefully turned the wagon and backed the stallion up until the back wheels rested close to the edge. Halting the horse before the slight incline, he applied the brake. A short while later, the stallion was free from the shafts and tied to a nearby tree. Cull's possessions were repacked into the saddlebags, and the horse was made ready to ride.

Cull changed clothes, throwing his traveller disguise into the mine and again donning the fine clothes of the petty lord. He looked at the soldiers' horses, still tied to the wagon, and regret showed on his face. He could not risk them wandering into the nearby countryside and giving away his hiding place. He had no choice but to leave them with the wagon and the dead.

"Don't get sentimental, ya auld fool," he berated, as he continued his preparations. Oil was scattered over the wagon and bodies until the smell of paraffin hung thick in the night air and raked at his throat. Cull stood back to inspect his work in the eerie light of the wagon's lanterns. Satisfied that all was well, he released the brake lever.

The wagon sat for a moment as if frozen in time, and then slowly, it rolled towards the gaping black hole. It quickly gained momentum when the back wheels dropped into the dark shaft, and the wagon teetered on the edge. The horses, realising their fate, panicked as they were dragged towards the pit. They whinnied piteously as they struggled against the lead rope, but it was no use. Cull had fastened their head-collars firmly, so that they could not struggle free. The wagon rocked for a moment on the edge of the abyss, and then it slipped into the darkness. The weight of the body-laden wagon pulled the struggling animals inexorably after it. One by one, they disappeared from sight.

Cull heard the crash as the dray shattered in the mine below and the loud 'whoomph' as the lamps ignited the paraffin. The screams of dying horses filled his ears. He stoically watched as the last of the animals was dragged to its death. Greasy, black smoke billowed out of the shaft as he stood watching.

Shaking his head, he turned and walked over to the stallion.

The steed was wide-eyed and jittery with fear, and Cull had to speak softly to calm the skittish animal. Eventually, it settled down and allowed itself to be led away from the smoking pit. Silence fell on the clearing as the well-dressed lord walked his steed down the hill to the roadside.

Looking left and right to make sure that the road was clear, Cull mounted up and turned his horse south, making for the river and the Great Marsh beyond. It had been a long night, but he still needed to cross the few miles of open ground before dawn. Shrugging off the urge to sleep, he kicked the horse into a trot and headed out. He trusted his mount's senses to guide them through the half-light of pre-dawn.

Chapter Eleven: Learning the Skills of Life

Maerlin woke early, her eyes still gritty and with a mild headache. She dressed in her new robes and went looking for some breakfast. When she left her room, she was surprised to see others already up and busy with the day. She stopped a freckle-faced girl with long, brown hair and asked her directions. Maerlin was directed down one of the corridors to the common room, where, she was told, novices ate, studied, and generally gathered. She followed the directions and soon found herself in a long chamber filled with girls of all ages, eating their breakfast.

"Maerlin, over here," yelled Cora, waving a slice of toast at her. "I didn't think you'd be awake yet."

Maerlin smiled weakly, still feeling groggy. "Is everyone else up?"

"Yes, we rise before dawn and sing our praise to the goddess as the sun comes over the Great Marsh. It's a wonderful way to start the day," explained Cora. "You look like you didn't sleep well. Is everything alright?"

"Mmm, oh yeah, just a bad dream, that's all. I guess all of this has knocked my brain sideways."

"Well, sit down and I'll go fetch you some tea. Help yourself to honey cakes," chirped Cora, slipping away to fetch Maerlin some tea.

When she returned, Maerlin smiled her gratitude. They ate for a few moments in silence, and Maerlin could feel the herbal brew slowly reviving her. The mist, which had clung to her brain since waking, began to lift like the sun warming the marsh and dispersing the fog.

"What am I supposed to do today?" Maerlin asked.

"I was told to bring you along with me to my classes for now and get you acclimatised. We have Healing Arts this morning and then Herbology, which is always interesting. This afternoon, I have training in Wild-magic, which means I guess you do too, and after that, it's Divination." Cora pulled a face. "I'm not very good at that."

The lessons were complex and extensive, and although Cora assured her that, with time, it would become easier, Maerlin still had her doubts. In Healing Arts, they spoke of parts of the body that Maerlin hadn't even realised existed, as well as healing points and sensitivities within the body. Herbology was even worse. They were each assigned one of the ancient oak trees within the sacred grove and were asked to communicate with the tree spirits within.

Maerlin was lost, but did not want to seem ignorant. She selected her tree and repeated the exercise she had done with Nessa, becoming one with the mighty oak. She quickly got lost in the ancient tree's awareness and did not hear Cora until the other girl shook her gently.

"Sorry!" she apologised as they headed for the common room and lunch. "I kept sensing something more when I was within the tree, but whenever I looked for it, it slipped away from my grasp."

"Ah! That'd be *Chornach*. She's the tree spirit in that tree. She likes to play games with novices. Don't worry," assured Cora "she'll show herself eventually. I had her tree for a while when I first came here. Just give her time and she'll come round."

"I thought it was just me, imagining things," Maerlin admitted. "I thought it was the poor night's sleep."

Cora's laugh was light and infectious. Soon Maerlin's heart lifted, forgetting her worries. "Let me tell you about my first experiences with *Chornach*. They might help you a little," explained Cora, and she proceeded to tell Maerlin a fascinating story.

Maerlin's worries lessened, and by the afternoon she felt confident enough to ask questions when she didn't understand.

Madame Muir, the Water-sister who was teaching the Wild-magic lesson, proved to be very patient and helpful.

"I want you to split into pairs for the next exercise and select one of the glasses of water I've provided. Maerlin ... why don't you stay with Cora? She has a natural ability with water anyway, so she'll make it easier for you. I presume Nessa *MacTire* has taught you the mind exercises?"

"Yes, Madame Muir," replied Maerlin.

"Good. So girls, I want you to start by enlivening the water and waking up the Elemental. Then, I want you to create a small vortex. Try to keep it under control, or we'll have water everywhere," Madame Muir instructed brightly, though from her tone she seemed she would be quite happy to have the room soaked.

"I thought only Water-magicians could use water?" Maerlin whispered to Cora.

"Oh no. Wild-magic users can use all of the Elements, but only to a limited degree. The Elemental with which they are blessed, however, gives them much greater ability, as the Elemental feels a closer affinity to the user. I can use Earth and Air Elements reasonably well, though Fire is a little more difficult for me. I guess that's understandable, with me being a Water-sister," explained Cora.

"What do I have to do?"

Cora smiled confidently at her new friend. "Clear your mind and go through the colours until the mind is black. You got that far in your lessons, I assume?"

Maerlin nodded, her mind already beginning the mental exercise. It had become almost second nature by now.

"Then, you focus on the water in the glass, but keep your eyes unfocused. Use your inner eye to see it instead," instructed Cora, letting Maerlin follow her through the exercise.

"I have it!" Maerlin exclaimed with surprise as the glass appeared in her mind.

"Is the image steady?"

"Pretty much, yes," Maerlin replied.

"Okay, then follow me through the exercise, and do what I do." Cora focused her attention on the glass, letting her mind go blank until the glass appeared firmly in her mind's eye. "Come, my dear friends. Come to my aid," she whispered "Come little ones, aid me in my task."

Maerlin watched the glass intently and felt the power being drawn in around her. The water in the glass shuddered for a moment, as if a tiny invisible fish swam close to the surface. The water was still clear within the glass, but as she studied it more, she thought that she could see ripples in the water.

"Come, sweet Undines. Come out and play with me," urged Cora in a soft whisper, as if speaking to a loved one. "Can you see the Elemental, Maerlin?"

"I think so. I can see movement in the water."

"Let's see if I can help," said Cora "Come, my pretty Undine. Rise up from thy lair and show thy beauty to the world. Let us bask in thy wonder."

The water swirled back and forth before Maerlin's inner eye. A tiny cone of water rose from the glass, defying gravity to rise upwards and swirl about.

"Blessed be," exclaimed Cora in a breathless whisper. "You honour me, beloved Undine."

A miniature fountain erupted, cascading upwards a hand's breadth before falling back into the glass.

Maerlin was transfixed. "That's wonderful!"

Madame Muir spoke from beside her. "I see that you're showing off again, Cora." Her tone did not sound displeased.

Cora's concentration slipped, and the water collapsed into the glass with an audible plop.

"Sorry, Madame Muir, I was just trying to show Maerlin the Elemental."

"That's alright, Cora," assured the teacher and turned towards Maerlin. "I think it's time for you to try it now, Maerlin. Nothing too fancy, just make the water move. That'll be enough for your first attempt."

Maerlin nodded and closed her eyes, suddenly very nervous. She could sense the others watching her as she cleared her mind. It took a few moments for her to find her inner peace. Finally, the white wall appeared and her concerns dissipated. Carefully, she made her way through the colours until she reached black and paused. Reaching out with her mind slowly as she had done with the tree, she moved her awareness forward towards the glass. Finding it, she fixed it firmly within her mind, sensing its coolness and clearness, almost tasting it on her tongue. Then she spoke, trying to copy Cora's soft whisper. "Come, spirit of the water." she whispered "Come forth for me."

The water remained calm and unmoving, giving Maerlin a momentary doubt.

"Come, little Undine, I beg thee. Come to mine aid," she pleaded, trying the more formal language she had heard others use when summoning Wild-magic.

The water remained placid within the glass, and Maerlin felt the awareness of others nearby. With a sigh, she forced herself to remain calm and refocused on the glass.

"You need to picture it in your mind, Maerlin. Show the Elemental what you wish it to do. Give it your guidance," Madame Muir encouraged.

Taking a few calming breaths, Maerlin pictured the water in the glass turning, becoming a small vortex, and again she spoke "Come forth, Sprite. Come out and play with me."

This time, the water quivered. The glass rattled slightly on the bench, and Maerlin focused harder on her task, picturing the water swirling faster.

"Come forth, little Undine," she encouraged. Her tone changed to one of joy as she saw the first tentative movements within the glass. Excitement filled her and her mind soared. She wanted to see the Elemental do more.

The water spun sluggishly in the glass, slowly gathering momentum as the Elemental sensed Maerlin's wishes and strove to comply. Maerlin focused harder, picturing the water in the mountain carne during a storm, its waters, choppy and wild. She urged the Elemental to greater efforts. The Undine gladly obeyed her request, eager to be free and unfettered from the confines of the glass.

Maerlin's concentration was suddenly broken as cold water splashed across her face. Cora laughed and clapped as Maerlin blinked in surprise. The table was covered in droplets of water.

"I'm not quite sure if that was what you had in mind, Maerlin ..." Madame Muir commented with a reassuring smile "... But for a first attempt, you certainly show promise. Next time, you might try for a little less of an exhibition, at least until you can control the Elemental. From what Nessa has told me, you have the potential to become a Storm-Bringer. It's been three generations since we've had one of those, not since Uiscallan Storm-sister. Let's hope that your skills become even half as legendary."

Turning to the rest of the class, her manner changed as she became businesslike "I think that's enough for today. Tomorrow, we'll be having a guest speaker in to show you all some Earth-magic. Tidy up please, girls, and then you may go to Divination," Madame Muir instructed, and then she added "Oh, I nearly forgot. Cora, can you bring Maerlin to the High Priestess's office? The Dream-catchers wish to speak with her."

*****

Cull made it to the village of Auldsmead without incident, though he was bone-weary by the time he arrived. His first port of call was the local priestess, situated in a little cottage on the outskirts of town. He bowed respectfully and explained his mission. He would need a boat to take him across to the Holy Isle, as soon as possible.

She gave him directions to one of the village huts, telling him whom he was to ask for. The villagers were still stirring, and the local fishermen had not yet left for the day. He would be able to get passage straight away and be on the Isle before darkness fell.

Thanking the priestess for her help, Cull handed over a leather purse; a donation to help the poor within her community. The pouch contained a tidy sum of money, enough to feed the whole village for the coming winter. The Boarite troop has recently been paid their monthly wages and had not yet had the chance to spend their earnings. Cull had no desire to keep the money himself. He kept only the paperwork from within the captain's saddlebag. The money might as well go to a good cause.

He followed the priestess's directions and soon he had negotiated passage across the swamplands.

Climbing into the flat-bottomed boat, he and his silent guide set off. Cull had long ago acquired the skill of sleeping pretty much anywhere. He pulled a light blanket over his head to ward off the flies and made himself as comfortable as possible. He was soon fast asleep. He slept throughout the morning, waking only when his guide announced their arrival.

A small party stood waiting for him. Three high-ranking priestesses greeted him warmly and led him to a guest chamber, where he could wash up after his long journey. Refreshments were also waiting, but Cull opted to bathe first. He was feeling grimy, and his muscles ached after the long trip. Once bathed, he changed into another black outfit of well-tailored expensive cloth. He had been planning for this meeting since he had left the Beggar-Lord. Cull decided on a well-trimmed goatee for his new disguise, and this suited his current apparel. Satisfied with his appearance, he filled a large pouch with coins and tied it loosely to his belt. Once all of his preparations were completed, Cull ate a light meal and left the room.

*****

Conal had spent the morning ambling around, and by early afternoon he was well and truly bored. His overactive imagination quickly conjured up a number of possibilities for amusement. They would while away the time until his new guardian arrived. He was in the process of sneaking into the girls' dormitories with an earthenware jar, which he had earlier filled up with an ant's nest, when he saw a new target for his amusement.

Walking down the corridor, looking clearly lost, was a well-dressed merchant. Conal quickly decided to hold off on his ant invasion. Slipping into one of the many alcoves, he dumped the jar of ants in the corner and hid in the semi-darkness, watching as the merchant passed him by.

The merchant was idly whistling a tune as he turned left and started towards the kitchens. Conal knew the layout of the Temple like the back of his hand and quickly considered his options. A plan emerged, one that suited him well for its double benefits, being both enjoyable and profitable. On swift, silent feet, Conal ran down the corridor in the opposite direction, taking the next left turn and hurrying to overtake the wandering merchant. Racing down the long corridor, ignoring the protests of the priestesses he flew past, he made it to the next junction and skidded to a halt. Pausing to catch his breath, he listened for the sound of footsteps approaching. The whistling merchant was getting closer. He had won the race, and now his plan would come into action.

The footsteps grew louder, riding boots clearly pronounced on the marble flagstones. Gauging his timing to perfection, Conal stepped back a few paces and raced around the corner. He collided with the merchant and brought the man down with him in a sprawl. Conal's nimble fingers grabbed the merchant's purse as they spilled apart. Deftly, Conal slipped the purse under his tunic.

The merchant came to his feet with surprising agility, a frown on his face as he stooped to pick up his broad-brimmed hat. "Where are you going in such a rush, boy? Is the building on fire?"

"Sorry, sir, beggin' ya pardon but I'm late for lunch, and the girls'll clear the table if they get the chance. I'll be left starving 'till supper," Conal mumbled in apology.

"Well, slow down on the corners, you foolish boy. You gave me quite a turn there," blustered the merchant as he flicked specks of dust off his hat.

Conal nodded his head and turned to slip away.

"Wait a moment, boy, I've not finished yet!"

Conal froze, fearing the worst.

"Where would I find the High Priestess's office?"

Conal breathed a sigh of relief. He had feared that the merchant had noticed his loss. Half-turning, he pointed in the opposite direction. "You take the second turn on the right, sir. You'll see a gilt-edged door at the far end of the corridor. That's the door you're looking for," Conal advised, before hurrying off.

*****

Cull had inspected the blonde-haired boy with the deep blue eyes, noting the fine weave of the tunic he wore and the Frost Dragon decoration on the left shoulder. He had found the one he was seeking. He turned and walked away, assessing the young heir. The boy showed potential. He had quick reflexes and soft hands. He patted the place where his purse had been. This might not be as bad an assignment as he had first anticipated. He might not be able to make a noble out of the rogue, but he could certainly make him a good thief, given time. He followed Conal's directions, and he soon found himself outside the High Priestess's door.

*****

"Ah, Maerlin, thou art here at last," the High Priestess greeted Maerlin and Cora as they entered the room. "Thank thee Cora. Thou may go back to thy lessons."

Cora nodded to the High Priestess and smiled briefly at Maerlin, before disappearing back through the door.

"Come, child, sit down," Ceila instructed with a friendly smile. "There's no need to worry. Thou art amongst friends here."

Four other women were sitting in the room. Two of them were speaking quietly together, while the other pair studied a pile of scrolls. As Maerlin sat, they all turned towards her.

"I've asked our Earth-sister, Nessa and thyself here to discuss thy dreams, Maerlin. The others are all Dream-catchers and adept in the art," Ceila explained, and Maerlin nodded to each of the women in turn as they were introduced.

Finally, her eyes met Nessa's and warmth spread through her. She had missed the companionship of the old healer.

"Hello, Maerlin. Have you been enjoying your first day on the Isle?" Nessa asked, puffing on her pipe. "Have you done anything exciting, yet?"

"Oh yes, Ness, I have. I managed to summon a Water Elemental, though it spat water all over me. I think I also had a brief encounter with a tree spirit, though I'm not too sure about that one."

"Excellent, dear, you're fitting right in. I've been invited to teach some Earth-magic to you and your classmates tomorrow."

"You're the guest speaker?"

"Yes, dear, I suppose I am. It's been quite a while since I taught here so I guess I'd be considered a guest speaker, now."

"Thou wast always an excellent teacher, revered mentor," praised the High Priestess, causing Nessa to wave away the compliment.

"But to come to matters of business," continued Ceila "If thou wilt excuse mine rudeness, time is short and I'm expecting an important visitor.

Maerlin, we wish thee to speak to us of thy dreams. From what Nessa has told us, they may be of some import. Canst thou recall these visions?"

Maerlin nodded before asking "Which dreams in particular?"

Ceila thought for a moment. "Let's go back to thy dream of the storm, the one before thy mother's death. Canst thou do that?"

Maerlin swallowed. Her throat had suddenly gone dry. Taking a deep breath, she began, recalling as much as she could about the dream. When she had finished, she answered a variety of questions from the panel of Dream-catchers. Finally, the room fell silent.

"Thank thee, Maerlin," said Ceila. "I am aware of the pain caused by this dream. Thou art brave to speak of it to us. Now, let's move on to more recent dreams. In particular, let us speak of the dream of which Nessa spoke. Tell us about the battlefield dream."

Maerlin cast back in her memory, and the dream came back to her as vividly as ever. It was a strong and powerful dream, and it left her feeling confused in many ways, but she explained the scene she had witnessed as best she could. When it was finished, she was visibly wilted. It had been a long and eventful day.

"Here, dear, have a drink of water," Nessa suggested, fussing over her for a moment while she recovered.

"Thanks." Maerlin drank down half a glass of the cool water and remembered her experience with the Undine earlier. When Maerlin had recovered, the Dream-catchers asked more questions, seeking further clarification on the contours of the ridge, and the armour worn by the combatants, as well as a better description of the magician. Maerlin did her best to reply accurately, and finally, they all seemed satisfied.

"She's speaking of the Battle of the High Kings, yet there dost not seem to be a fortress there at the time. She must have seen the original battle, but some things within the tale do not match our archives," stated Veola, one of the Dream-catchers.

"Veola, dear," Nessa pointed out "Is it possible that these historical facts have been recorded wrong, or that Maerlin remembered them wrong, between sleep and waking?"

"Aye, both are possibile, for sure," agreed the Dream-catcher.

The High Priestess nodded her agreement. "It was definitely Storm-sister Uiscallan she spoke with, and the Dragon-lord himself on the battlefield. I don't understand how Uiscallan could know of her presence, however; for history does not state her having Dream-catching abilities."

"Who is to say what was and was not omitted from the archives," Nessa pointed out.

"Hast thou any other dreams that thou canst recall?" Ceila asked.

Maerlin nodded. Taking a breath to collect herself, she spoke of her dream of darkness and the rat attack, and of waking to find Conal's ferrets in her bed.

"Some of this could be circumstantial, I think …" suggested Veola, after some consideration "…, but it seems that Dubhgall the Black's crow apparition is more than just coincidence. His appearance once is foul news, but twice is a warning which must be heeded."

"Who is Doo-gal the Black?" Maerlin asked.

"He's Lord Boare's sorcerer, as he was his father's before him and his grandsire's, and great grandsire's before that. No one knows how long he has been linked with that family, but our archives confirm his presence at Dragon's Ridge at the battle with Conal's great-grandfather."

"Conal? What's he got to do with all this?" Maerlin asked.

"Conal is the heir to *Clann Na Dragan*, dear. I thought I'd told you that," Nessa explained.

"No, Nessa, you didn't. You kept calling him Dragonson, and I gather some people are after him. What are *Clann Na Dragan*, anyway?"

The Dream-catchers all looked surprised at Maerlin's ignorance, until Nessa spoke. "Remember Sisters. Maerlin was raised high up on the Mountain of the Gods. She knows little of the world beyond her mountains and even less about Dragania's politics."

She turned to Maerlin and explained "Conal's father was the High King, dear. His family have been High Kings of Dragania since his great-grandfather slew the High Boare. That was in the Battle of the High Kings at Dragon's Ridge. The newly-victorious Dragon-lord built *Dun Dragan* on the ridge to commemorate his victory, and he took the symbol of the Frost Dragon as the totem-beast of his people. Peace reigned in the land, and we prospered under his guidance. That was, of course, until the current Lord Boare raised an army and defeated Conal's father. The Boarites are now seeking to kill the last remaining *Dragan* heir. Then, Lord Boare hopes to usurp the throne of the High King with the help of his sorcerer, Dubhgall the Black."

"So, is that why we've been avoiding all those Boarite soldiers, and why Conal has been hiding all this time?"

"Yes, dear," Nessa replied "He cannot proclaim himself King of *Clann Na Dragan* until next spring at the Gathering of the Clans. He needs to wait until after his rites to manhood on his fifteenth year. Even then, it'll be a risk. He's still very young to raise an army and defeat Lord Boare. It was only with Uiscallan's help that his great-grandfather defeated the High Boare all those years ago. Dubhgall's magic is very powerful."

"Are there any other dreams, Maerlin?" Ceila asked. "They might also speak of Dubhgall's interference."

"No, I don't think so," Maerlin replied. "Oh … there was one other dream, but I saw no crow in it, or Dubhgall the Black."

"When was this?" Nessa asked.

"It happened last night, Ness. It was horrible!" Maerlin went on to describe her dream, ending with the slaughter of the sleeping troopers.

It was at that point that a knock came to the door, and a well-groomed man interrupted them. "Begging ya pardon, High Priestess. They told me to present myself, as soon as possible."

"Lord Cull, I presume?" Ceila asked, and smiled when the man nodded his head. "Come in, good sir. I think we're pretty much finished here."

Ceila turned to the Dream-catchers. "Thank you, Sisters. We'll stop there for the day. We'll speak more of this on the morrow."

The Dream-catchers rose as one, nodding to the High Priestess as they left the room. Nessa followed them out. Maerlin, however, paled and remained glued to her seat in shock.

"It can't be!" she murmured as she shrank farther into her seat.

The High Priestess turned and asked "What's the matter, Maerlin?"

Maerlin pointed at the well-dressed merchant in horror, stammering "It's him! He's the one from my dream."

Cull frowned. "What's the girl talking about?"

The High Priestess looked at Maerlin before speaking "I was told that thou wouldst be able to take on this unique task, but I have to admit, I had my doubts. The item in question is of great value to me and to the whole country. Tell me, Lord Cull. Is it true that thou single-handedly killed twenty soldiers, last night?"

Cull blinked with surprise, looking from Maerlin to the High Priestess. "How, in the Nine Hells, did you …?"

Ceila nodded. "... So it's true then?"

"Yes … I had to. Lord Boare sent men after the boy. They were amateurs, and I dealt with them," Cull explained. "I was told to ensure the boy's escape. We've been watching over the lad while he lived within our demesne, but when he opted to leave, we had to give him time to reach sanctuary."

"Thou didst well, Lord Cull, and we are in thy debt. The Beggar-Lord has always had the blessing of the goddess's Order. Our objectives are similar. But tell me … what of this troop?"

"Lord Boare is as persistent as a louse on a horse's back. He's always nibbling away, seeking blood, don't ya know. He wasn't going to give up with the death of a couple of his assassins. I knew that he'd send troops out to scour the countryside, so I set up a little trap to deal with them."

"... And they're all dead?" the High Priestess pressed.

"Begging ya pardon if it offends your holy ways, but we live and die on the streets of Dragania. Life is cheap, and heaven is far away. We might have similar objectives, but our methods differ greatly."

"It might be these differences that will aid us in our quest. Hast thou met the boy, yet?"

"Aye, I have. He ran into me, and robbed my pouch," Cull answered with a grin. "He's got good reflexes for a cub, but he needs a little training."

"Remember, Lord Cull. The boy is to be the next High King, not a master thief. Thy task is to keep him alive until his Rites of Manhood," Ceila warned.

"I don't need to be reminded of my task, Ma'am," Cull replied. "I'll see the boy stays safe until he's reached his title."

"You can't be serious!" Maerlin protested, indignantly. "You're not letting this killer near Conal, are you?"

The High Priestess, who had forgotten about Maerlin, turned and frowned. "Hast thou any better ideas, Maerlin? Thou, of all people, should know his efficiency and resourcefulness. Dire times call for dire solutions."

"But isn't there another way?"

"The boy wilt not stay within the safety of the Isle, and therefore, he needs a guardian. It needs to be a powerful guardian to take on the might of Lord Boare and the cunning of Dubhgall the Black. We have little choice in this matter," Ceila declared.

Maerlin sank back in the chair, clearly unhappy.

Cull turned to Maerlin. "I take it that you and the prince are friends?" he asked. "Don't worry, lass, I'll look after him as if he was my own son. No harm'll come to the lad while I'm around. I swear."

Maerlin looked into those cold, killer-eyes, eyes that she had first seen in her Dream-catching, and she relented. She could see the sincerity in them now. "If you do, I'll hunt you down and curse you to the Nine Hells."

Cull smiled softly, respecting the gutsiness of the young novice.

"I think we'd best summon the *Dragan* prince," Ceila suggested, studying the two.

"That won't be necessary, Ma'am. He'll be along any time now," Cull predicted with calm assurance.

"Oh, and why is that?" Ceila asked, her eyebrows arching with curiosity.

"Well," Cull explained with a wicked grin. He produced a finely-crafted knife from within his robes "While I was allowing him to steal my purse, I was busy stealing his dagger. I'm sure it'll dawn on him, sooner or later. It won't be long before he comes looking for it."

The High Priestess laughed. "I think we might've finally found a suitable guardian for him. You are truly a gift from the goddess, Lord Cull."

Cull grinned and shrugged. "Perhaps …"

Chapter Twelve: Conal's Guardian

It didn't take Conal long to discover the deception. He had searched the purse as soon as he reached the safety of the alcove. When he found only a handful of worthless copper farthings, he cursed his bad luck and the duplicity of merchants. Moments later, he noticed that his dagger was gone. It must have fallen off during his mad dash, or when he collided with the merchant.

It was a very special dagger. It had been given to Conal by his father shortly before his death, and he scoured the corridors searching for it. When all other options had been covered, the truth finally hit him. He had been robbed. He could hardly believe it. That bumbling old goat of a merchant had robbed him of his father's dagger and walked away with all the confidence of a master thief.

By the time he reached the High Priestess's office, he was so incensed that he didn't even bother knocking. He burst into the room, turned to glare at the merchant, and shouted "You slimy old sneak-thief!"

"Conal! That's no way to treat our honoured guest," Ceila protested.

"But he's a thief! He stole my dagger. It's right there in his hand. Look!" Conal objected. "Give it back to me, at once!"

"That was a business transaction, young sir," Cull informed, his manner becoming haughty. "We exchanged goods, which I guess you could refer to as quid pro quo. That's hardly theft."

"WHAT!" Conal protested. "No! You stole it from me."

"Young sir. What is it that you hold in your hand, pray tell?" Cull asked.

Conal looked down at the stolen purse and flustered "It's a money pouch, but there are only copper farthings in there. There's not enough money in there to buy a decent meal."

"That was my money pouch, was it not?" Cull calmly clarified.

"Yes … but that's not the point."

"Let me get this right … you have *my* pouch of coin, and I have *your* dagger. Is that correct?" Cull waited for but a moment, more for effect than to give Conal the chance to reply "That's what we in the trade would refer to as bartering, young sir. That's the exchange of goods for coin, or other goods. It's a very common practice throughout the land. I'm sure that you must be familiar with the concept!" Cull flung his arms skyward in a dramatic fashion, before continuing "I'm grievously insulted. How dare you call me a thief? Would you renege on the barter after the deal is struck? If so, that's your own problem. It has nothing to do with me. You accepted my pouch of coin with all the eagerness of a cat in the creamery."

"But you stole it. It's mine," protested Conal.

"Enough of this, Conal," Ceila demanded, making an effort to sound cross, even though she was enjoying Conal's predicament. "I think thou should apologise to Lord Cull this very instant."

"WHAT! But he stole my father's dagger. The man's a scoundrel, Ceila." Conal protested, trying desperately to make the High Priestess see sense. "He's nothing but a cutpurse!"

"... And an assassin!" Maerlin added.

Conal hadn't noticed Maerlin until now. She was sitting quietly in the chair and her interruption hadn't helped him one bit. It knocked his chain of thoughts completely off.

"You do me too much honour, please," Cull objected, holding his palms up, as if to ward off a compliment. "I merely try to be all things to all people."

"Look ..." Conal demanded. The conversation was getting completely off the point "... just give me back my knife!"

"Oh no, I can't do that!" Cull replied "That wouldn't be right, at all. I'd be the laughing stock of the trading community, if I did that. My name would be mocked on every street corner. My wives would die of shame, weeping in each other's arms! My many children would turn away in disgust, and when I became weak and infirm, they'd leave me to beg like a commoner! No one would come to mourn me when I died from some unmentionable pox, and I'd be buried in the Pauper's Plot, with lime as my only coffin!"

"I don't know who you are, thief, or why you're here, but listen to me," Conal growled. "That dagger belongs to me. It's my birthright, and it's not for sale, so give it back right now." Conal moved forward, his fists clenched.

"...Or else?" Cull asked calmly. "The last time we clashed, you lost out. I doubt you'd fare any better off this time around."

Conal paused, red-faced with anger.

"Sit down, Conal," ordered the High Priestess.

He glared defiantly at the merchant, who waited calmly, dagger in hand.

"SIT DOWN!" Ceila commanded, in a voice that broached no argument. Conal reluctantly sat down next to Maerlin, who for some reason was smirking at him.

"That's better. Now, I think we need some introductions ..."

"... But Ceila ..." Conal began.

"... Enough!" Ceila ordered, warding off any further protest. "As thou all know, I'm Ceila, High Priestess of the Order of Deanna," she continued; a pool of calm within the stormy room. "This here ..." the High Priestess pointed at Maerlin, "... is our latest novice, Maerlin, Air-sister of High Peaks. She shows great promise in the use of Wild-magic, and she's also a Dream-catcher. For example, it was Maerlin who dream-caught thy little adventure last evening, Lord Cull."

"Ah! So that's how she recognised me."

"The unruly boy with the stupid pout and the bad manners ..." snipped Ceila as she turned towards Conal "... is Conal *MacDragan*, heir to the throne of *Clann Na Dragan*, and generally a loud-mouthed, sticky-fingered, spoilt brat!"

Ceila glared down at Conal and met his angry gaze squarely. Her expression dared him to interrupt her as she continued her introductions. "I gather that the two of thee have already met earlier and had a brief trade. One it seems that our young prince now regrets ..." She held her hand up firmly to prevent any comment from Conal, who had opened his mouth to protest. "... Finally, let's come to our revered guest, Lord Cull of

Manquay. I believe he's another king in the making, if my intelligence is correct. He's the heir to the throne of the Beggar's Guild. He's a beggar, thief, spy, and assassin, to name but a few of his many talents. Some of his skills are well-guarded secrets, which we will not venture into. He is, however, clearly sent here by the goddess and none shall gainsay Deanna's wisdom ..." She smiled at the three of them, pleased with her introductions and summaries, before adding the punch line "... Oh, and Conal, I nearly forgot. He's also thy new guardian."

It took Conal a moment to comprehend the last remark. "What?" he asked in almost a croak. Conal had clearly misheard some vital piece of information as he had been too angry to listen properly.

"Art thou deaf, Conal? I said that he will be thy new guardian."

"You've got to be kidding me!" Conal protested. "The man's a rogue. I doubt he's competent enough to be a gardener, let alone a guardian. You've been conned by his slippery tongue, Ceila."

"Who do you think made it possible for you to sneak around Manquay at night, stealing all that money without a buy-your-leave from the Thieves' Guilds? You've never even paid the Guilds their share of the booty. That's a deadly offence, in case you didn't know. Who do you think it was that smoothed things over with Guild of the Cutpurse, boy?" Cull continued shattering Conal's illusions. "No one picks pockets in Manquay without their say so; not even a spoilt, little princeling. You'd have been gutted like a fish a long time ago had I not interceded on your behalf," Cull assured the blank-faced prince. "I grant you that over time you've learned the basic rudiments of pick-pocketing and even a bit of burglary, which isn't bad considering you've lacked any proper training, but let's be real here, shall we? You wouldn't be here today without my protection. Apart from waylaying drunks, your abilities as a thief are, to say the least, clumsy! Were you even aware of the existence of the Guild of the Cutpurse, or for that matter, the Guild of the Silent Intruders?"

Conal was flummoxed and rose to protest.

"SIT DOWN, CONAL!" Ceila reprimanded "Hear us out before opening thy mouth. It might be wise, *just this once*, to use thy brain *before* thy tongue makes thee look any stupider than thou already are."

Conal had never seen Ceila so angry. She had never spoken to him in such a manner. In shock, he sat back down.

Composing herself, the High Priestess continued "Thou hast expressed a wish to leave the sanctuary offered to thee here, Conal. This I understand, for it cannot be easy for thee to live in a land of women and tranquillity. Such a life is not in thy nature. The *Dragan* blood, which courses through thy veins, seeks something more. Nevertheless, let us face some basic facts. Lord Boare seeks thy demise, rest assured on that. The magic we placed into thy dagger can only obscure thy presence from magical scrying, not from human eyes. There are Boarites everywhere these days, and many of the poor wouldst sell their very souls for a few coins. The world is a perilous place, Conal, and if thou think that thou can survive in it unguarded, then thou art truly a foolish boy. I cannot believe such a fool would be thy father's son. The *Dragans* had always been intelligent, if betimes impetuous."

The comments stung Conal, but they got through to him, and he considered his options carefully.

"Thy father laid a burden on my shoulders, Conal. He beseeched me to watch over thee until the time came for thy Rites of Manhood, should the need arise. I would not shame this Order, or myself, by giving thee poor advice. He wished thee to claim what is rightfully thine, and the Order of Deanna supported him in this. It is in the interests of all in Dragania that thou should become the next High King. We cannot have it fall into Boarite hands again," she explained, kneeling down to take Conal's hands and look deeply into his eyes. He could see tears welling there as she pleaded "Conal, please accept my wisdom in this. If thou dost leave, accept this man to be thy guide and guardian. He is the best there is, and he wilt see thee sitting upon thy throne on Dragon's Ridge, as was thy father's last wish."

"She speaks the truth, Conal," Cull rumbled. His haughty manner had disappeared as the pretence of being a merchant left him, "Your father spoke to Broll before the Second Battle of the High Kings. He wanted the Beggar-Lord to watch over you also, as we had watched over him during his earlier years."

"You knew my father?"

"Aye, but that's a long story, lad." Cull offered up the stolen dagger.

Conal accepted the knife with a nod of gratitude, tucking it into his belt.

"Tis a good blade, lad. Your father chose it well. It's lightweight and it has been well-crafted. It looks like it was made by one of the Master-smiths in *Ard Pect*. I watched you kill with it only last week and it cut through that Boarite's armour like butter."

"You saw that! But ... it was dark in that alley."

Cull laughed. "Let's just say that I've the eyes of an alley-rat."

"It's a good blade ..." Conal agreed, after a few moments of silence "... but do either of you know where my father's sword is now?"

Cull and Ceila looked at each other. The High Priestess turned to Conal. "I've been told that some of thy father's men slipped away from the battlefield after his death. They took his body with them. They hid him in an old burial chamber near to *Dun Dragan*. They feared Dubhgall's magic arts and did not want the High King's body desecrated. If thou seeketh the legendary sword, *An Fiacail Dragan*, I suggest that thou look for that mound. He lies in a tomb beneath a sacred circle of stones. If it is not lost forever, then this is the place to look."

Conal listened, deep in thought. He knew the stone circle she referred to. He had often gone riding there when he lived at *Dun Dragan*. The locals avoided the burial mound. They were frightened by its legends of dark magic, but Conal had never been concerned by its dark past. He had always found solitude there. "I know the place you speak of. It's called The Twelve Warriors and the Maiden," Conal replied, his face a mask of determination. "I'll go there and reclaim my father's things. They belong to the Dragon Clan, and he has no more need of them," he announced. "The sword is still needed in the land of the living."

"Don't be stupid, Conal!" Ceila objected. "That area is swarming with Boarites at the moment. They hunt sympathisers of *Clann Na Dragan*. It's far too dangerous."

"Ceila, how long do you think it'll be before some grave robber comes along and discovers his body? It's not safe to leave the sword there," Conal insisted. "It must be retrieved before it is lost or worse still, falls into the hands of Lord Boare. He'd have little opposition to his claim for the High Kingship, if he got his hands on that blade. It's the symbol of the High King."

"But Conal!"

Cull interrupted "No, the lad's right. It must be retrieved and soon. I've been stupid not to have seen this already. I'll go and fetch the weapon myself. When I return, I'll collect the boy and take him someplace safe."

"Oh no, you don't. I'm coming with you," demanded Conal. "I want to see my father's remains, and I'm certainly not staying here. Ceila asked me to wait a few days at most. It's half a moons' ride north to Dragon's Ridge. That means I'd be stuck in this stinking swamp for at least another moon. There's no way I'm sticking around here for that long."

"It's too dangerous, boy. I can't risk taking you there." Cull insisted "Anyway, you'd slow me down too much. I work better alone."

"That's fine. I'll go on my own," Conal retorted defiantly as he turned to the High Priestess. "Thank you for your hospitality, Ceila. I'll be leaving, first thing in the morning."

Ceila blinked at the announcement, but it was Maerlin who spoke up "I'm coming with you, Conal. You might need my help."

"What!" Conal exclaimed. The others echoed his surprise.

"If Lord Cull isn't going to help you to retrieve the sword, someone's going to have to. I know a little magic and I can ride a horse. Anyway, Conal, you're my friend and I won't let you go alone."

"But thou hast hardly been here a day, Maerlin," Ceila protested. "Thou need to stay and study. Thou should both stay and let Lord Cull retrieve the weapon."

"I'm going to get it, and I don't need any help from magic-wielding witches," Conal argued.

"Oh really! Tell me, Conal, how thou wilt get past the guards unseen?" Celia asked. "I have no doubt of Lord Cull's abilities. He is, after all, a master thief, but not thee. Thou dost endanger thyself too much on this quest, Conal. A competent magician might be useful to thee."

Cull was not happy with the way the conversation was going. "Very well, I'll take the boy when I go to fetch the 'pig-sticker' … but only the boy."

"What about me?" Maerlin asked.

"Oh no! I don't need a girl along as well, thank you," Cull replied "Dragging the royal brat along is bad enough."

Conal frowned and considered protesting.

The High Priestess hesitantly held up her hand. "Wait! Much though I dislike saying this, I believe that Maerlin and her mentor Nessa should go on this quest too."

"Whatever for?" Cull asked.

"I believe it is the goddess's wish," Ceila informed them with a sigh. "Maerlin, it seems, is inextricably linked to the heir to the Dragon throne, as well as Dubhgall the Black, and even thee, Lord Cull. If thy mission is to be a success, then she wilt need to be present. Whether we like it or not, the goddess will have her way on this, believe me."

"You can't be serious. How, in the Nine Hells, am I going to get two children and a priestess into the heart of *Dragan* country? Didn't you just say it was swarming with Boarites? That's to say nothing of the magical skills of Dubhgall the Black and his acolytes," Cull pointed out, hoping to make the High Priestess change her mind.

"I'm sure thou wilt think of something, Lord Cull," she assured him calmly. "Don't worry about Nessa *MacTire*, though. She's long been away from the isolationism of the Holy Isle. Thou wilt find her quite pragmatic. She could be the most worldly of all the goddess's Sisterhood. Have no fear of that."

"This is ridiculous!" Conal exclaimed, resenting Maerlin for forcing herself onto his quest. "This is my idea. It has nothing to do with the goddess, or the Order."

Ceila smiled softly at him. "Everything in creation is of interest to Deanna, and from what we've heard of Maerlin's dreams; she is closely linked with thy destiny, Conal."

"We don't need Maerlin along on this quest," Conal insisted. "What use is she going to be? We won't have any need of her dreams, will we?"

"Hast thou a gift for Divination, Conal *MacDragan*? I can send thee off to the revered Druidic College in *Ard Pect*, if that is the case ..." the High

Priestess replied, with an arched brow "…after your Rites of Manhood have been completed."

Conal flushed and bit his lip.

"You just want to go off on your own, so you can bask in all the glory. You just want to be the hero, don't you, Conal?" Maerlin accused, hitting the nail on the head.

"Don't be ridiculous!"

"I bet you do."

"Give me strength!" Cull mumbled. "That's all I need. Listen up, you two! If you keep arguing like this, I'll leave the pair of you behind and be damned with any prophecies."

Maerlin and Conal stopped, though they continued to glare balefully at each other.

"Well! Now that that's all decided, I think I'd better go and find Nessa. She will need to begin preparations," Ceila announced. "I'll leave Conal under thy care, Lord Cull. Thou canst become better acquainted. Maerlin, I'll show thee to thy next class."

"Aw! Can't I stay, too?"

"Thou wilt need all the study time that thou can get, while thou art amongst us, Maerlin. This quest will take some time to plan. In the meantime, thou must take every opportunity to learn as much as we can teach thee. It will help thee to prepare for thy upcoming trip. I doubt that thou wilt have free time to play with thy newfound friends, but … we all have to make sacrifices."

Maerlin did not like the sound of that, but it was too late to change her mind, now.

*****

Conal's gloating was brief, before Cull burst his bubble.

"Can you read, boy?"

"Of course I can read ... Why?" Conal wondered where the topic was leading. He had been taught to read by his father's tutors, but had found it tedious, so it had fallen by the wayside over the last few years.

"That's good. I believe that the Order has an excellent library vault somewhere. Go there and dig out every scroll you can find relating to the following topics ..." Cull paused, gathering his thoughts. "... We'll start with the geography of Dragon's Ridge, the surrounding countryside, and the history of the entire region. Once you've done that, you can study the history of your family going back to your great-grandfather and also that of the Boare's. I want you to study maps of all the land between here and there. Also, find out what you can about the various Clans and their allegiances to the two greater Clans. Pay particular attention to any cultural differences and folklore." Cull paused, looking sharply at Conal "Are you gifted with a brilliant memory, boy?"

"Erm, no ... why?"

"Then I suggest you pick up a quill and start taking notes."

"Why do I need all this stuff?" Conal protested.

Cull sighed loudly before answering "What's the first rule of warfare?"

Conal wracked his brain for a moment and came up blank. "No, I'm sorry. I can't remember that one. I think I was told it once, but it was a long time ago!"

"Give me strength!" Cull muttered, looking heavenward. "The first rule of warfare is 'Know thy enemy'. The second rule of warfare is 'Know thy friends', and the third rule is 'Know thy battlefield'. If we are going to travel across the country, through enemy territory to bring back that big 'pig-sticker' that your father called a sword, then we'd better be prepared for any eventuality. So I want you well-versed in all the important details and a lot of unimportant ones, too. They're the ones that can be the difference between success and failure."

Cull walked towards the door, while Conal frantically scribbled notes. "Oh, and I nearly forgot. We'll start on your physical training tomorrow morning. Meet me at dawn on the jetty and we'll establish your daily routine. Sleep well, boy ... you're gonna need it."

Cull left, leaving Conal to sink his head on the table and groan.

Chapter Thirteen: The Next Morning

Conal's day began at dawn, when he staggered sleepily out of his room. His new guardian had instructed him to be waiting by the jetty when the sun appeared in the east.

Cull arrived as the sun peeked over the misty horizon, and they began to run three circuits around the island. Each trip was over a three-mile hike over rough ground. In places, the ground was boggy, sticking to the feet and dragging on Conal's weary muscles. In other places the footing was firmer, and the rough uneven surface strained the weary tendons and threatened to sprain Conal's ankles.

As they jogged, they could hear the sound of the priestesses singing.

Despite all the time he had spent on the Holy Isle, this was the first time that Conal had actually been awake to hear them. The song followed them as Conal jogged after Cull, who set a gruelling pace throughout.

By the end of the run, Conal was wheezing and panting. He was almost eager to be sent to the library so that he could rest his aching legs. He was not, by nature, an early riser. He tended to sleep in during the morning and wander around after dark, getting up to mischief. He had begun the morning after only a few bells sleep, and by the end of the third circuit, he was dead on his feet. Cull, however, had other ideas and led him off to face his next task.

A makeshift gym had been set up in one of the empty warehouses, and into this Conal was led. Here, there were ropes hanging from the rafters, benches leaning against walls at odd angles, and other assorted paraphernalia. These were used to drain every possible reserve of strength from Conal's aching muscles.

"You're not tired already, are you, toe-rag?" Cull goaded. "Did you not do anything useful at that tavern? You wouldn't last a week on the streets."

The tirade niggled at Conal's pride, forcing him to more and more effort, until sweat wept from his aching body. When the exercises had finished, Conal lay gasping for breath, slumped over one of the benches.

Cull poked him in the ribs. "It's time for some sparring now. Let's see what you've left in you, lad, and what those flat-footed sergeants taught you."

"What?" Conal whined, hoping for a reprieve. "You've got to be kidding ... I'm exhausted."

"Didn't I tell you to get a good night's sleep?" Cull reminded, ignoring the protest.

"I couldn't sleep, so I went for a walk and did some thinking."

Cull would hear none of it. Picking the prince up by the scruff of his tunic, he dragged Conal over to a makeshift sparring ring "Choose a weapon," Cull ordered, pointing to a rack nearby.

Conal walked sullenly over and inspected the weaponry. Seeing a short-sword amongst the assorted weapons, he tested its balance. He swung the sword back and forth a few times, getting used to its weight as he limbered up. "I'll take this one."

Cull shrugged indifferently to the boy's choice and selected a hayfork.

"Okay, lad, now we'll see what you're made of. Come on ... attack me."

"Aren't you going to arm yourself properly first?" Conal asked. "This thing's sharp, you know. It could hurt you."

Cull grinned wickedly.

With a sigh, Conal shuffled forward. He took up his position as his father's sword-master had taught him. His blade was pointed towards Cull's chest, his knees slightly bent and his body positioned side on, to limit the target area to his opponent. His back was straight, and his wrists were relaxed and ready to strike. Conal felt assured and confident, despite his weary limbs. His teachers had always complimented him on his abilities with either sword or knife. He tried to ignore the insolent smirk on Cull's face as he readied himself for action. Anger simmered up inside him. He was getting fed up of Cull's goading remarks. Conal was confident of his ability with the sword and he decided to teach his new guardian a lesson. His anger brewed inside as he prepared himself, easing the aches in his body and giving him renewed strength. It would be a short and painful sparring session, of that Conal felt sure. Seeing Cull's relaxed pose only irritated Conal further.

"Well, lad? Don't tell me that you hid behind the ladies' skirts the whole time you were growing up. I would have thought your father would have taught you to use a sword, at least."

At the mention of his father, Conal's anger boiled over. With a yell of rage, he aimed a swift thrust towards Cull's neck. The thrust was meant to nick Cull's flesh. It was meant to be a warning of things to come, so that Cull would take him serious and prepare to fight.

Cull hadn't even limbered up before the fight. He just slouched there with the lightweight fork held casually in his hand. He was still sneering at the boy when the thrust began. As Conal's blade shot forward, Cull's wrist moved with lightning speed. His body swayed to the left, away from the sword thrust, the fork coming up like a viper and connecting with the blade. With a flick of the wrist, Cull's fork snagged the sword between the tines. As he twisted the fork, Cull's bodyweight and the long shaft came into play. As the twist continued, Conal's wrist bent back under the pressure, and before he knew it, the sword was forced from his hands. It flew a short distance across the room and scraped along the stone floor. Pain shot up through Conal's wrist, bringing tears to his eyes.

Cull then attacked, with calm precision. He swung the fork around in a wide arc, its whistling wooden handle finding contact with the toes of Conal's right foot.

Crying out, Conal fell to the floor and grasped his foot as pain shot up his body. A sharp blow cracked against his elbow, numbing the funny bone there. This was followed up by a strike to the head, directly behind the ear. Conal curled defensively into a ball to protect his more vulnerable parts from further attacks.

The sudden flurry of blows stopped, and Conal lay there, recovering from the onslaught.

"Stand up, lad, and tell me what you've learned?" Cull ordered.

Conal looked up. He could see the old man's hand, offering assistance. He climbed painfully to his feet and considered his moves and what he had done wrong. His thrust had been perfect, and yet, he had been disarmed by a mere garden implement. No matter how many times he replayed the attack and counter in his mind, he couldn't understand how he had been disarmed so easily. "How did you do that?"

"I used your own training against you, lad; that and your disrespect for my weapon of choice. There are a few lessons to be learned here, so take note. Firstly, your opponent can always be beaten by the element of surprise, so use your head as well as your sword. Soldiers tend to rely heavily on their training, and their heads are rarely used at all. Secondly, although your stance and thrust were good, I beat you. Why? Because I knew that your attack would be one of a few limited options, all of which I had covered," Cull explained. "You fought by the military rulebook. I will teach you to fight by the code of the street. You can learn to maim and kill in ways that you never dreamed of, and with weapons that you had never even realised existed."

Cull spun the fork between his fingers. "This is a hayfork, but a broom or a hoe would be just as affective. They're lightweight, and they can be moved at speed with a mere flick of the wrist."

Cull flicked the fork, stopping it an inch from Conal's exposed throat. "With this much momentum behind it, it'd slice through your jugular and larynx as affectively as any sword. Don't forget that. The cut might not be as clean," admitted Cull, "but you'd still be dead."

"If you look at the target areas that I selected, you'll see that they were not text book. Nevertheless, they are very effective. If you ever have to suffer the pain of an ingrown toenail, you'll appreciate how many nerve endings there are in that region, and how much pain can be caused by a short, sharp, shock to the toe. The elbow is another good target area. It's almost impossible to grip a sword properly when your funny bone has been jarred. A blow behind the ear will leave your head ringing like a bell, and it will impair your vision. A jab in the throat will leave you gasping for breath and incapacitated. I can teach you about these and many more. I can also teach you the use of garrottes and poisons for quick, silent deaths or slow, lingering ones."

"But there's no honour in that," Conal objected. "It's a cowardly way to fight."

"I seem to recall you stabbing a militiaman in the back, boy, while he was urinating in an alley. Was that honourable?" Cull reminded.

"He was a Boarite assassin. He'd been sent to kill me," Conal retorted, his face flushing with anger. "He deserved to die."

"He was a man. Never forget that, boy. He isn't the one you need to kill. He's just one of many such lackeys. One day, you'll have to kill Lord Boare. That man is a skilled swordsman and a born killer. Nevertheless, let us discuss this issue of honour, for it's a valid point. Honour is for the man with an army at his back. He'll quickly lose the respect of his men, if his leadership is besmirched. In a dark alley, when you're outnumbered and poorly-armed, honour is the toll of the death bell. Honour is the loser's lament. When the time comes for you to lead an army, you'll not need the tricks that I can teach you. Until then, they're the passage to your future kingship, so learn them well. That'll be enough for today, boy. Go and get cleaned up. You can spend the rest of the day in the library. I have things to prepare. Meet me back here at sundown and we'll work out again," Cull instructed.

"We're running again this evening?" Conal whined. "But I ache all over."

"Then you'll sleep well tonight, and you'll have no need for midnight jaunts."

*****

Cora woke Maerlin in the pre-dawn light and dragged her up the hill to where the priestesses and novices were silently gathering.

The High Priestess arrived last, as Maerlin stood shivering in the dampness. Ceila greeted the worshippers with a warm smile, before turning east to the soft glow of the breaking dawn. An orange haze broke the horizon, a prelude to the coming day. It brought light to the thick mists around the Holy Isle. Lifting her arms skywards, Ceila uttered the ceremonial phrase "Come forth, blessed Lugh. It is time for thee to warm the world," and then she started to sing.

The hymn she sang was ancient, giving thanks to the sun god, Lugh, for the warmth he brought to the land, and to the goddess Deanna, for her blessings. Others joined in after the first few lines, facing the morning sun and shining back its blessing with the warmth of their smiles.

*****

The Dawn Chorus Hymn

Come forth, blessed Sun and bring light into the darkness,

Cast away all shadows, from the spirit and the heart.

Let your warmth and radiance, bring a new and joyful day,

Where new life is everywhere and children laugh and play.

A Blessing to the goddess Creator of the Earth,

Giver of all life and everything of worth.

We sing the Dawn Chorus, in praise for all you give,

Your blessing on our children and on the life we live.

The sun will rise each morning, with you to guide his way,

Your hand will touch each petalled flower and show them the new day.

The fox beneath the hillside, will curl up; fast asleep,

Safe in the knowledge that the world is in your keep.

Birds awake and sing thy praise, in the glory of the dawn,

They sing in joyous thankfulness, of the gift of a new morn.

Each morning as the day breaks and the sun comes from the east

We praise the glory of thy gift and break our morning feast.

So it was in childhood and to this very day,

And will be forever. This we hope and pray.

Maerlin listened to the words and the joy with which they were sung. She felt the sun starting to warm her face, and the song filled her spirit. One by one, the priestesses and novices took up the hymn, bringing new harmonies into the song. As it grew, the glory of its simple praise filled Maerlin with a deep feeling of love.

When the song finally ended, it drifted around in the Great Marsh, sending echoes back to the Holy Isle. It was as if the song never actually died, it just danced around in the mists. The birds in the marshy reed beds took up their own song in praise of the dawn. The world seemed filled with the goddess's blessing.

"That was wonderful," Maerlin exclaimed. "You do this every morning?"

"Yes," Cora replied. "It helps to keep us focused on our duties and reminds us of the beauty of creation."

Maerlin nodded, still wrapped in a warm magical glow of the occasion.

"Come on, Maerlin. It's time to break some bread and begin the day's lessons," Cora urged, clasping Maerlin's hand and dragging her towards the common room. After a quick breakfast, Cora outlined the day's study, which seemed to Maerlin much fuller than the previous mornings.

"How are we going to fit all that in?"

"We aren't …" Cora corrected "... You are. You've been given a load of extra lessons, though I don't know why."

"Oh … no!" Maerlin moaned, and she began to explain the events of the previous day.

"You're going on an adventure! That sounds like fun," Cora squealed in excitement, jumping up and down "But won't that be dangerous?"

"I guess," shrugged Maerlin with indifference. Her mind was still daunted by the additional lessons she now faced.

"Awww, I want to come, too," Cora whined. "I can be useful, you know. Can you talk them into letting me come along, Maerlin?"

Maerlin vividly remembered the frowns on Cull and Conal's faces, at the prospect of her going along. "I doubt they'd go for that. Even Ceila would disagree to it, but I'll see what I can do."

"I'm sure you'll think of something, Maerlin," Cora assured.

Maerlin did not feel the same confidence.

*****

After Cull had finished the morning training session, he was satisfied with the boy's efforts. Time was short, however, for him to teach the young prince enough to ensure his survival. Cull would have preferred to hide the prince away in a nice inconspicuous city where they could melt into the sea of humanity. Nothing there would draw attention to an old beggar and his young apprentice. Shrugging off his doubts, he went in search of Nessa.

When he found her, he was surprised by his first impression. She was unlike any priestess he had met before, although she was dressed in the same white robes as the other priestesses of Deanna. She wore it with the casual authority only obtained by a few. Her eyes were sharp and lively as she greeted him.

"The High Priestess wishes for you and the young novice Maerlin to join me," he began gruffly.

"So she has advised me," informed Nessa noncommittally, between puffs of her pipe. "I can't say that I'm happy with the idea. I've just rushed halfway across the countryside to get Maerlin here, in the hope of giving her some education. Now, she's taking off again."

Cull was relieved that the witch didn't fill her sentences with thees and thous. They tended to make conversation difficult, and he had never understood why many within the Order insisted upon this archaic form of speech.

"I'm glad we're in agreement. I'll inform the High Priestess of our decision to leave her behind, right away. Then, I'll be able to go and fetch this damned pig-sticker on my own," Cull replied, feeling the worry lifting off his shoulder.

"You misunderstand me, Lord Cull. I didn't say that. Much though I dislike the idea, I'm forced to agree with Ceila. The hand of the goddess is indeed in this. She clearly wishes Maerlin to go on this quest. I, for one, don't intend to let Maerlin go out into the world in her present condition, without some guidance," Nessa assured him, her resolute face partially obscured behind the veil of smoke.

Cull's heart sank. "Condition, what condition?"

"She's been given the gift of 'Wild-magic'," Nessa informed him. "She has more than I've seen in anyone in a long, long time."

"Wild-magic?"

"Some women are given a gift by the goddess Deanna. It manifests itself at the time of their change, when the moon goddess, Arianrhod, blesses them for the first time," Nessa explained, closely watching the man's expressions. "Only a small number are given Deanna's blessing, and in the initial stages, it can be a dangerous and uncontrollable phenomenon. Maerlin was given this gift. It's something we refer to as 'Wild-magic'. I have the blessing also, but her gift far surpasses my own. She has the potential to become a 'Storm-Bringer', perhaps the greatest Storm-Bringer ever to have lived."

"I don't know what in the Nine Hells you're talking about, priestess."

"Let me tell you a story, Cull. I was in the mountains, heading for the pass into the Broce Woods, last spring. Word came to me of a young girl who, if rumour was correct, had predicted her mother's death. Such things are of interest to me, and it is my task to investigate them for the Order. So I headed towards High Peaks, which lies on the southern edge of the Mountain of the Gods, to check it out. You see, if the rumour was correct, then the girl has the potential to become a Dream-catcher," Nessa explained, pausing to puff on the long clay pipe.

"Before I arrived, more tales reached me. It was claimed that she could summon thunderstorms and bring lightning down on those who annoyed her. Needless to say, I hastened my journey and soon reached Maerlin's village. As I arrived, I witnessed a storm of immense power. Two houses were destroyed in the storm, and the cattle and sheep had stampeded all over the mountainside."

"They always get summer storms up in those mountains."

"Very true, but you'd have to have been there to see this one. They build strong houses of stone up there, well able to withstand stormy weather.

Some of those houses had been blown apart by lightning and ferocious winds. It was a freak of nature and Maerlin, it seems, was the catalyst."

"You mean she can set storms on people?"

"No, not yet, but she may be able to do so, given time. It's been known to happen in the past, though it's a very rare gift. At present, she's more like … a lightning conductor. Her anger and frustration attract the storms to her."

"Oh, bleedin' marvellous. That's all I need," Cull groaned. "And I thought my problems were bad enough."

"It's not all bad. She's gradually learning some amount of control. I've been teaching her all summer now, and she's come a long way. She hasn't lost her temper in a while, and we've only got drenched a handful of times," Nessa informed, with a wicked grin. She was clearly enjoying his consternation. "It's only when she dreams and her control mechanism is down that we have to worry. Being a Dream-catcher as well as a Wild-magician brings its own complications. You should've seen the night sky, the evening before last, when she dreamed about you."

"Oh for the love of Dagda!" Cull moaned "A prince who thinks he's a master thief and a novice who thinks she's a weathervane."

"Look on the bright side," Nessa explained. "You'll have me along as well, just to make life interesting."

Cull kept his opinions on priestesses to himself. He'd curse the Beggar-Lord, if he didn't love the old man like a father. "I never understood why Broll has this obsession with helping out your Order. We've enough concerns in this world without interfering with the Otherworld," he grumbled. Digging out his tobacco and papers, he rolled himself a cigarette.

"Broll is clearly a wise man, Cull. Deanna has more interest in this world than the Otherworld. His aid will surely be noted by the goddess."

"She certainly isn't looking after his health," Cull complained, bitterly. "He's being eaten-alive inside though he tries his best to hide it."

"Each of us comes to death, Cull. There's no avoiding it. Not even the priestesses of the Order of Deanna can gainsay Macha's will, when she rides forth to collect her dues." Cull knew she spoke the truth. Nessa puffed again on the pipe, changing the subject for she could clearly see Cull's grief for the Beggar-Lord's imminent death. "Tell me, Cull. How are you going to get us all the way across the country and up to Dragon's Ridge?"

"I haven't the foggiest idea on either the direction to take or the method. I recently disguised myself as a traveller and that might be as good a disguise as any."

Nessa considered the idea. "I like it! It has merit. We could disguise ourselves as *Na Teincheor*, and the Boarites wouldn't give us a second glance. That'd be an excellent disguise."

"The only problem is that I sent the wagon down a mine shaft and burned it. I don't suppose there's another such wagon hanging around on the island. If I'd have known that I'd need that wagon again, I'd have emptied it out and thrown the bodies down the mine shaft, instead," Cull grumbled, puffing on his cigarette and adding to the room's smoky atmosphere.

"Leave the wagon to me," Nessa assured. "I have my uses as you'll find out. We'll find you another wagon though it may take a few days to procure. I guess we'll need suitable clothing also, to play the part," Nessa considered, talking out loud as she chewed on the problem. "I'll go and speak with Ceila. You can deal with the other problems. I'm sure there'll be a few."

"That's an understatement," Cull grumbled. "The boy is completely spoilt and as lazy as a hound dog. The girl is a walking storm, and I haven't got a clue which route to take. It'll take days to go through all the possible permutations. That's to say nothing of the boy's training. He'll never be able to fit in as a *Teincheor*. He's much too fair and striking to be anything other than a *Fear Ban*."

"I'm sure with a few days of training in espionage that you'll have him playing the part. I'll do my best to make sure that Maerlin is mentally prepared for the quest." Nessa paused a moment before adding "I hear that you have Conal working out every morning?"

"That I do, and evenings too. He'll need hardening up for this journey, and he'll need to improve his fighting skills. At the moment, he fights like a soldier's whelp," Cull commented with a smirk. "I'd hate to wager on him in a bar-room brawl."

"Can I ask a favour of you?" Ness asked. "Would you mind taking Maerlin along with you, when you're practising? She'll be doing a lot of mental exercises over the next few days. Enough to make her head throb like the worst hangover you've ever had. Some physical exercise will help relieve her stress. We wouldn't want her to explode, or we'll all get washed into the ocean."

Cull shrugged, not seeing any problem with it. "It might actually be useful. It'll give the young prince some competition. There's nothing like a bit of rivalry to bring out the best in someone."

"Thanks, Cull, that'd be great. They won't argue too much if you keep them busy."

Cull rolled his eyes and grinned mischievously "I'll do my best."

And so it was that Maerlin found herself racing around the marshy landscape each morning with Conal and Cull. Conal's limbs ached from the strain and the bruises of battle training, while Maerlin's head throbbed with a continuous migraine, but slowly as the days progressed, they hardened up and accepted their arduous regime.

Chapter Fourteen: Putting Plans into Motion

The intensive training sessions lasted longer than expected, as Cull and Nessa made ready for the coming journey. The leaves were beginning to mottle with the first hints of autumn, and the morning chill became more noticeable in preparation of the coming winter.

Each morning, Nessa would walk to the High Priestess's office and ask "Any news?"

Each day Ceila would look up and smile softly. "No, Ness, I'm sorry, but I'm sure we'll have news tomorrow."

"Could the birds have got lost or killed?"

"I sent your request as urgent, Nessa. One bird might fail to reach its destination, but not three. Thou art just going to have to wait another day or two."

Nessa would nod and turn to leave, gnawing on her lip in concern. She had promised Cull that she would provide the wagon for their journey, and she knew that Cull waited anxiously for news of its arrival.

Letters had been sent by the Order's army of Fan-tail doves, to each of the nearby towns and cities, requesting the priestesses there to look for a suitable vehicle. The letters did not state the reason for this unusual request in case a courier bird fell into the wrong hands, but such explanations were not necessary. Whatever the High Priestess required was for the betterment of the Order. Therefore, the search had gone out.

After weeks of searching, there was still no response, and Nessa was beginning to worry. She hated to inform Cull of her failure, but she couldn't put this off any longer. Walking away from the office, she set off for a hike around the island to clear her mind. Her thoughts turned to the other details she was responsible for. The disguises, at least, were going well. The novices were working diligently on creating the distinctive clothing of the travelling families of *Clann Na Teincheor*. The clothes would be ready within the next two days. She had this much time left to procure the wagon and have it hauled to one of the villages at the edge of the Great Marsh.

Some of the priestesses had been working on various potions and dyes. These, would darken the skin and hair. The dyes would need to be impervious to water and hard-wearing. Their skin would need to be a rich, nutty-brown tone: similar, in fact, to Maerlin and Nessa's own colouring.

Clann Na Teincheor originated from the native Pectish Clans, who had first ruled those lands now taken over by the *Fear Ban*. They had been evicted from their tribal homelands during the great invasion, some two centuries previous. Since then, they had evolved their own distinctive sub-culture.

The companions' hair would need to be the raven-like black so common amongst *Na Teincheor*. This too, was well under control, with the final testing being done on the dyes today. Cora, Maerlin's newfound friend, had been the first to volunteer to help with the project and had gone so far as to try out the newly-made dyes, to see if they worked properly. The girl had also been busy helping out with the needlecraft, whenever free from lessons. She was eager to be of any help she could be in the coming quest.

When Nessa had asked Cora about her heavy workload, the girl had replied "Maerlin is my friend. I'll do all I can to help her. She's working very hard, so I'd feel tardy if I wasn't lending a hand when it's needed."

Cora smiled warmly and went back to her needlework, working on the fine intricately patterned embroidery of a traveller woman's costume.

*****

The day before, Maerlin had tentatively approached Nessa. "Have you a moment, Ness?"

"Certainly, dear, what is it? Are you having any problem with your lessons?"

"No, it's not that … it's just …" Maerlin paused, seeking a good way to proceed "I was wondering if Cora could come with us," she blurted out, twisting her braid nervously as she watched Nessa's expression closely.

Nessa blinked with surprise and kicked herself, mentally. She should have seen this one coming. "Sit down, Maerlin," she instructed and patted the bench beside her "Why exactly do you want Cora to come along?"

Maerlin had obviously anticipated just this question. "Well … I've never had a best friend before, and it seems such a waste to lose my first one, before I've even got to know her properly. Also, she's been here longer than I have and she'd be able to help me to with my lessons," Maerlin replied, hardly pausing for breath. "She's very good, you know and she's a Wild novice too, a Water-sister. That might be useful on this quest. You're Earth and I'm Air, maybe someone with Water might come in handy, and then there's …"

"...Hold up there, before you get ahead of yourself," Nessa interrupted. "Maerlin, it's not up to me to decide. This is Conal's quest, and Cull's the one in charge. I was dragged into this because of you. I haven't got much of a say in the matter. While you're at it … don't you think Ceila should be consulted, too? Cora has been placed into the care of the Order, and the High Priestess is responsible for her well-being. Cora's family wouldn't appreciate her being placed in any danger."

Seeing Maerlin's forlorn expression, Nessa advised "Why don't you start by asking Cull? He's liable to be your hardest nut to crack."

"He scares the hell out of me, Ness. I wouldn't have the nerve to ask him. I was hoping you'd ask him for me."

"Me! Why me? This was your idea," Nessa pointed out.

"Well ... you're much better at this sort of thing than I am. No one ever says no to you," Maerlin argued.

Nessa sighed, feeling the burden falling upon her shoulders, to add to the weight already there. "I'll tell you what I'll do. I'll speak to Ceila for you and see what she says. There's no point in antagonising Cull, unless we have to. If Ceila agrees, then I'll go with you when you speak to Cull, but you'll have to do the asking. Is that fair?"

"I guess so," Maerlin reluctantly agreed and hugged Nessa. "Thanks, Ness. I knew I could count on you."

*****

Now, Nessa had another problem on her plate. She had asked Ceila about it. She had reiterated all of Maerlin's arguments, hoping that the High Priestess would say no.

After a few moments' thought, Ceila replied "Thou wilt never get Cull to agree to it, though."

"What!" Nessa protested "I was hoping you'd say no."

"Why? I think it's a great idea. Maerlin makes some valid points. She could learn from Cora, and Cora needs to spend more time out in the world. She's from the Western Isles, and she needs to broaden her horizons. But as I say … thou wilt never get Cull to agree to it."

"Don't 'thou' me, *Ceila Ni Madra-Uisce*. This isn't my idea. Why don't you ask him?" insisted Nessa, puffing indignantly on her pipe.

"Awww … but Ness," wheedled the High Priestess, bringing fond memories of a different time, when Ceila was Maerlin's age. "Thou hast always had a way with men. They melt like butter in thy hands. Surely, thou wouldst be better-equipped to speak to Lord Cull than me?"

"Pah! Don't give me that … I know what you're trying to do! You're as bad as Maerlin. I won't do it, I tell you. D'ya hear me, I won't do it!"

"Yes, I guess thou art right, Ness. It's unfair of me to place such a burden on thee. I guess we should just forget about the whole idea," Ceila answered demurely. "Please forgive me. I was merely trying to do Deanna's bidding."

Nessa groaned and shook her head in disgust, feeling the weight of responsibility nestling firmly on her shoulders. Ceila embraced her old mentor, and left with a knowing smile.

Nessa was left with no choice. She would have to be the one to ask Cull. If she put some effort into it, she was sure she could win him over. Nessa didn't mind, one way or another, whether the girl came along or not, but Ceila had cleverly manoeuvred her into a position of guilt, forcing Nessa's hand. She would have to take on this arduous task.

Nessa continued her walk as she mulled over her problems in her head. Her thoughts returned to the original conundrum. Where was she going to find a traveller's wagon? Everything else hung on this.

Finishing her circuit, she headed back to the common room, and sat down on one of the benches, feeling despondent. She would have to find Cull and give him the bad news. All their work on costumes and potions would be for nothing. Without a wagon their plan was useless.

"Ness!"

Digging into her pipe to clean it, Nessa refilled the bowl, hoping that a quiet smoke would calm her.

"Nessa! Have you gone deaf in your old age?" The question broke through her thoughts, making her look up. Veola, one of the Dream-catchers, was standing before her, looking perplexed.

"Sorry! Did you say something? My mind was elsewhere."

"Ceila's looking for you … something to do with a pigeon."

"A pigeon … don't you mean a dove?" Nessa asked. "Has she got a dove for me?"

"She's got a whole loft full of the smelly, wee critters. You know that, Ness! All I know is that she ran past me, grinning like an Imbolc hare. She was looking for you and clutching one of those white pigeons."

"It's a dove, Veola, a Fan-tail Dove," Nessa corrected absently. Clearly, the woman was no ornithologist.

"Whatever!"

Giving up, Nessa lifted her skirts and hastened away, seeking out the High Priestess. They nearly collided, moments later, in the corridor.

"Ah, Ness, we're in luck. A message has come through from Manquay. Ester has found thee thy wagon, though it's in need of some repair. She has arranged for Captain Bohan to bring it down the river and deliver it to the village of Auldsmead. It should arrive tomorrow, at the latest. Let's hope that it's good enough for thy needs."

Nessa felt like jumping for joy, and she hugged Ceila as she beamed. "It'll do. It'll have to do. Even if I have the bare bones of a wagon, I can work from there and fix it up. I'll go and give Cull the good news."

Nessa hurried away, lighter of heart now that at least one of her burdens had been lifted, and silently she gave thanks to the ever-resourceful Ester.

183

Cull was cleaning up the gym after the morning session when Nessa found him.

"I thought you'd been avoiding me," was Cull's greeting.

Nessa flushed, for she had been doing exactly that. "I've been a bit busy, sorry," she apologised. "How's the training going?"

"It's good, very good. The boy has a lot of fire in his belly. He'll make a ferocious fighter when he grows up. He's just like his father. It must be true what they say about the *Dragan* blood."

"You should have met his grandfather, Cull. He looked like a god fallen to earth, and he had that same sultry smile that'd make all the ladies swoon. He was an outrageous flirt!"

Cull looked at the priestess in surprise. "You can't be that old?"

Nessa grinned, while her mind filled with warm memories of her first love, with a handsome young man with dazzling, blue eyes. "The goddess has been kind to me, but that's another story. How's Maerlin coming along?"

"The girl has spirit. She's a feisty wee critter, that's for sure. Her weapon-skills aren't much at the moment, but she makes up for it with her gutsy attitude. I wouldn't want to be the one to stick his hand in that hornet's nest. Someone could get badly stung if they riled that wee lass up. That's without her using any of that magic stuff," Cull reported. "She's also fleet-footed. She runs like a whippet, even on this boggy ground. I guess it's all that running up and down mountains. Her upper arm strength is good enough, but her legs are superb. She can run for miles and hardly break a sweat. To tell you the truth, she's growing on me," he admitted with a sly grin "But keep that to yourself."

Nessa smiled, knowing what he meant. She braced herself for the impending storm. "Cull, I was just wondering ..."

"...Did you find a wagon yet?" Cull interrupted. "I'll need to begin re-planning, if you haven't found one."

"Yes, actually, I did. It's due to arrive in Auldsmead on the morrow. I'll sail over there this evening, to wait for its arrival."

"Auldsmead, you say. That's where I have the stallion stabled, excellent. I guess that means we'll be heading north via Manquay. It's as good as route as any I suppose. At least, it keeps us out of Boarite country. So, when do you expect it to be ready?"

"Well, I gather the wagon's a bit run down, but I'll get the local craftsmen working on it, right away. It'll be ready in a couple of days, I'm sure. Cull, I was just wondering …"

"… It all sounds great. Good job," Cull replied, cutting off her question for the second time. "And I suppose the other preparations are underway?"

"Yes, yes. They're testing the dyes today. Cora, Maerlin's friend, has volunteered to try them out. She's been working very hard these last few weeks. The High Priestess thinks it would be a good idea …" Nessa paused and started again "Well, we were both wondering …"

Again Cull interrupted, his eyes glistening with enthusiasm at the prospect of beginning the quest. "… I'm sure it'll be fine, Nessa. I'll leave these minor details to you. You can handle them without my input." He was already turning towards the door. "I'll go and work on the maps. Let me know how the wagon's coming along and when it'll be ready."

"But Cull …" Nessa tried again, in an effort to get the question out.

"…I leave it in your capable hands, Nessa. I'm sure you'll be able to manage any trivial detail," Cull assured as he headed off to the library. Nessa was left burdened by the decision.

"Oh, Deanna! Why do you always do this to me?" Nessa murmured, looking skywards as she dug out her pipe. "He's gonna kill me when he finds out about this. Either that or everyone else will when I tell them that Cora can't go."

Nessa sat down on one of the benches and filled her pipe, ignoring the smell of stale sweat that permeated the warehouse. For a long time, she just sat there, puffing away on the long-necked pipe and contemplating her dilemma, until finally the decision came to her. Feeling the burden of responsibility upon her shoulders, she left the makeshift gym. She headed towards the potion class to watch over the coming tests, hoping to pull Cora aside and speak with the novice.

During the late afternoon, Nessa left the island, a worried look on her face as she headed for the village of Auldsmead. When she arrived at the riverside docks, she was surprised to find that Captain Bohan had already delivered the wagon.

The wagon sat, looking forlorn, on the dockside. Even in the poor light of dusk, Nessa could see that it was in desperate need of attention. "Well, there's nothing much you can do about it tonight!" she murmured to herself. With a shrug of her shoulders, she turned from the wreckage of a wagon and walked away. Soon, she arrived at a well-tended hut on the outskirts of the village and rapped on the weather-beaten door.

The warm glow of a fire lit up Nessa's weary face as a plainly-garbed old priestess opened the door and inspected her visitor. Concern etched the old woman's face as she greeted Nessa with all the bluntness of long acquaintance. "Your face looks like a pit-bull's, after he's been licking the piss off a stinging nettle, and then deciding to take it out on a hornet's nest! Whatever's the matter with you this time?"

"The goddess is tormenting me, Bess," Nessa announced despondently. "Was I too vain in my younger years? The world seems to be getting harder with each passing moon."

"That's such a heap of bovine excrement Ness *Mac Tire*! Come inside and grab a seat by the fire. I'll open a couple of bottles of my homebrew mead, and we can light up a couple of pipes. Then, you can tell me all about it." Bess took her friend's arm and pulled her into her cosy little home.

During the remainder of the evening, Nessa spilt her heart out to her oldest and dearest friend. She spoke of her doubts, as well as the coming quest. She explained everything they were planning to do, the hard decision that had been placed upon her shoulders, and how she had dealt with it. One bottle of mead became two and then three as the room slowly filled with the pungent odour of pipe-smoke, and the fire died down to embers.

"You always show the world a strong face, Nessa. You've done that ever since we came here as children. You could've left the Order long ago, but your pride wouldn't let you. No one would have denied you your chance to be the High Queen, but you denied your own heart. You opted for duty

186

over love. You broke that poor boy's heart back then, and I think you broke your own too."

"Please, Bess. Don't bring that up again! It was the right decision at the time. We all knew it. He needed to wed into one of the ruling Clans. He needed to strengthen his claim to the throne. He couldn't have done that by wedding a Pectish girl like me. There'd have been uproar, if he'd married a *MacTire*!"

"Pah! You just like being a martyr, Ness, and I'm getting too old to listen to such nonsense. Listen here and mark my words. You made your decision back then, and it's old news now, though I told you that you were being foolish at the time and on more than one occasion since." Bess raised an eyebrow, which said more than words ever could. "You've made a decision now, and in my mind it's a good one, for what that's worth. You can't please everyone, Ness, and the burden has fallen to you. That's life, and the goddess chose you because you were always able to handle such tough decisions. You always chose duties over self, even when it broke your heart. Me, I'm happy to spend my days tending this small community. I watch them being born and I watch them die, as I have done these last sixty-odd years. We each choose our own paths, Nessa, though I would've chosen that golden-haired boyo in a heartbeat, if it'd been me he was making moon eyes at," Bess goaded her life-long friend, finally getting a smile out of Nessa.

"Enough of that," protested Nessa, half-heartedly. "I'm sick of hearing about it. Ya bring him up every time we meet. You're like that demented jackdaw you used to own; the one that kept saying 'bloomers', over and over again. Why ever did you teach it that word, anyway?"

"I tried to teach it lots of things …" Bess objected "…but the stupid bird just got stuck on that one word and that word alone."

The two women then discussed other things, talking long into the night.

In the morning, Nessa walked down the muddy street with a bounce in her step. The weight of worry had left her during the night. "Whatever the goddess wills," she had decreed on waking. She was finally confident with her decision.

As she walked down the narrow street, she accosted each of the village's craftsmen in turn, with polite but firm requests for assistance. None of the artisans was brave enough to look Nessa in the eye and tell her that they were too busy. Therefore, a small procession assembled on the quayside.

"Gentlemen," Nessa announced as she pointed at the dilapidated wagon. "This is the small task that I beg your generous assistance on."

"What … that!" the local wheelwright exclaimed. "You can't be serious. That piece of junk needs torching. I could make you up a nice new undercarriage. It'd be a far better job."

Nessa looked pointedly at the wheelwright, as the other craftsmen nodded their agreement. "Have you an undercarriage to hand, right now?"

"Not likely!" he blustered. "They're made to order. It'd take me at least a fortnight to build it, even if I set my other work aside and leave that to my apprentices."

"That's no use to me. I need a working wagon within the next two days. I must be ready to leave by then. You'd better pull your boys off whatever other jobs their working on and get them on this one, too."

"We can't do that!" the blacksmith protested. "We've orders to finish."

"Has Deanna and our Order not blessed you and your families?" Nessa asked sternly. "Your trade would be nothing without the blessing of the Order. Your wives would give birth unattended. Your sick, left to die. Have we not always given our help in times of need?" she demanded, glaring at the craftsmen. "Surely, you can spare a couple of days for your benefactors?"

"We're grateful to the Order, Ma'am, there's no denying that …" replied the wheelwright, wringing his cloth cap. "…but what you're asking is impossible. Even with the help of our apprentices, working night and day, we couldn't repair this wreckage within a week."

Nessa smiled, for she knew that the job was as good as done. "Don't worry about that, gentlemen. With the goddess's help, all will be achieved in good time. Instruct your families to offer a prayer each evening to Deanna, and I'll go and fetch some of the priestesses to lend you a hand."

The blacksmith shuffled his feet, clearly agitated and looking for the right words.

"Was there something on your mind, smith?"

"Without rising insult to the fair ladies of the Holy Order, Ma'am, this is complex work, and it needs skills that have been learned through years of training."

The other artisans stepped nervously away from the big-shouldered smith. Clearly, he had overstepped the mark, but Nessa merely smiled. "Let me show you all something."

Stepping between the shafts of the wagon, she cleared her mind as the workmen gathered around. "Spirits of the Earth come forth," she whispered in a guttural voice. "Come forth, my sweet Gnomes, and assist me." She drew in her magical energies and summoned Earth Elementals. The ground trembled slightly and then all became still.

Nessa focused on the ash shafts, and she merged her mind with the old timbers. She sought out flaws and rot within the wood. The left shaft was rotten in the core, a common problem with old ash, and a weakness that could not be healed at this late stage of its life. The right shaft, however, was still sound, if a little dry and brittle. Pushing her healing powers into the wood, she worked it back to life. When she was satisfied, she focused her mind and spoke a single audible command "Bend."

The wood creaked as the shaft twisted and turned before the astonished artisan's eyes. Nessa continued to force healing energies into the wood as she bent the long, thin shaft to a 90-degree angle. Turning to the blacksmith with a cheery smile, she asked "Any questions?"

The men shook their heads in amazement. Their eyes were still locked on the twisted wood.

"I think that'll be all then. If you gentlemen will begin, I'll be back shortly."

Nessa left the craftsmen to begin the job of renovation. She returned in the early afternoon with three other Wild-magicians: one from each of the four Elements. The priestesses soon assessed the situation and began helping out, using their unique skills. Apart from the abilities that they could muster through Wild-magic, and the other forms of magic at their disposal, they also had a great effect on the general speed of the project. Whenever two artisans argued over how a particular task should be done,

one of the ladies would quickly step in with a softly spoken question "Is there a problem here, gentlemen?"

Differences were quickly resolved, as egos were set aside under the watchful glare of the priestesses.

By dusk, the job was well underway, with the wheels repaired and the undercarriage re-fitted. The wagon had been dismantled and checked over, inch by inch. Then, it was reassembled with parts replaced where needed. It would all be finished in time for the following evening, including a fresh coat of paint and a new canvas covering. The harnesser was also been busy cobbling together a set of old harness for the black stallion. It would be ready in time to pull the wagon.

All was going according to plan, as Nessa led the priestesses to Bess's hut for the night. They would begin again at dawn, while Nessa returned to the island to check on the other preparations.

Chapter Fifteen: The Long Road

Nessa found herself swamped. She and Cull were finalising the packing and loading of the gear into the flat-bottomed boats. These would be ferried across the Great Marsh to the village beyond. Nessa had only a few moments spare in which to speak to Maerlin about her recent decision. "Maerlin dear, I'm afraid that Cora cannot come with us. She has another path to follow." Seeing the hurt in the novice's eyes, she added "I'm sorry, Maerlin. I know that you two have become close, but you'll just have to trust me on this."

"But Ness, couldn't you ..." Maerlin began.

"... No, Maerlin," Nessa interrupted, cutting off any further argument "I can't. Please don't argue with me on this. Now go and help pack the last of the herbs before Cull mixes them up or Conal breaks all the vials."

Maerlin hurried off with a face that would curdle milk. She started to stow baggage onto the barge with a vigour that made Nessa wince.

Conal seemed particularly happy with the prospect of leaving. The long days of preparation had gnawed away at his impatient soul. Dressed in the colourful garb of a *Teincheor*, he looked a completely different boy to the one who had arrived. His short golden hair was as black as a raven's wing, and his skin was the colour of seasoned oak.

The others were similarly disguised. Cull had only needed to dye his grey-brown hair, for his skin was already swarthy from years of living outside. Maerlin and Nessa had needed the least preparations of all, with only a change of clothing and a different hairstyle. Maerlin's long single braid, so typical of the mountain folk, had been re-plaited by Cora into many tiny braids, which now hung down her back. Tiny colourful beads hung from the bottom of each braid, and these rattled whenever Maerlin moved her head.

The two girls had spent some time, the night before, braiding each other's hair in readiness for the trip. It all seemed such a waste now to Maerlin as her friend would not be coming.

Maerlin realised that Nessa must have spoken to Cora earlier in the day, for she had not seen her friend all morning. Tears welled up in her eyes as she imagined Cora's distress. She had been so much looking forward to Cora coming along. Tears dripped down onto her new blouse. Maerlin continued her work, but they kept returning to blur her vision.

Finally, all was packed and, as if waiting for this moment, the High Priestess arrived to see them off. Ceila walked gracefully over to speak to her former mentor. "Take care of thyself, Nessa. My heart aches each time thou leave. I wish I could come with thee, but my duty lies here. Watch over thy wards and know that we will pray for thy safe return."

"Stop that, you're getting all mushy on me," scolded Nessa as they embraced. "You know how much I hate goodbyes."

Nessa hurried away to do some reshuffling of the packages.

"Lord Cull," addressed the High Priestess "I've known thee for but a short time, yet my heart and seer's eyes can see the goodness within thy gruff heart. I pray thee, watch over these children and bring them back to me. Our hopes and prayers go with thee."

"I'd rather your prayers were for Broll. His need is greater than mine. I'll do all I can to make this a success," he assured. He took the High Priestess's hands in his own and kissed her fingertips lightly.

"Go with the blessing of Deanna," she blessed him softly, touching her hand to his forehead in formal blessing.

She turned to Maerlin and looked long into her sad eyes. "Come, child." she offered, and Maerlin ran forward to the comfort of the High Priestess's arms. They hugged silently for a few moments, while Maerlin shook, tears flooding from her. The High Priestess waited patiently for the worst to pass and then lifted the girl's head and kissed her on the forehead. "Go with Deanna, dearest Wind-sister and hurry back to thy place here."

"I will, Ceila, I will." Maerlin promised. "Can you pray for Cora, and tell her I'll be back soon?"

"I have seen thy paths, Maerlin, in the visualizations of time during my Dream-catching. Do not worry about thy newfound friend, for thy destinies are entwined. She will be with thee always. Nothing could keep thee apart. Such is the goddess's wish," proclaimed the High Priestess

"Now go, before my robe is ruined. Thou wilt see me again, Dream-catcher. Look for me in thy dreams."

Maerlin headed for the boat, leaving the High Priestess standing with Conal on the jetty.

"Conal. Heir of *Clann Na Dragan*," Ceila began "Thou hast changed much since thou first came here, and I'm not talking about thy recently acquired disguise. I have watched thee grow from a small boy into the man I see before me, for in truth, that is what thou art, even if thy Rites of Manhood is still some moons away."

She stroked the downy hairs on the boy's jaw line, a silent testimony of the beard that would soon grow there. "Even this last moon, thou hast filled out and broadened at the shoulder. Lord Cull must have worked thee hard, but thou wilt need all that strength in the coming moons."

Conal shuffled and reddened beneath his darkened skin.

"I'm sorry, Conal. I didn't mean to embarrass thee, though soon, thou wilt be a great charmer and such compliments will be a norm for thee. Let me give thee one piece of advice before thou leaveth me." She paused and smiled at the boy who would soon be a king, if the goddess willed it "Do not forget thy heart, Conal. Thy head is full of vengeance for thy dead father, and this could blind thee from thy true duty. Follow thy heart as thou walketh the land, for thy destiny is great. Upon thy words and deeds lies the destiny of a nation, not just thine own fate. Wilt thou remember that for me?"

Conal looked into her concerned face and nodded. "I'll try, Ceila." He struggled through a constricted throat and finally added "You've always been a great ally to my Clan. I thank you, Ceila, for all your patience and effort."

Ceila smiled as she dragged Conal into her warm embrace. "Thou truly art coming into thy manhood, Conal. Go with Deanna and with my prayers. Let us both hope that thou need not return to the Holy Isle. Thy pranks have giving me enough grey hairs already," she teased as she released him.

Conal ran to the boat and climbed aboard. Soon, they were heading out into the swamp. Ceila stood patiently, watching them slip silently into the reeds. She hoped that her vision had been misinterpreted.

"Guard them well, Deanna," she prayed as they disappeared into the mists.

*****

They arrived at the village with a couple of bells of daylight left. They had time to inspect the beautifully-refurbished wagon. This would be their home for at least a full cycle of Arianrhod's moon. As they packed their belongings into the small space, each of them wondered whether it would be big enough for their needs.

Finally, it was Cull who broached the subject. "This isn't going to work. We've way too much stuff here. I want everyone to go through his or her belongings and discard anything that isn't *absolutely essential*."

"You can't be serious," objected Nessa, thinking of all her herbs and vials.

"I am indeed," Cull insisted, digging out maps and books from his own packs. "We might be living in that wagon for a while. It isn't going to fit everything, so start re-packing."

It eventually took three attempts to shed all the unnecessary bulk from their belongings. A large pile of discarded items grew beside the wagon. In it were assorted weapons, clothes, books, maps, make-up, combs, cooking utensils, and trinkets, along with other items decreed by Cull as of no definitive use. Even Conal's ferrets' cage had been removed, though only after a local hunter had agreed to take care of them. Cull had insisted that they go, or that they could forget the whole expedition.

"That looks better," Cull declared with a note of satisfaction. It was still going to be cramped within the wagon.

"Let's hope that this weather holds, or we'll be killing each other before we reach our destination," said Nessa. "I think we might as well sleep at Bess's place tonight and get at least one good night's sleep before heading off. Come along everyone, I'm sure she'll have a good stew waiting for us."

*****

Maerlin slipped quickly into a troubled sleep that night …

194

She found herself wandering through dark and ancient woodland. She wandered through the immense trees, until she came into a clearing. In it, a group of warriors sat talking around a fire. One warrior stood, and the others fell silent to hear him speak. The speaker was dressed in a massive badger-skin cloak over a linen tunic and a grey, woollen kilt. He was short and bulky in stature, as were his blade brothers. Each of the men fashioned short, bristly, black hair and affected two bleached stripes running from their foreheads to the napes of their necks. They were all armed with heavy war spears. Each warrior also had two vicious-looking triple-bladed daggers.

Maerlin glided closer, to listen to the speaker. It had been two years since she had heard the Old Tongue spoken. She had not spoken the language since her mother's death. Occasionally, her mother would sing in Pectish or when she got annoyed or excited, she had been known to slip into her native tongue. Maerlin had always been an inquisitive child, and after a little coaxing, she had persuaded her mother to teach her some of the ancient language of the Pectish Clans. It had always sounded exotic and colourful, and Maerlin had been a keen student. Within no time, the two of them could hold conversations together, but her mother had made Maerlin promise not to speak the tongue to anyone else in the village. Maerlin, already aware of the physical differences between her and the other children, had agreed. Now, two years since her mother's death, the language was slow in coming back to her, but soon, she could make out enough of what was being said.

"I agree with Clansman Bulliac. It is time to stamp out this threat to our sacred lands. For too long we have suffered the constant gnawing of Clann Na Torc upon our woods. Let us gather together the Setts and rid this curse from our territory, before it's too late. Their arrogance is great indeed to threaten the Great Truce of three generations. I say we should go to war. What say you, Brothers?" The fierce warrior brandished his daggers, so that the wicked triple-blades glistened in the firelight.

Warriors jumped to their feet, baying for blood and shook their weapons in response to the call for war.

"Send out runners this night for a meeting of the High Council. I will raise the War Banners, and we will put an end to this impudent Boare."

The clearing rang out with war cries, before the warriors dispersed.

Maerlin turned away, slipping back into the dark forest. As she did so, she noticed a shadow moving along the edge of the clearing. Had she not turned at that precise moment, she would have missed it. It too had been crouching quietly, listening to the meeting. The shadow's movement had caught Maerlin's eye.

Straining, she tried to make sense of the dark figure, but she could see no features. It was just a shadowy humanoid form that slipped through the trees and away from the clearing. Acting on instinct, she followed. The shadow moved faster, forcing her into a run to keep it in sight as they hurried through the woods.

She forced her dream-self on as the shadow raced ahead, and her speed increased to match the fleeing shade. They sped along at breakneck speed, until the woods blurred with the speed of their race. Suddenly, they burst onto a vast open plain of grass.

The moon was up, giving her better light, but still she could not see the features of the one she followed. Intent on its destination, it raced across the plain, faster than a galloping horse. Urging herself on, she followed, curiosity pushing her to greater effort.

Finally, the shadow slowed before a great, round tower. It stood high upon a hillock. The shadow slipped around the tower and vanished from sight. Maerlin followed and found an arched doorway set flush to the cold grey stone.

For a moment, she wondered at the purpose of this isolated building in the middle of the vast plain. Was this a watchtower? She also wondered at her location, for she had seen nothing like it in the mountains or near the Great Marsh. Her curiosity, however, drew her back to the door of the tower.

Danger lurked inside. She could feel it, even now, yet she was drawn to open the door and look beyond. Who, or what, was the shadow? Why had it been spying on the meeting in the woods? These things she had to find out.

She tentatively touched the door, feeling its rough, grainy wood beneath her palm, and a chill run through her body. As she placed her weight on the door, she could feel her body being drawn through it and into the darkness beyond. Her dream-form walked through the insubstantial timber with no more resistance than she would meet while walking underneath a waterfall. In fact, it left the same chill on her skin.

She found herself in a dark chamber with small pools beneath her feet, and she could hear the sound of water dripping from above her head. She had been here before and remembered another dream of darkness. Stumbling slowly forward, her heart filled with dread, she strained to make out details of the chamber.

"You are foolish, girl, to follow me into my lair. Did the rats not teach you anything?" a voice asked from the shadows. It was the same raspy voice she had heard before. It was a voice that caused her to shudder with revulsion.

"Who are you?" Maerlin asked, and then she remembered the Dream-catchers' discussion "Are you the one they call Dubhgall the Black?"

The shadowy figure moved closer, laughing in a hollow, raspy way. "Ah! It seems that I'm famous ... or should that be infamous? What have those dried-up hags from the foggy knoll told you? Have they told you of your impending doom or of the folly of your quest? Did they tell you that you are to be the ultimate sacrifice, the tool with which Lord Boare wins his High Kingship?"

"No, they did not, but I think you are a weaver of lies. Your tongue is like that of a serpent," Maerlin challenged, holding her terror in check and drawing upon her anger. "It's always flickering away, hypnotising its prey."

"You're a brave girl, but your cause is lost. The Dragan-cub will never see his manhood, let alone his crown."

"You're wrong," Maerlin replied hotly, glaring at the dark form. "Tell me, Dubhgall. Why is it that a sorcerer of your skill and reputation is working as a lackey for Lord Boare? Is he that good of a master, then? Does he throw you a bone, occasionally, if you've been good?" she goaded, hoping to keep the shadowy magician off-balance.

"Master! Lord Boare is not my master!" the shadowy magician hissed "He is but a means to an end; a tool to be used. Do I look like a hound dog to come to heel at a master's word? I am the greatest magician to ever live. None can stand against me."

"What about Uiscallan Storm-Bringer? They told me that she defeated you at the First Battle of the High Kings?"

"That harridan was lucky on the day, but I outfoxed her in the end," Dubhgall rasped as he paced across the room. "Do not mention her again. She was unworthy of consideration."

"What happened to her?" Maerlin asked. Her curiosity was piqued.

Dubhgall laughed. It was a chilling sound. "Have those island hags left you in the dark on that, too? Did they not tell you of her madness? The Storm-Bringer could not gain control over her own powers. Love blinded her and made her weak. In the end, Uiscallan was consumed by her love and fled. She could not stand by and watch her golden-headed warrior bed another for his wife," Dubhgall gloated with a sly chuckle. "It was I who instigated her downfall. I, who planted the doubts in the High King, I was the one who made him believe that he must marry a highborn and cast aside the Pectish witch. The foolish Dragan believed the dream to be an omen. None questioned him. The stupid Fear Ban accepted his decision with relief, happy in their own bigotry."

Maerlin listened, trying to make sense of the tale. All the time, her eyes sought a means of escape.

"So, why do you need Lord Boare, if you're such a great magician?" she goaded. "I think you're all shadowy words. You're just a sad, demented, old fool with no real power. You rely on other people's fears, and you weave your magic with lies, deceit, and illusions."

Dubhgall spun and charged towards her, rage emitting from his shadowy form. "You think this, do you? You, who is yet to know the true meaning of power," he yelled "I will show you power!"

The sorcerer drew from his inner pool of magic and muttered an incantation. An angry buzzing filled the room as smoke poured forth from the wizard's fingers. The noise grew louder, and small forms darted out of the hazy smoke that gathered around Dubhgall's shadowy figure. As the buzzing increased, angry insects flew towards Maerlin.

Maerlin staggered back, swatting at the hornets that surrounded her, as Dubhgall's hollow laughter bounced around inside her head. She looked for an escape route, but none showed itself as the first of the hornets embedded its fiery sting into her outstretched hand.

198

"Am I not the greatest magician? Beg now and I will let you live. Beg, before it is too late!"

Maerlin bit back her cry and channelled her rage. Closing the pain she felt into a box within her mind, she cleared her brain of her fear and evoked a Fire Elemental as she had been instructed. "Come, sweet Salamander," she murmured. "Come forth, for I desperately need thy aid …"

"Fall to your knees, girl, and beg forgiveness for your impertinence."

Within the darkness of her mind, Maerlin focused on the flame. Holding it tightly inside her mind, she coaxed it to greater life. Her head pounded as she held onto the building power. Finally, she could hold the Salamander within her no more.

"Come, child, before it's too late," the sorcerer was saying. "Kneel down and call me Master, and I will let you live. Walk away from the hags on their foggy hideaway and become my acolyte. I can feel the power within you, but you will never come to your full potential under the guidance of those self-serving harridans."

Maerlin focused on her outstretched hand, which writhed with angry insects, and she uttered one word aloud, putting every ounce of her anger into the sound "Burn!"

The flames burst forth from her fingers, reaching out to envelop the swarm and then onwards towards the dark figure of the sorcerer. Hornets fried instantly as the very air was consumed with flames. Dubhgall flinched backwards in surprise. The room lit up brightly so that each detail of the stonework was etched within Maerlin's mind; that and the look of shock on the face of Dubhgall the Black.

An intense wave of pain hit Maerlin, causing her momentary feeling of triumph to dissipate as her body went into shock. Maerlin's legs buckled and gave way, her vision blurred and darkness enveloped her.

She heard Nessa's voice calling her name "Maerlin! Maerlin! What is it?"

Blinking back tears and clutching her hand, Maerlin looked up to find herself in Bess's hut.

"My hand! I've burned my hand!" Maerlin wailed as she looked down at the charred flesh.

Nessa inspected the wound briefly before grabbing a nearby water pitcher. Grasping Maerlin's wrist, she plunged the swelling hand into the cold water until it was fully submerged.

"Keep your hand in there until I can fetch my lotions," Nessa commanded, and then more softly she added. "It'll be fine, dear. Don't worry."

The others had gathered in the doorway, peering into the bedroom to see what the commotion was.

"What's going on?" Cull grumbled, wiping sleep from his eyes.

"It's nothing, Cull," Nessa informed as she barged past him "Maerlin's had another one of her dreams, and somehow, she's managed to get herself burned. That's all I know for now. I'll know more by morning. Take the boy and go back to sleep. There's nothing for you to do here."

*****

Later, with her hand bandaged, and with lotion on her face and neck to ease the swelling of the hornet stings, Maerlin related her dream to Nessa and Bess. The lotion soothed the worst of the pain, so that only a dull throbbing ache remained, but Maerlin could not sleep.

"Didn't I teach you to be careful when using Wild-magic, Maerlin?" Nessa reproached. "You're lucky to still have a hand left."

"But it was only a dream, Ness!" Maerlin protested. "I didn't think I was going to really burn."

"Dream or not, if you summon an Elemental, it'll come to your bidding. You're lucky that most of the energy went into the Dream-catching, and only a fraction of it slipped here. You could have burned the house down," Nessa explained as she handed the girl a soothing drink. "Let's hope you gave Dubhgall as much of a fright as you gave the rest of us. You must have given him enough, anyway, to have escaped his trap. Drink your tea, Maerlin, before it gets cold. It'll help to lessen the shock."

Chapter Sixteen: The Long Race North

Cull and Conal rose as dawn was lighting the eastern skyline, and the group quickly ate some breakfast.

Soon after, they were heading down the quiet street to the wagon and harnessing up the horse. As the grey mists drifted around them, they waved goodbye to Bess and left the village. They were heading north to meet up with the Western Highway. The morning sun was well up when they reached the junction and turned east, heading down the cobbled road towards the city of Manquay.

A few miles farther on, Cull pulled the horse over to the side of the road and called for a halt.

"We'll set up camp here. Sort out some feed for the horse, Conal," he ordered, handing over the reins. Leaving him to un-harness the stallion, Cull rummaged around in the baggage and pulled out a short-sword.

"What's that for?" Nessa asked in alarm.

"I think we're being followed. Call it a hunch, but I get the feeling someone's behind us," Cull announced. "Stay here and look after these two. I'll be right back."

"But it might be an innocent traveller!" Nessa protested. "Don't kill anyone just because of a stupid hunch."

Cull grimaced. "Don't worry, I'll be careful," he assured as he slipped into the trees and vanished from sight.

"Damn that man, and damn his instinct," Nessa cursed, straining to see back down the road.

"What's the matter, Ness?" Maerlin asked.

"Nothing, dear, just fetch some water for the horse, will you?" Nessa instructed.

They set up camp, Nessa regularly looking down the road, waiting for Cull's return. It wasn't long before he reappeared. He was leading a dun mare by the reins. A body lay slumped across the saddle. As he neared, they could all see the angry scowl on his face.

"Ah, well! There goes nothing," Nessa muttered as she braced herself for the coming storm.

Cull marched forward and lifted the body from off the saddle, laying it onto the ground and rolling it over.

"Cora!" Maerlin gasped in surprise and ran to her friend's side. She could see a large bruise on the side of Cora's head. "Have you killed her?"

"She'll live. I just knocked her over the head," Cull growled as he looked at the others. "Does anyone know why she was following us?"

Nessa braced herself and announced calmly "That'd be because I told her to."

Cull blinked as they all looked at Nessa in surprise.

"What do you mean ... you told her to? Why, by the Seven, were you having us followed?" Cull growled.

"It was the only solution." Ness looked him squarely in the eye. "She was to join us at nightfall, but your instincts were sharper than her skills as a tracker. I should have expected it, considering that she's from the Western Isles."

"Why, by Deanna's monumental paps, was she going to be joining us at nightfall?"

"She's coming with us, of course," Nessa replied, matter of fact. She pointedly ignored Cull's blasphemous remark.

"And just when was I going to be informed of this?"

"At nightfall, I guess," Nessa replied calmly "It was, after all, you who agreed to it."

"What do you mean, I agreed to it? That's the first I've heard of it," Cull protested, spittle flying.

"I distinctly recall speaking to you on this matter, or should I say, trying to speak to you on this matter. As I recall, you kept interrupting," Nessa announced. "I said to you …"

"…When was this, exactly?" Cull demanded.

"There you go again, butting in. Did no one ever teach you that it's rude to do that? I can see that we'll have to work on some of your bad habits, but first, I need to dress that bump. We don't want her to get a concussion," Nessa declared, lifting her medicine bag down from the wagon.

"Hang on! Just when exactly did I agree to this?" Cull persisted, trying to get a grip on his fraying temper. He was getting nowhere against Nessa's calm demeanour.

"You said to me … and I recall the conversation quite clearly, you told me 'that you'd leave it up to me to decide'."

"…I was talking about 'minor matters'. Not something like this …" Cull protested. His temper was bubbling to the surface again.

"And how, pray tell, am I supposed to decide which matters you consider minor, and which are important enough for you to stop and listen to, when I ask for your advice? I'm just dying to hear the answer to this …" Nessa's tone was thick with sarcasm, and Cull could only bluster.

"…Well, I'm not having it … she's going straight back," he insisted. "I don't need another slip of a girl getting in the way. Having one half-trained novice tagging along is bad enough. How, by the Dagda's blessed cherries, did she even get across the marshes in the first place? I booked every available boat to ferry our gear across."

"She has her own means of travelling over water. She's a novice of Wild-magic, Cull, and a good one at that," Nessa replied as she inspected the bruising on Cora's forehead. "Her speciality is Water Elementals. It was one of the simpler tasks I set for her. She succeeded in all of them, it seems."

"What tasks were these, Ness?" Maerlin asked, while smothering the large bruise with salve.

"I gave Cora three tasks to prove that she was worthy of this mission," Nessa informed. "She'd be of no use to any of us if she couldn't pull her own weight. The first task was to keep the tasks themselves a secret, even from you, Maerlin." Seeing the look of hurt in the novice's eyes, Nessa added "I'm sorry, Maerlin, but it was the only way."

"Why was that?" Maerlin asked.

"Because we needed to leave before Cull and Conal found out. I didn't want to spend days arguing about it. We're *not* going to have any argument over it, either," Nessa stated, looking hard at Cull, who was busy grinding his teeth.

Cull glared back, still unconvinced, but curious enough to ask "...And what were the other tasks?"

"Cora needed to find a way to get herself disguised, so that she could pass as one of us, but without raising undue questions. She volunteered for each potion as you can see from her appearance, and then she managed to find some suitable clothing. I can only presume that she stayed up late at night, working on them to have them ready."

"What was the third task?" Conal asked.

"...That she finds her own way across the Great Marsh and follow us. I can only assume that she either stole or bought a horse from the village. She succeeded at all of her tasks and did them well. I won't see her sent back now," Nessa declared, adamantly.

"...But what about the High Priestess? Surely she'll object ..."

"No, actually, when Maerlin first asked me about this, Ceila was the first person I went to. I'd foolishly hoped that she would nip this idea in the bud. She agreed with Maerlin, however, and I was overruled. I went to Cull and I tried to speak to him about it, hoping that he would refuse, but he wouldn't even discuss it. He just said 'It was up to me to sort out any minor details'," Nessa explained, doing a fair impression of Cull's voice.

"Therefore, after a lot of soul searching, I made my decision. The girl is coming along and that's final," Nessa insisted "Now, I think we'd better get her inside, so I can check that wound out properly. Maerlin, a cup of tea would be nice and some of them currant scones that Bess baked for us. Cull, Conal, if you would be so kind. Be careful when you lift her into the wagon?" They all looked at her in amazement until she added "Well ... we haven't got all day you know."

And so, the group was now five.

As they travelled down the road later that afternoon, heading towards Manquay, Maerlin slipped her hand into Nessa's and confided "I'm sorry, Ness. I shouldn't have doubted you. Can you forgive me?"

"Of course, dear. You forgot the first lesson I taught you again, didn't you?"

Maerlin recalled the lesson and smiled. "I guess I did. Anyway, I just wanted to say sorry and thanks for helping."

"Maerlin, I personally didn't think it was a good idea, but the goddess Deanna kept putting things in my path until she eventually changed my stubborn mind. Sometimes, she needs to batter me around the head a bit to make me see sense, just as I do you. My mentor grew many a grey hair during such sessions, and I'm sure I will too. In the end, we all learn, with the help of Deanna."

*****

They settled each night in one of the many hazel or birch groves along the roadside. Each day, they headed farther east until they came to Manquay. There, they opted to circle around the city walls, rather than tempt their fate within. Cull ordered them to camp early that evening, a few miles north of Manquay. Taking Cora's dun mare, he rode back towards the city, to speak with the Beggar-Lord.

They hid the wagon in a thicket beside the road and jumped up nervously every time they heard a noise. None of them slept well as they awaited Cull's return. They sensed the danger this close to the city walls. Finally as the dawn lightened the eastern sky, they heard the sound of hooves approaching. Conal quickly drew his sword and rose to see who it was, but Nessa forced him back into the thicket with a sharp command "Wait! That's more than one horse approaching. Stay down."

Conal nodded agreement, hiding behind the bush with his sword ready. Maerlin quickly took up position beside him. She was armed with a steel-tipped quarterstaff.

"Oh, Deanna! What has that man been teaching you?" Nessa hissed in exasperation as she looked at Maerlin. "How, in the Nine Hells, are you going to use that with a burned hand? Can you tell me that?"

"I'll manage," Maerlin replied with a stubborn set to her jaw line. She was determined to fight if the need arose.

"Just refrain from using any magic, dear. I like my hair just the way it is," Nessa ordered, only to groan a moment later as Cora emerged from the wagon, clutching a dagger, "Oh, no, not you as well?"

Cora, at least, had the good grace to look guilty. The novice's head was still wrapped in bandages above her eyebrows.

The horses drew near and stopped and then they heard a voice call out "It's alright. It's only me."

"Cull!" Maerlin and Conal shouted together, bursting out of their hiding place to greet the beggar-spy.

Cull was towing a line of horses; his face was a mask of worry.

"What news, Cull?" Nessa asked.

"We've got trouble coming up behind us. Hitch up the wagon and get ready to leave. We'll need to cover as much distance as possible today. There's been a Clan rising in the north," he explained "A Boarite fort has been attacked during the night. Word of it has travelled faster than a messenger pigeon could fly. Lord Boare is sending his army north to quell the rebellion."

"The Brocians?" Nessa asked, recalling Maerlin's recent dream.

"How, in the Nine Hells, did you know that?" Cull demanded.

"Maerlin saw them meeting during a Dream-catching. That answers your other question, too."

"What other question is that?"

"...The reason why the Boarites knew of the attack so soon. They knew about it even before it happened. Dubhgall had been watching the Brocians meeting, too. That's how Maerlin got herself burned. Dubhgall lured her into a trap after the meeting. She had to use her magic to break free."

"Why would the Brocians go to war? It doesn't make sense," Conal asked. He had recently been studying the different Clans during his afternoon respites from the exercise field. Cull had even been quizzing him to make sure he didn't spend the afternoons napping, instead.

"I haven't a clue, Conal. They usually keep to themselves and stay inside the Broce Woods. Even the hamlets on the eastern edge of the Woods rarely see them," Nessa explained. "The Brocians venture out only during darkness. From what Maerlin has told me, it seems Lord Boare has been encroaching on their territory."

"What? But there's been an agreement since Conal's great-grandfathers time," Cull growled. "Didn't anyone teach Lord Boare about his family's history? The last war with *Clann Na Broce* was a long and bitter struggle. That fool should know. It was his ancestors that started it. It only really finished when *Luigheagh Dragan* got them to sign the Great Truce."

"Good news, then. That should keep the Boarites busy," Conal added.

"Far from it, lad! If we were heading anywhere else but north, it'd be great, but we have to go through the Broce Woods on the way to Dragon's Ridge. This was exactly why your ancestor brokered the Great Truce in the first place. We're going to get caught between the Brocian warriors and Lord Boare's conscript army. They're already landing on the docks of Manquay, and the vanguard will be marching north, any time now," Cull explained "That's why I stole the extra horses."

"You stole them?" Nessa exclaimed. "Why didn't Broll give you some horses?"

Cull grinned at her. "Well, there are two reasons, actually. Firstly, I was a bit pushed for time and I needed good quality mounts and …" He paused for effect, happy in his own cunning "… secondly, it just so happened that Lord Boare and his generals were picketed at one of the expensive hotels, nearby. I thought it might irritate them, when they found themselves walking in the morning."

"You play a dangerous game, Cull," Nessa warned.

"It's the only way to play. It's so much sweeter that way," Cull chuckled.

207

As the birds began their dawn chorus, they set off on the Northern Highway. Nessa drove the wagon while the others rode their stolen horses.

As it turned out, Cora was not a good rider, having spent most of her life on a small island. She was capable enough while the horse was walking, but precarious in a trot. Thankfully, the wagon cancelled out any chance of galloping.

"Maerlin, Conal, can you ride on either side of Cora until she learns her seat. We don't want her to end up with another lump on her head," Nessa suggested. "I should've seen this coming when Ceila told me that she needed to broaden her horizons. Ceila was always good at understatements."

The group travelled at a slow trot for most of the morning, occasionally slowing to a walk to let the horses rest.

*****

For the next three days, they kept up a steady pace, rising early and riding until late, only stopping to rest the horses. Cora was becoming steadier on her horse with each passing day, but both the novices had become saddle sore and ached from stretched muscles. By the end of the third day's hard riding, even Cull was feeling the pace.

"We can't continue like this, Cull," Nessa declared, voicing his own thoughts.

"What choice do we have? We have to stay ahead of that army. If we let them overtake us, we'll be bogged down in the middle of their supply train. It probably spreads all the way back to Suilequay."

"What if we go cross-country? We could head northeast, towards the Broce Woods? Wouldn't that work?"

"It'd slow our pace considerably and make it harder on the horses, especially the cob."

"Well, we can't go on like this, Cull. What else can we do?" Nessa asked.

"Aye, I suppose you're right. We'll change course in the morning and head for the edge of the woods," Cull agreed, with a sigh of resignation.

"We can skirt around them and cut east towards Dragon's Ridge from there."

*****

The following morning, the group headed over the hilly countryside. The going was rough over the drumlin countryside at the foot of the mountain range. They were constantly going up and down hills, and each valley held either a brook or a boggy area into which the wagon sank nearly up to its axles. The heavyset stallion sweated and toiled through each of these dips, his muscles straining and his lungs bellowing with his exertion. The going was painfully slow.

"This is going to take days at this rate," Cull barked at Ness, anxious to be moving along, before the impending war progressed any further. "This wagon wasn't designed for travelling cross-country."

"We're just going to have to leave it behind then, aren't we?" Ness responded as she scanned the horizon. "Look! There's smoke rising over there. It might be a village. We'll head that way and see if we can trade the wagon for some pack animals."

"What about our disguises? They'll be useless without the wagon."

"Then, we'll just have to discard those too, Cull," Ness shrugged with indifference, turning the wagon to face the trail of smoke. "Have you any better ideas?"

Cull saw no alternative, so they slogged on, heading for the trail of smoke until they crested a small hill. Finally, they looked down at the source of the smoke. It was not, in fact, a village. It was the remains of a wooden fort, and it was still smouldering from a recent attack.

"Maybe we should skirt around it and keep heading for Dragon's Ridge?" Cull said "I don't like the look of that, at all."

"No, Cull. I need to go down there and see if there's anyone still alive. I'm a healer of Deanna. There may be people down there in need of my healing arts."

Cull nodded with resignation. "Conal, stay here with the wagon and mind the girls."

"I think they'd better come, too. It'd be better if we all stuck together. Whoever did this might still be around," Nessa pointed out.

Cull scanned the horizon before nodding agreement "Very well then, here, you'd better be armed and ready for danger." He started handing out weapons to Maerlin and Conal.

"What about me?" Cora asked.

"Are you trained in arms, girl?" Cull growled. He had been avoiding the novice as much as possible, and Cora had likewise avoided him.

"...A little. I used a trident in mock battles when I was a younger," she answered, not meeting his eye.

"Maerlin can teach you the rudiments of the quarterstaff," Cull instructed "Until then, stay close to Nessa."

Cora's shoulders slumped. Her face was a mask of bitter disappointment.

"Don't wander off, anyone. Stick together," Cull commanded as he drew two short-swords for himself. They rode cautiously towards the smoking ruins of the ring fort.

"This was freshly built," Nessa noted as they rode through the gates. "The timbers are showing no signs of age."

"How far is this from the edge of the Broce Woods, Nessa?" Cull asked, surveying the damaged wooden walls.

"I'm not really sure. It can't be far though, only a few leagues. Why?" Ness asked as she looked around. There was plenty of blood on the ground, but they had found no sign of life or death.

Cull directed them towards the remains of the main building. It still smoked from the recent fire. "If Lord Boare has been building forts all around the Broce Woods and across the Plains of the Dragon, he'd need a lot of timber. This might be why the Brocians are all riled up. The main source of timber in these parts is in their territory."

They stopped before the smoking remains of the main building and dismounted silently. Cull signalled that the rest of them should stay put and moved cautiously forward. He placed his hand on the charred remains of the door and pushed it gently aside, to peer into the gloomy interior of the building. The place reeked of charcoal and burned flesh. As he peered within, he could see patches of light amidst the dark recesses. The roof must have partially caved in. He looked down the long corridor towards another set of doors, at the far end. Other doors led off to the left and right.

"Wait here," he ordered. "This place could collapse at any moment."

As if to prove him right, timber creaked loudly in the wind. Cull braced himself and stepped into the smoky building. He walked carefully forward, using his naked blade to push each door slowly open as he passed. Peering inside each in turn, he found the rooms empty and vandalised.

Broken glass and discarded weaponry lay on the packed-earth floor, but no clue could yet be found as to who had assaulted the fortress. Finally, only the double doors at the end of the long corridor remained. Cull braced himself before entering. The smell of scorched flesh was getting stronger with each tentative step.

Wrinkling his nose in anticipation, Cull pushed open the doors. The fire must have been at its hottest here, and the hinges on the doors had buckled and partially melted in the intense heat. As the doors swung open, they creaked ominously. The heavy timber dragged and strained on the already warped metal of the hinges, and then one of the doors fell with a loud crash. Dust and soot rose into the air, making Cull cough as the room shuddered with the reverberations.

He stood in the doorway, ready to race towards the exit as the whole room creaked ominously and threatened to collapse. Finally, it settled, and silence descended on the room like a shroud. Through the swirling smoke and dust, Cull could see the headless remains of the garrison soldiers. They had been piled high in the centre of the room.

Biting back the meal that threatened to rise from his gullet, Cull stalked forward and inspected the dead. Many wounds covered the charred remains. He noted long, triple gashes on the bodies of the dead, confirming the attacking force's identity.

"Brocians," he muttered as he gazed down at the distinct wounds on one of the soldier's chest. Three long gashes went from the dead man's shoulder to his hip, biting deep into the flesh and scraping bone. Another three puncture wounds were found, just below the soldier's solar plexus. A killing thrust through the heart and lungs. These wounds could only have been made with the distinctive Brocian three-tine dagger, a *Tri-crub*.

He wondered why the Brocian warriors had taken their enemy's heads. It had been many years since they had practiced headhunting. Turning away from the corpses, he searched the Hall for the missing heads, but without success.

"There's none left alive?" Nessa asked quietly from the door.

"Bull's pizzle!" Cull cursed, his heart suddenly racing with the surprise. He had not heard her approach. "I thought I told you to wait outside!"

"I heard the crash and came in to see if you were injured," she informed him, not taking her eyes off the heap of charred remains.

Cull nodded. Taking a deep breath, he reported "They're all dead. At least, I hope they are. I'd hate to see what they do to the survivors." He paused a moment before adding "You're from around the Broce Woods, Nessa. You know *Clann Na Broce* better than most. Why would they take the heads?"

"I don't know, Cull, but I fear we'll find out before too long," Nessa predicted. "Let's get out of here. There's nothing we can do for them. They belong to Macha now. Deanna's blessing is of no use to them."

Nessa turned and walked away, leaving Cull to face the deathly silence on his own. Shaking off the feeling of dread, he headed towards the sunlight.

"What's in there?" Conal asked "Did you find anyone?"

Cull ignored the question, looking around. "Where's Maerlin?"

"She was here a moment ago," Cora confirmed.

"Maerlin!" Nessa shouted, looking around "Maerlin, where are you?"

It was then that they heard the scream.

Chapter Seventeen: Beginnings and Endings

Cull swung around and pointed towards the far side of the main building.

"She must be round there. Come on!" he ordered as he charged off. Conal and Cora were hot on his heels. Nessa followed, as fast as her feet could carry her.

As they reached the corner of the building, another scream erupted.

"Stop doing that!" an anguished voice called out as they raced towards the stables at the rear of the building. Cull charged around the corner and skidded to a halt. Before the stable stood Maerlin; her quarterstaff poised and ready for her next attack.

The man before her was tall and gangly, dressed in a blue serge suit with fine embroidery stitched along his short cape. He wore his blonde hair long and ratty, and he sported a short goatee. His sword lay on the ground before him, and he was nursing an injured hand.

Maerlin lunged, her steel-shod staff whirling close to the man's head.

"Stop that!" he yelped, dodging hastily away.

"You started it!" Maerlin accused. Though she barely came up to the man's chest, she had clearly come out the better in their confrontation.

"What on earth is going on here?" Nessa demanded. "Maerlin, put that down and leave the poor man alone."

"But ... he attacked me!" Maerlin insisted, glaring angrily at the gangly stranger.

"I thought you were one of those barbarians, coming back to take my head! I'd been quite content to hide in the stable, until you kicked the door in. What else was I supposed to do?"

"Maerlin, leave him be," Cull ordered, marching forward and lifting up the discarded sword. The rapier had seen better days. "Were you planning to tickle her to death with this?" he asked "This blade's covered in rust. I doubt it'd cut butter, even on a warm day. You'd've been better off farting at her."

"I have little use for weapons," explained the man, shifting nervously from foot to foot. "It's more for show than anything else. It was meant to discourage brigands during my travels."

"This isn't the healthiest place to wander around, in case you hadn't noticed," Cull muttered, throwing the man his rapier. "Here. We mean you no harm. Can you tell us what happened here?"

Instead of reaching out to catch its handle, the man shied away from the weapon, letting it fall to the ground. "It … It happened last night … shortly after sunset," he stated hesitantly. "They came out of the dark like blood-thirsty demons and killed the guards at the gates. Before anyone knew it, they'd swarmed into the fort and were killing everyone in sight. I was in the Hall, singing to the Captain and his men, when the door burst in and they fell upon us. We didn't stand a chance. Many of the soldiers weren't even armed. They were drunk on cheap mead."

"How is it that you survived, when everyone else is dead?" Cull asked suspiciously.

"I don't know, honestly, I don't. The last thing I remember was a short, bulky man with white stripes in his hair. His features were masked by war paint, and he was running towards me with a spear in his hand. I grabbed Aoife and tried to protect her, lest the barbarian do her harm. I covered her with my body and pleaded to every deity I could think of ..."

The strange man was relaxing a little as he narrated, embellishing the tale with body language and facial contortions "... His face was a mask of purest hatred. He was clearly possessed. His eyes were red with rage, and spittle flew from his lips. I tell you, the barbarian was insane. Aoife and I were surely doomed. I closed my eyes waiting for the killing blow, but it didn't come. I trembled with fear, and the goddess, Macha, swam before my eyes. The world stopped as my life pass before my eyes. Finally, when death did not swoop down to embrace me, I looked up into that demonic face …"

Shuddering, the man continued "... He looked down at me and then over at my sweet Aoife. I could see a hint of intelligence behind those wild, barbaric eyes. The Seven must have heard my pleas and touched the barbarian's soul, for instead of thrusting his spear into my heart, he cracked me over the head with it."

The man lifted his long hair away from his forehead to show them the nasty swelling near his right temple. It was as if he wanted to confirm the might of the blow, before continuing with his narration. "For a moment I saw stars, and then the blackness of the tomb. I must have been out for a good while for when I awoke; I was lying on the ground outside. Aoife was lying beside me, and the Hall was in flames. The horde had fled back into the night, and the sun was breaking through the morning mist. I swear to you, and not a word of a lie, I knelt there, cradling my sweet Aoife in my arms and I wept, thanking the Seven Greater Gods for protecting us."

"Where is this woman you speak of?" Cull asked, his eyes scanning the shadows of the stables behind the stranger.

"Oh no!" the man explained, waving his hands about, as a bright smile lit up his face. His smile brought out a new radiance within his features, which had been hidden before. "Aoife is my harp. I'm a poet and a singer … an entertainer if you will. Perhaps, you might have heard of me …" he added hopefully.

"Of course!" Nessa declared, interrupting them "That's why he survived. It's so obvious now."

"What … why?" Cull asked, clearly bewildered.

"The Brocians … they thought he was a bard. That's why he still lives."

Seeing the blank expressions on the others faces, she explained further "The Brocians, or *Clann Na Broce* to give them their proper name, are one of the ancient Pectish Clans that lived here before the invasion of the *Fear Ban*. Their Bards, like the Brehons and the Druids, are sacred to the Pects. *Clann Na Broce* may live deep within the Broce Woods, but they are as much Pects as the Wolf and the Bear Clans in *Tir Pect*. Their lands may be in Dragania, but they've never forgotten their heritage or culture. They wouldn't kill a bard. To do so would bring down a terrible curse on their heads. It's a sacred *Geasa* to them, a serious taboo."

"So you're a bard then?" Conal asked, never having met a real bard before.

The singer flushed, clearly uncomfortable with the question. "Well, not exactly a bard, as such, though I've always held true to their own high standards. Alas, I didn't have the honour of their fine tutelage. My folks were far too poor to pay the fees of the Bardic College. It's been said, however, that I can sing the birds out of the trees and recite battle epics to raise the bodies of the fallen," he boasted with a slightly arrogant air.

"I fear that those within the Hall would beg to differ, singer," interrupted Cull sourly. His comment had the desired effect on the singer's boastings. "So the Brocians won't kill a bard, is that what you're saying, Nessa?"

"Yes, Cull. At least, that's the best possibility I can think of."

Cull thought for a moment. "Good ... then he can come with us. We might have need of his services before too long."

"What?" Nessa asked.

Maerlin glared venomously at the singer. "You can't be serious!"

"What are you talking about?" the bard asked, nervously. "Where exactly are you going?"

Cull sighed and tried to explain "We are, at most, a half day ahead of Lord Boare's vanguard. They'll have seen that smoke rising, the same as we did, and they'll have sent someone to investigate. I'd imagine that they'd send a full platoon, at the very least," he summarised, looking at the others, one by one. He sighed again. It was clear that they still didn't understand his reasoning. "Let me put it this way. When they come over that hill and see what's inside this Hall, they're going to be mightily vexed. Then, they'll start looking for someone to blame. Now maybe, just maybe, our bardic friend here has enough of a gift of the gab to explain how he survived the attack while everyone else was butchered. I wish him the best of luck with that. We, however, are up to our necks in Dung Alley without a shovel between us. They'll follow those wagon tracks straight to us, and we'll end up decorating the nearest tree, if we're lucky. Alternatively, they may decide to drag us back to that accursed sorcerer, to use for his fiendish spells. Do we all agree on that?"

"Yes. I see what you're getting at ..." Nessa agreed "... But what's the singer got to do with us?"

"We're heading into the Broce Woods, by the shortest route possible. That way, we'll only have one enemy to face. If we bring the singer along, we might live long enough to tell about it afterwards."

"Oh, no, I'm not going anywhere near those woods," insisted the singer. He dug through the straw nearby. "It's full of Pectish barbarians. Aoife and I will head into the mountains."

"You won't make it, believe me ..." Cull assured, calmly "... And running will only make you look guilty. Your best bet is to come with us. We've already ascertained that the Brocians won't harm you. You're as safe as houses with them."

"You're crazy," accused the bard, pulling a harp free from the straw and inspecting it closely. "I think I'll just stay here and explain it all to them, like I did to you. It worked once, so I'm sure it'll work again."

"Ah, that's the point though, isn't it? We have Nessa here." Cull pointed towards Nessa. "She's from these parts and knows about the Brocians. The Boarites, on the other hand, are an ignorant bunch of arrogant thugs. They tend not to wait for explanations, at least, not from the likes of us. Well ... I'll say no more. The choice is entirely yours."

The harper, by now, was busy packing his few possessions into a sack.

"Oh, by the way," Cull added "What's your name?"

The singer looked up. "I'm Taliesin Larkstongue."

"Never!" Maerlin protested. "I don't believe that for a moment."

"Maerlin, don't be rude!" Nessa scolded. "If he says that's his name, then it must be. Bards don't lie."

Taliesin coughed, as if some dust was tickling the back of his throat. "Alas, the girl speaks the truth. It was not my *real name*, but it's been my ..." he paused, seeking the right phrase "... *Stage name,* shall we say, ever since I became an entertainer. I thought it'd bring me good luck to be named after such a famous bard."

"Your luck's just run out, singer ..." Cull commented dryly "... But don't worry. We'll be heading back this way in a moon or two. We'll cut down your body or what's left of it and give it a decent burial ... erm ..." Cull paused for a moment and then added "... How exactly do you spell Taliesin? I've never been that great with my letters ..."

The bard paled visibly, unable to reply.

"...Well, never mind, I'm sure we'll manage. Come along, Ness. We'd better be getting out of here. We best leave the poor fellow to his prayers," Cull announced in a fatalistic tone as they headed back to the horses.

Nessa hid her grin and followed, saying loud enough for Taliesin to hear, "Maybe, we should kidnap him ... it'd be for his own good. That blow on the head has clearly muddled the poor man's brains. It isn't right for us to leave him here to face his doom."

"No, Nessa," Cull replied firmly. "Every man should choose his own fate. It's not up to us to force another destiny upon him. It's probably the goddess's will. She might want him to serenade her in the Otherworld."

"...Wait! I've changed my mind," the singer shouted, dashing after them. "I've heard that the people of the Broce Woods recognise true talent, when they hear it. This could be my big chance."

Cull winked at Ness as he continued walking. "Well ... only if you're sure, Taliesin."

*****

"You better grab yourself a mount, Ness, and you too, Taliesin. We'll be leaving the wagon here."

"What about all of our gear?" Nessa asked.

"You can stay with it, if you want, Ness. My priority is to get these children to safety, and complete our mission. We'll need to ride and ride fast. My instincts tell me that some cavalry are going to arrive, any time now. That smoke will draw them like ravens to a battlefield."

Taliesin had run back to the stables, while they argued. A raucous bellowing soon erupted from within.

"What in the Nine Hells is making all that noise?" Cull asked, as Nessa finally agreed to abandon her precious herbs.

The singer appeared a moment later, pulling hard on a lead rope that stretched back out of sight. The bellowing was coming from within the stable, and presumably, from the other end of the rope.

"Come on, Gertie. It's alright. The smoke's died down now," Taliesin coaxed, before being dragged back into the stable by his mysterious mount.

"Larkstongue, my ass!" Maerlin commented. "He couldn't talk his way out of a privy."

"Watch your language, dear," Ness reprimanded "It's bad enough that Cull curses like a drunken sailor, without you starting."

"Do you need a hand there, bard?" Cull offered. "We're in a bit of a hurry, you know."

"No, I'll be just fine. I'm just blindfolding Gertie. It works on horses, so I'm sure it'll work for her, too."

They looked at each other, wondering just who or what Gertie was. They didn't have to wait long, however, before Taliesin led the reluctant creature out into the sunlight.

It was taller than a horse and covered in dull, brown fur. Its hide looked like an old carpet that had seen better days; better years even. Once the blindfold had been removed, it revealed a face that would curdle milk and make babies wail inconsolably.

"That's one ugly son-of-a-horse you've got there," Cull commented as he watched Taliesin try and clamber onto the creature's back.

The creature bellowed again, a phlegm moan of forlorn discontent.

"It sings in fine key, too!" Maerlin exclaimed as she backed nervously away from the monstrosity.

They inspected it from a safe distance, wondering what sort of creature it was. Eventually, it was Cora who braved the ridicule and asked "What exactly is that thing?"

Taliesin had, by this time, managed to get onto the creature's back, though he looked distinctly uncomfortable. "It's a dromedary." Seeing their lack of comprehension, he added "A one-humped camel."

"Where, in the Nine Hells, did you get that thing?" Cull asked.

"I was told that she comes from a far-off land in the east. From a place that's hot and dry, and covered with sand. They call them the 'ships of the desert', and they use them instead of horses. I won her in a dice game," Taliesin confessed. "I've tried to sell her a couple of times, but no one seems to want her."

"I wonder why," Maerlin teased.

"Can't you just steal a horse? I'm sure the garrison won't object," Cull remarked. "We need to get moving, and that thing doesn't look too agile."

"Oh, she can run all right. Don't worry about that. Anyway, there aren't any horses. The Brocians took them all. For some reason, they never ventured into Gertie's stall. I guess they were wary of her."

"Damn!" Cull cursed, realising that they now had another problem. "Nessa, you're going to have to take the draught horse. He's a good, comfortable mount, but he'll be slower than the rest."

"Okay, but I'll need a leg up. He's a bit taller than I'm used to," Nessa admitted.

Soon, they were racing northwards again. At first, the horses were nervous around the camel and shied away from the huge beast. It proved, however, to be fleet enough of foot, if a little ungainly. It easily kept pace with the other mounts. Nessa and the heavy stallion drifted gradually to the rear, being the slowest of the party.

They raced down the last hills and onto the Plains of the Dragon. The tops of the trees marked the Broce Woods ahead of them. To their east, there was nothing but grassland that went on for miles and miles. To the west rose the Mountain of the Gods, shadowing majestically over the rest of the Great Pectish Mountain Range. Eagles Reach lay on the northern side of it, while High Peaks lay on the southern side.

"We're almost there," Cull encouraged as he urged the others on. "Head for that small hillock; the one with the tower on it. The woods aren't far beyond it."

Maerlin looked up at the mention of a tower and dread filled her heart. She pulled her horse up sharply. "No, Cull! Don't go near that tower."

"What!" he exclaimed, pulling his own mount up beside her "Why ever not?"

"That's Dubhgall's tower. We need to stay well away from it. I've been there in my dreams."

He looked up at the tower and at the safety of the woods beyond. "I guess we could circle off ..." he began.

"There are riders, right behind us!" Taliesin yelled in a panicked voice, urging his mount to greater effort with a stick.

Cull turned to look behind them and groaned inwardly. Cresting the last rise were at least thirty riders. They were less than a mile away and racing after them.

"They've seen us," Taliesin hollered as he raced past.

Cull could see the cavalrymen urging their horses on. Turning back to Maerlin, he yelled "It looks like we've no choice now. Ride, Maerlin."

They sped across the plain at breakneck speed. Nessa was slowly falling farther and farther behind. Cull looked back as they raced towards the tower. "Hurry, Ness," he shouted. "They're gaining on you."

"I know, I know," Nessa replied "Get them into the trees."

It was then that the camel bellowed a shriek of pure fear and bolted. Taliesin hung on grimly as the beast shot past the others, eyes rolling around in its head.

"Look ... on the tower!" Maerlin yelled, pointing towards a shadowy figure standing on the parapet.

"That's all we need!" Cull cursed "Bleedin' magic!" He urged his mount nearer to the others. "Make for the treeline, hurry!"

Just then, Cora screamed. Her mount was twisting frantically as if to shake off some unseen attacker. "Help!" she yelled as she sawed on the reins, but the horse had its bit firmly between its teeth. Her efforts were useless.

They were passing the tower by now, and Cull looked up to see the evil grin on the old sorcerer's face. He was already beginning to chant another spell.

Another scream drew Cull's eyes away. As he watched, Cora's horse bucked in a frenzied effort to free itself from the invisible tormentor. Even a good rider would have had difficulty staying in the saddle of the bucking thoroughbred, but Cora didn't stand a chance. She was flung high into the air and sailed into the long grass. Her shriek of terror was cut short as she landed heavily and rolled to a stop.

Cull raced over, his heart in his mouth. Leaping from his mount, he hurried to Cora's side. "Cora! Are you all right, lass?"

The novice gave no response. She was either dead or unconscious. He didn't have the time to find out which. Quickly, he pulled her limp body onto his mount's withers and clambered back into his saddle. Gripping her clothing, he spurred the horse towards the woods.

Looking ahead, he noticed that Maerlin was struggling with her own mount, but she was still heading towards the trees. Conal and Taliesin were waiting there, anxious for the rest of the group.

Cull glanced behind, his heart pounding as he searched for Nessa. At first he couldn't see her, and a cold fear gripped him, thinking that she had been captured. Then he spotted her. She was only a few yards ahead of the cavalry. They were baying with anticipation now, sensing success. Their long lances were pointing towards Nessa, eager to pierce her flesh. Her mount was flagging with exhaustion and failing fast.

"Hurry, Ness," he yelled, willing her on.

Nessa waved him away, urging him silently to get the others to safety. Cull's mind raged as he was caught between his responsibility to the children and his urge to go back and protect the priestess.

As if reading his mind, Nessa yelled to him "Save the children!"

Turning around to check on her pursuers, she yanked hard on the stallion's reins and turned the horse sharply to the side, heading directly towards the dark tower. Cull could only watch in horror as she charged straight at the stonework, not even slowing as she drew near. Her pursuers momentarily lost momentum, confused by her sudden change of direction. Cull could only look on as Nessa kicked the last vestiges of strength out of her mount. She raced headlong for the arched doorway at the tower's base. At the last moment, her horse reared, refusing to run into the solid object. It stopped in its tracks, swerving away as it tried to change course, and Nessa was propelled forward, out of the saddle.

"NOOoooo!" Cull yelled as he watched transfixed. Nessa sailed through the air and landed against the door lintel with an audible crack of bone. She rebounded off the door frame and into the tower. It was as if the door had disappeared on contact. He could hear the others screaming from the edge of the woods, but for a moment, he was lost in shock. The cavalry unit divided; a few dismounting and running towards the tower, while the rest turned to face Cull. Only then did his senses return. Pulling his horse around to face the trees, he kicked the animal hard in the flanks and rode for his life.

"Don't let them get away, you idiots!" he heard the raspy command from the watchtower. "I want them all!"

Cull gripped Cora tightly, as his horse galloped across the flat ground. Death breathed down his neck as he raced before the Boarite soldiers. Their baying followed him and urged him onward.

"Get into the trees!" he bellowed, waving to the others. "Hurry!"

He knew that it was all lost. It would take a miracle to save them now. He was within feet of the woods and ducking down to ride under the lower branches, with the sound of pursuit loud in his ears, when the first spear whistled by over his head.

Chapter Eighteen: The Brocians

More spears flew past Cull's head, striking the onrushing cavalrymen. They flew out of the undergrowth into the charging horses. Cull's horse was fully committed to entering the woods, but when he realised that the Boarites had stopped under the barrage of spears, he hauled on the reins to slow his breakneck speed.

"Brocians! Fall back! Fall b ...!" the Boarite commander was ordering, before slipping from his horse. A spear was embedded in his chest. It didn't take long for his men to realise the danger they were in.

Soon Cull was alone at the edge of the woods.

"What are you doing? Get back there!" the sorcerer cursed. "You mangy cowards, attack them or I'll cut out your livers!"

"Hey!" A voice called from the shrubbery behind Cull. "If you stay out there much longer, the Dark Mage will surely kill you."

Cull turned, looking around for the speaker. He could see nothing within the shadowy undergrowth.

"Spirits of the Dark One, come to my aid!" the Mage demanded. "Smite down these wretched creatures who have failed you."

Cull spun back round, fear rippling up his spine in anticipation of another magical assault. Luckily, this time, he was not the intended target.

As he watched, a dark swarm gathered on the tower above the wizard. It became a thick, seething mass, covering his upper arms as he chanted. This, he hurled like a huge ball, towards the fleeing cavalrymen.

Realising their danger, the Boarites urged their weary mounts on. Cull could see, however, that it was a losing race. The black cloud swarmed towards the soldiers, descending on the last of the group. A blood-curdling scream came from the soldier and his mount as they were enveloped by the cloud. It smothered them with its darkness. When the cloud rose, moments later to continue its hunt, all that remained of man and beast was the clean white bones of their skeletons.

"By Cernunnos!" Cull cursed as he watched the black swarm pull down its next victim.

"You're crazy, old man, to tempt the Dark Mage," commented the voice within the undergrowth, bringing Cull out of his shock.

Shaking away the image that would haunt his sleep, Cull slipped into the trees. He didn't get far, however. Swinging silently from the boughs, a dark figure knocked him from his saddle. Cull rolled as he fell, taking the impact easily on his shoulder. As he rose, his hand was already reaching for his sword, as his eyes searched for his attackers. Men fell from the trees like monkeys. Others burst out of the undergrowth. Some even sprang up from the very ground itself. Each of the warriors was armed with either heavy spear or the triple-bladed *Tri-crub* daggers of the Brocians. Their skin had been painted a mottled grey-green, so that only eyes and teeth stood out. Their hair was covered in leaves and twigs, helping them to blend into their environment. Each man wore a large badger-fur cloak and a grey, woollen kilt.

"If you draw that blade, old man, you will die," the Brocian before him warned with casual assurance. The warrior's eyes were calm pools as he waited for Cull's reaction. Only the tension in the forearm muscles gave any hint of the man's readiness for battle. Cull recognised the voice as the one who had spoken to him, moments earlier.

He froze with his sword halfway out of its sheath. "Where are the others?" he asked as he silently counted his opponents. Nine men stood before him, and he knew that others waited at his back. There were too many of them to take on with any chance of success.

"I see your eyes, old man. Don't do anything foolish. We are all trained warriors, not foolish *Torc* conscripts. We aren't those pathetic excuses for men used by the Boare. Your companions are alive and unharmed … for now. We are not slayers of children or bards. The High Council will decide your fates. Will you come without a struggle or will we have to kill you?"

Cull reluctantly slid the sword back into the sheath and relaxed his posture, raising his hands in submission. "All right, I surrender," he agreed, while he readied himself for any opportunity that might arise.

A sharp blow from behind hit Cull at the base of the neck, followed rapidly by another to his temple and Cull's knees gave way. As he slipped into unconsciousness, he felt them roughly bind his arms and legs.

*****

When he awoke with a groan, Cull found himself secured firmly to a tree. Blinking back the pain, he strained to make out any sounds. He had been blindfolded. The bindings were tight, and much though he twisted, he could not slacken them.

"You'll lose skin like that, old man," reproached the Brocian, his tone light and unconcerned by Cull's attempts to escape. "You should stop fighting against your bonds. It's a futile gesture. There are others who would rather kill you than take risks, so your life is in my hands."

"What do you want?" Cull asked, giving up his struggle for the moment.

"I want answers. You bring many mysteries with you, old man. I dislike mysteries so I want some answers."

"Why did you save us?"

"I'm the one asking the questions, but I'll give you this one answer, then you must answer mine. You were running away from the Boarites, who appeared to want to kill you. This means that my enemies could also be your enemies. Even more, it seems that the cursed Dark Mage wanted you captured. It is not often that the Dark Mage takes such a personal interest. I decided that your party might be of more use to me alive than dead. Let us hope that I'm not disappointed. Now, tell me who you are?"

"We're just a family of travellers. We came across a burned-out fortress and decided to help the bard. We were scared, so we thought to hide out in your woods, knowing that Lord Boare would blame us for the deaths of his men," Cull lied, giving as much truth to the story as was prudent.

Pain shot through Cull, making him wince. The sharp tines of a *Tri-crub* were digging into his chest.

"Do not feed me lies, old man. I didn't bring you here to listen to fairy tales."

"I'm telling you the truth!" Cull protested. The three points dug deeper, breaking his skin.

"Maybe you'll speak more truth if I torture one of the others, the boy perhaps?"

"Have the Brocians fallen as low as to torture children now?" Cull growled through gritted teeth.

"Listen to me, old man, for I weary of this game. We are at war. The niceties of peacetime have been put aside. I will get to the bottom of this before you die, one way or another."

"So you intend to kill us after all?" Cull replied.

"That's not for me to decide. However, I will know whether you bring danger into my Clan, before I take you to the High Council. I would prefer straight talk and a peaceful conclusion, but I'll take whatever I need, if I have to. I must be sure that my Sett is not in danger," informed the Brocian. "So let us be civilised and speak the truth, if not as friends, then at least as people with a common enemy."

Cull wondered just how much to tell this man. The Brocians could assist their cause. They could be potential allies for Conal, but many factors were as yet unknown. Cull could not decide.

"Okay, I'll make it easy for you, old man. Let me tell you some of the things I do know," continued the Brocian. "You're dressed like *Clann Na Teincheor*, the travelling folk. Your disguises are good, but you are not Pects. Your skin is like ours, as is your hair. At a passing glance, you could easily be mistaken as one of that Clan, but I'm not so easily fooled. The boy's eyes are those of a *Fear Ban*. No Pect would possess eyes that blue. This makes me wonder whether you are spies, sent here to find our Setts and plan an attack. Are you spies, old man?"

Cull tensed again, expecting another jab of the Brocian dagger. "We are not spies! Did you not see one of our comrades fall? Did you not see the Boarite soldiers, hot on our heels?"

"Aye, I saw the woman fall. The Dark Towers are cursed by ancient magic, and only shamans can enter one of them and survive. That particular tower once stood within these very woods, hidden from the eyes of the *Fear Ban*. That was always so, until these last three years.

228

Now, our woods have shrunk as the soldiers of *Clann Na Torc* come with their axes and their saws. They harvest our trees like wheat and ferry them across the plain to build their fortresses. The *Fear Ban*, it seems, are not content with the lands that they've already stolen from the Pects. They are hungry for more."

"They're chopping down that many trees?" Cull asked in surprise. "That tower must be half a mile away from your woods."

"It once stood three leagues within our territory. It stands on land decreed during the Great Truce as solely the property of *Clann Na Broce*. These woods are out of bounds to the *Fear Ban* axes. Thus, it was sworn by *Luigheagh Dragan*, himself. Now, Lord Boare and his Mage are taking away our lands, bit by bit, and this pillaging must stop! They venture too close to our sacred sites. This cannot be tolerated any further."

Cull considered the Brocians words, his mind racing.

"So now it's your turn, old man. Tell me why you hide within the guise of *Clann Na Teincheor*? Tell me why the boy speaks like a city dwelling *Fear Ban*, yet the girl is from the mountains? The other girl, we have not spoken to yet, but the brooch she wears next to her heart is distinctive of the Island folk. Why have you people come together? What brings you into our lands?"

"Cora! Does she live?"

"Ah! One of you has a name, at least. She is from the Islands then, to be named after a handmaiden of the sea god. Yes, the girl lives ... for now, though her wounds are beyond our healer's skills. She rests in the hands of the goddesses. Whether she wakes or not, will not be decided by mortal men. Deanna and Macha are haggling over her soul."

Cull felt guilty. He had not always treated Cora fairly. Now he regretted his behaviour and wished that he could have done more. "What of the woman who fell? Is she alive?"

If Nessa was here, she may be able to heal the novice.

"No," replied the Brocian with some regret in his voice. "I'm sorry. She did not make it. Though, by her sacrifice, she gave you the time you needed to reach the woods. Tell me about this brave woman? She should have songs sung to praise her in the Otherworld."

Cull felt his heart grow heavy. "Surely there's a chance that she survived? Could you not send men out under the cover of darkness and search for her?"

"It will soon be dawn. You have been out for some time. My men have already been out onto the plains, but they found no trace of her. There is blood on the lintel of the tower door, much blood, but no tracks could be found. She must have fallen into the tower, therefore, she is dead. Ancient wards protect those towers. To enter one of those dark places is to kiss Macha's sweet lips. There is no hope, believe me on this. Many a foolish warrior has disappeared forever, after entering one of those towers. You should mourn her loss, as is fitting."

Cull took a few deep breaths to clear his head. Nessa was gone. She had always seemed as durable as an oak tree, but she was gone. Even Deanna's servants must submit to the will of Macha. She had told him that, herself. What must the others be thinking? Maerlin would be distraught with grief.

"Speak to me of the woman, old man. It is good to speak fondly of the dead," coaxed the Brocian.

"Her name was Nessa *MacTire*. She lived on the edge of the Broce Wood, with the charcoal settlements on the eastern fringes, or so I've been told," Cull recalled. "These settlements have always lived in peace with the Brocians. They never harvested timber that was not dead or diseased, as per the terms of the peace agreement within the Great Truce. Nessa was a healer and a priestess ..."

"Nessa of *Clann Na MacTire!* The priestess of Deanna and the famed healer, surely you are mistaken? The Elders of *Clann Na Broce* have always praised her work during the Plague Years. This cannot be the same Nessa you speak of."

Cull shrugged. "It is said that the priestesses of Deanna are blessed with longevity. I honestly don't know if we are talking about the same person. I've only known her for a short time."

"We will arrange for the rites of passage for your companion, once our shamans recover her body. She must be given fitting tribute as a priestess of Deanna. She was clearly a great woman," promised the Brocian. "Why were you travelling with one of that Order? Why have the Orders become embroiled in the politics of men?"

Cull remained tight-lipped, not wanting to say too much, but knowing that he must come up with a plausible reason. No such reason came to mind.

"I see that you still hold some reservations, old man, though now is not the time for such," the Brocian commented with a sigh. "I'll make this easy for you, as I can appreciate your predicament. You have been left with the responsibility for these children, and I can sense that this is a new burden for you. Am I right?"

Cull nodded slightly, seeing no harm in acknowledging the truth of this.

The Brocian pulled hard at the bonds that bound Cull to the tree. Cull tensed in anticipation of a dagger thrust, but the Brocian merely sliced through the bonds and stepped away.

"What's this?" Cull asked as he rubbed feeling into his chafed wrists and pulled off the blindfold.

He was alone with the Brocian, in a clearing in the woods. He studied his captor more closely, trying to gauge the man through the thick layer of camouflage and war paint.

"I'm releasing you into my care. My instincts tell me that you are a deadly opponent, but a loyal friend. I hope that I will be proven right in my decision. Come and see that your companions are unharmed," instructed the Brocian "Perhaps then you might speak more freely. I warn you though, do not raise your arm in threat or you will be cut down, and do not attempt to escape. There are many unseen dangers in the woods of *Clann Na Broce*."

Cull followed the man through the woods, rubbing life back into his wrists as he walked. They walked for a while and eventually came to another clearing. It was still dark, and Cull had difficulty seeing much in the limited moonlight that filtered down through the trees. The Brocian, however, walked swiftly on, never catching any of the unseen obstacles that snagged on Cull's clothing.

"How can you see in this darkness?" Cull had thought that he had good night vision from years on the city streets. The woods, however, were far darker than the streets of Manquay ever got.

"We are nocturnal, old man. We come out at dusk and sleep during the day."

"But you were at the edge of the woods, yesterday. Why was that?"

"We are at war, so we sleep lightly in our Setts. We keep a watch over the Dark Tower and all along our borders, the same as you would post sentries during the night."

"That makes sense, I guess, but why are you nocturnal?"

"We like it that way. It's more peaceful. We have few natural enemies. Wolves and bears tend to treat us with respect, as do the other forest creatures. Our only threat is our fellow man, and since the Great Truce there was little of that … at least, not until recently."

They walked on, heading uphill until the Brocian stopped. Cull nearly walked into him. "Why've we stopped?"

"We are here," informed the Brocian, stooping and moving aside some leaf mould.

"Where?" Cull looked around at the empty woodland.

"This is my home, old man. Welcome to my humble abode. I am *Vort Na Broce*, War-Leader of the Southern Dell Sett, and you are now my guest," announced the Brocian formally. An eerie green light spilled forth as the Brocian levered up a hidden door. It revealed a shallow tunnel leading into the bank of the hill.

Cull would have never suspected an entrance before him, it was so well concealed. He was sure that even in broad daylight, he would not find the entrance unaided.

"In Pectish society, it is considered good manners to offer your host a name," Vort prompted, observing his guest in the soft light.

"Oh, erm … Cull. They call me Cull."

"Welcome, Cull. I see that you've a small name, to go with your few words. How is it that a leader of men can have such a short name?"

"I like it that way," Cull replied, succinctly.

"Then call me Vort, if that'll make you more comfortable," Vort instructed, still holding the trapdoor open for his guest.

Cull stepped over the threshold and walked down the corridor. The tunnel walls were made from woven hazel rods. Vort shut the door behind them, closing out the night and the woods.

"Where is this light coming from?"

"It's a fungus that we cultivate. It gives off sufficient light for us to see by."

They came to another circular door, made out of the same intricate weaving. Cull stopped before it and looked back at his host.

"Please … enter. Your friends are waiting within," Vort assured.

Cull found the ornately-carved handle, noting absently its knot-work design of badgers at play. Lifting it up, he pushed the door inwards and stepped into a large circular chamber.

"Poppa! Poppa!" Two small infants ran to greet the Brocian. He swept them up, one in each arm and whirled them around playfully.

"Ah, boys! Where's your mother?"

"She's with the sleeping girl, Poppa," replied one of the youngsters, while his little brother pointed helpfully towards one of the side rooms.

"Good, lads, now run along and play. It's safe outside, but you've only a short while until bedtime," Vort instructed, letting the boys down.

"Aw, Poppa! We've been stuck inside all night," the older boy protested.

"Then you'd better hurry. It'll be dawn soon, and you both need your sleep."

The boys fled quickly, running into the passageway and squealing with pent-up enthusiasm.

"My sons," Vort explained with pride.

"So I gathered," Cull grinned, beginning to like this fierce warrior.

"Let's go and see our patient, shall we? My wife, Orla, is a good healer. She'll do all that she can to help your companion."

Vort led the way into a bedchamber. It was crowded with Cull's companions.

"Cull!" Conal exclaimed. The others turned.

"CULL!" Maerlin wailed as she dashed into his arms, weeping.

Cull held her, a little uncomfortable in his new role as consoler.

"We thought you were dead, too!" Taliesin was forced to stoop slightly in the low chamber.

"Is everyone all right?" Cull asked, looking at each of them in turn. Finally, his eyes came to rest on Cora. An attractive Brocian woman was tending to the novice's bandaged head. He presumed that this was Vort's wife.

"We're fine," assured Maerlin. "At least ..."

Cull could see the tears welling up in Maerlin's eyes.

"...Oh, Cull. Cora won't wake up!"

"Hush, child. I'm sure she'll be fine. These things take time. I'm sure she'll wake up anytime soon. She'll be right as rain. Just you wait and see."

Chapter Nineteen: The Harper's Lament

Conal walked quietly through the dawn mist, following the sound of a harp. The mournful music rang out clearly in the dawn air, and a lump came to Conal's throat as his thoughts turned to Nessa. The music continued, its source hidden within the mists, giving it a surreal quality which touched Conal's soul. Silently, he offered up a prayer to Deanna, the goddess of life, in the hope that Nessa would be granted a seat beside her in the Otherworld.

A voice joined the haunting music, its tone filled with sadness. The language was unfamiliar to Conal. The voice was a rich baritone that blended well with the soft notes of the harp. Although Conal did not understand the words, their sentiment was clear. It was a song of sorrow and loss, and it cut through mere words to reach deep within. Conal sought out the source of the haunting music. Cresting a rise, he looked down into the hollow beyond. A magnificent waterfall filled the valley, small and yet breathtaking in its beauty. From Conal's position, he could see the shadows of fat trout, swimming languidly in the dark water. Taliesin was sitting on one of the pool-side rocks, playing his harp as he sang. He was lost in concentration.

Conal crept closer on silent feet, not wishing to disturb the bard's song. The valley was a natural amphitheatre, and the background noise of the waterfall complemented the soft notes. When he was as close as he dared, Conal sat down to listen.

The lament ended, but the echoes of it drifted around the valley before disappearing like ripples on a pond. Finally, silence descended on the valley, save for the waterfall. Taliesin was still lost in thought, and he had not moved since finishing the lament. Eventually, Conal coughed, to catch his attention.

Flinching, Taliesin spun round. There was a momentary panic in his eyes.

"Sorry," Conal apologised. He hadn't intended to startle the harper. "I was just listening to your music."

"That's alright, lad. I'm just a little jumpy after the last few days. Come, sit beside me," Taliesin invited. "It's Conal, isn't it?"

Conal rose and went over to sit beside the harper. "Yes, it is."

With all of the recent chaos, they had not managed to talk. After a few moments of shared silence, Conal spoke "I've never heard that song before. It's very sad. What is it?"

"It's called *Fherdiagh's* Plight, and it's in the Old Tongue. I thought it was appropriate, given our surroundings. The Brocians, like the other Pectish tribes, still speak that language."

"What's it about?"

"It's about love, loss, death, and betrayal. It's part of an ancient saga. I'll translate it for you sometime … but not today," Taliesin promised. "My heart's too heavy to do it justice."

"Why … what's bothering you?"

Taliesin looked at Conal and sighed. "I'm thinking of giving it all up and going back to farming. I've had little or no luck since I started singing. These last few days in particular have been hard. There's been too much death and destruction lately. I might as well just face facts. I'm never going to be a bard. It's not in my destiny."

Conal turned to look at the singer in surprise. "Why? You've clearly a gift for music. If you sing like you just did, I'm sure it'd be fit for any King's table."

"And what would you know about royal tables?" Taliesin teased. He was still unaware of Conal's true identity.

Conal realised he'd spoken out of place. They didn't know the singer well enough to tell him the truth, yet. He flushed with discomfort and fobbed off the remark. "I know what I hear."

"You've a good heart, Conal, but I'll never be a bard."

"The High Priestess of Deanna once told me that I should follow my heart and not my head. It was sound advice; advice that you should listen to, too. If you really want to be a bard, then you'll be one. You've got the skill and maybe the determination. Don't give up so easily, just because of a few minor setbacks."

"Minor setbacks … what does a young lad like you know about setbacks?" Taliesin grumbled.

Conal glared at the singer. "I might be young, Taliesin, but I've had more than my fair share of setbacks. I was orphaned before my seventh summer. Since then, my life's been a constant battle to survive, yet I'm still here, and I'm still striving towards my goal. I could've given it all up and accepted an easier life, but I didn't. Just because I'm young doesn't mean I don't know about life."

Taliesin blinked in surprise. After a moment's thought, he grasped Conal's shoulder warmly. "You know something, Conal, I think you're right. You don't act like most boys your age. Forgive me. I'm just feeling a bit lost at the moment."

"I know what you mean."

"So tell me, Conal, what is this goal you speak of? I know so little about any of you."

Conal flushed. "I can't tell you at the moment … I'm sorry."

Taliesin shrugged. "It must be big indeed for you to be so secretive. What is it you plan to do? Have you found a secret diamond mine, you're keeping to yourself? No, wait, I know … you're going to become some swanky lord with his own castle, with servants at his beck and call," he joked, ruffling Conal's hair.

Conal gritted his teeth, and his eyes flashed with anger.

"Hey! I'm sorry, Conal," the singer apologised, seeing Conal's reaction. "I was only kidding around. Whatever your goals are, I wish you well with it. I'm sure you can achieve anything you set your mind to. Please, excuse me and my big mouth. I was never the brightest apple in the barrel."

Conal relaxed, seeing the genuine concern in the singer's eyes. "Forget it, Taliesin. I'm a little on edge, today, that's all. So, were you any good at farming?"

Taliesin laughed. "Hardly! My father said I was the worst farmer's son he'd ever seen. I think he was happy when I finally ran off, because the farm would go to my younger brother. He's very pragmatic and hard working; a perfect farmer's son. I was always too lazy, and a bit of a daydreamer. I would get lost in my own world while the sheep wandered away, untended."

"If that's the case, I'd stick to singing, if I were you. I've a feeling that someday soon, you'll have a tale to tell and a King's table to tell it at. You mark my words," Conal predicted solemnly.

"Maybe you're right, Conal … thank you. You've lightened my heart. I know! Why don't we sing a cheery song together? Will you join me in a verse or two?" Taliesin asked with a lopsided grin.

"Oh, no! Your one-humped friend has a better voice than me, and I'm not kidding. I can't hold a single note," assured Conal. "I'll leave the singing to you, Taliesin, but can you sing a happy song for Nessa? I think she'd have preferred that to a dirge."

Taliesin nodded. "Of course I will, Conal, though I'll have to tune Aoife first, to do the song justice."

Conal headed back to the Sett to see if there was any news on Cora. The sound of the merry ditty echoed through the woods behind him.

*****

"Is she really gone?" Maerlin asked.

"Aye, lass, she is," Cull replied.

They were sitting on one of the cots, in the guest rooms. Maerlin was still wrapped around Cull's waist, as if afraid to let go. They had been sitting quietly like that for quite some time. Neither of them had felt the need to speak until a moment ago.

"I miss her."

"We all do, lass. There'll be many who'll miss her. She was that kind of a woman. I always thought she had a sort of regal quality," Cull said with a smile. "Maerlin, I know it's hard to think about this after such a loss, but we need to put her death behind us. Do you understand? We can't let her death stop us from going on. She'd not have wanted that."

"I know," agreed Maerlin, though her heart was still heavy with loss.

238

"Maybe you'll want to stay here with Cora until she wakes. I can always go on ahead with Conal. We can pick you up again when we return," Cull suggested.

Maerlin was torn between her desire to see this quest through and her wish to stay with her injured friend "Can I think about it?"

"Yes, of course, though Vort says we'll need to travel tonight to the High Council. He wants us to go to *Broca* and speak with the Elders there."

"Have you told him everything?"

"No, lass, there's a whole lot in everything. Some of it, I don't even know."

"Is that wise?"

"I trust him," said Cull simply "He's a very clever man. Don't let the face paint and his fierce expression fool you into thinking he's just another stupid warrior, Maerlin. I'm sure that Nessa taught you that looks can be deceiving."

Maerlin smiled a soft, sad smile. "You bet. It was the first thing that she ever taught me, and one she hammered home whenever possible."

"Well, Vort's like that. I think before this adventure is over, we're going to need his help, maybe even tomorrow at the High Council meeting. I gather that not all the Brocians will be as happy to have us amongst them. They are a secretive people and not used to having strangers in their territory. I think we need to let the singer in on our little secret, too. We'll need his help almost as much as we need Vort's. If we're going to be successful at this Council meeting, we're going to need all the help we can get."

"Very well then, if you think it's for the best." Maerlin accepted his wisdom as she had Nessa's "I'll go with you. After that … we'll see where the goddess leads us."

"You've started speaking like a priestess already, Maerlin. Next thing I know, you'll be theeing and thouing all over the place," he teased. "Lord Cull, pass me thy plate, if thou wouldst be so kind," he mimicked with a grin. "Dost thou want one potato or two, Lord Cull?"

Maerlin giggled and slapped him playfully. "You won't catch me speaking like that. Not even Ceila is that bad ... well, not quite."

They both laughed, their troubles momentarily forgotten.

"Come on, lass. Let's go and look in on Cora and see whether she's improved," Cull suggested, his heart feeling lighter than it had all day.

Maerlin jumped to her feet, and her smile stayed as she took Cull's hand and led him from the room.

*****

Sometime later, Taliesin rose to leave. He covered his harp in her protective casing, before taking one last look at the pool.

"You sing the Old Tongue like a native, bard. That's unusual for a *Fear Ban*."

Taliesin turned to find a group of Brocians standing nearby. He wondered how long they had been there. He had not noticed their presence before, their clothing blended so well into the surrounding woodland. The speaker was an old man. He was grey and weathered by time, and yet he stood proudly and spoke with quiet confidence.

"Tell me, bard. How is it that you know our language so well?"

"I was raised in a small village on the Screaming Plains, close to the border with *Tir Pect*," Taliesin replied. "There was an old man who lived there, a Pect. He'd worked there for many years as a farmhand. When he wasn't working, he was a *Seanachai*. He was very gifted with the harp, and he had a great skill in storytelling. I spent much of my childhood sneaking out of an evening to listen to him weave magic with words and music. He taught me many stories and songs, and he took me away from my humdrum life into a place of magic and dragons, heroes and villains. It was he who taught me to play."

Taliesin caressed Aoife lightly, his calloused fingers feeling the grain of the age-old wood as he recollected "Just before he died, he called me into his hut. I could see that he was being called by Macha. Death was mere heartbeats away. Every breath was a battle. You could see it in his eyes." Taliesin looked to the old man for understanding.

The Brocian nodded.

Taliesin continued his story "The old *Seanachai* called me to his bedside, and much though I feared his imminent death, I sat down beside him. He asked me to bring him his harp. I'd never touched such an instrument before. I'd only ever practised on poor substitutes, by comparison. I did as he asked and placed in reverently into his gnarled hands. His whole face lit up with joy. He caressed the strings lightly, making sweet music without effort as his mind drifted between the worlds. All I could do was sit there and listen. I was hypnotised."

The memory brought fresh pain to Taliesin, and he wiped a tear from his cheek as he had done seven years earlier.

"After a while, the *Seanachai* stopped, and we sat in silence for a long time. He rested between this world and the Otherworld, and I was lost in the world of my own imagination. Then he called out to me. 'Geordie,' he said. That was my name back then. 'Geordie, will you grant me a dying man's wish?' My heart went into my throat. I'd never seen anyone die before. 'Yes, of course!' I replied 'What can I do?' The *Seanachai* smiled. It was like he could see things that no mortal could possibly see. He always had that quirky smile about him," Taliesin explained with a wry grin of remembrance.

"'Take care of Aoife for me, will you, Geordie? Don't ever let her get as old and rundown as I am,' he begged. My heart nearly burst when I realised what he was asking of me. I was too dumbstruck to reply, so he reached out and handed me his beautiful harp."

"She had been made by the *Seanachai*, during his time at the Bardic College in *Ard Pect*, and he loved her greatly. She was as beautiful as the day she was first tuned. I took the harp from him, and I swear to you, my hands and knees were shaking. I hadn't been so nervous since my first kiss!" Taliesin explained.

The Brocians smiled at his expression. His tale had touched all of them.

"'Play her for me, Geordie,' he asked 'Let me hear her sweet voice one more time.' Though I was all thumbs, I did my best to treat the harp with the respect she deserved. I played her, and the *Seanachai* closed his eyes and drifted off. I played for a long time, getting used to the feel of her. I guess time just slipped away. When I finally finished and looked up, I realised that the *Seanachai* had slipped away, too."

Taliesin paused, as his emotions threatened to overcome him, but the story demanded to be finished, so he wiped his eyes away and cleared his throat. "That night, I buried him, and it was the last time I ever tilled the earth. When I'd finished, I lifted up his harp and walked away from the farm. I've never returned."

"That's a powerful tale, bard," said the old Brocian, his eyes shining with sadness.

"I'm not really a bard." Taliesin admitted, needing to clear up any misunderstanding "I'm just a dreamer."

The Brocians stood silently, contemplating the confession as they would any important announcement. Finally, the old man spoke. His voice was clear and assured as he offered them his words of wisdom "This morning I sat here and I listened to a bard playing. He played one of the great epics, and he played it with great skill. The song lifted my soul and wrung at my heart, for there was a gift in the bard's fingers and in his voice." He paused and the others grunted in agreement. "Then, the bard told me a tale in tribute to his friend and mentor. It brought tears to my eyes and warmed my ageing bones. There was deep compassion in the telling. My ears, they know a bard when they hear one. My spirit, it knows a bard when it feels one," declared the old man. "They speak to me, so that I can tell the world. They tell me that I've been honoured and that I should return this honour where it's due. So I say to you, bard, you are most welcome here."

The old man looked around to the others and received their nods of agreement. The consensus had been given, and no one disagreed with his wisdom. Smiling softly at Taliesin, he turned and walked away, leading the Brocians back to their Sett. He left the harper contemplating his words.

*****

Cull called a meeting together. It was held in the room in which Cora lay sleeping, as Maerlin was reluctant to leave her side. He looked over at Conal and at the novices for a moment, while he prepared his thoughts. Finally, he turned to their host, Vort, and to the harper, Taliesin. "I've asked you all here for a reason. I think it's time to put you all in the picture, so that you know what you're getting into. I ... we, need your help, and so I think you deserve the truth ... the whole truth, before you make any decisions."

Conal's eyebrows rose with momentary concern, before he nodded in resignation.

"Firstly, I apologise for any deceit on our part. It was not our intention to deceive *Clann Na Broce,* far from it. We still hold faith to the Great Truce."

Vort opened his mouth, about to speak, but Cull raised a hand to hold off any interruption.

"Our disguises were not meant for you, but rather, they were meant to deceive Lord Boare and his minions. We have good reasons for this. As you said yourself, Vort, the boy's eyes are far too blue to be anything other than a *Fear Ban*. Well, you were right about that. What you don't know, however, is just who the lad is ..."

"Cull ..."

"No, lad, I think it's time we trusted these people. I pray to the Seven that my instincts are correct about them, but we have far more to lose by being silent, then we have to gain by speaking out."

The look on Conal's face showed his reservations, but he fell silent.

"Where was I? Ah, yes, the lad. Let me see, how can I put this?" Taking a deep breath, Cull finally blurted out the truth, keeping it plain and simple so as not to add to the confusion. "The lad here is Conal *MacDragan*, son of the last true High King and heir to the Dragon Clan."

Taliesin's jaw dropped in shock and even Vort looked surprised, though a twinkle glittered in his eye as he digested the information. Neither said a word as Cull continued "So, you see, we had very good reasons to hide behind the guise of *Na Teincheor*. Had he fallen into the hands of Lord Boare, the future of Dragania would be in peril. It is my belief, and that of the Order of Deanna also, that he is destined to become the next High King. Should we fail in this task, dark times will befall us all; *Fear Ban* and *Pect* alike."

"You tell an intriguing tale, Cull, and yet, for some strange reason I find myself believing it." Vort's eyes glittered with curiosity. "But, if he is the son of the *Dragan*, why are you bringing him here? The Plains of the Dragon are swarming with the conscripts of *Clann Na Torc* at the moment, and we even saw Dubhgall the Black in the Mage's Tower. Have you lost your mind?"

Cull grimaced, as Vort's words echoed his own thoughts on many an occasion. "We have come north for a reason, Vort. We have come to reclaim Conal's father's sword, the pig-sticker you know as *An Fiacail Dragan*. We think we know where it is hidden, and we must prevent it from falling into Lord Boare's hands."

"Cull, will you please stop calling the sword of the High Kings, a pig-sticker? It deserves some respect."

Cull ignored Conal's complaint. His gaze was locked on the Brocian's.

"You really know where *An Fiacail Dragan* is hidden? People believe it lost," Vort asked.

"There's only one way to know for sure, and that's to go and look, but as you say, the Plains of the Dragon are swarming with Boarites. We need to get beyond *Dun Dragan*. Can you help us, Vort?"

The Brocian's face fell as he considered the request. "I'm sorry, but it's not that easy, old man."

"Why not?"

"I can't make this decision. The War Banners have been raised, and *Clann Na Broce* are at war with the *Fear Ban*. The Great Truce brokered by *Luigheagh Dragan* is broken and my clansmen have donned their war paint. I have been elected War-leader of the *Broce*. I was the one who raised the War Banners, and petitioned the High Council for war. I cannot put aside my *Tri-crub* and war spear without the consent of the High Council. We will need to go and speak with them. We will leave tomorrow and head for the great city of Broca. There, you will get your decision, Cull."

Cull nodded grimly, before turning to the harper.

"...And what about you, Taliesin Larkstongue, will you come with us and help us? I'm sure that our case will be stronger if we have a bard along to speak for us."

"I'm not a bard," Taliesin protested, not for the first time. He fell silent for a few moments before continuing "However, if what you say is true, this adventure would make an epic ballad. I'd never forgive myself if I missed the chance to tell it. I'll do what I can to help."

Cull smiled and felt some of the weight of worry lifting off his shoulders. "Thank you. I hope you never live to regret your decision. Now, I think it's time for bed. We've a big day ahead of us."

*****

The rat crawled through the darkness, seeking out some safe refuge. She knew that she would soon be hunted, so she moved as quickly as her broken body would allow. She needed to find shelter, and soon, for others would smell her blood and begin their hunt. The rat found a hole within the wall and slipped inside.

Luck blessed the rat as the hole was empty. It was narrow and ended in a small alcove. Turning around within the tight space proved to be difficult, and it was a painful experience, but fear of attack gave her the strength of will she needed to persevere. Finally, safe in her hidey-hole, she hunkered down and assessed her injuries. The broken bones could not be fixed, leaving one of her front legs useless and her ribs cracked. The bleeding, however, was lessening now. The wound was beginning to clot. Carefully, lest she reopen the wounds, the rat licked herself clean. After a time, she drifted off. Her rest proved to be short-lived, however, for it was not long before they disturbed her.

Sniffing noisily, the first amongst them came, sensing the intruder within his territory. He was big and lean, a born pack-leader. He would have the pleasure of the kill, and he would feast on the choicest flesh, which was why he had ventured first into the narrow tunnel.

She waited, feigning death while her ears strained for the right moment. Timing was critical. Timing was life or death.

The big male moved closer, sniffing the air and tasting the trail of blood. Impatience was his enemy; that and his hunger. There was little fresh food to be had in his domain. It was a place of famine or feast, and his pack was starving. The fallen one lay as still as a carcass as he approached. The scent of blood filled the air and encouraged the pack-leader to act. Thinking the stranger dead, he hurried forward, eager to begin the feast. He would gorge himself on her tender flesh before dragging out the remains to his subordinates. His hunger made him careless. His jaws dribbled saliva in anticipation of the coming feast.

She held her breath and lay as still as death until the very last moment. Only then did the injured rat attack. As the leader's head brushed against her whiskered face, she opened her powerful jaws. His jugular was before her, exposed, and into this soft area she quickly sank her teeth.

He squealed in protest, the noise frightening the others who lurked in the darkness beyond. He writhed and scratched in desperation as his lifeblood burst free, but she did not release her hold. It wasn't long before his thrashings grew weaker and finally, he died.

The rat's carcass pressed down heavily upon her, and his thrashings had re-opened her wounds, making her feel queasy. She lay beneath him for a while, regaining her strength before crawling free of his weight. His corpse now blocked the passageway, but at least he stopped the others from attacking her while she slept. Sleep was what she needed now, to give her time to heal.

Hunkering down behind his cooling body, she closed her eyes and drifted off.

Chapter Twenty: The Broce Woods

Maerlin sat beside Cora, holding the unconscious girl's hand as she watched over her. She willed her friend to wake up. The Sett had long since fallen silent, as one by one the others had fallen asleep. Now, only Maerlin remained awake. She sat in silent vigil over her friend's sleeping body. Her eyes were heavy and threatened to close, her mind teetering on the cusp between consciousness and slumber while Maerlin strived to stay awake. It was a losing battle, however, and eventually her brain slipped into sleep.

Maerlin drifted through layers of mist, dark and light, floating up into the sky and looking down upon the Broce Woods. She called out in exhilaration, and her cry echoed around her. It was the cry of a merlin, like the one depicted on her mother's pendant. Looking down at herself, she was surprised to see the sharp, crisp wings of a bird of prey, the strong, sturdy tail. Testing her wings, she tried some aerial acrobatics, sliding into a dive and then curling off to skim the upper branches of the trees. Shrieking her joy, she climbed again and turned southwards towards the Plains of the Dragon.

She could see the Mage's Tower ahead, and Maerlin slowed to a more cautious speed as she came nearer. A huge raven was circling the dark parapet, a bird of ill omen. It was one of the Dark Angels of Macha, the goddess of war and death.

She remembered an earlier dream where Dubhgall had transformed himself into just such a bird, when fleeing the First Battle of the High Kings. Seeing the bird again, she veered away. Her sharp hawk-eyes surveyed the surrounding countryside. It was useless. There was no sign of Nessa. With a heavy heart, she knew that the healer had truly gone. She had needed to see it for herself, nevertheless, before acknowledging the painful truth.

Again, the hawk shrieked, but this time it held a note of pain and loss, rather than joy.

Maerlin slipped away, heading back to the woods and her sleeping body.

Waking with a jolt, Maerlin stifled a sob of mourning. Nessa's loss weighed her down. Gripping Cora's hand, she rested her head on the quilt. She needed to calm her beating heart and gather her wits together. Her mind was dull with grief and weariness ... and again she slipped away into the mists.

The mist swirled around her, and she found herself in darkness. Fear gripped her as she recognised the Mage's Tower. Struggling against the rising panic, she fought against her terror. Think of a white wall, she admonished herself. Do your exercises. Calm your mind.

After a few moments, her heart steadied. She sensed that she was alone. Dubhgall was not here. He might still be sailing on the breeze outside or he might have gone to report to Lord Boare.

Maerlin wondered why she had been drawn to the tower again, as she meandered around the chamber. Light, I need light, she told herself. "Spirit of fire, come to my aid. Come forth for me, bright Salamander."

Carefully this time, keeping a firm grip on the Elemental she summoned, she pictured a tiny flame sitting above her open palm. When she was satisfied with the image, she released her will to show the Elemental what she wanted. The Salamander eagerly obeyed, and the room filled with its soft glow.

Rats squealed at the sudden flare of light, running away from a hole, where they had been gathered. The pack sought hiding places within the farthest shadows.

Maerlin's flame flickered for a moment, her mind distracted by the sight of the rodents. She calmed herself, and the flame steadied. "Damn it! I hate rats!"

Maerlin walked to the door, seeking out any sign of Nessa. She could see nothing, save a small splattering of dried blood near the door. Closing her eyes, she reached out for her guardian. For a moment, she even thought that she sensed her nearby, but then the feeling was gone. Had she just imagined it? Could it be a memory of the passage of Nessa recently like the ripples on a pond after the falling of a stone? The ripples are not the stone, but they give testament of its passage on the surface of the water. Maerlin wondered if this was what ghosts really were.

"This is futile! Leave this place before he returns. You won't escape him so easily, next time. He'll be prepared for your minor cantrips, and he'll easily counter your spells. This is foolishness." The voice in her head

even sounded like Nessa's. Maerlin shuddered. She could even picture her mentor's face, though it seemed to blur and fade, as memories often do. She could hear Nessa berating her for her stupidity, and she silently thanked the dead priestess for her wisdom. Nessa must still be watching over her from the Otherworld, guiding her in times of danger. Whether it was the spirit of her dead guardian, or her own fickle subconscious, it brought Maerlin back to reality. Releasing the Salamander, Maerlin sought out her body, fleeing the tower.

*****

Again, her dream-self wandered through the fog.

"Maerlin, what's happening?" a voice urged from the mists. It was a voice that Maerlin recognised.

"Ceila, is that you?" Maerlin asked in surprise.

"Hush, now. Thou mustn't make too much noise! Others may hear thee."

"Sorry, Ceila, you surprised me."

"What's happening, Maerlin?"

Maerlin trembled, unable to speak of Nessa's death. She didn't want to hurt Ceila. Nessa had been the High Priestess's mentor, too. They were obviously close.

"It's Nessa. She's dead, isn't she?"

"How did you know that?"

"I'm a Dream-catcher, Maerlin. I see things. I haven't time to explain. What about the others?"

"Cora sleeps and she won't wake up!" Maerlin blurted.

"Hush child! Thou needeth to be strong! Trust in the will of the goddess."

"Why would Deanna take them from me?" Maerlin protested. "It isn't fair!"

"Fair ... what's fair got to do with it?" Ceila admonished. "Thou cannot see the bigger picture, only fragments of the whole. Who art thou to judge her wisdom? Later, thou might see things differently, once thou hast seen more."

Maerlin was silent, her grief making her sullen. "It's my fault entirely, I got them into this. I wanted to go with Conal on his adventure. I dragged them both into this."

"Don't say that!" Ceila scolded. "Thou art being foolish, child."

"No! It's my fault. I hate myself, and I hate this quest. I'm sick of it. I'll let Cull and Conal go on, and I'll wait for Cora to wake up. Then, we'll return to the Holy Isle. Or maybe I should just go back to High Peaks instead and live like a hermit in one of the caves on the Mountain of the Gods."

"NO!" the sharp command came from the mist. "Thou MUST continue with thy quest."

"I've had enough! I've put enough people in danger already. What use am I?"

"The goddess chose thee, and thou must see this through," Ceila demanded, getting more agitated. "If thou leaveth the quest, it might kill them all. Please I beg thee, stay with them, Maerlin."

Maerlin was unsure, but she could hear the panic in the High Priestess's voice. "I don't know," she said after a few moments of silence.

"Promise me thou wilt do this, Maerlin."

"I'll think about it. That's all I can promise."

"I will pray for thee, then. Go with Deanna ..."

"Ceila?"

No reply came from the mists.

"Ceila!" she repeated with more urgency. The mists stayed as quiet as a morgue. "Damn it!"

*****

250

Maerlin awoke, gritty-eyed and disoriented. Sitting still, she collected her thoughts and remembered her dreams as she had been taught during Divination lessons on the Holy Isle. She meditated on the dreams and tried to fathom out their mysteries. Something didn't make sense, she realised, but she couldn't grasp what it was. Just as she was getting some clarity from her dreams, her concentration was broken by the sound of the door opening. Cull walked in, accompanied by Orla, and the thought was gone.

"No change?" Cull asked, looking down at Cora.

"What ... oh no, she hasn't stirred." Maerlin rubbed her throbbing head.

Cull came over and patted her on the shoulder. "It'll be all right, Maerlin. She'll pull through," he assured, though a flicker of concern showed in his eyes.

"I must feed the Sea-girl, Cora," explained Orla in halting *Sassenaucht*. "There's more stew by the fire, Little Hawk," she added, pointing to the large common room and its central hearth.

Maerlin blinked and looked sharply at the Brocian woman. "What did you just say?"

"I said I must feed your friend. There's some for you also, in the pot by the hearth."

"No. What did you just call me?" Maerlin demanded, agitated now.

Orla looked confused. "I'm sorry. Did I say something wrong? Vort told me that you were called, *An Maerlin*. That's 'little hawk or little thief in Pectish. Did he get your name wrong?"

"No," murmured Maerlin, "I'm sorry, that's my name. It's just ... oh never mind."

Memories of her parents calling her Little Hawk came flooded back to Maerlin, bringing with it a great wave of loneliness. As emotion threatened to overcome her, Maerlin dashed from the room, leaving the others to look up at her, as she hurried outside.

Tears had started to run down her cheeks before she got through the outer door. She rushed blindly across the valley. Staggering through the woods,

251

she cried like she had never cried before. For the first time since leaving her village, she was feeling homesick. She missed her father's quiet assurance and comforting silence. She realised just how much she missed his calm manner within her life. Sitting on the stump of a fallen tree, she hugged herself and cried until her weeping subsided into sniffles. When her tears ran dry, she just sat, head in hands, lost in her own thoughts.

*****

"Here. I've brought you some breakfast ... or is it supper?" Conal asked, holding a bowl of steaming stew out to Maerlin.

"I'm not hungry," she murmured as she tried to fight of her headache. She felt him sit down beside her, but kept her face hidden within her hands.

"You'll be no use to anyone if you starve yourself to death, Maerl," Conal said. For once, his voice wasn't confrontational. "Here ... try a bit of it, at least. It's actually quite tasty."

"What's in it?" Maerlin murmured, still not looking up.

"I don't know ... it's a stew. I was afraid to ask."

Maerlin looked up at Conal, but she couldn't be roused from her sombre mood. "I'm not hungry."

"You'll need your strength, Maerlin. It's a long haul to the Brocian city."

"I'm not going. I don't belong here. I shouldn't have come in the first place. It was stupid of me, and now I've got Nessa killed and maybe Cora too." Tears welled up in her eyes again.

Conal placed a hand tentatively on her shoulder. "Maerlin, that's nonsense," he said softly. "Listen, you've been a great help on this journey. We'd have been lost without you. Don't give up on us now, Maerlin, please. We've lost so much already. I think Ceila was right when she said we needed you. You belong on this quest."

"Why ... what've I done? All I do is mess things up. What is it ... do you need someone to cook and clean for you?"

Conal glared at her. "The choice is yours, Maerlin. We'll be leaving shortly." Placing the bowl of stew at her feet, he marched off, muttering under his breath.

Maerlin regretted her comments almost immediately, but it was too late to take them back. He had tried to comfort her, and she had behaved like a spoilt brat. She sat there for a long time, feeling guilty and trying to decide what to do.

*****

The others were ready and waiting below Vort's Sett. A group of Brocians stood watching. Cull looked around at the twenty or so warriors waiting to escort them to *Broca*.

"Where are your own horses, Vort?" There were only three horses and the camel in the clearing.

"Horses are of no use in these woods," Vort explained. "Don't worry. We'll take it slow, so that you can keep up."

"But I thought you rode? What happened to all those horses you took from the fort?" Cull asked.

"They make an excellent stew. The meat is very lean and tasty, but it's too tough for a good roast."

"You mean we've been eating horse-meat!"

"Yes ... why? Is there something wrong?" Vort asked, perhaps worried that he had broken some taboo of the *Fear Ban* and failed in his duties as a host.

"No, it was lovely. It's just ... well ... we aren't used to eating horses, that's all," Cull explained. He decided that some diplomacy was called for and added "Thank your wife for her hospitality and for looking after Cora."

"I will," promised Vort, pleased to see that his guests were happy.

Cull looked around the woods, hoping to see Maerlin, but the girl did not show. "It looks like we're down to three. We'd better get a move on."

Vort walked over and spoke to one of the Brocians gathered outside the Sett. It was the old man, who had spoken to Taliesin by the waterfall. They embraced warmly and spoke quietly for a few moments. Then, the old Brocian handed Vort a rolled-up piece of cloth.

Vort slipped it reverently into his pouch before taking up his position at the head of the Brocians. He looked towards Cull for confirmation to proceed.

Cull took one last look around the clearing, hoping that Maerlin would appear. When there was no sign of her, he reluctantly nodded to Vort. "Let's go," he said with a degree of sadness.

Vort made a gesture and three of the Brocians set off to scout ahead. Vort allowed a few moments to pass, giving his scouts ample time to break a trail before setting off. The rest of the warriors followed in single file, setting a ground-eating pace.

"Hang on!" a shout came from the hilltop. "Wait for me!"

"Maerlin." Conal smiled with relief.

Maerlin ran down the hill towards them, skirt flying, as she sprinted through the trees. "Hang on, I'm coming with you."

Luckily, Cull had packed her gear, just in case. "You left that a bit close. I thought we'd have to leave without you."

"Sorry everyone, I needed some time to think," she replied as she mounted her horse.

Vort had paused at the edge of the clearing and he smiled over at her.

"Lead on, Vort," Cull confirmed.

*****

They rode into the dusk and the light faded. Vort ordered the out-runners to use torches to guide their way. These special torches contained the same eerie, glowing fungi that the Brocians used in their homes. Cull reasoned that this made sense when you lived in a forest. Fire was always a threat.

The leaves had already started to fall, and autumn was approaching fast, this far north. Coolness descended on the woods as they rode along.

Maerlin felt the chill and pulled her cloak more tightly about her body. Her head still ached, and she could feel cramping in her guts. By now, she knew the warning signs, but she had none of Nessa's herbs left to ease the pain. It would only get worse over the coming days.

They rode through the night at a steady trot. They only stopped for long enough to rest the animals. The Brocians showed no signs of weariness as they ran. They maintained a steady, mile-eating jog.

As the sun was beginning to lighten the woods, Vort halted. "We must go on foot from here. Our scouts will look after your mounts."

"How far is it?" Cull asked, looking around the dense woodland. The trees here were ancient. Immense beech, oak, and ash dominated the woods with the occasional holly and sycamore interspersing and fighting for light. He doubted that this part of the wood had seen an axe in centuries.

"It's only a couple of miles farther on," Vort encouraged. "If we run, we'll be there before the Council breaks up for the dawn. I've sent a runner ahead to tell them of our approach."

"Why can't we bring the horses?" Conal asked.

"You'll see," assured Vort. "Can you run?"

"We'll manage," confirmed Cull. He was glad that he had recently put Maerlin and Conal through their rigorous training regime.

They set off; bringing only what they could easily carry. The rest of their belongings were left with the mounts. At first, the pace was easy enough and the ground flat, but soon they came to a gradient, which got steeper by the moment. Taliesin fell farther and farther behind, clearly unfit for such exertion. He was further hampered by the weight and bulk of the harp, Aoife. He had adamantly refused to leave it behind. Its case constantly snagged on undergrowth and hampered his movements.

"Where is he taking us?" Taliesin asked between gasps.

"I don't know," wheezed Conal. For all his recent training, he was only slighter better off. "I think they've hidden a mountain in these woods that we didn't know about."

Vort led them over the top of the hill and stopped, looking only slightly flushed after his uphill jog.

Maerlin, being the fleetest of the companions, was the first to join the Brocians. She stared in amazement at the vista before her. "Wow, that's awesome!"

A few feet in front of them hung a narrow rope bridge. It swayed gently in the breeze, and spanned across a large ravine. The bridge was intricately made and over a hundred feet in length. It led across the emptiness to another wooded hill. On the far side of the ravine, Maerlin could see smoke rising above the treetops. They had reached their destination.

"Welcome to the ancient city of *Broca*," Vort declared, as Cull and Conal crested the hill. "The ancestral home of *Clann Na Broce*."

Taliesin clambered up the last few feet on hands and knees, panting heavily. He collapsed on the ground and crawled forward to look over the edge. Looking down into the ravine, the harper groaned loudly. "I'll take the other way across!" Taliesin turned and quickly retreated away from the edge.

"There's only one entrance into the city, bard. Is that a problem?" Vort asked.

Taliesin paled and said nothing.

Maerlin skipped lightly onto the swaying construction. "Look at that view!"

Cull was watching the bard, who had gone as white as a sheet. "What's up, Taliesin?"

"Is that thing safe?" Taliesin looked nervously at Maerlin, who was skipping along the bridge like a mountain goat.

"Of course it is," assured Vort, before pointing out the river below to Maerlin. "This is where the River Man begins its journey to the sea."

"How far down is it?" she asked excitedly, looking through the slats of the bridge to the water below.

"About two hundred spans," said Vort. "The city's builders picked this location for its defensibility. It's the only city in Dragania that has never been ransacked. Only once has the city been under siege, and that attack failed. When the rope bridge was cut, the attackers fell to their deaths on the rocks below. When they realised that they were in for a long and protracted siege, they withdrew, though not without heavy losses. That was before the signing of the Great Truce."

"I can't go over that!" Taliesin announced emphatically. "Sorry, Cull, but I'm suddenly not feeling very well."

"Are you scared of heights, Taliesin?" Cull asked.

"A little," Taliesin admitted. "Normally, it's not that bad, but that …" Taliesin pointed with horror at the rope bridge "...that's a nightmare come to life. I can't cross that! My legs are like jelly just looking at it."

"Don't worry, Taliesin," Vort assured. "We can help you across."

"Oh no, I'll be fine, right here, thank you very much! Maybe I'd better just go back and check on Gertie," Taliesin suggested, rising to his feet and turning to leave.

"Don't be so pathetic, Taliesin," Maerlin teased, who by now was happily swinging on the ropes.

"Stay out of this, Maerlin," Cull warned.

"Look ... I can't!" Taliesin edged farther away from the edge.

"I'm sorry, my friend, but I must insist. You must go over the bridge. The High Council will want to speak to you all." Vort was clearly uncomfortable with the predicament.

"But you were going to leave Maerlin behind at your Sett?" Taliesin pointed out.

Vort looked down, decidedly uncomfortable. "Erm, no actually I wasn't. My men were watching over her the whole time. If she had not come willingly, she would have been brought."

257

"What?" Maerlin snapped, her voice rising up an octave.

"Please! I've tried to be civilised about this, but my hands are tied. I have been given strict orders, which I intend to obey. I was instructed to kill all trespassers; but at my own discretion, I could capture them for questioning. I decided that in your case, I would make such an exception. I believe that you deserve a fair hearing, and I have taken a great risk in bringing you here. It is here that your fate will be decided."

"You can't be serious!" Cull growled angrily as the Brocian warriors reached for their weapons. "What about your promise of hospitality?"

"Stop!" Vort signalled his men away. "That, I hope, will not be necessary."

Turning to Cull, he looked earnestly at him as he tried to explain "It's not my intention to harm you, or your companions, Cull. You should know that. Please, I beg you, do not make too much out of this small matter."

"Too much!" Maerlin exclaimed.

Cull looked at the Brocian for a moment and then he sighed, knowing that an argument would get them nowhere. "I trusted you!"

Vort felt the sting of accusation within that simple statement. "I have not broken my vow of hospitality, nor will I. I will speak at the meeting and seek the best possible conclusion," Vort assured. "But I must insist on all of you being present. The bard, in particular, will be an asset to you. My father spoke to him yesterday and it seems Taliesin is fluent in the Old Tongue."

"I wouldn't go that far!" Taliesin protested, now realising the identity of the old Brocian.

Vort ignored the comment and continued "You'll need someone to translate the discussion for you, as I'll be there as a witness. I won't be allowed to speak to you during the hearing."

"So this is going to be a trial, then?" Cull asked, only now realising the full meaning of the Council meeting.

Vort winced at the word trial, which was very close to the truth, and he realised how this could be perceived. "Please, I beg you, trust me in this. I will do my best to help you."

Conal had been listening to the discussion, one hand on his sword, ready to defend himself. "I don't like this one bit!"

"Neither do I …" Cull murmured "… but it doesn't look like we've a choice."

"The bard will be seen as a good sign," Vort assured them. "Having him speaking on your behalf will help your case. Bards are well respected for the truth they speak."

"But I'm not a bard! I keep telling you that. Why doesn't anybody listen to me?"

Cull felt like throwing the obstinate singer into the ravine. Their lives were in his hands. A minor technicality such as his bardic status was of little concern to Cull. He was more worried about them all staying alive.

"My father spoke to you of that, Taliesin. He has vouched for you, but it shows the honour of your words when you speak the truth. I will inform the High Council of my father's blessing when I present his war banner. I carry his authority as one of the Elders." Vort placed a hand on the rolled up cloth that he had been given before they left.

"Be that as it may, I'm not crossing that bridge," Taliesin insisted stubbornly.

"We could carry you over," offered Vort in an effort to find a peaceful solution.

"Over my dead body," retorted Taliesin hotly.

"I'm sure that won't be necessary, though perhaps unconscious might be easier for you. Which would you prefer?" Vort asked with a grim look on his face.

Cull looked from one to the other. Quickly, he stepped between them.

"Taliesin, can I have a word?" he asked, placing his hand on the gangly singer's shoulder. Cull turned him away from the ravine.

"Don't try and talk me into going across that bridge, Cull. I won't do it."

"I wouldn't dream of it," assured Cull, calmly. His hand slipped across the other man's shoulder. "I can see that it'd be a complete waste of time."

"Really?"

"Really," assured Cull. He clamped his fingers firmly into the base of Taliesin's neck. As the bard flinched and tried to struggle free, Cull squeezed the nerve-endings more firmly, exerted further pressure.

Taliesin slumped, with Cull's hand still clasped onto his neck. His hand followed the taller man down, until the harper hit the ground, already unconscious.

"What're you doing, Cull?" Maerlin demanded, rushing over to Taliesin's side. "You've killed him!"

Cull frowned. "Did Nessa teach you nothing about healing, lass?" he demanded. "Why is it that every time you see someone lying on the ground, you accuse me of murder? He's unconscious, for crying out loud! I squeezed on the right pressure point, that's all."

"Awesome!" Conal exclaimed, his eyes wide with excitement. "Can you teach me that?"

"Conal!" Maerlin glared at him.

"What … I was only asking."

Cull turned to Vort. "I think he'll be safe to carry over now."

Vort nodded at the older man, a look of relief on his face. "Thank you, Cull."

"Yeah, right," Cull shrugged and stomped onto the bridge. "Let's just get this over with, shall we?"

Chapter Twenty-One: The Brocian High Council

The rat slept and healed a little, before the pack returned.

She had woken earlier, hearing their squeals of fright and wondered at the cause of the disturbance. Silence had resumed, and she had slipped back into slumber.

Now, she could hear them again, but not this time in fright. They were gnawing at the hindquarters of the big male. Hunger had driven them back to the carcass, and they were slowly eating their way through it. She waited in the darkness, knowing that this was inevitable. It was as sure as the sun rising and setting. She was old, very old in rat years, old enough and wise enough to know such things.

The carcass before her started to shift as the rats pulled it out of the hole and feasted upon their deceased leader. She let them eat, hoping that they would have their fill and leave her alone. She needed more time to heal. She was not yet ready to face the world.

The rat pack feasted, and for a while the injured stranger was left in peace. She slept lightly, waiting for their return.

It was a day later, maybe longer. It was hard to judge time in the perpetual darkness, more so when you were delirious with blood loss and pain. All that she knew was that some time had passed and she had slept some more, before she heard the tentative scrapings of another rat at the entrance to her hole. They had come back. The hunger of the pack had returned.

The newcomer was still too weak to fight off a hungry pack, but she braced herself and waited for the first rat to squeeze through the hole. They would want to know whether she had survived the recent confrontation. They would want to know if there were easy pickings within the hole.

It was another male. She could smell his rank, musky scent. His battle-scarred nose, inched forward into the hole. He was not as eager as his predecessor. This one was more cautious. This one may yet live to fight another day. He came slowly within lunging range. Timing it perfectly, she lunged forward, screeching loudly as she snapped her jaws before his twitching whiskers. It cost a great deal of effort to make the lunge, but the cautious one quickly retreated in fright.

The rat pack abandoned their hope of a second, easy meal. She had killed their leader and was still able to fend off another attack. The rats retreated, and waited, with all the patience of their race. Eventually, the injured rat would need to leave the safety of the hole. There was no food or water within. She would have to come out, or die. They could wait for the meal to come to them, where they could attack it in numbers.

*****

Cull stomped angrily across the swaying bridge. The others hurried to catch up. When he reached the far side, something caught his eye, and he stopped and waited for Vort. "What, by the Nine Hells, is the meaning of that?" he demanded, pointing at the offending articles.

"That's magic, or so I've been told," Vort replied with evident disgust. "I don't understand how such things work, but I'm told that it's a very powerful spell."

"Sweet Deanna!" Maerlin exclaimed when she saw the objects.

Spread out, at ten pace intervals all along the ridge, stout poles had been stuck into the ground. Each of these spears had been decorated with the decapitated head of a Boarite soldier. The air buzzed with flies as the pale and bloodied heads gazed sightlessly across the river, tongues hanging from limp lips, forever silent.

"That's horrible!" Maerlin shuddered in revulsion, yet her eyes refused to look away from the macabre scene.

"It's bleeding obscene, that's what it is!" Cull growled. "Is that really necessary?"

"You'd have to ask Dorcha about that. I know little about magic," Vort replied with a scowl. "Praise Cernunnos for granting me the simple skills of a hunter and warrior."

"Why are they there?" Maerlin demanded. Such barbaric acts did not compare with her teachings of magic on the Holy Isle.

"From what I can gather, and I stress my ignorance in this matter, they create some kind of magical barrier through which Dubhgall the Black cannot probe. He's known to have power over men's dreams. These 'trophies' act like a screen. They stop him roaming through the city causing trouble in men's minds," Vort explained. "I cannot be sure that it works, but our High-shaman swears by them."

Cull ground his teeth in anger. It confirmed his suspicion of all things magical. "It ain't bleedin' right, whether it works or not! That's no way to treat the dead," he grumbled, stalking past the decapitated heads.

Vort glared darkly at the heads for a moment, before replying "I totally agree. It would be very hard for me to feast in the Hall of Heroes, without my head."

*****

"He's waking up," Conal hissed.

"It's about bloody time, too!" Cull said with relief. "If I'd have known he was gonna sleep this long, I'd have punched his lights out instead. At least that way, I'd have got some satisfaction out of it."

"Well, it's your own fault," reminded Maerlin, primly.

"Mmm?" Taliesin murmured, slowly waking.

"According to Vort, it'd be good to have Taliesin speak on our behalf, so he better get his wits together. From what you've managed to translate, Maerlin, this isn't going too well."

They had been sitting in the vast amphitheatre, deep underground, for the past bell or more. The High Council, a group of thirteen Brocian Elders, sat upon a raised plinth before them. The other Brocians sat in rising rows of benches, listening intently to the various speakers.

All of them spoke in the Old Tongue, the traditional language used daily by the Brocians. This meant that Maerlin was forced to translate, as best she could, to Cull and Conal. She was barely managing to keep track of the conversation as the debate was heated and the dialect confusing. To make matters worse, although she understood a lot of the words used, the phraseology left her confused, and therefore, unwilling to commit to translating its possible meaning. "A lot of this doesn't make any sense to me," she kept saying again and again as she tried to translate.

Certain things were obvious, however. One of the speakers, an ageing fellow, his face hidden in a great, black cloak, spoke with such venom in his voice that it left no one in any doubt of his opinion.

Another mild-mannered Brocian was gesticulating in such a manner as to express the need for reason and calm.

The last of the speakers to rise, and the one still speaking, was Vort.

"Wake up, damn it!" Cull demanded, elbowing the harper sharply in the ribs. "We need you."

"What! What?" Taliesin spluttered. "Where are we?"

"We're in the High Council meeting," Maerlin explained, helping Taliesin to sit up so he could look about.

"How did I get here?" Taliesin demanded as he blinked with surprise.

"Don't ask!" Cull growled. "Stop asking stupid questions and listen to what they're saying. We need to know what's happening."

"Who's rattled your cage?" Taliesin retorted, perplexed by Cull's angry outbursts.

"Just do it, will ya?"

Taliesin frowned, making the most of his silent expression of dissatisfaction, before turning his attention to the speaker.

"Well?" Cull persisted, only a few moments later.

"Give me a chance, Cull. I'm just getting the hang of their dialect. I use Pectish for songs. I'm hardly fluent in the Old Tongue, you know! In songs, you remember a phrase and repeat it. This isn't the same thing at all."

"But what are they talking about?" Cull's frustration was coming to the surface.

"They're talking about the *Fear Ban*, which I assume is us, though it could be the Boarites. It's a loose term, which generally refers to all the foreigners who invaded the Pectish kingdom. It refers to their pale skin and blonde hair."

"But we've lived here for generations," Conal objected.

"It seems the Pects have long memories, Conal, and they know how to hold a grudge," commented Taliesin dryly. "They still view Dragania as part of *Tir Pect*. The Pects would be considered cousins, as would the other southern Pectish Clans, such as the mountain people of Eagles Reach and the traveller families of *Clann Na Teincheor*."

"Aren't the mountain people *Fear Ban*?" Maerlin asked. "I was the only dark-skinned person in my whole village … apart from my mother."

"You're from High Peaks, Maerlin, which is on the southern peak of the Mountain of the Gods. The northern half, which is closer to these woods, is the territory of *Clann Na Seabhac*; the Hawk People. That's why it's called Eagles Reach," Taliesin explained. "They live in relative peace there, as few venture that far up the mountain."

"Never mind the geography lesson, Taliesin. What are they saying?" Cull demanded.

"From what I can make out, some of the Brocians want us to be sacrificed to Cernunnos. They feel that the god of the hunt would look favourably upon their war with *Clann Na Torc*, if such a sacrifice was made," Taliesin translated. "Vort is suggesting another way. He is saying that *Clann Na Dragan* has always been fair in its dealing with *Clann Na Broce*. He's pointing out that they have never broken the Great Truce. He is saying something about aiding in the search for *An Fiacail Dragan*."

"Excellent, Taliesin," Cull encouraged. "Keep going. You're doing grand."

"They're asking him something about his father, something about his duty to the banner? Oh, I think I understand it now. They're saying his duty is to war. He petitioned the High Council to go to war, only a few weeks ago. He demanded that they raise their war banners against the *Fear Ban*, and they're asking him to make his mind up. Does he want war or peace?"

"But it was the Boarites who were cutting down the woods, not us," Maerlin protested, remembering her dream.

"Some of them can't see a difference between us. They say that you've disguised yourselves as Pects, but you are *Fear Ban*. This duplicity isn't helping them to trust us."

"I didn't disguise myself as anything, apart from a few clothes," Maerlin objected hotly. "I've spent my whole life looking like this, and I've been getting stick about it ever since I was born."

"That may be so, but you must remember something, Maerlin. Much though you have the features of a Pect, you speak with the tongue of a foreigner. You speak *Sassenaucht*, and you consort with the 'Invaders' ... with the *Fear Ban*," explained Taliesin, though he knew she wouldn't understand. He was having trouble with it, himself.

"Can we get back to the debate?" Cull asked.

"Sorry," murmured Taliesin and returned to his translation. "Vort is speaking of the damage done to the woodlands of his Sett by *Clann Na Torc;* that's the Boarites. He's telling them that we share a common enemy. That we, too, are at war with Lord Boare and his Dark Mage."

"He's got that bit right," Conal growled, sitting tensely on the edge of his seat. "That festering weasel killed my father, decimated my Clan, and is trying to steal my throne."

"I'm not sure that they'd agree with your claim to the High Kingship of Dragania, Conal," Taliesin ventured, delicately broaching the subject. "As far as they're concerned, your father and his fore-fathers before him were all a bunch of usurper tyrants. They stole the crown from its rightful owner, the High King of the Pects. Technically, they stole it from the Boarites who in turn stole it from the Pects, but those are mere semantics. To them, the clans of the *Fear Ban* are all the same. They're nothing more than Reaver pirates who stole half of the kingdom of *Tir Pect* and made it their own."

"But that's ridiculous!"

"Shut up, Conal! Now isn't the time to get into politics. I want to know what they're saying."

Conal gave Cull a dirty look and sat back sullenly.

"And don't start pouting either. You look awfully silly when you do that," Cull instructed, though he hadn't even bothered to look round at Conal.

Maerlin giggled and received a nasty glare from the pouting prince.

Taliesin grinned at the two youngsters, before Cull again demanded him to translate.

"Vort is suggesting that it could be beneficial for *Clann Na Broce* to look beyond their own borders … to seek allies," Taliesin explained.

The crowd broke into angry heckling. Clearly, this had not gone down too well with some in the chamber.

Vort held up his hands for silence, his face earnest.

"He's saying something about their history, about another time when they marched out of these woods to make war on the men of *Clann Na Torc*."

The heckling grew louder. Individuals within the crowd were calling on him to leave.

Vort's face remained calm, though his eyes turned to flint. He laid his father's banner gently aside and drew forth his *Tri-crub* daggers. These he held up high, and the crowd fell silent.

Only then did he speak, but his tone was no longer conciliatory. His manner had changed, clearly some etiquette had been broken and some insult made.

"He's calling for a Blood-truth, whatever that is?" Taliesin reported. "He's saying that as the *Broce Mor,* he has a right to be heard. I presume that means that he's their elected champion, their War-Leader. He is saying that they either follow his leadership or seek another in his place. He is demanding the right of a Blood-truth." Taliesin apologised. "I'm sorry, Cull. This has me lost."

"Don't worry, Taliesin. You're doing better than the rest of us."

Cull was getting worried. This 'Blood-truth' didn't sound good. He had heard of similar ideas before, and it didn't bode well.

Vort had, with dramatic ceremony, ripped off his tunic, leaving him dressed only in his grey kilt. He was calling something out as he marched angrily around the arena.

"What's he saying?"

"He's demanding that someone come and speak the truth to him," Taliesin advised. He, too, sensed that things were about to turn nasty.

The crowd had fallen silent, but now they began to shout loudly. Fists were raised, but none stepped forward to meet his challenge.

Again Vort called out, his face livid as he raised both of his *Tri-crub* into the air. As Cull and the others watched in horrid fascination, Vort slowly drew the lethal three-tined daggers across his own chest. Six long gashes wept blood as he bellowed his challenge to the assembly.

A loud war cry answered him from the upper chamber, and the crowd parted to reveal the challenging warrior.

He was a huge bear-like man with a long, black beard and bristly hair. He stood nearly as tall as Taliesin, though he was at least twice as wide. Thick cords of muscles bulged as he strutted forward to take up the challenge. He ripped off his tunic and cast it aside in a flourish as he stomped down the steps to the arena.

"Bolcha! Bolcha!" Men within the crowd chanted. Others took up Vort's name and shouted support for the smaller warrior.

The chamber shook as the two warriors circled each other warily.

They were already taking tentative mock-lunges at each other, when one of the High Councillors stood and raised his arms for silence. The shouting subsided to a murmur as the crowd submitted to the Elder's authority. "*Vort Na Broce* of the Southern Dell Sett, it is your right as War-leader of the *Broce* to call upon this Council for a Blood-truth. Is that your wish?" Taliesin translated to the others.

Vort glared around the chamber before raising his voice and answering. "I'll not stand by and have my judgement questioned. It was I who spoke to this Council of the need for war against the *Fear Ban*. It was I who raised the war banners against *Clann Na Torc* because my own Sett was under the greatest threat. It was the High Council's wish that I lead this war and now some question my ability. Let the truth be told in blood!" Taliesin repeated for the others, the look on his face a mask of concern.

The High councillor nodded in agreement and turned to the large warrior, speaking loudly, for all to hear.

"What's he saying, Tal?"

"He said, *'Bolcha Na Broce* of the Westward Dell Sett, do you wish to challenge the War-leader's wisdom? Do you wish to lead *Clann Na Broce* to war?' This doesn't sound good."

"But he's huge. He'll massacre Vort," Maerlin objected. "We have to stop this."

"Stay out of this, lass," warned Cull. "I suggest you pray to your goddess for some divine intervention, but I'm telling you, stay out of it. I don't think they'd want us to interfere."

"He's right, Maerlin," Taliesin confirmed. "The Pects consider such ceremonies sacred. They'd kill us for interrupting."

By this time the crowd had begun to cheer again. Bolcha had taken up the challenge.

The two men stepped warily around the central area, occasionally taking short lunges at each other, while the crowd worked themselves into a state of frenzy.

*****

Vort drew forth a little of his pent-up anger, letting it build inside him as he watched Bolcha's eyes. They had fought before, and they knew each other's strengths and weaknesses. However, this was a Blood-truth and not a sporting competition. Warriors had died from the wounds they received during a Blood-truth.

As he circled, Vort gripped his daggers lightly. They had been forged specifically for him and fitted snugly into his palms. He assessed his opponent as he waited for the fight to begin in earnest. Bolcha was a good fighter. He was strong and confident, and if he was allowed to use his superior strength, he would win. Vort would need to stay out of his reach. His only hope was his speed and dexterity.

Seeing an opening, Vort darted forward and slashed one of his daggers at his opponent's belly. Bolcha's dagger came down to meet the thrust and the two blades rang out. Bolcha's other *Tri-crub* thrust forward; his longer reach threatening to stab Vort in the neck.

Vort parried the thrust with his left-hand blade, deflecting the blow. The talon-like daggers locked together and Vort fought to dislodge his blades. A test of will ensued as they strained for dominance.

Vort's muscles strained as he struggled against Bolcha's superior upper body strength, but he could not relax his hold for a moment. If he did so, he would lose his daggers and then his life. He bared his teeth and locked eyes on his opponent.

Bolcha's sneering face looked down at him as he exerted greater and greater pressure on the entangled blades. Vort knew that he was losing. He needed to find a way out of this test of strengths. Swinging his foot, he aimed a kick at the other man's groin.

Bolcha twisted, and the blow landed harmlessly on his thigh, but it gave Vort the chance he needed. Keeping his bare foot on the other man's thigh, he vaulted up and over his opponent, and his blades slipped free.

The crowd cheered wildly as Bolcha spun around and charged at Vort.

Vort was turning to face his opponent and was caught by surprise at the speed of the attack, but managed to roll free of the wild lunge. The two men circled again, each testing the other's defences with small slashes or thrusts.

*****

Maerlin's head throbbed badly. The headache had been troubling her over the past few days, and the heat and noise of the chamber was making her feel nauseous. Her hair tingled as she watched the fight, sensing magic in the air. Surprised and a little curious, she tried to identify the source of the magic. Weary and stressed, she tried to calm her mind, but the fight kept interfering with her concentration.

270

*****

Vort's temper was coming close to boiling point, giving him the strength he would need to defeat the bigger opponent. He growled at Bolcha and lashed out with his daggers. The blades clashed and created sparks as steel met steel. The glare in Bolcha's arrogant eyes only fed fuel to his anger. Bolcha was already convinced of victory, though no blood had yet been spilled. The big warrior was a renowned bully and had long desired the title of warlord of the Clan. He had been the first to back Vort's motion for war, but had been disappointed when Vort had chosen others to be his captains. Vort had seen the glow of excitement on Bolcha's face as he beheaded his victims with slow deliberation. Vort had been sickened that day, at the gruesome task they had been set for the warriors by the High-shaman, Dorcha, but it was clear that Bolcha relished the task. He was a cruel and mean-hearted man.

That was why Vort had chosen others to be his captains. Bolcha's warriors followed his leadership through fear rather than respect and trust.

Channelling his anger, Vort attacked, forcing the bigger man backwards as his *Tri-crub* rained down in a flurry of over-arm blows. Vort fed his anger into the attacks, releasing some of the restraints that bound his hidden nature. He felt light-headed as he slipped further into the combat. He danced as he fought, letting the natural rhythm of life and war take him beyond his consciousness. His growls became a song of praise to his totem-beast, the badger. He gave himself over, just a little, to his rage.

*****

The air around Maerlin had become charged, as it did before one of her storms. She concentrated and was sure that there was magic within the room, but it was not coming from her. Much though she was fearful and anxious, she was maintaining her control just like Nessa had taught her. So, where was the magic coming from, she wondered? She looked for the source, focused on the chamber with her mind's eye. Before her, she could clearly see the warriors; even see their auras as she allowed her inner senses to take over. She spotted the magic almost immediately and her senses focussed on the tiny glow. It was not a form of magic that she had been trained in, but it existed, nevertheless. It was growing before her inner eye.

*****

The counter-attack came, as Vort knew it would, and he fought hard to block Bolcha's blows. The sounds of the baying crowd slipped away from Vort's consciousness as he deflected the attacks. He was being forced backwards by the ferocity of the blows, unable to stand his ground against them. The whistling sound of metal cutting through air sang in his ears and mingled with his own song.

It was only a matter of time before blood was drawn, and as he drifted more and more into his battle trance, time ran out for Vort.

The blow struck him across the cheek and three thin razor-sharp lines appeared on Vort's flesh. Pain shot through his face as he strove to keep away any further blows. Yelling out, letting his rage consume him, he counter-attacked. His blades came up and clashed with Bolcha's. Again, their *Tri-crub* became entangled.

Bolcha towered over Vort, breathing heavily as he pushed Vort's arms backwards. The warriors gripped the floorboards with their bare feet, straining with their outstretched arms. Tendons protested at the pressure they were being forced to endure, and Vort's arms were pushed further and further back. He could only pull his blades downward to prevent his shoulders dislocating under the strain. Vort was becoming ensnared in the bigger man's arms.

The *Tri-crub* slipped from Vort's hands as the pressure upon his wrists became too much. Bolcha wrapped his heavily-muscled arms around the smaller man's back, in a vice-like bear hug. Vort felt Bolcha's blades digging into his back as he struggled, but Bolcha had a good grip and exerted more and more pressure.

Vort felt his ribs creak under the bear hug and sensed his body growing limp. He was squeezed tighter and tighter. Fury boiled in his mind as he hung there, being slowly crushed under the powerful grip. His body began to tingle all over. He could feel the intense heat on his skin. He was light-headed, and his bones screamed in agony as they began to contort. He had felt this sensation once before and he knew what it meant, but he was dying and he could do nothing to prevent it from happening. He fought against Bolcha, and he fought against his own body at the same time.

Vort sensed his body being lifted off the ground, as Bolcha's arms strained to crush him. It was not Bolcha's way to kill quickly, and so, one by one, Bolcha's own blades were discarded. He needed a better grip on Vort's back, in order to finish him off.

Vort groaned as heat and pain coursed through his dying body. His brain was a seething mass of red anger, as his last breath was squeezed out of his lungs. Soon, he would pass to the Otherworld. Pain shot through his back as Bolcha strained and put additional pressure on Vort's spine. Macha's breath was sweet on his neck as if death was eager to embrace him. Vort's consciousness slipped farther away, and he was no longer able resist his own inner struggle. He was dying, he knew that now, and the secret that he had held since his youth no longer mattered. In that final moment, as Vort accepted death, his secret burst into life. It was free at last.

The crowd had long since fallen silent, sensing the imminent death. Only moments remained. Soon, it would all be over, when Vort's spine snapped in two.

*****

Maerlin gripped the bench tightly until the wood creaked in protest. Her inner eye was locked on the battle. She watched the magic grow until it shone like a gigantic firefly in her mind. She could not believe what her senses were telling her.

*****

A growl of bestial rage erupted from within the arena, and for a moment, Bolcha paused. Surprise turned to shock, and then as quickly into panic, as razor-sharp teeth sank into his neck, gnawing into the soft flesh beneath. Sharp talons ripped into his thighs causing him to cry out, as much in astonishment as fear.

Bolcha looked down, and his eyes widened as realisation finally dawned on him. His eyes were looking deeply into the eyes of *Clann Na Broce's* sacred totem-beast. Dread filled him. He suddenly found himself wrestling with a huge, ferocious badger.

Bolcha struggled to cast the demonic animal away, but the badger's jaws were already locked onto his neck. The animal's claws were digging tightly into his back, and they clung on fiercely against Bolcha's struggles. The warrior's hands grasped the animal's head, desperate to release his throat from the vice-like grip. He could feel the beast's jaws biting deeper, as they tightened over his windpipe. The Brocian knew that a badger would not release its grip until it had heard the sound of bone or cartilage breaking.

The animal shook its broad head, sinking its teeth deeper. Its mouth filled with blood as it gnawed inexorably into the warrior's neck. The jugular vein erupted under the pressure, only moments before the windpipe collapsed. The demonic beast continued to worry at the wound, tearing at the flesh until blood gushed across the chamber in a thick fountain of red gore. Only then, did the beast release its hold.

Bolcha collapsed, clutching at his neck in a vain attempt to stem the flow. His eyes were already glazing over and his feet rattled on the wooden floor, as his nerves fought against Macha's will but the goddess of death won out, as always. Within a moment, the beating feet stilled and only a carcass remained. Macha had harvested the spirit of the fallen warrior.

The huge badger, its muzzle still slick with the warrior's blood, glared around the chamber. It was seeking an exit. It growled threateningly at any who blocked its passage. Seeing the doorway at the rear of the chamber, it rushed forward, lashing out at anything that stood in its path. Cries of panic were heard, as people fled from the blood-splattered apparition. In moments, it was gone. Dismay replaced panic.

The agitated Brocians looked down on the body of Bolcha and whispered to each other.

"What in the Nine Hells just happened?" Cull demanded. The same question was asked many times over in the Old Tongue, as the Brocians tried to make sense of the chaos. No sign of Vort could be found, save for his discarded clothing and daggers. He had vanished during the melee.

Taliesin looked around him, his face pale. "It can't be!" he exclaimed "It's just a myth ..."

"What're you talking about, man?" Cull demanded. His eyes were still fixed on the dead warrior.

"It can't be," repeated the astonished bard. "It's impossible!"

"It was Vort!" Maerlin explained. "I saw it!"

"What was Vort? Where is he, anyway?" Cull asked.

"Vort changed into that badger."

"What! Don't be ridiculous," growled Cull, not believing what his own eyes had witnessed "Vort's not a shape-shifter. That's just fairy tales. You can't really do that. No-one can."

Maerlin shrugged. "Dubhgall the Black can. I've seen him change into a raven. Anyway, I'm telling you, Vort changed into that beast. That's what I saw."

Taliesin was becoming agitated. "This is incredible! The legends speak of members of the different Pectish Clans being able to transform into their totem-beasts. They would have to be powerful shamans though, not warriors. Anyway, it's just a myth." His eyes gleaming with excitement, Taliesin added "This is fantastic. I can't believe my own eyes."

"All well and good, if it happened," Cull said, still unconvinced "But what does it mean for us?"

"It happened, Cull, believe me. I can see these things better than you can. I've been trained for it," Maerlin assured.

"Taliesin?"

"What?" he asked distracted. "Oh yes … the consequences, right! I'm really not sure. I haven't the foggiest idea what the Brocians will make of this. Vort won the battle, but will they view it as cheating?"

Conal had been sitting quietly, listening to the conversation. Now, his studies came back to him. "The Pectish Clans hold this sort of thing in high esteem," he declared. "They refer to it as Form-melding."

"Oh and how would you know?" Maerlin demanded. "Are you suddenly an expert on shape-shifting?"

"Cull had me look up the histories and cultures of the different Clans within Dragania, when we were on the Isle."

"That was clever of me," remarked Cull "though, in truth, I was just trying to keep you out of trouble. I didn't think you'd actually do that much studying. Well done, lad."

Chapter Twenty-Two: The High Council's Decision

The silence had grown ominous, and the rat could smell the fear in the air. The Dark Mage must have returned. She had not heard his arrival, but the other rats knew. They had scurried into hiding.

Now was the time for her to leave. The hungry pack would not venture forth while the Dark Mage remained, unless of course, he summoned them. If such a command came, they would hasten to his call. Their continued existence depended on it.

Crawling forward, keeping the weight off her injured forepaw, the rat slipped quietly out of her hole and waited for the right time to continue.

A child lay strapped to the altar; she could see it clearly in the torchlight as she hid within the shadows. Fighting back her natural urges, she watched as the Dark Mage prepared his sacrifice.

It was hard to fight down the fear, but she forced herself to sit and watch as the child cried out in pain and begged for mercy. Finally, the sacrifice passed to the Otherworld. The rats, it seems, would not go hungry this night.

The injured rat was not thinking of food, however. She had other things on her mind, and she waited patiently for the right moment to act. She tensed as the Dark Mage drew power, ready to cast his spell. She sensed his change and saw his body glow through her inner senses. His form blurred, his shape blending into the shadows around him.

Now was the time to act, while the rat-pack was still in hiding, and the Dark Mage was distracted by his spell. The injured rat summoned her last remaining strength, trying to be as quiet as possible. As the mage was engrossed in working his magic, she put her own plan into action.

Dubhgall finished his spell. When it was completed, his form changed. Where he had once stood; there now perched a huge raven. It cawed loudly as it flapped up and landed on the body of the sacrifice. Quickly, it feasted on the tender parts of the Macha's feast: the eyes of the innocent. Gobbling down the white orbs, it clacked its razor-sharp beak in relish before taking to wing. Soaring upwards, it circled and climbed until it reached the open door of the parapet above.

He would be gone for some time, she hoped, as she struggled to climb the stone steps of the tower, one at a time. She would need to reach the parapet before his return. Ignoring the pain in her side, she hopped up each step, until she reached the top. Exhausted, she fell out of the trap door and lay exhausted on the stone flagstones of the roof of the tower.

*****

The High Council had finally called the meeting to order, and after some consultation, they had closed the chambers for the day. The weary councillors needed time to rest and ponder the startling revelations.

Cull and the others had been escorted by a number of armed warriors to a set of suitable chambers. The escort had been polite, but firm. Their weapons had not been returned, though Taliesin had been allowed to keep his harp.

Now, they sat and waited, wondering what lay ahead.

"We should get some sleep," suggested Cull half-heartedly, though they were all too much on edge to sleep.

"Is there any chance of a song, Tal?" Conal prompted, looking at the harper.

"I'm not really in the mood for singing, Conal, though I thank you for the thought. I doubt whether my song would cheer you," replied Taliesin. He was busy cleaning the already pristine harp.

"Could you just play a little music, then?" Maerlin begged. "Please … my head is fit to burst and a little distraction would help."

Taliesin looked at Maerlin's forlorn face and nodded. "All right then, a tune perhaps," he agreed and placed Aoife in his lap.

He tuned his instrument, taking the time to check each of her many strings in turn and then together, for what seemed like an age to the others. They didn't object, however, for even this simple task sounded melodious. When Taliesin went through some simple progressions to relax his mind and loosen his fingers, they were convinced that he had already begun to play.

His mind calmed with the joy of playing his beloved harp. He played a soft, soothing tune filled with the imagery of swans, lakes, and balmy summer evenings. Soon, he was transported to another place and the real music began. He drifted through his imagination, and the harp brought his visions to life, creating pictures and moods to suit his intricate plucking.

By the time he had finished, a bell had passed and the others were fast asleep. A harper might have been insulted to have his audience fall asleep on him, but Taliesin smiled. They had been through a lot these last few days, and a good night's sleep, or rather a good day's sleep, would do them the world of good. His own soul was lighter also, and he settled down on one of the bunks and soon drifted off.

*****

Vort awoke, naked and covered in blood. Memories came flooding back to him of his battle with Bolcha. Visions filled with animal rage. Feeling his skin crawl with revulsion, he bent over and vomited up the half-digested blood in his stomach.

"No! This cannot be," he moaned as his mind relived the battle.

Looking up through the cover of trees, he sought out the sun and gauged the time. It was nearly noon by his estimation, and the people of the city would be sleeping. Only sentries would remain awake, and he knew how to slip past them to reach his destination. He would have to face the judgement of the High Council, but to do so naked would only add to his humiliation.

It was then, that he remembered that he had other worries; much greater than his nakedness. Picking himself up, he snuck back into the city, considering his options as he went.

*****

Cull woke with a start. A hand was covering his mouth.

"Relax, Cull. I mean you no harm," hissed a voice in the darkness. "Get up quietly and we'll go and wake the others."

The room was blacker than Macha's wardrobe, but Cull recognised the voice. "What, by the Seven, are you doing?" he growled.

"Shush! You'll wake the guards!"

"How did you get in here without waking them?" Cull asked.

"I know the city better than most, Cull. I trained here when I was Conal's age. There are myriad tunnels running through the city, almost forgotten by the citizens of *Broca*. I've an inquisitive nature, so I spent some time learning all about them. Now, enough questions … get dressed."

"Can I have a little light please, Vort?" Cull fumbled around in the darkness, looking for his tunic.

"Oh, sorry, I'd forgotten about that." A green glowing torch lit up the room. "Now hurry up and we'll go and wake the others."

"Hang on! What are we being so secretive about?"

"We're leaving, of course, while the city sleeps."

"What? Why are we doing that? I thought you'd won the duel?"

"Let's just forget about that … if it's all the same with you," murmured Vort, not meeting the other man's gaze.

"Why? I thought you Pects approved of that sort of thing. I thought it meant that we were going to be in the clear."

Vort gave a sardonic laugh. "I thought you had a better grasp of politics than that, Cull. I'm a warrior not a shaman. Warriors aren't supposed to have the ability to Form-meld. It's a sacred thing … a shaman thing. During the meeting with the High Council, the man who spoke out the most vociferously against you was Dorcha, our High-shaman. I wouldn't recommend waiting around for his opinion on this matter. I don't know about you, but I'm leaving before his sacrificial dagger can rip out my heart."

"But he can't do that. You're the Clan Champion," objected Cull, trying to come to terms with the information.

"Given time for leveller heads, I'm sure that you would be right, Cull, but we might not have that long. If my father had taken his seat at the High Council, I might have had a chance. However, with him guarding the

Southern Dell Sett, my life is in danger, and therefore, so is yours," Vort pointed out as he moved towards the door.

"You're going to run away rather than face them?"

"You think that I should stand before my people and have them pass judgement on me? I've shamed my family ... my Sett. How can I face the High Council when everyone witnessed my dishonour? I lost the Blood-truth. I should be dead."

"But you won! The other warrior is dead."

"I didn't win, Cull!" Vort hissed angrily. "The beast within me won. Don't you understand? I was dying. I'd lost the Blood-truth," explained Vort "And as I was slipping away, it managed to escape my will. *It* killed Bolcha, not me."

"I'm not so sure that the High Council will see it that way. Shape-shifting is part of your Pectish mythology."

Vort looked hard at Cull before commenting "I thought you were a pragmatist, Cull, not an optimist. You could be right. If you wish to stay and find out, I wish you well, however, I'm leaving. I thought you might want to go and retrieve *An Fiacail Dragan* ... but perhaps not."

"The what?"

"You know ... the Dragontooth. The sword of *Clann Na Dragan*," explained Vort.

"Oh! I see." As he finished dressing, a thought came to him "What about our weapons? Can you get our things?"

"Your personal gear is already in the common room. You can collect it before you leave. The mounts, however, I cannot get for you. There isn't time, and you're better off without them."

"What, no mounts? How're we supposed to get to Dragon's Ridge without mounts?"

"We'll run," explained Vort. "We'll be safer on foot, and we'll be harder to track."

Cull hated the idea of losing their mounts. "Hang on a moment. You said 'we'. Are you coming with us?"

"Have I any choice? It looks like my destiny is wrapped up in yours. If the young *Dragan* cub can defeat the Boare, then I might have helped win this war for my Clan."

"But it'll take us days to return to the Southern Dell Sett and then head north on foot," Cull objected. "Can't we take the horses? We could outrun your clansmen."

"You can't outrun *Clann Na Broce* in these woods, Cull. Not even with me as a guide. Believe me when I tell you this, we are safer on foot. Anyway, we won't be going to my Sett. We'll be going straight north, through the woods and on to Dragon's Ridge."

"North … why north?"

Vort shook his head in exasperation. "Cull, I spent so long trying to get you to speak to me and yet you remained silent. Now, I want you to be silent and you plague me with questions. Come, let's wake the others and leave before it's too late. You can ask me more while we're running."

"I've seen you run, Vort. I won't get the breath to ask you the time of day."

Vort grinned at Cull before slipping out of the room.

Soon, everyone gathered together in the common room, where they found their weapons and gear sitting on the table.

"I suggest you travel light," Vort instructed as he watched them get ready. "We'll need to move quickly and quietly, if we are to slip away undetected. We've a long run north."

"Run? Did he say run?" Taliesin asked.

"Yes, Taliesin, he did," confirmed Cull.

"But what about Gertie … they aren't going to eat her, are they?"

"Taliesin, I'm sure your camel will be safe. My clansmen are wary of her. They aren't convinced that she isn't at least part demon. I doubt that anyone would eat her," assured Vort "From the smell of her, I'm not even sure whether or not she's edible. I certainly wouldn't want to eat her."

Maerlin had woken up with a headache again. It felt like she'd had this headache forever, even though she knew it was only a few days. The idea of running all day with her stomach cramping and her head throbbing didn't appeal to her, but she kept silent. When she learned, however, that they would not be travelling back to the Southern Dell Sett but heading north, she wasn't happy. "We can't leave Cora behind. She's all alone. They'll kill her when they find out we've escaped."

"Maerlin," assured Vort, "Cora is staying in my home as my guest. No one of the Southern Dell Sett will raise a hand against her, and they will protect her against any threat. I've sent my warriors back to the Sett to help defend it. They'll speak to my father about what has passed here. He'll know what to do. Don't worry about your friend. She is safer there than she would be with us."

"Why? Are we heading into danger?"

"We should be safe enough for the first day. We'll only need to avoid the Clan patrols. I know this land, and I know how to slip past my clansmen unseen. After that, however, it gets more difficult. We'll need to cross the Plains of the Dragon. At the moment, it's swarming with Boarites. Even travelling at night, it'll be a dangerous journey." Vort looked at each of them, reading their thoughts "We need to leave now, if we're going to leave at all. It's up to you."

Conal spoke first "I still don't understand something. Why aren't you staying to see what the High Council decides?"

"You're welcome to stay, Conal *MacDragan*, but I won't," assured Vort "However, if you want to retrieve *An Fiacail Dragan*, I'll help you to get there."

Conal thought for a moment and nodded. "Let's go. After all, that's what we came here to do, isn't it. So, what are we waiting for?"

Cull grinned in agreement.

Maerlin had been sitting, holding her stomach to relieve the cramps, but looked up and gave a brief nod.

They turned towards the singer.

"This isn't your fight, Taliesin." Conal admitted "But you're welcome to join us. I'll have need of a bard at some point in the future, if I'm successful."

Taliesin decided quickly "It'll be an epic tale. What bard could refuse the chance to witness it, first hand?"

"Then it's agreed," said Cull, getting to his feet. "Lead on, Vort."

Vort led them to a small door, set in one of the walls of the chamber.

"That's the broom closet, Vort. I've already looked in there," Conal said as he watched the Brocian open the door.

"Yes. That's what it looks like, but looks can be deceiving," said Vort as he stepped over some implements, into the narrow cupboard.

They heard the soft click as Vort fumbled with the back wall, and then, the soft swish of a false wall being slid aside.

"Shall we?" Vort asked with a grin. He led the others into the cupboard. Behind the broom cupboard was a narrow passageway. It was dark and covered in cobwebs, but of sound construction.

"How did you find this passage?" Conal asked, taking a torch and heading down the tunnel. "It's amazing."

"The builders of the city felt that some emergency exits would be useful. There was always the small possibility of an attacking force breaching the bridge before it was cut. I spent a long time studying old scrolls in the city's library. I was looking up Form-melding at the time, but I came across some ancient plans by accident. My original research got waylaid, at that point. I spent many a happy bell or two after that, finding routes into restricted places," Vort reminisced with a grin.

"Restricted places? That sounds like fun," said Conal. "Like what exactly … no, let me guess … the Treasury?"

Vort coughed. "Well, no. Actually, I was more interested in the women's dormitories. Orla, my wife, was staying there at the time," he confessed. "The tutors frowned on young people meeting without supervision."

Maerlin had been thinking of something else and changed the subject "Vort?"

"Yes, Maerlin, what is it?"

"You were looking up shape-shifting, or Form-melding, as you call it? Does that mean you've done this before?"

For a few moments, the tunnel fell silent. Vort cursed himself for opening his mouth. Form-melding was not a subject he wished to discuss, but it was too late now. Reluctantly Vort spoke of his past "When I was about Conal's age, I Form-melded during a fight. Luckily, the other boy escaped with only a bad bite. It was a foolish fight amongst friends, but it got out of hand. It terrified us both. He swore to keep it a secret. He even lied to his family about the bite on his leg. We've never spoken of the matter since, and I've worked hard to keep the beast at bay," Vort confessed. "The only other person to know about my curse was my father. He was the one who treated the leg wound. He too conceded to my wish for secrecy, though he wanted to shout it from the treetops. He was very proud of it, but he respected my wishes. Now, the beast has finally killed someone, and my secret is out. Maybe I should've taken my father's advice and announced it at my Rites of Manhood. Somehow, during my trials at the Spring Fair, I managed to suppress the beast for long enough to hide it from the priests of Lugh. I had no wish to become a shaman. My eyes were always drawn to the *Tri-crub* blades and the ways of the warrior."

"But, it was always inside you?" Maerlin pressed, remembering the magical glow that she had seen during the Blood-truth.

"Oh, yes. I've fought hard to beat the beast over the years, but it's always there, lurking in the shadows," Vort admitted. "I can feel it growing in me whenever my blood heats up."

"I know that feeling …" Maerlin agreed, with a wry smile. "… And yet you've managed to suppress it without any proper training. That's incredible."

"Well … I was doing fine until now."

Maerlin was impressed. Before Nessa's guidance, she had been creating havoc whenever her temper got the better of her. Even with Nessa's training, she still made some blunders as could be testified by her bandaged hand.

They hurried down the dark passageway and found a flight of stairs, which they started to descend. This tunnel had not been used for a very long time. The cobwebs hung like curtains across their path and the dust lay like snowdrifts on the floor.

"Are you sure this is the right way? I'd have thought we needed to be heading upwards to the surface," Cull asked, rubbing cobwebs from his face.

"This is the right way," assured Vort. "We're heading down into the gorge. From there, we'll follow the river upstream to its source."

Soon, they could feel a faint breeze on their faces, confirming an entranceway ahead. They turned the last spiral in the staircase and squinted against the bright light.

Looking up, high overhead, they could see the rope bridge. Steps led down from where they stood to the river below.

"Where to now?" Conal asked.

"We go into the river. It's not too deep here. At this time of year, it'll only reach your calves. Even in midwinter, it's only waist high."

"My boots are going to be ruined," Taliesin complained as he followed the others.

"You can always take them off, Taliesin. It wasn't a concern for the designers of the city, as my people don't wear shoes.

Cull grinned as Taliesin struggled out of his high boots. He, like Maerlin, was well used to walking barefoot.

Conal pulled off his own boots, though his were not as fine as the bard's. "I guess if we're planning on running later, I'd rather do it in dry boots."

They waded through the icy-cold water, heading north. Vort directed them to stay in the shadows on one side of the river, making it harder to be spotted by anyone above. It took the rest of the afternoon to wade sufficiently upstream to reach the end of the gorge.

Vort knew that by now, their disappearance would have been noticed. It would take a while longer for the passageway to be found. They still had some time, but they would need to be very careful. Their passage through the secret tunnel was impossible to hide. Their tracks in the thick dust of the floor and the broken cobwebs could be easily seen. Before nightfall, their pursuers would be at the riverside entrance. From there, they would have to split up or choose a direction to hunt. He hoped that they would head south and knew that the river would leave no traces of their passage to follow. Logic dictated that he would go south as the river veered eastward towards the Southern Dell Sett. By now, they would probably know that he was leading the group. Cull and the others could not have known of the ancient passageways, very few Brocians even did. They must conclude that Vort, or one of the men of the Southern Dell Sett, was helping the *Fear Ban* escape. The obvious escape route was south, but the skilled trackers of *Clann Na Broce* might not be so easily fooled.

Conal was making for the bank, eager to get out of the water and put his boots back on.

"Hold it, Conal," Vort hissed. "We must stay in the water."

"Whatever for?" Conal protested. "It's freezing in here. I can barely feel my toes anymore."

"It's just for another couple of miles," urged Vort "The trackers will be as eager to get out of this water as you are, *MacDragan*, and they'll expect us to climb out as soon as possible. The banks here are clay, and they'll be like writing on a scroll to the men who hunt us. We must continue for a while longer in the water and hope that they think we've headed south."

"But we're exhausted, Vort," pleaded Maerlin, her head throbbing as much as her feet.

"Three miles upstream there's a waterfall. There, we'll find a suitable place to hide until dawn," Vort explained, stressing "We must not be caught out in the woods after dark. Please, trust me on this, stay in the water until we reach the falls, and I can promise you a safe place to rest."

"Our feet are already frozen. Another couple of miles won't make any difference. Lead on, Vort," said Cull.

Vort knew just how skilled the Brocian hunters that he was competing against were. He had trained with the trackers. He knew just how much danger they were in. They would have to be very careful to avoid any risk of discovery. He led them onwards, encouraging them with smiles as he went.

Finally, they reached the waterfall and he called a halt. Standing knee-deep in the pool, Vort handed Cull one end of a coil of rope. "Follow this rope and it'll guide you through the darkness."

"What darkness? The sun hasn't set, yet," asked Cull. "Where is this hiding place?"

"Through there," answered Vort, pointing to the deepest part of the pool, beneath the falls.

"You've got to be kidding me," protested Taliesin.

"Why do you *Fear Ban* say that?" Vort asked, not expecting an answer. He went on to explain "There's a cave behind the falls. To get into it, we need to swim underwater, through a narrow passageway. It comes out behind the waterfall and can only be reached from two ways. One is through this pool, and the other is through a narrow chimney on the island above," Vort pointed towards the top of the waterfall "Believe me. There's no safer hidey-hole in these woods."

"How did you find it, then?" Taliesin asked, looking dubiously at the cold, dark water.

Vort smirked as he remembered. "We used to come here for midday swims, when we could sneak away from our tutors. Naturally, when I noticed the underwater passageway, I wanted to find out what was at the other end of the tunnel."

"We ... who exactly is we?" the bard persisted.

"Only my wife and I. We never showed it to anyone else. It was our secret hideaway."

"You seem to make a habit of being secretive, Vort. I hope you aren't hiding anything important from us ..." Taliesin pointed out, a little petulantly.

"...Again," added Cull with a hint of bitterness.

Vort frowned. "If you've a better idea, feel free to share it."

No one ventured any alternative suggestion so Vort dived into the pool. Swimming to the centre, he turned back to the others. "Just follow my guide rope and you'll find the tunnel," he instructed "I'll see you on the other side." Taking a deep breath, Vort dived beneath the dark water.

"That man's awfully annoying, you know," grumbled Taliesin.

"Aye, I've noticed that," Cull grinned. "He's useful though."

"Aoife's going to complain for a week if I give her a bath," protested the harper. "There has to be another option?"

"It's up to you, Taliesin, but the rest of us are going to follow Vort," said Cull. "If there was another way, I'm sure he'd have mentioned it. Just be thankful that we aren't wearing armour."

The bard pouted. "I'll be along in a moment. You go on ahead."

One by one, they dived beneath the water, following the rope down into the subterranean tunnel. Maerlin swam out first, shivering with the cold. There, she paddled for a few moments, getting used to the shock of the cold on her body. Filling her lungs to their full capacity, she sunk beneath the water and groped for the guide rope.

Quickly, she pulled herself along, hand over hand, deeper and deeper into the pool. She slipped into the tunnel and wriggled forward along the rope. It was totally dark in the tunnel and she was forced to find her way along by the feel of the rope in her cold hands. It was her only guide. Her lungs craved for air as she frantically swam through the darkness. She was starting to consider turning back, panic building inside her, when she saw the green glow of a Brocian torch ahead.

Maerlin burst from the water, coughing and spluttering, to find Vort's extended hand. With his help, she climbed up onto the rocky floor of the cavern and gasped for breath. As soon as she could, she wrung the excess water from her clothes. Shaking the water from her braided hair, she looked about the cavern.

It was about twenty feet wide. The narrow pool, into which she had emerged, lay at its centre. High overhead, she could see the orange glow of the setting sun through a hole in the roof. Bits of trees and debris hinted at the creator of the cavern. Many a winter storm must have gradually worn away the solid rock, to carve out this tiny cave.

Shivering, Maerlin searched for dry kindling as Vort waited for the next swimmer.

Conal spluttered to the surface a few moments later, as Maerlin was forming up a small cone of twigs to build a fire. He was followed quickly by Cull. "By Dagda's blessed plums, that'd wake you up!" the beggar gasped as he squeezed the water from his clothing. They all stood shivering, watching Maerlin as she tried to summon a Fire Elemental into life within the tiny cone of sticks.

"You'll get a lot warmer if you fetch some firewood," she pointed out dryly, when their standing over her had become annoying "All that shivering and chattering your teeth isn't helping me to concentrate."

Looking abashed, the others headed off. Soon a decent fire was crackling; lighting up the cavern with a bright orange glow.

"Where's the bard?" Vort asked with concern. Taliesin had not yet appeared.

"He's whining over getting that damned harp wet," explained Cull. "I guess he's working himself up to the swim."

Just then, Taliesin appeared, shivering as he climbed out of the pool. He inspected his harp carefully, even before wringing the water from his own clothes. He had filled the space within the harp's protective satchel with sphagnum moss to further protect the instrument from the cold water.

"Aoife dear, I'm so sorry," he murmured "I waxed her heavily before I wrapped her. Hopefully, she'll survive the ordeal," Taliesin muttered. No one was listening.

It wasn't long before they started to warm up. Steam rose from their damp clothing. They huddled around the fire and made themselves as comfortable as possible. Once they had dried off sufficiently, they settled down and fell into troubled sleep.

Chapter Twenty-Three: The Hunted

Vort awoke, surprised to find that he was trapped in a cage. The room was dark, but not so dark that the Brocian could not see. His well-trained eyes peered out of the cage bars at the circular room beyond.

Before him, a figure dressed in a black cowl and robes, sat waiting. He was known to Vort, who growled in hatred at his presence "You! I should have known!"

"Ah, the beast awakens," goaded the shaman, standing and walking towards the cage.

"What's the meaning of this?" Vort growled, barely containing his anger as he gripped the bars.

"Well now, let's just call it a precaution, shall we. We wouldn't want you to slaughter any more innocent people now, would we?"

"Release me at once, Dorcha!"

The High-shaman smiled; a cold, hard smile of pure hatred. "You want me to release your beast. Do you want to roam free like the wild animal you are?"

Vort shook the bars, his anger bubbling to the surface.

"They will not bend, warrior. They are magically warded, so you can save your strength, Vort Mac Aiden."

"Why have you imprisoned me? What is this place?" Vort demanded, as he looked around the stone-walled room.

"This is one of the many towers that dot the landscape, Vort. They're a good place to hide you. None of your brave warriors would venture into one of these magical buildings. Only spell-casters can enter this building unscathed, but you're a shaman now, aren't you Vort?" Dorcha goaded.

"Leave me alone, you lousy maggot." Vort growled. "I'm no threat to you. I've no interest in becoming a shaman."

The shaman prowled the room, staying just beyond Vort's grasp. "Ah, but that's the problem, isn't it. You've become a threat to me, Form-melder ... Tell me?" the shaman asked, as if in casual conversation "Have you had this ability long?"

Vort considered silence, but knew it would be useless. The shamans had ways of gleaning knowledge from within the brain. Hating himself for his fear of the magician, he reluctantly answered "I changed once before, when I was a child. It was horrible, and I've fought against it ever since."

"But you can tell me how you Form-meld into the Totem-beast?" the old shaman coaxed. "You can tell me how you make the magic work?"

Vort smiled, realising something important. "Does this mean that you can't do this yourself, Dorcha?" he goaded. "I was told that you were the most powerful Clan shaman alive. Your sycophants even claim that you are as powerful as Dubhgall the Black. Yet, for all of your powers, you can't take the form of our totem-beast. Is that what you're so worried about?"

Then he realised the full extent of his threat to the shaman.

"Ah! I can see that you finally see the light. Not satisfied with becoming the Clan Champion, you're now treading on my territory."

"You can have it, Snake-tongue! I've never wanted the ways of the shaman. I've no time for your trickery and your lust for terror. The ways of the warrior are purer and leave the soul untainted."

The old shaman ignored the snide remarks, changing tack. "Tell me Vort. Was the taste of your brother clansman's blood sweet to your lips? Did the death of Bolcha bring a secret joy to your heart? Did the animal within you bay at the moon like a wolf-pup?"

"You always were a sick and sordid excuse for a human being, Dorcha. Go rot in the Nine Hells," growled Vort, spittle flying from his lips as his anger grew.

"Ah, I can see the Beast within you now. It's hiding, but I can see it in your eyes. Come out and play, Beastie. Cast off this hollow shell you have chosen to hide behind."

Vort fought to control his anger, gritting his teeth and glaring at the shaman. His skin felt tighter and his brain throbbed as he battled for dominance over his inner-self.

"Pain!" Dorcha commanded, casting a yellow powder into Vort's face.

Vort's head filled with agony as the powder settled on his flesh and burned into his skin. "I'm going to kill you, you putrid worm, if it's the last thing I do."

"PAIN!" the shaman commanded, doubling the sensation of burning on Vort's flesh. "Come forth, my wee Beastie. Come! Come and kneel to your Master."

Vort's bones creaked as they contorted. His self-control was waning under the magical powder's continual torment.

"GGGGGGGGgggggettttttt offff meeeeeeee!"

"Come Beastie. Come and lick my feet. I will leash you and house-train you," Dorcha tormented.

"NOOOooo! Stoppp this!!Ggggggggggrrrrrrr!"

The Beast lashed out in frustration, its razor-sharp talons scraping uselessly off the magically-reinforced metal bars. It plunged its jaws between the bars, seeking to reach its tormentor. The shaman stood laughing, just beyond the creature's grasp.

"What a cute little Beastie we have. Lie down and heed your Master, Beast," Dorcha commanded.

The Beast gripped the bars in its jaws and gnawed at the metal, seeking escape.

"PAIN!"

Squeals of anguish and rage filled the room. The pain came in waves, never completely letting go, before coming back again. Vort rolled around on the rocky floor, trying to dislodge the yellow powder that was causing him so much torment.

*****

His cries soon woke the others, none of whom had been sleeping very well. They rushed forward and tried to wake him, but without success. Seeing his body spasm with seizures, they grabbed hold of the thrashing Brocian.

"Hold him down!" Cull ordered. "He's having some kind of seizure!"

They grappled with the unconscious warrior. Vort's strength was incredible. Even with all four of them sitting on him, he continued to thrash about and growl menacingly. His eyes rolled about in his head, and his mouth dribbled froth and blood as he struggled.

"We have to do something!" Conal urged.

"Vort, wake up!" Maerlin yelled, but the warrior did not respond. She sensed the magical power growing within the sleeping Brocian and blurted out a warning "He's changing! He's Form-melding. We have to wake him up."

Vort body shook violently. His howls of rage and pain filled the cavern. One by one, they were thrown away. His eyes were open, but he did not see the companions before him. Vort fought against some unseen enemy, within his mind.

It was Taliesin who came up with the solution "Throw him into the water," he suggested. Together they pounced on the warrior and with one almighty heave; they lifted Vort off the ground and threw him into the pool. Time slowed as Vort sailed through the air and landed with an almighty splash.

An echo of the watery splash reverberated around the cavern as they stood around the pool and waited. It wasn't long before Vort burst out of the water like a geyser. Spray flew everywhere as he gasped for air. "What're you doing?" he demanded. Climbing out of the water, he wrung the excess water from his long hair.

"You were dreaming," explained Taliesin. "You were having a nightmare and you were starting to change … I … we thought it best to wake you."

"So you tried to drown me!" Vort exclaimed, unable to fully remember his nightmare.

*****

Cora awoke to find that she was alone, in a strange room. Her head throbbed a little, but otherwise, she felt fine. She looked around. "Hello?" Her voice croaked with thirst. Cora strained to listen and she could hear people speaking in the next room. She tried again, hoping to catch their attention "Hello. Is someone there?"

The language they spoke was very similar to that spoken on the Western Isles, and she could understand the conversation after a moment

"I'm telling you. I heard something."

"You're imagining it, father."

"I might be getting old, daughter, but I'm far from senile. Come. We'll see who is imagining things."

A moment later, the room was lit up with an eerie green glow, and two strangers entered the bedchamber.

One was a Pectish woman, only a few years older than Cora and she had soft, friendly eyes. She smiled down at Cora and spoke haltingly in *Sassenaucht* "I'm glad to see that you're finally awake. We were getting worried."

Cora studied the man beside her. He had strong Pectish features, similar to those found on the Western Isles. His face was a web of soft wrinkles, and he had long silver hair and a full beard. His eyes were milky with age, but they held a friendly curiosity about them. They looked wise and assured. They reminded her of her own father's; King Mannaman the Wise.

"I told you she was awake," he said. His voice was rich and assured, just like her father's, too. His manner was one of light-hearted scolding. He had spoken in the Old Tongue; in Pectish. Then he spoke again, but this time in *Sassenaucht.* "Welcome to my home. You are safe here. You are our guest."

Cora looked from one to the other, as questions flooded her brain. "Where am I?" she asked, trying to remember how she had got here.

"Ah! She speaks in the Old Tongue," pronounced the old man. "I knew she was an Islander. I told you so!"

"Yes, father, you did, and I never doubted you." Turning to Cora, speaking in Pectish, she asked. "What can you remember?"

Cora thought for a moment before answering "Sorry … nothing much. Where am I? Wait ... Maerlin, where's Maerlin?"

"That's good. It looks like your mind is still working. That's always a good start. The rest will come in time." Orla sighed with relief. "My name is Orla. *Orla Ni Tirloch Broce*. I'm the wife of *Vort Mac Aiden Na Broce* of the Southern Dell Sett."

Cora looked blankly at the woman, not comprehending.

The old man cleared his throat "You're going too fast, Orla, give her a chance. The girl's only just woken up. Here … let me try." He turned to Cora and explained, slowly "You're in the Broce Woods, lass. You're in one of the Setts of *Clann Na Broce*."

Memories rushed back to Cora, "Maerlin … Conal!"

"They're fine. They've gone to the High Council with my son. They'll be due back shortly," he placated, placing a comforting hand over Cora's.

"What about Cull and Nessa?" Surely, Cora thought, Nessa wouldn't leave me if I was unwell?

A shadow fell across Aiden's face, and he gripped her hand tighter. "I'm very sorry but the one you call Nessa didn't survive," he explained with sadness in his voice. "I'm sorry for your loss."

"Oh, no!" Cora moaned, tears rolling down her cheeks.

Orla came forward and sat down beside her, placing a comforting arm around Cora's shoulders.

Just then, a commotion sounded outside. Loud voices could be heard calling out. Others responded in shock and concern.

"What in the Nine Hells is going on out there?" Aiden demanded, getting to his feet.

"Have they returned already?" Orla asked.

"I doubt it. I'd better go and find out. I'll be right back." The old man patted Cora's hand and left. Orla continued to comfort the distraught novice.

Sometime later, Aiden returned. His face was a grim mask of concern.

"What's wrong?" Orla demanded.

"There's been trouble at the High Council. It ended in a Blood-truth …" he began, pondering how much to tell his daughter-in-law.

The blood drained from Orla's face as she shook her head in disbelief. "Vort's not dead. I'd know it if he was dead," she blurted out, her voice pleading for confirmation.

"No, he's alive, but … there's a problem." Aiden took a deep breath and continued "Vort ordered our men to return to the Sett and they've run all the way here to bring us the news. They tell me that something happened at the Blood-truth, something I know that Vort prayed would never happen again."

"What happened, father?" Orla pleaded. "Please, tell me."

"When Vort was a boy, he got into a fight with *Liam Mac Phelim Broce* of the Eastern Dell Sett," he explained, deciding to start at the beginning. "Vort lost his temper during the ruckus and Liam was quite badly injured. He still limps to this day when the weather's cold …"

"…What are you telling me, father?" Orla pressed.

"I shouldn't be the one telling you this," Aiden grumbled. "My son should be telling you this, but he hoped to keep this a secret, even from you …"

"Father," Orla pleaded. "Just tell me what is going on."

The old man sighed and murmured "Forgive me, Vort." Looking at the girl that he had come to know and love as a daughter, he tried to explain "The truth of the matter is that Vort is a Form-melder. Liam was injured when Vort bit him."

There was a moment of shocked silence before Orla shook her head. "No, that cannot be, Father. Vort is a warrior, not a shaman. Anyway, we haven't had a Form-melder in the Clan for many, many years, and it's never been a warrior. There must be some mistake. They've got it wrong."

"Orla-daughter, believe me," confirmed Aiden. "Vort can Form-meld. I've seen the evidence of it with my own eyes."

"But what's that got to do with a Blood-truth?" Orla asked with a feeling of dread.

Aiden sighed and took Orla's hands in his own. "Bolcha challenged his authority and they fought a Blood-truth. Dorcha must have put him up to it. Vort was losing the battle, but Bolcha was not content to win first blood. He wanted to humiliate Vort. He wanted to kill him. Vort was dying, it seems, and in his dying moments, he lost control and Form-melded. The totem-beast within him killed Bolcha. My son's a good boy and his heart is true. He did not wish to trouble you with this thing, but now it troubles our whole Clan."

Orla stared at her father-in-law, tears running silently down her face. "Where is he?" she finally asked. "I must go to him."

"He's gone, daughter," Aiden replied, his foggy eyes filling with tears. "The messenger told me that Vort feared the High Council's reaction to the Blood Truth, not for himself, but for those under his protection. He had sworn them as his guests and he would not endanger them. Vort has fled the city and taken them north to Dragon's Ridge. He has cast himself into exile."

"No!" Orla wailed. "NO!"

Aiden pulled her close, rocking her gently as she sobbed.

Cora lay forgotten in the background, a voyeur to this intimate moment. She sat silently and waited, trying to make sense of it all.

"We must send out scouts. We must go and bring Vort home," spluttered Orla. "We cannot leave him out there on his own."

"Daughter, we can't do that!" Aiden explained, though his own heart was heavy. "Dorcha has demanded his death. He's accused of aiding the *Fear Ban* in their escape. The shaman was always a spiteful snake, and he must feel threatened by this revelation. Our duty is to guard the Sett for now and resist Dorcha's men when they come. I must go to the High Council and speak to them, make them see sense. In the meantime, our men will be needed here. They need to protect the Sea-girl. She is our guest, Orla. She cannot be given up into the hands of Dorcha and his acolytes. She would surely die under their cruel knife. You know this."

"But father …" Orla objected.

"… No!" Aiden replied sternly. "Would you shame your husband's house and his Sett? Would you shame my son's honour by letting the poor girl into that monster's hands?"

Shocked into silence by Aiden's tone, Orla saw beyond her own grief. Wiping her eyes, she nodded acceptance. "You are as wise as your name, *Aiden Crionna*. I'm sorry," she apologised. She would not shame her husband by showing any sign of weakness when the shamans came. For come they would, and soon. "We must prepare for their arrival. We must hide her somewhere that they cannot find her."

"Hiding her won't work. The shamans can see deep within a man's soul. Secrets are hard to keep from them."

"Then, what are we to do?"

"It's simple. We must refuse them entry. We have no choice."

Her mind worked out the ramifications of the action. "But … we can't do that. They could kill you, father."

Aiden grinned, showing no concern. "I am not so old that Dorcha and his whelps can scare me. I'm a High Councillor and the High Elder of this Sett. Dorcha couldn't risk the wrath of the Council by killing me without a trial. He'd be forced to bring me before the Council, and there, I could plead my case, and that of my son."

"He's a dangerous opponent, father," warned Orla.

"Daughter, it'll take more than a second-rate shaman to kill me. Now come, we need to put on our best clothes and organise the Sett. We have visitors due shortly."

They stood to leave, Cora forgotten, until she spoke up "Wait!" she said "Can I help? I want to help."

From the little Cora could make out, trouble was brewing, and her friends were at the heart of it. Cora wanted to assist these people who would risk all to save her.

They turned to look at her, pausing a moment before Aiden spoke. "Cora, you are our guest. This is not your war to fight."

"Hang on!" Cora protested "My friends and I have got you into this. Please … let me help."

"There is little that you can do, Cora … unless you can make yourself invisible," Aiden joked. He turned to leave, his mind already on the task ahead.

Cora thought for a moment and then called out. "Wait!"

Aiden turned to look at the feisty, young novice. "What is it? We have much to do."

"There might be a way ... Is there a lake nearby? A well, perhaps, or some other water source?" Cora asked.

"There's a waterfall nearby, with a pool below it. It's just beyond the Sett," Aiden confirmed.

"Perfect! Show it to me. I have an idea." Cora struggled up from the bunk.

"But you should rest, Cora," objected Orla.

"I'm fine, believe me. I'll be better once I see the water," assured Cora. "I'll help you get your husband back, I promise, but first, let's deal with these shamans."

The two women assessed each other in silence, before Orla nodded. "Show her the waterfall, Father."

Aiden considered objecting, but curiosity was a family trait. He wanted to know what the island girl had in mind. "It looks like I've been outvoted," he replied, leading the way out of the Sett.

*****

"What dost thy mean, thou cannot penetrate it?" the High Priestess demanded.

The Dream-catchers avoided her gaze, only one of them having the courage to answer her "Ceila, we cannot get through the fog. It is beyond our abilities."

"But surely a concerted effort could break through. We must see what's happening in the north," Ceila urged. She marched back and forth, thinking of a way around the problem, and all the while, remembering the vision she had seen before the companions left.

"We've tried everything, but there's been no trace of Nessa for days."

"What about Maerlin, or Cora?" Ceila asked.

"Maerlin's been masked from us since she left the Isle, and Cora disappeared a few days ago. It's like they don't exist," protested the Dream-catcher.

Ceila whirled around on the priestess, anger in her eyes. "No, don't say that! They can't all be dead."

"But Ceila ..." ventured another of the Sisterhood, in an effort to placate the High Priestess.

"Listen to me," commanded Ceila. "Bring in every novice with Dream-catching potential if you have to, but find me a way to break through that mist. I want to speak with Nessa, Maerlin ... any of them. I'd be happy to speak to Conal's ferrets, at this point in time. One of them must be found. Now go!"

The priestesses hurried away. No one could remember the High Priestess being so upset, but no one understood why their efforts at Dream-catching were being hampered. Someone, or something, seemed to magically be blocking their Dream-catching, and as yet, they couldn't break through.

Chapter Twenty-Four: The Plains of the Dragon

They waited in the cavern until sunlight lit up the hole in the roof of the cave. They were aware that outside, the woods were swarming with Brocian scouts hunting them. Finally, Vort signalled that it was time to leave.

"We don't have to go swimming again, do we?" Taliesin asked, concerned about the damage to his harp.

"Fear not, bard. We'll be going upwards this time." Vort pointed to the narrow chimney above.

"How are we going to get up there?" Taliesin asked, gauging the climb.

"I'll climb up first and lower a rope down. It'll help you get up if you have any difficulty," explained Vort. "If the worse comes to the worse, I can always pull you and Maerlin up."

Maerlin looked up, gauging the hand holds of the climb with an experienced eye. "What do you mean? I can climb that," she asserted. "I might be a girl, you know, but I'm a mountain girl. We learned to climb before we could walk."

"There's no need to get in a huff about it, Maerl," said Conal. "Nobody said you were useless, just because you're a girl."

"Ha! I can outrun you, Conal *MacDragan*, and I can damn well out-climb you too. Just you wait and see," Maerlin challenged, her temper flaring. "You might be the prince of some poxy country I'd never heard of until recently, but you'll always be a stable boy to me."

"Stable boy!" Conal gasped. "I was never a stable boy. That was just a disguise, you stupid ..."

"Children!" Cull interjected quickly, sensing a pending argument. "Let's just get on with this. I know that none of us slept well, but let's try to keep it friendly, shall we?"

"She started it!" Conal objected.

"I didn't. He did," she accused, pointing at Vort.

Vort winced. "I was only trying to be helpful," he mumbled as he headed for the cavern wall.

Tying the rope around his waist, he scaled the side of the cavern. It was not an easy climb as the wall leaned inwards towards the hole in the roof, but the stone offered plenty of hand and footholds.

He made it to the top without incident and climbed out of the hole and onto the rocks above, where he rested for a few moments, catching his breath. Then, he walked over to one of the sparse trees on the island and wrapped the end of the rope around it, before heading back to the hole.

"Okay, next one up," he shouted down.

"Me first," Maerlin demanded, reaching for the rope.

"Hey! No way. I'm next." Conal snatched the rope from her.

"Stop it, the pair of you!" Cull commanded. "I'll put you both over my knee and tan your behinds, if you keep this up."

They both looked at Cull guiltily.

"Taliesin, you can go next. That way, you can help Vort."

"Who … me?" Taliesin asked. He would have been happy enough to go last.

"Is there another Taliesin, around here?" Cull asked, handing him the rope.

Taliesin tied the rope around himself. Testing the knot a few times, he hefted the harp case over his shoulder and began to climb.

Eventually, they all made it onto the small rocky island without incident.

"Where to now, Vort?" Cull asked.

"We stay in the river until it veers to the north, that way we'll leave no tracks. It's shallower up here and won't be as bad."

"How long is it until it bends?" Taliesin asked.

"It'll take us about three bells, and then we'll strike east for the rest of the day. We should reach the plain before nightfall."

"Is there a place to rest up … a place to hide?" Cull asked.

Vort shook his head. "We'll need to keep going. If we stay in the woods, my clansmen will find us. Once out in the Plains of the Dragon, however, we're no better off. The Boarites patrol it heavily. We must make a dash for Dragon's Ridge and the tomb beyond. Once there, we'll be able to rest."

"What about afterwards ..." Conal asked "... after I've got the sword?"

"I'd suggest hiding out in *Tir Pect* for a while. There is mountainous country along the western shoreline that leads all the way down past Eagles Reach and beyond. If we're careful, we can make it down there during the spring, but not before. The snows will be coming soon, this far north."

"But won't the High King of *Tir Pect* object to our presence?" Taliesin queried.

"Only if he finds out," Vort said. "I have some cousins living in the lower mountains. They'll offer us shelter."

"Let's worry about that after we get Conal's pig-sticker, shall we?" Cull suggested "Lead on, Vort."

The Brocian nodded and headed upstream.

"I do wish you'd stop calling my father's sword a 'pig-sticker', Cull," Conal complained indignantly. "It's the most famous sword on the continent and the symbol of the High King. Don't you think it deserves a little bit more respect?"

"Yeah, right!" Cull said indifferently.

*****

Cora inspected the pool like a child with a new toy. She loved water. The feel, look, smell, sound, and taste of it, in all its forms. Gently, she stooped and stroked the dark waters of the pool, as if caressing a loved one. "It's beautiful," she gasped.

"I'm glad you like it. I've always found it a peaceful place," said Aiden "But this isn't getting us anywhere."

Cora turned and looked at the Brocians, wondering how to explain her plan. "I'm a novice of Deanna. I have certain blessings from the goddess, in particular with water. I've never attempted to do what I'm about to do, but I've studied others who've done it."

"You mean to say you don't know what you're doing?" Orla asked.

"I know the theory …" Cora confirmed "... I've just never actually tried it before. But don't worry. It'll either work, or it won't." Cora omitted to tell them what might happen if she failed.

"Can we help?" Orla asked.

"Yes, you can. There's a danger of me getting 'lost' if I stay underwater for too long," Cora explained "As soon as the shamans are gone, you'll need to come and fetch me back."

"What are you planning to do?" Aiden asked "...Back ... back from where?"

"You'll see, soon enough. Listen to me carefully, Orla. When you come, you'll need to swim into the pool and call out my name. Keep calling me, for I may be … distracted by the water."

Orla's face was a mask of concern as she listened.

"If I don't return, go and fetch some salt … a whole pile of salt! I want you to throw it into the water. That should get my attention. Do you understand?"

Orla nodded and repeated her instructions.

"When the shamans come, they'll be looking for me. They may seek me in your minds, as well as in your Sett. I want you to put me from your thoughts. Focus your whole attention on Vort. If you do this, it will act like a wall. Their magic will have trouble penetrating it. Do you understand?"

They both nodded.

Cora smiled encouragement and turned to face the water. Stepping calmly to the pool's edge, she slipped the robes from her body until she stood naked as the day she was born. Her light skin dimpled in the cool air, and her breasts puckered in anticipation of the cold water. She stepped into the pool, her mind going through the exercises she had learned at the Holy Isle until she was ready. Cora concentrated on the dark waters. "Spirits of the water come to my aid," she urged, summoning Water Elementals to her "Come forth, sweet Undines, I beseech thee. My need is great."

The Brocians watched in silence.

"Come, beautiful Undines, creatures of my heart. Caress me and let us become one."

They came eagerly to her; many lithe, sleek creatures, stroking her naked thighs and calves.

She walked farther into the pool, so that the water covered her stomach and then her breasts and shoulders. The Undines continued their caresses as she summoned more of them to her aid "Come, Undines. Come and embrace me," she urged as she sank beneath the water.

In her mind, she directed the Elementals. As Maerlin had seeped her consciousness into the ancient oak, so Cora seeped her very being into the pool. Pushing her magical abilities to their limits, she forced herself deeper and deeper into the multi-consciousness of the Water Elementals, embracing them in a way that was far deeper than merely physical. Her whole spirit was enveloped in the water, becoming one with it as she disappeared from sight.

Her breathing became the slow breathing of the pool, absorbing the oxygen from the air around it, letting out its breath through evaporation. Her heart slowed to nothing as the cold seeped into her very essence. No trace was left of her existed to the human eye, and the Brocians gasped in surprise.

"That's impossible!" Orla searched the pool for the novice.

"I have seen some amazing things in my long life, daughter of my heart, but this beats them all," Aiden exclaimed, picking up the robe and hiding it amongst the rocks.

The Dream-catchers burst into Ceila's rooms, waking her from her troubled sleep.

"We found Cora!" they announced.

"Yes, I know. I found her too, but she's disappeared again," the High Priestess informed them "I had her firmly in my mind. She was there and then she slipped away. How could that happen?"

The others related their own experience. Cora had finally appeared out of the mists. It had taken them some time to focus on her, but they eventually tracked her back to her body and saw through her eyes. What they saw, however, made no sense.

There was no sign of her companions. Cora was evidently in some woodland with two strangers. None of the priestesses knew who or where they were. As they watched, Cora stepped into a pool and blinked out of existence. Each of the Dream-catchers had woken with a shiver of cold.

"She can't just disappear," objected Ceila. "Surely one of thee can tell me what's going on here?"

No answer was forthcoming, adding to the High Priestess's frustration.

"I want to know every piece of woodlands from here to *Tir Pect*. I want that waterfall identified. They have to be out there someplace."

The Dream-catchers hurried off, eager to be away from the High Priestess's wrath. Ceila had not slept well since the companions had left, and she was deeply troubled by this mystical fog.

"Wait!" Ceila commanded. "Summon all the Water-sisters. I need to speak to them immediately."

*****

The raven was perched upon the Dark Mage's shoulder, accepting morsels of meat from him. Its injured wing was healing nicely, and it would soon be able to fly.

"Have another piece," the hoarse voice urged. "You'll need it to regain your strength, Little Macha."

The bird cawed and flapped its wings, exercising the newly-healed bones.

"Yes, that's right," the Mage urged, as the bird gobbled down more of the meat "Eat and grow strong, Little Macha. We'll soon feast on the bounties of our Mistress."

The bird fought against its natural abhorrence of the Mage. Soon, she would be strong enough to fly. She had been granted this second chance at life. She had even been provided this old fool to heal her and make her well. She would serve her Mistress's will, as always.

"Come Little Macha. Gaze into the bowl with me and see what lies within."

The raven looked into the bowl of steaming entrails and saw beyond it, into the magical vision.

She saw a wooded area and within it, a group of humans wading through the shallow river.

"See, Little Macha. Look who's coming to dinner."

*****

The group crouched on Vort's signal. They had left the riverside and had been moving cautiously through the woods, in an effort to get well clear of them before nightfall.

The Brocian held a finger to his lips. Vort sensed something ahead. Signalling for the rest of them to hide within the piles of rotting leaves that littered the forest floor, he crept forward, throwing leaves over his cloak as he went, to help camouflage his presence. The others waited in silence, hardly daring to breath.

Vort was gone for a long time, but eventually he returned. "It's all clear."

"What kept you?" asked Cull.

"There were some sentries guarding the wood's edge," Vort explained "We're fine to move on, now."

"You didn't kill them, did you?" Maerlin asked. Her voice was filled with worry.

"Of course not, Maerlin, they're my clansmen. I wouldn't kill them. Fortunately, I knew their commander and we had a few words. He's agreed to send them on a patrol. It should take them a while, so we'll be able to slip past while their gone."

"That was very kind of him. How did you manage that?" Cull asked.

Vort grinned like a cat in the creamery. "I sneaked up on him and held my dagger to his throat while we discussed the issue."

"I've always found that to be a good start," commented Cull dryly.

"That's what I thought …. Anyway, I pointed out that if I was able to do that to him, I could kill his men with equal ease. I suggested that it would be prudent for his warriors to look elsewhere, and after some consideration, he conceded my point," explained Vort. "Of course … once I'd let him go, he attacked me. After I'd broken his nose, his honour was satisfied, and he withdrew his men."

"I see," commented Cull. "That was very diplomatic of you."

Vort shrugged, a wicked grin etched on his face. "Shall we go? He'll be back in a while, so we really should be moving along. I'd hate to humiliate him in front of his men."

Cull shook his head. "Let's go."

They headed ever east, keeping to a steady jog until they reached the edge of the woods. Here, Vort called another brief halt.

Tall grass swayed in a light breeze for as far as the eye could see. The sun was off to their left, glaring as it neared the horizon and making it hard to look in that direction. When satisfied that it was clear, Vort signalled and sprinted across the grassland. The others followed, looking constantly for any signs of danger. When Vort was satisfied with their distance from the woods, he slipped to the ground, signalling the others to do likewise. Digging out his water container, he swilled water around his mouth before speaking "Do as I do," he instructed, pulling a single-bladed dagger from his clothing. Digging into the ground, he quickly cut a circle around his body with the knife. The others watched, wondering what he was up to. Vort then peeled back the sod, using the knife to cut excess soil from the turf, leaving only a thin layer of roots and earth attached to the grass. He worked quickly and carefully, until the circle of grass came free of the prairie. This, he draped over himself like a cloak.

"What are you doing, Vort?" Cull, like the others, had been watching the Brocian with growing curiosity.

The warrior shook loose earth from the grass cloak and smiled at Cull. "If we're spotted, the Boarites will charge towards us. We'll simply slip away through the grass and lie under these cloaks, like this." Vort showed them how it was done. "We'll disappear from sight. After searching around for a while, the Boarites will think they imagined us. It's very easy to imagine things after a day of riding across these plains. The ever-moving grass plays tricks on your eyes."

"You've done this before, I take it?" Cull thought he knew the answer.

Vort gave him a malicious grin and motioned for them to cut their own grass cloaks.

Soon five large clumps of grass were heading north-east, while the sun slowly set.

"Keep behind the person in front," Vort instructed. "You'll make less of a mark in the grass that way."

They passed two patrols, before the sun slipped behind the horizon. Both times, Vort was able to spot the patrols in time to hide. As the last of the sun slipped behind the horizon, Vort called a short halt and discarded his grass cloak.

"We should see Dragon's Ridge, once we crest the next rise, or at least we would, if there was enough light. The moon will not crest the horizon for another two bells, so we should be able to slip past the remains of *Dun Dragan* unseen."

They set off again, trusting on Vort's night vision to guide them. When they crested the next rise, however, they all stopped in their tracks.

"By the Seven, would you look at that?" Maerlin exclaimed as she gazed ahead. Fires spotted the prairie like stars in the sky. "What in the heavens is that?"

311

"Our scouts had reported heavy troop movements along the Northern Highway, but this is incredible. The Boare must have his whole army out there," Vort murmured.

"Why has he brought his whole army here? Surely, he isn't planning to invade the Broce Woods?" Cull asked.

"I don't know, but it's going to be a nuisance for us, one way or another," Vort replied, though he was also concerned for his clansmen.

"Whatever the reason, the night is passing us by. I'd hate to be caught out here in the moonlight, trapped in the middle of that army," prompted a nervous Taliesin.

"The bard has a point," agreed Vort and led them around the encamped army.

They moved in silence, eyes avoiding the campfires of the Boarite soldiers, to prevent their night vision becoming impaired. It took them some time to slowly make it beyond the army, having to do so in fits and starts, while Vort scouted ahead for sentries. The moon was already cresting the horizon when they finally made it beyond the last campfire and hurried northwards. They were close to their final destination now. Only the awareness of the huge army at their backs reminded them to tread cautiously, as they headed towards the burial mound.

Chapter Twenty-Five: The Burial Mound

Cora's spirit drifted through the calm waters. She played with the river trout and caressed the sleek boulders of the pool. The sound of the cascading waterfall was music to her ears, complimented by the lapping of the tiny waves on the rocks. She was at one with her element and in ecstasy.

All the troubles of her life had dissolved into nothingness after her transformation. Her past was a distant memory as she drifted contently within the cool, dark waters. Her life as a novice seemed a half-forgotten dream.

Something nagged at her consciousness, however, like a gnat that buzzed in her ear. It was the sound of a name being called out. There was something vaguely familiar about the name, but it was of no concern to her. She ignored it and concentrated on the sweet music of the Water Elementals.

Again the buzzing came, an urgent whine disturbing her meditation. Like a sleeper refusing to wake at the sounds of morning, she turned her consciousness away and ignored the annoying sound.

She sensed a distorted splash in the water. This was not the sweet sound of a trout jumping for flies, but the sound of a something foreign hitting the surface of the water. The pool rippled as the splash extended outwards in rings. For a moment, calm descended again on her watery consciousness, and then the screaming began.

Pain shot though Cora's mind as salt mingled with the fresh water. It filled her very essence, burning as it seeped outwards to fill the pool. It enveloped her with its tangy taint. Cora shook with terror, but more terrifying still were the cries of her beloved Water Elementals. They shrieked and slipped away from the ever-expanding salty water. To the freshwater Elementals, the salt acted like an acid, burning their soft skins, and Cora's ears filled with their terrified cries as they fled away from the poisoned waters.

Her mouth filled with water, and she began to choke. The magic of the Elementals had left her; deserted her. As if waking from a pleasant dream, only to find herself trapped in a nightmare, she was frightened and lost.

Cora was back in the world of men. She was drowning in the bottom of the pool.

Again, she sucked in water, filling her lungs as she struggled to breathe. Her mind reeled in confusion, while her limbs struggled instinctively towards the surface.

She burst onto the water's surface with a loud gasp. She was wild-eyed and pale. She looked around her like a newborn child, seeing the world for the first time. Then, reality hit her like a hammer-blow, and she fell backwards into the water, sinking beneath the water.

Hands grabbed her and hauled her struggling body back to the surface.

"No! No, please, let me die!" Cora pleaded in hysteria, longing to sink back into the heavenly world she had left so suddenly. She tried to pull away, tried desperately to retreat beneath the water.

A sharp slap caught her across the face, stunning her into silence. Hands grabbed her and hauled her out of the water. They carried her naked body onto the rocks, where warmed cloaks were wrapped around her icy skin. She was blue with the cold, her skin almost translucent from her time submerged. Cora spluttered and coughed up water, and then vomited violently. Brine mingled with vomit in her mouth. Moaning in shock, she curled into a ball and wept her young heart out.

"I'm sorry, Cora. I'm so sorry," Orla apologised.

Cora was so cold that the warmth of Orla's body felt like fire where their skin touched. It caused her to shiver violently. Her muscles twitched spasmodically with a life of their own as her blood began to pump sluggishly through her veins.

Orla was blubbering something about a shaman being in the village the whole night, searching. Cora, still in her shock, barely comprehended what was being said. She yearned to slip back in the pool, to be as one with the water. It felt like her very soul had been torn from her body, leaving an empty shell behind.

Slowly, her body warmed, and as it did so, her memories returned, making her time in the water, seem like an ethereal dream. Cora was exhausted, more tired than she had ever been in her whole life. Her very spirit ached, not just her flesh and bones, leaving her unable to rise.

They carried her to the Sett and laid her down beside the fire. They fed her warm broth and herbal teas, in an effort to rouse her from her zombie-like trance. Cora drifted in and out of consciousness as her mind rested from the rigours of her magic.

After a long time of troubled sleep, Cora woke, and though she was still very weak, she struggled from the bed and went in search of Orla. She needed to speak to the Brocian woman, urgently.

*****

Sometime later, the two women sat together on Orla's bed, hugging each other as they sought solace from the troubles of their worlds. Neither spoke. Their needs went far beyond words, more intimate and personal. Finally they slept, still wrapped in each other's arms. This time, their sleep was untroubled.

When they woke, much later and still entwined, they awoke as one, refreshed and ready for the night ahead. Cora looked over at her newfound friend. "We need to go and find them. They're in grave danger."

Orla nodded. She had also witnessed the dream message. She had dreamt of the beautiful woman in white robes, and she had heard the urgency of the High Priestess's message. Though she didn't recognise the woman within the dream, the woman was clearly a person of authority and knew Cora and the others.

"I'll wake Aiden at once and speak to him. I'll make him understand," Orla promised.

When they reached the common room, however, they found Aiden already awake and speaking with the other Elders of the Sett. They had also had a vision of a fair woman in white.

"I've sent runners to the other Setts, telling them where Vort and the others are heading. Even if they are against us, they'll send their warriors to help recapture them. They'll bring my son back to face the High Council."

"But they could kill them!" Cora was still unsure of the intricate politics of the Brocians.

315

"Not if I'm there to make sure that justice is served," Aiden assured confidently. "We leave with the ringing of the next bell. We'll bring as many warriors with us as we can muster. We'll need to be in the vanguard of the *Broce* forces. That way, we can ensure that Dorcha's lackeys don't interfere."

"I'm coming with you," Cora insisted, her tone dismissing any argument.

"So am I," added Orla. "The women of *Clann Na Broce* are trained at arms. We can fight beside our men."

The Clan Elder looked at the two women, seeing the bond developing between them and the steely gazes of determination on their faces. "It's been a long time since the women of *Clann Na Broce* fought alongside their menfolk, but it isn't without precedent. If you're sure about this, Orla, then so be it," Aiden agreed.

As the women turned away to prepare themselves for the journey, he spoke again "Orla, my daughter ..." he continued, causing Orla to turn and meet his rheumy eyes "...You fill my heart with pride."

"Thank you, father. You have always been the rock to support me, as you are to the whole Sett."

*****

Cull could see the white stones, glowing in the moonlight. The companions lay in the long grass a short distance from the burial hill, waiting while Vort scouted the perimeter. He wanted to be sure that no Boarite soldiers lurked in the long grass around the hill, before proceeding.

Two ravens were perched on the standing stones above the mound. Their dark shadows stood out against the marble dolmens of the mystical ring. Cull had always hated these Angels of Death. He fished a sling from within the many pockets of his baggy coat and searched around for a suitable stone.

"What're you doing?" Maerlin hissed.

"I'm going to kill those cursed Death-birds," Cull hissed back, pointing at the two black shadows perched on the stones.

"No, you're not!" Maerlin grabbed his hand to stay the shot. "They're servants of Macha. Don't you know that it's bad luck to slay them?"

"They'll wake up the whole army if they start to sing," Cull insisted.

"Can you hit them both with one shot?" Taliesin whispered "If you kill one and wake the other, it'll make enough noise to wake the dead. On a still night like this, its cawing will carry for miles. Maerlin's right. Leave the birds be."

Cull reluctantly nodded. "I guess you're right. I just hate those damned Death-birds."

"They're just birds, Cull! Anyway, it's better not to tempt the goddess of death." Conal's gaze was fixed on the huge mound. "If we're quiet, we should be able to sneak into the mound without waking them. Leave them alone and hopefully the goddess will feed elsewhere."

They could see Vort, stealthily crawling towards them, and soon he was crouching beside Cull and the others.

"It's clear out there," confirmed Vort "There are no fresh tracks anywhere near the mound, so we can get inside, and not a moment too soon. The sun will be up shortly."

"Great ... let's go." Cull rose to his feet. On his signal, they scurried forward, moving as quietly as they could through the long grass. They were soon nestled against the side of mound.

The burial mound was an ancient man-made structure, older than the knowledge of the bards. Long, long ago, a people long since passed into obscurity, had brought immense stones and tons of earth to this site and built this giant structure. Their reasons for doing this had long since been forgotten. The mound stretched for fifty paces in diameter and rose to the height of four men. The banks of the mound were made of large white stones knitted closely together. These glowed eerily as if they had stolen some of Lugh's magic and held it within them, to be released during the time of darkness. The stones sloped upwards at a sharp angle, and the mound was capped with a green sward of grass. On the top of the mound stood the mystical ring of gigantic granite stones, standing like ancient statues in the night. These dolmens were the Twelve Warriors. These symmetrically placed menhirs circled around a central altar stone. The Maiden Stone lay flat on the earth like a table. Local lore told tales of dark times, in the deep past, when this stone was used for human sacrifices. It is said that once, the Maiden Stone had been used as an altar to the Elder god, *Crom Cruach*; the evil snake-god who was banished by the Seven Greater Gods who now ruled the heavens.

On the eastern side of the mound, where it faced the morning sun, a small passageway lay partially hidden in the tall grass. It was to here that the companions crept. A broad stone lintel, intricately carved in ancient runes and scrollwork, marked the entrance. The secrets hidden within its ogham runes had long since been forgotten.

The entranceway was narrow, making it a tight squeeze to crawl through, into the dark chamber beneath. The passageway headed down at a slight angle so that, at midsummer, the rising sun would fill the inner chamber with the first rays of Lugh's light.

Vort went in first to check for danger. His night vision was the best in the group. A narrow corridor ran directly from the entrance to the main chamber, and three smaller chambers led off from that room to form a cross. The tomb smelled old and musty, with no trace of recent occupation that Vort could recognise. No faint odour of food, alcohol or smoke lingered in the chambers, to hint of recent occupation by man. Neither was there the smell of armour oil, urine, blood, or sweat; the scents which lingered wherever soldiers had been picketed. Satisfied that no one had been in the tomb recently and no danger lurked in the side chambers, Vort activated one of the green bundles of fungi and lit up the interior of the tomb. This was the all-clear signal for the others, and they quickly clambered into the corridor.

Conal was eager to see his father and was next into the chamber. He pushed through the narrow confines and was soon in the passageway. The green light drew him onwards, to where Vort stood in silent respect.

Entering the main chamber, Conal paused and looked around. The wrapped remains of a long dead hero had been placed on the floor in the corner. This must be the original occupant of the burial mound. He had been carefully removed from his central plinth, to be replaced with the body of the High King: Conal's father.

The raised plinth stood in the room's centre, perfectly situated to bathe fully in the first rays of the midsummer sun, in the beam of light known as the Light of Heroes. Such a light was claimed to be a blessing from the sun god, Lugh. Conal's father had been laid to rest with as much respect

318

as possible after his final battle. The body had decomposed, hiding the mortal wound that had slain him as much as it hid his features. Conal looked at the regal armour and fine cloak, and he recalled his last memories of their time together. His father's parting words had been distracted, his mind elsewhere. The King's thoughts had been on the impending battle as he said farewell to his only son.

The two had not been close since the death of Conal's mother. It was as if the sight of the boy haunted the father. The King was reminded of the loss of his beloved wife every time he looked at his son and it tore at his heart. Nevertheless, he had loved his son, and he had done his best to ensure his survival. That much was evident from the arrangements he had made with people such as Ceila.

Tears welled up in Conal's eyes and ran freely down his cheeks. He stood in silence, looking at the body of the dead King. So many unsaid words lay between them. So much put aside for a later date, a better time; a time that never came.

The others gathered around in silence, none venturing further, lest they disturb him.

Eventually, Conal took a step forward, and then another. Each one, slow and tentative, but bringing him closer to the body of his dead father. While the others waited silently, he placed his hands on his father's gauntleted fists; fists that still held the legendary *An Fiacail Dragan*. Conal silently prayed to Deanna, the goddess of life. When he had finished, he paused a moment in thought and prayed again. This time his prayer was shorter and more succinct; a ritual prayer to Macha, the goddess of death. To ignore the dark goddess was never a good idea. His father had been a warrior and therefore, in some morbid sense, a servant of the dark goddess. He prayed that Macha would guide his father's spirit in the next world, where the High King would feast in the Hall of Heroes, as was fitting.

Wiping his eyes, he turned to the others. "Must we leave him here?" he asked, though he knew that they could not carry the body to safety.

No one spoke for a while, each knowing the truth, but none saying it. Finally, it was Maerlin who spoke; the girl who had lived in ignorance of the politics of Dragania her whole life, and until recently, had not even heard of the Boarites or the Dragons. She was the one who came up with the solution. "Is this not a King's chamber, Conal? Is there a more fitting place for a hero to reside?"

Conal thought for a moment, his heart still troubled. "What if the Boarites find him? They'd desecrate his tomb!"

"Perhaps ..." ventured Maerlin "... I could move the lintel stone a little, so that it was narrower. The Light of Heroes would still enter, but no one larger than a small child could gain entry. Would that help, Conal?"

"Can you do that, Maerl?" he asked, remembering some of Maerlin's other attempts at magic.

The novice looked him in the eye and replied "I honestly don't know, but I can try, Conal. I'll do my best. That's all I can promise."

"Fine, then let's do it," agreed Conal. "I've no desire to spend the rest of the day here with the dead. Let's seal up the chamber and head north before dawn."

Cull shook his head. "That won't work, lad. We'd never make it in time. There's nowhere to hide around her for miles. Conal, listen to me," he urged "We can spend the day in one of the side chambers and leave at nightfall. When we leave, we'll let Maerlin seal the tomb. We'll have the whole night to slip away. I'm sure Maerlin can't move that stone without making at least some noise. If we do it now, the whole place will be swarming with Boarites. That's to say nothing of the Dark Mage's acolytes."

Conal didn't like the idea of staying, but he knew that Cull's words made sense. After a moment's hesitation, he nodded and moved away from the corpse.

"Haven't you forgotten something?" Taliesin asked, stopping Conal with an outstretched hand.

"What's that?" Conal manner's was more gruff than usual.

"The sword, lad, *An Fiacail Dragan*," answered Vort. "Isn't that why we came?"

Conal sighed, shaking off his melancholy and inspected his father's sword. It had once been his great-grandfather's sword, and it had been used in the legendary First Battle of the High Kings, long ago. Since then, it had become the symbol of the High King. Its basic shape was similar to many other such swords. The blade stood over half a man's length long and almost a hand's-width wide at its thickest. The hilt had been designed for either a one or two-handed grip. There, however, the similarities ended. The hilt was wonderfully crafted into the form of a dragon. The beast's wide jaws clenching the blade, making it appear like a tongue, bursting from its mouth. The dragon's jaws spread wide to act as blade-breakers. The body of the silver dragon was hidden within the dead King's gauntleted grasp. It was a beautifully sculpted hilt; fit for any King, but what made the sword unique was its blade.

The bards claimed that the blade was crafted from the canine tooth of the last of the Frost Dragons. It was for this reason that the sword had got its name; *An Fiacail Dragan*: the Dragontooth. It was said that the combined magical powers of the Order or Deanna had gone into crafting the blade, and that they had imbued the weapon with their magic. In the green light of the Brocian lamp, it glowed with a life of its own, attesting to the possible truth behind the legends.

Conal had seen *An Fiacail Dragan* cut easily through armour and flesh without nicking the magical weapon. The blade shone with a warm, golden glow, so unlike a steel sword. It never felt cold to the touch, not even on a winter's day. Running his hand over the exposed blade, Conal experienced a shiver of delight. It couldn't really be made from a dragon's tooth, he thought, but whatever its origins, the sword was clearly steeped in magic.

The sheath of the sword was still strapped across his father's shoulder, baldric fashion, and carefully, Conal unclasped the buckle and pulled it free. The prince discarded his own sword and buckled the empty sheath across his own shoulder. Then, almost hesitantly, he reached towards the sword. His fingers were drawn to the legendary blade. He felt a thrill of excitement at the prospect of possessing such a mythical weapon. He touched the gauntleted hands that were clasped protectively over the dragon-shaped hilt.

The others watched in silence, holding their breaths.

Conal looked down at the blade of the High King and then at his father's helmeted face. The moments ticked by as the others waited. They had come a long way and risked much for this moment.

321

"Well?" Cull finally asked, getting impatient. "Are you going to take the pig-sticker, or not?"

Conal turned to look at his mentor, his expression unreadable.

"Well?"

"No, Cull. Let him keep it ... at least for a little while longer. I'll get it later, before we leave," Conal replied. Turning, he stalked away, to rest in one of the side chambers. Maerlin, sensing his unease, followed him, but Conal was in one of his taciturn moods. He ignored her presence. The two of them settled down in silence within the darkness. Each was lost in their own thoughts. They found comfort in their shared silence as they had before on the Lurching Otter.

Vort looked over at Cull and shrugged.

Letting out a sigh, Cull headed to the opposite chamber. There, the three men made themselves as comfortable as possible within the cramped confined of the chamber and prepared to sleep.

Chapter Twenty-Six: The Dragontooth Sword

Cora rode through the trees at the head of the column. Over a hundred warriors had left the Southern Dell Sett, men and women of the Brocian sub-clan. The only ones to remain behind were the old, the infirm, or those too heavy with child to fight. These, were left to guard the Sett while every able-bodied warrior raced north to rescue Vort.

Other warriors emerged from the woods as they proceeded. They had come from the nearby Setts. These warriors had fought alongside Vort and respected him. The numbers rose steadily, and Cora soon lost count of the amount of warriors that raced through the woods. Orla and Aiden ran along beside her horse, with other close family members: the vanguard of the hurriedly-amassed army.

By the time they reached the edge of the woods, the warriors had become a horde. The war banners of many Setts flew in the autumn breeze as they gazed across the expanse of moonlit grass. At the tree line, they called a halt. Some planning would be needed before entering enemy territory.

"Send out scouts," ordered Aiden. His order ran through the gathered horde. Others were still arriving as the scouts headed out across the prairie. Each of the scouts selected a spot of grass and 'skinned' the prairie to make grass cloaks, as Vort had done earlier.

Still men gathered, and inevitably, some of them were shamans. They headed towards Cora and the banner of the Southern Dell Sett. Soon, an argument erupted over who was to lead the Clan into battle.

"...But, there's no Champion here to lead this expedition," demanded a shaman. He was a haughty-looking fellow with a hooked nose. "We should elect a new Champion before we proceed."

Aiden growled menacingly at the shaman. "We have a Champion already, Belik. He's out there somewhere and possibly in danger. I won't stand by and let you, and that snake-tongued master of yours, elect another Champion in his absence."

"The High Council has ordered his return to face trial. He has broken sacred traditions," Belik insisted.

"No. Actually, the High Council didn't say that. It was Dorcha who made that demand," Aiden clarified angrily, spittle flying from his lips. "The High Council agreed that we should ask Vort and his companions to return, so that we can get to the bottom of this matter. There's a big difference. Don't flap that slippery tongue of yours at me, shaman, or I'll rip it out of your mouth."

"Father, calm yourself. Angry words will get us nowhere," Orla urged.

"With no Champion to take the lead …" Belik demanded "… I insist that Dorcha lead this expedition. He is, after all, the High-shaman and a man of great wisdom."

"A shaman … leading the *Clann* to war?" one of the warriors protested "Never!"

Others rumbled their agreement.

"I realise that such an option would go against tradition. It has never been done before. However, neither has it been known for a warrior to Form-meld," Belik pointed out "But your Champion seems to have no problem flaunting traditions."

Aiden spoke again, containing his temper, if barely "And where is the High-shaman, Belik? I see no sign of Dorcha. Is he still lurking about in one of his towers? What dark deed is he up to this time?"

"I'm sure he'll be along at any moment," Belik replied "Maybe, I should manage affairs in his absence."

"How would you like to read the future in your own entrails?" Aiden offered; pulling out his *Tri-crub* and letting it glitter in the moonlight.

The shaman paled visibly and stepped back "That's … that's … that's no way to speak to a shaman," he protested nervously, eyeing the gathered warriors. None of the warriors interjected on the shaman's behalf. Some even grinned maliciously.

Finally, one of the warriors spoke up "With Vort unable to defend his honour, we should elect *Aiden Crionna* in his stead. That way, Vort's honour is preserved."

Other warriors agreed, nodding and cheering.

"Well, Father? Will you protect my husband's honour?" Orla asked, beaming with pride at the gesture from the assembled warriors.

Aiden was lost for words, his throat suddenly thick with emotion, but he nodded his acceptance.

A cheer ran through the Clan, and the shout went up "Strength to the Southern Dell Sett!"

It echoed across the woods and prairie as others took up the chant and bellowed it out in defiance of the gathered shamans. *Aiden Crionna Na Broce* of the Southern Dell Sett had not felt such pride since his son took up the role as War-chief. He cleared his throat while he waited for the cheering to subside. It went on for a while longer before he raised his hands for silence "Warriors of *Clann Na Broce* ..." he bellowed "... Follow your captains. You all know the ways of the Badger Clan. Let us go to war!"

Another cheer rang out across the land as the warriors surged forward. As they ran, they broke up into groups of fifty or so warriors, each following an elected captain. They ran north in single file, following the banner of the Southern Dell Sett, and the one solitary rider.

The light in the eastern sky heralded another day as the warriors advanced.

*****

The horde of *Clann Na Broce* advanced north, while their scouts cleared the way ahead for them. The scouts rose up from the earth around Boarite patrols, killing them swiftly before they could give warning of the advancing warriors.

By late afternoon, the Brocian scouts had found the army of Lord Boare, and they had pulled back to warn the advancing horde. Aiden learned that the Boarites outnumbered his own warriors, two to one. This was to say nothing of the magicians within Lord Boare's ranks.

The Brocians knew well the legendary powers of Dubhgall the Black. Without the skills of Dorcha, they had no shaman strong enough to offer them protection. Dorcha was still missing, leaving his acolytes like lost sheep. None of the other shamans offered aid to the warriors. They would have to face the coming battle without magical assistance.

Aiden did what any wise general would do under such circumstances. He ordered out more scouts and had his men slip into hiding amidst the tall grass. Within a short while, the warrior horde of *Clann Na Broce* had disappeared. Only a lone horse could be seen, standing on the prairie.

"Are you sure we can't kill your horse?" Aiden asked again, though they had discussed this matter at length before.

"I'm certain," insisted Cora. "I'm still feeling weak and I haven't the strength to run, believe me. Even riding is hard at the moment. Anyway, the horse isn't endangering us. If a patrol saw it and rode this way, it would be massacred, long before they could get near enough to investigate."

The novice was right and Aiden relented.

"So what's the plan?" Cora asked.

"We wait until dark and then we attack," explained Orla, matter of fact. "We'll fall on them before the moon rises and be gone before they finish bleeding to death. That is the way of the *Broce*."

"But how can you fight without moonlight? Aren't you going to risk killing each other by mistake?"

"We'll be able to see in the darkness, but the Boarites won't. Therefore, we'll have the advantage," explained Orla. "We'll fall upon them as they sleep, like winter wolves on newborn lambs. Before dawn, the army of *Clann Na Torc* will be decimated. They will no longer be a threat to us."

Cora shuddered as the image came to her mind. "How does that help us get to the others?"

"They'll be found a little farther north, Cora," Aiden explained "We'll break away from the main attack and go around the Boare's men, amidst the confusion of battle. While the Boarites are being slaughtered, we'll race to the Twelve Warriors, and hopefully, we'll find them there. We should reach the burial mound by midnight and be safely back in the woods before dawn."

"But why attack at all?" Cora asked "Why not just go round them in the darkness and leave them alone?"

They looked at her with expressions of dismay.

"We are at war with the Boars of *Clann Na Torc*," Orla explained. "They have felled our sacred trees and invaded our territory. They have broken the terms of the Great Truce. They must pay for these crimes. They must forever tremble in fear of *Clann Na Broce*."

"Isn't that a bit ... barbaric?" Cora suggested, still not understanding the need for open warfare.

They looked at her with incomprehension.

*****

Dubhgall watched. Tonight, would be the eve of Samhaine. It was a very magical time for Necromancy and the other Dark Arts. It was a time when the boundaries between the world of the living and the Otherworld were at their weakest; a time when the dead could cross over and walk amongst the living. It was almost time to achieve his goal. He had been working hard towards this day. Years had gone by as he patiently orchestrated the key elements to his bidding. It was finally within his grasp, but he must not lose focus so near to the end.

Absently, he fed tender morsels to the injured raven as he watched the steaming entrails within the bowl. The child had been a true innocent, and her bowels gave a clear image of the battlefield. "Look, Little Macha! Look at what our Mistress has brought us to feast upon. She will have her fill this night," he cackled, petting the bird.

The raven focused on the bowl, fighting off her revulsion at being handled. She forced herself to remember her Mistress's mission and resisted the urge to peck out the old man's eyes.

The vision in the bowl changed under the Mage's direction and showed another scene.

The Boarite army were busily preparing for the expected attack. Lord Boare stood amongst his men, urging them on to greater effort, anticipating the coming victory.

Dubhgall waved his wrinkled hand over the bowl and another scene appeared. He looked down at the burial mound. Everything seemed quiet until the Mage concentrated and refocused. Amongst the long grasses, some distance west of the hill, a large force of Boarite soldiers waited in hiding.

"Look, Little Macha. The final pieces are falling into place. The Boare has heeded my request and sent some of his Elites for the coming event. I knew that the prize I promised him would be enough to tempt him. I couldn't have trusted this job to his Lordship's pathetic conscripts."

Where other troops would have become restless and fallen asleep, the Elites continued to maintain vigilance. They took turns, silently watching the mound and the surrounding grassland, waiting for the anticipated signal.

"Come, Little Macha. It's time for you to stretch that injured wing of yours," Dubhgall commanded, as he drew forth his magical powers.

Two ravens flew north-easterly. As the sun sank in the west, they landed on the standing stones in a flurry of feathers. This time, one of them changed shape and the Mage stood on the Maiden Stone, awaiting the coming events.

*****

It was almost dark when Cull woke the others and they ate a quick meal.

"It's almost time to leave," Vort advised, having just peered out of the entrance.

"Thank the Seven." Conal was eager to be gone. He found the tomb depressing, and he wanted to be away from it as soon as possible.

"Is it clear outside?" Cull asked.

"I can't see anything, but I haven't been outside yet. I was waiting for the sun to set," Vort replied "Should I go and check now?"

"No ... You'd probably better wait until we're ready," said Cull. "A little while longer isn't going to make any difference." Turning to the prince, he asked "Do you still want to take the sword, lad, or will you leave it here with your father for safe keeping?"

Conal still wondered what he was going to do. He couldn't risk the magical sword falling into the hands of the Boare: besides, it was a family heirloom, and so, it was rightfully his now. "I think I'll take it with us."

"Okay. I guess it's time to retrieve that pig-sticker," Cull prompted. "You might want to leave your own sword in its place. A hero should be armed in the Otherworld."

Conal nodded and lifted his discarded weapon from the floor. "That's a good idea, Cull. Thanks."

The others readied themselves to leave as Conal walked over to the High King's remains and placed a hand upon *An Fiacail Dragan*.

"Rest in peace, Father," he prayed. "May they feast you well in the Hall of Heroes." Conal gripped the dragon-shaped hilt and prised it from his father's clenched fists.

Suddenly, a blinding flash of light erupted as the sword came free. The loud bang of its detonation echoed throughout the chamber. Strange green smoke billowed around the tomb as, blinded and deafened, the comrades tried desperately to escape.

They stumbled into one another, coughing and spluttering as they staggered away. One by one, however, they were overcome by the toxic gas and slumped into unconsciousness. The bodies of the fallen further hampered the escape of their comrades. The first to collapse was Conal, followed quickly by Maerlin and Taliesin. The greater bulk of the two other men slowed the effects of the poisonous gas. Vort was the last to fall, being the farthest away from the body of the dead King when the trap went off. He was climbing out of the entrance when the fumes finally overtook him. As he slipped into unconsciousness, he could hear the raucous laughter of Death Angels, summoning Macha to reap her harvest.

Chapter Twenty-Seven: The Battle of Dragon Ridge

The Elites heard the raven's harsh song, and they knew that the time had finally come. They hurried to where the Dark Mage stood, waiting by the burial chamber.

"I'd give it a short while before you drag them out," Dubhgall suggested. "That gas will need a little time to dissipate."

The Dark Mage turned and headed back to the standing stones to prepare for the coming ritual. Soon, he estimated, the battle would begin at Dragon's Ridge. Why was he always drawn back to this battlefield? It was like replaying destiny, over and over again. How long had it been since that first battle, the one that history referred to as the Battle of the High Kings? So much had happened since then. So many sacrifices, each Samhaine, to sustain him over the long years of his protracted life, and yet his task was still not complete, but the end was finally in sight.

His old bones were aching more with each passing day. It had been a long year since the last rite, but soon, he would feel rejuvenated. He hoped that his sacrifices were well received by the Dark One. The final threat would soon be eliminated.

$$*****$$

Cora had been unable to sleep. Few amongst the Brocian Horde had. They were waiting for darkness to fall. Finally, the sun set in the west, signalling that it was time to begin.

Orla came forward in the half-light and handed something to the novice. "Here, chew on this."

"I'm not that hungry really," replied Cora, whose stomach was twisting with nerves.

"It's not food, silly. It's called *Suiladorcha* root," explained Orla. "It tastes nasty, but it'll be very handy once it gets dark."

"I've never heard of it before. What is it exactly?"

"It's a plant that only grows in the deepest part of the Broce Woods, near to *Broca*. It's a tiny green flower. You could easily miss it, it's so small. You'd think it was a blade of grass," explained Orla. "The roots, however, are thick and strong. Our shamans prepared the root using special magic. They will heighten your senses, and in particular your night vision."

Cora bit into the root. After a moment or two, her mouth filled with vile-tasting juices as her saliva worked on the dried root. "Ugh! It's disgusting."

"You've got that right, but chew it anyway. It'll help," advised Orla.

A harsh barking began nearby, short and hollow. It was carried across the plain and taken up by others within the horde.

"What's that?" Cora asked, looking at the barking warriors.

"It's time for us to dance for Cernunnos," proclaimed Orla, her face flushed with excitement. "That's the summons to war."

Cora hurried to her horse, still chewing on the disgusting root. "This root isn't working," she said. "Perhaps, I need to be a Brocian for it to work properly."

"Don't worry about it. It takes a little time to work into your system. Just keep chewing," assured Orla as she took up her place beside Cora's horse.

Aiden ran up to them, carrying his war banner. He too, was chewing on a root.

He smiled up at Cora and asked "Are you ready?"

"I'm as ready as I'll ever be."

Aiden raised his head and yelped three short barks. His signal was relayed along the line of warriors. Almost as one, the warriors of *Clann Na Broce* surged forward.

The sun was disappearing, leaving only a faint hint of orange on the horizon. The warriors headed northwards at a walk, letting their muscles loosen after the long time of inaction. Soon, they picked up the pace and moved forward at a steady jog.

Cora realised that the sun had finished setting as the orange glow had disappeared, yet she could still see clearly. Her vision was similar to that on the night of a full moon, but she could see no moon visible. Her vision should be nothing but utter blackness.

She could make out the features of the painted warriors beside her, even the individual blades of grass as her horse cantered forward. Turning to her other senses, she listened to the horse's breath, which seemed loud to her highly-tuned ears. She realised that she could actually hear the horse's heart beating in its chest, and a thrill went through her at this new sensory awareness.

She focused on her sense of smell. Her brain registered the scent of horse sweat and leather in the air. She also detected the sweeter scent of pollen as her horse disturbed the long grass. Human sweat and the rich tang of the *Suiladorcha* root assailed her nostrils along with many other scents she struggled to decipher.

She could smell wood smoke. It was coming to her on the breeze, from Dragon's Ridge, where Lord Boare's army was waiting. She wondered if they had any idea of the imminent attack. Would they have noticed the disappearance of their scouting parties? One way or another, she and the Brocians were about to find out.

They crested the hill in silence. Before them, they could see the campfires of the Boarite army; a myriad collection of small orange glows that made their eyes blink after the darkness of the open plain.

"*BROCE ABÚ!*" The sudden roar came from the horde, over and over again as they charged down the hill "*BROCE ABÚ!*" Cora found herself carried along in the surge as the clansmen charged.

She could see the shimmering of Brocian blades and spears, glittering in the orange glow of the campfires. A trumpet blew within the Boarite camp, a panicked wailing of terror. The trumpeter desperately tried to rouse the sleeping troops, warning them of the surprise attack.

Cora clung to her horse, glad that Cora and Aiden were protecting her, as they broke through the outer pickets.

Boarite soldiers hurriedly regrouped before the amassed horde of *Clann Na Broce,* and the forces met with a resounding clash. The air rang with the sound of men dying.

Cora shuddered as her heightened senses struggled against the gory information being fed to her brain. She watched in horror as soldiers were cut down before her eyes. A path was being carved through the enemy, and she followed in the wake of the lead warriors.

Aiden and Orla remained at her side, deflecting any attacks that came her way with brutal efficiency. They were making steady progress through the outer regions of the enemy camp. It was then that the world burst into light around them.

The dazzling light shone down from the Dragons Ridge in huge beams. Night turned suddenly into day. The Brocian charge shuddered to a halt, as warriors shielded their eyes against the glare. Some stumbled forward, trying to continue, but the waiting Boarites cut them down.

"It's a trap!" Orla warned.

"What is that light?" Aiden strained to see through the brightness.

"The sun god, Lugh, is falling on our heads!" a warrior cried out, teetering on panic.

"No ... It's magic," Cora assured, though she did not know of any magic that could create such brightness.

Her eyes watered as the light seared into her brain, the effects of the root heightening the already bright illumination.

A horn blew from the ridge, loud and long, and the Boarites surged forward at the signal. The light shone from behind them, so they were not as blinded by its intensity. They yelled abuse as they cut down the blinded warriors of *Clann Na Broce*. Lord Boare had been holding back the majority of their troops, until the magical glare halted the Brocians' charge. Now the Boarite conscripts had the advantage of both numbers and surprise. They quickly made use of it.

"Fall back!" Aiden roared. "Fall back!"

Cora desperately dredged through her brain for a counter-spell to lessen the effects of the blinding lights. None would come to mind.

The Brocian warriors were forced backwards by the full might of the Boarite infantry. Deadly hails of arrows rained down upon the closely packed warriors, and many more were felled by the disciplined spear work of the Boarite conscripts.

*****

The Dream-catchers watched the battle in horror.

"Is there still no sign of the others?" Ceila asked as she watched the vision in the Seers pool.

The gathered priestesses shook their heads.

"They're still hidden by the mists, Ceila," a Dream-catcher informed the High Priestess.

Ceila frowned and walked away from the pool, pondering the decision she was about to make. As a rule, the Order of Deanna remained neutral in such disputes, but they had sat on the fence for too long in the matter of Lord Boare's attempts to gain the High Kingship. Prepared for the argument that would ensue, Ceila announced "I will contact Cora Water-sister and offer her our assistance."

"What! You can't do that, Ceila," one of the priestesses objected. Others nodded their agreement. "We don't interfere in the politics of the Kingdom."

"Can we stand by and allow Lord Boare to desecrate the throne of Dragania? Can we watch while he turns the Kingdom into chaos, as his great-grandfather did?" Ceila protested; her face flushed with anger. "We will intercede on the Brocians' behalf. One of our Sisters is with them, and her companions must be nearby. Does anyone here wish to challenge my authority on this matter?"

None offered further dissent.

"Summon our best magicians. We will need their aid in this battle, and the blessing of Deanna."

Summoning her Dream-catcher magic, Ceila melded with her Sisters and focused on the image of the young novice, far away.

"*Cora,*" Ceila called. "*Cora Water-sister, heed my call.*"

The plain lit up to the south of the burial mound. This was the signal that Dubhgall had been waiting for. His acolytes had sprung the trap on the Brocian Horde. Now, his ceremony could begin.

"Macha, goddess of war and death," he chanted in his croaky voice "Come and witness my adoration. Come! Summon your Dark Angels to feast amongst the harvest I have brought for you."

Dubhgall walked around the Twelve Warriors, lighting similar bright magical flares to those used on the Dragon's Ridge. These torches, however, did not need the burnished steel shields behind them to direct their brightness. Shadows scurried away from the stone circle to reveal five slumped forms, secured firmly to the ancient dolmens.

The Boarite Elites formed a defensive ring around the burial mound. Their task was to guard against any attacker that might slip past the battlefield to the south. Dubhgall the Black, and his pet raven, stood by the Maiden Stone in the centre of the ring of dolmens. The Mage was reading carefully from an ancient magical tome.

"Mother of Darkness, come to me. Taste the sweet flesh of the sacrifice that I bring to thee this night," Dubhgall intoned.

The raven, which had been sitting on his shoulder, flapped its wings and cawed in response.

"Yes, Little Macha. Your Mistress is coming," cooed the Mage as he continued.

The companions hung limply in the ropes that bound them to the stones. The Mage walked amongst them, studying each of them in turn. He came forward and stood before the beggar, Cull. With a touch of the Mage's hand, Cull awoke. "What!" he rumbled as he looked around.

"You must be the one they call Cull," said Dubhgall. "Wake up, alley-rat, and witness the real ruler of Dragania."

The magician walked on, coming to the prone figure of the gangly harper. Placing his hand on the singer's forehead, the Mage woke him from his toxic slumber. "Wake up harper, you are needed here. Look around you and take careful note. I'll be expecting a great epic out of you before this night is out," Dubhgall commanded, heading farther around the circle of stones.

"Ah, the Royal Whelp!" he sneered as he woke Conal. "Wake up boy. It's time that you inherited your birthright. Tonight you will follow your father into the Hall of Heroes ... or should that be the Hall of Fools?"

Conal shook with rage, taking in the scene before him. "You knew, didn't you? How did you find me?"

"Soon, all will be revealed, *MacDragan*," Dubhgall assured as he removed the dagger from Conal's belt. "When the High Priestess placed a charm on this blade, it caused me no end of trouble. Someday soon, I will deal with that meddling Sisterhood and their swampy Isle. I will teach them not to tamper in my affairs, ever again. But, for all their cleverness, they missed one vitally important detail. Do you know what that was, Conal? They masked you from my scrying eyes, but they forgot to mask another. Her fate is entwined in yours. This was written in ancient text, many eons ago for all to see; at least, for those who can understand such things. Yet the foolish priestesses left her unprotected. All I had to do was patiently watch her grow. I knew that she would come to you one day. It was written in the stars. She led me right to you, and I was able to watch you through her eyes."

"Maerlin!" Conal gasped, as understanding hit him.

"Ah! Well done, *MacDragan!*" Dubhgall exclaimed, as he slapped the boy's cheek condescendingly. "Yes, it was the girl. She led me to you, and through her, I learned what you had planned. It was so easy to set a trap for you, and you arrived right on time. Did you know that? I hope you appreciate all the effort I've gone to, hurrying you north for this very special occasion."

"What occasion?" Conal asked. "Why go to all this trouble? Surely, you don't need the Dragontooth sword?"

Dubhgall laughed. "You stupid boy, I've no need of *An Fiacail Dragan*. However, I'm sure that his Lordship, the Boare, will be grateful for retrieving it, but that's all. No, boy. What I wanted was something with much more magical power than that."

"What's that then?"

"Clearly, some of your lessons have been lacking, boy. Tonight is Samhaine. It's a time of great magic. Tonight, I'll perform a very powerful spell and bring youth back into my old bones," explained Dubhgall. "You've foolishly brought me, not one, but two sacrifices; you and Maerlin. I have two virgins to slay on the Maiden Stone, a double feast for the Dark One to bring me back my stolen youth. Tonight, I will gain the vigour I need to complete my lifetimes work. No longer will I need that pathetic despot to shelter behind and pamper. Never before have I been able to sacrifice a servant of Deanna, and a Wild-magician at that. She will make a magnificent offering!"

The Mage walked on, pleased as he saw comprehension dawn in Conal's eyes. The next person to be woken was Vort. The Brocian looked up and growled a curse. "Dorcha! What's the meaning of this? The High Council will have you banished when they hear about this."

The Mage laughed. "Vort, oh, Vort, you were always such a fool. You take men too much at face value."

"Vort," Conal explained. "That's Dubhgall the Black. That's Lord Boare's pet."

"No, Conal, you're mistaken. That's Dorcha. He's the Head Shaman of *Clan Na Broce*!"

"I'm telling you, Vort. That loathsome scum is Lord Boare's pet mage, Dubhgall the Black!"

"It can't be!"

"Silence!" Dubhgall commanded and flicked a casual finger at the prince. Conal convulsed in pain as the spell struck. "The prince is correct ... at least about my identity. I am, however, no one's pet," Dubhgall growled as he walked on to the last of the companions.

"Wake up, Maerlin, my pretty little novice. Wake up and witness your doom," he chirped as he released Maerlin from her magically-induced sleep.

Maerlin looked into the face of her nightmares. A face that she had seen so often in her dreams; and one that she had come to dread.

"So, we meet in the flesh, at last. I'm so glad to see you here, believe me. I've been looking forward to this meeting, since long before you were even born."

"Dubhgall the Black!" Maerlin cursed. "How did you manage this?"

"I told you before, Maerlin, I'm the most powerful magician alive. I must admit, however, that it was you who helped me. I warned you that those stupid priestesses had led you astray. Now, they've giving you up as a sacrifice, while they hide away in their stinking swamp. They refuse to participate in the politics of Dragania, and so, they allowed you to be lured here. They left you without protection."

"I had Nessa!" Maerlin objected.

"Ah yes, the old hag. Tell me, Maerlin, where is the old crone now ... when you need her most?"

Maerlin glared at the Mage as she fought back tears. Her body had been wracked with cramps and headaches for days. She was feeling weak, but the mention of Nessa further deflated her waning spirit.

"She left you, didn't she? They all did. They didn't even give you a simple charm to mask your presence. They gave the prince some protection, but not you. They placed a ward on his father's dagger, so that I couldn't find him, but you ... you, they left as a lamb to be slaughtered," Dubhgall explained "You, they betrayed, and because of their incompetence, you have betrayed your companions. You've led them all here to their deaths."

Maerlin shuddered, knowing that the Mage's words were true. She had brought about Nessa's death, and now, the others would die because of her foolishness.

"Don't cry, Maerlin. I'll give you some good news. When I've finished here ... when I've defeated the Brocians and burned their precious woods to ashes, I'll march my army up the mountain, to that little hovel you once called home, and I'll raze the place to the ground. The whole village will be crucified for the pain that they have caused you. You see, Maerlin, I've watched you grow, and I know all about you."

Maerlin blinked back her tears and looked up at the Mage's gloating face. She pleaded "No ... not my father."

"Your father! Surely you don't still have feelings for that drunken fool! Where was he when you needed him most? He sold you off to the hags of the Isle. He hit you and he humiliated you in public. He scorned you and rejected you," yelled Dubhgall. "He's a maggot, and his death will be slow and painful. I promise you that!"

Dubhgall walked away, leaving Maerlin to sob as she hung dejectedly from her bindings. "Let the ceremony begin!" He commanded, waving some of the soldiers forward. "Bring me the witch-girl."

The Boarites grabbed Maerlin and unfastened her bindings. Gripping her firmly, they dragged her forward to where the Mage stood, waiting by the Maiden Stone.

"Leave her alone, you Boarite scumbag," Conal yelled. "Fight me instead, you yellow cowards."

Dubhgall grinned at him "Wait your turn, Dragon-boy. Your time is nearly upon you. But first, I'll start with the girl's sweet young flesh ..." Turning to the soldiers, he commanded "Strap her to the stone."

Terror filled Maerlin as she was lashed to the central stone. She was bound, hand and foot, spread-eagled across the cold granite.

"Have you ever wondered why this is called the Maiden Stone?" Dubhgall hissed into Maerlin's ear. "It was on this stone that powerful Mages slaughtered virgin sacrifices to the Elder god, *Crom Cruach*. He promised the magicians longevity, if they offered him worthy sacrifices. Only through the uncorrupted blood of the pure can the Ritual of Life be ensured. Your blood, and your fear, will seep into the stone to sate the ancient god's hunger, and your life-essence will soak into me. You will die, Maerlin ... so that I can live."

"No," Maerlin moaned. "Please, no!"

The raven flew off the Mage's shoulder and landed on the Maiden Stone, walking up the stone to look into Maerlin's eyes.

"Little Macha, you must wait to feast on her eyes," Dubhgall chided, playfully. "I need her to witness the horrors that I've planned for her, before you dine on her sweet orbs. Be patient, my pet."

The raven squawked in protest, flapping its wings as it hopped away from Dubhgall's outreaching hand. "You will have them soon enough, Little Macha. I promise you that," assured the Mage.

Giving up on catching the bird, Dubhgall signalled to the waiting soldiers. "Strip her," he ordered, as he turned away.

Maerlin's screams echoed across the plain as her clothes were roughly torn from her body. She wriggled and lashed out vainly at her tormentors.

The coldness of the stone seeped into her skin, making her shiver. Maerlin could hear her friends shouting protests, but the sounds were hollow, as if from a great distance. Her mind was retreating within itself, in an effort to shield her from the coming horrors. Would her death be quick and painless, or would the Dark Mage draw it out to savour her anguish, before she finally became the Macha's feast? Maerlin couldn't help but wonder. Her imagination tormented her with thoughts of all that was to come.

"Begin the ritual," ordered Dubhgall. He began to chant from the dark text in the ancient grimoire before him.

One of the soldiers stepped forward eagerly, hoping to gain the Mage's favour. He was a heavyset man with an ugly, pox-riddled face and small, beady eyes. His face was covered with bushy eyebrows and a greasy beard. Stepping up beside Maerlin, he leered down at her naked body, fuelling her apprehension.

"What a sweet little thing," he cooed, as he leaned forward and licked his sour-smelling tongue across her face. Maerlin gagged at the rank odour of his breath and struggled against the ropes that secured her to the Maiden Stone.

"Leave her alone, you motherless pig-swill!" Conal cursed.

The Mage stopped chanting for a moment and glared at Conal. "*MacDragan*, if you open your mouth again and interrupt me, I'll personally cut out your tongue and feed it to my raven. You can slowly choke on your blood while I watch." Dubhgall went back to his spell as Conal blanched, sure that the Mage would keep his promise.

The soldier pawed at Maerlin's naked body, leering at her suggestively.

Maerlin's skin writhed with revulsion as she watched her tormentor. "No!" she whined, struggling to break free. Her wrists and ankles bled where the ropes chaffed her skin, but her bonds remained tight.

All the while, Maerlin could hear Dubhgall's droning as he chanted his spell. The raven watched the soldier intently, perched beside Maerlin's head; its beady obsidian eyes never blinked.

The soldier clambered onto the stone. Maerlin could smell his rank, sweaty odour as he pressed his loathsome body down on top of her.

"Get off me, you rancid warthog," she cursed, struggling to dislodge him. His beady eyes grew more excited with each thrash of her body. Looking up at him filled her with dread. She could read his evil intent and it horrified her. Fighting back her growing terror, Maerlin looked away, wishing to hide herself away from his lecherous gaze. Her eyes were again drawn to those of the raven.

"Help!" she pleaded to no one in particular. No one could help her now.

Pain washed over her as the soldier thumped her in the rib cage.

"Pay attention, Witch-girl!" the Boarite growled. "I'm going to make you feel pain like you've never known it before."

Maerlin glared defiantly at him, drawing phlegm and spitting it directly into his face. Feeling her anger rising, she cursed "I hope you enjoy your time in the Nine Hells. I hear the demons can do unimaginable horrors to a man's soul."

This time, his punch caught her in the jaw; a hard, bone-shaking blow that made Maerlin's eyes water before she slipped into unconsciousness.

Her peace was short-lived, however. Warm liquid splashed across her face, and the acrid taste of urine filled her mouth, causing her to choke and gag. Desperately, she turned her face away from the flow, but couldn't prevent it hitting her cheek and upper body. The soldier had stood on the Maiden Stone and urinated on her to wake her up. Now he stood there, laughing at the horrified look on her face. "You're not getting away from me that easy. I need you wide awake while I work. You're not allowed to go to sleep on me."

Stooping, he raised his hand to his face and gathered up the phlegm deposited there and wiped it across Maerlin's thigh, grinning at her revulsion.

"What are you doing, you idiot?" Dubhgall roared "Can't you understand simple instructions, you great lummox? I want her to be in pain. Stop toying with her and hurt her, or I'll show you what I means by pain."

The soldier flinched away from the Mage's threat. He was well aware of the dangers of annoying the Dark Mage. Lifting his fist, he struck a sharp jab in her solar plexus making her gasp for breath and strain against her bonds.

"Pain! I want more pain!" Dubhgall demanded, coming closer. "Can't you do anything right?"

The Brocian rained blows down on Maerlin's body, while she thrashed about on the stone in an effort to rid herself of her tormentor. Dubhgall was standing beside the stone, yelling encouragement, when a flash of silver shimmered before his eyes. His looked down and noticed the silver pendant hanging around Maerlin's neck. His face blanched at the sight of the silver hawk. He gaped at it in astonishment, before staying the soldier's arm "Stop!" he commanded.

"What's the matter, Sire?"

Ignoring the brute, Dubhgall gripped Maerlin's hair and lifted her head off the Maiden Stone. "Where did you get this pendant?" he hissed angrily. He was clearly surprised by the sight of the silver medallion.

Merlin looked up at the Mage through swollen eyes. Images of her mother's face came to her, and with it, she found some defiance. "I thought you were the all-powerful Mage, Dubhgall. You should know that already. You must be slipping in your old age."

"Answer me, girl, while you still can!"

"Or what...? Are you going to have him beat me some more if I refuse?"

Dubhgall shook her violently. "Answer me!"

Maerlin glared at him with hate-filled eyes. She would not answer his question, no matter what he did.

Dubhgall slapped her already swollen cheek, before stomping back to his magical tome. It was as if a dark shadow of doubt hung around his heart. Something was clearly troubling him. Shaking off the moment of doubt, Dubhgall picked up his grimoire and commanded "Continue ..."

Maerlin's tormentor nodded and rained blows down on her body as the Mage's chanting again filled the air.

Her companions struggled as they watched Maerlin being systematically beaten. Vort growled menacingly as he strained against his bindings. They were becoming more bestial with every passing moment. As he started to Form-meld into his Totem-beast, one of the soldiers stepped forward and sharply rapped him over the head with the butt of his spear. Vort slumped against the dolmen, stunned.

Maerlin groaned and thrashed about on the Maiden Stone under the brutal treatment she was receiving. Her pleas for mercy fell on deaf ears. They merely goaded her torturer to greater cruelty. Lifting her hand, the Boarite prised one of Maerlin's fingers back slowly. He laughed loudly as she screamed out. A bone finally snapped under his pressure, and waves of pain flooded through Maerlin, as he wiggled the broken finger about. Maerlin's brain fled from the reality around her, as she slipped into shock.

Chapter Twenty-Eight: The Maiden Stone

"Maerlin!" a voice whispered urgently in her head. "Maerlin! Listen to me before it's too late."

Maerlin realised that she had been hearing the voice for some time. It was a niggling sound that had been there in the background, but she had not noticed it before.

"Maerlin!" the crackly voice repeated urgently.

"I'm dying," protested Maerlin, hoping for release from the constant pain. "Leave me alone."

"Maerlin, dear!" the voice chided "Will you stop this nonsense and listen to me?"

"Go away, Dubhgall!" Maerlin dismissed. "Let me die in peace."

"You're not going to die, Maerlin, so stop all the melodramatics!" the voice scolded sharply. The voice was getting stronger, now that Maerlin had acknowledged its existence.

"Who are you? Why are you bothering me?" Maerlin demanded as she floated in a sea of pain.

"You must stop this!" the voice persisted. "Pull yourself together, Maerlin."

"Leave me alone," moaned Maerlin. "I'll be dead soon, and then I'll be free."

"Oh really ... and what about the others? What about Conal? He'll suffer and die after you? Do you want that? What about all of your friends?"

"No! Leave me alone. I can't do anything to save them," Maerlin protested, but the presence in her mind continued to berate her.

"Don't you understand, Maerlin? The Mage is feeding on your fear and pain. It's making him younger by the moment. He'll continue to hurt you

until you prove to be of no more use to him. Then, he'll do the same to Conal ... and to Cora too, if she's captured."

"Cora? She's safe in the Broce Woods!" Maerlin objected. Concern for her friends drew her further away from her melancholy.

"Listen to me, dear. Cora is at Dragon's Ridge with the warriors of Clann Na Broce. The Mage has ordered her capture!"

Maerlin struggled to free herself from the invisible tormentor who probed at her weary brain and tortured her mind. "You're lying, Dubhgall. I know you too well. You're a serpent and a deceiver, and you have always lied to me. You've deceived me before with your illusions, but I can hear the hoarse cackle of your voice."

"You're wrong, Maerlin, and will you stop trying to dislodge me from your brain? It took me long enough to get in here in the first place." The voice sounded vaguely familiar to Maerlin.

Doubt still lurked in Maerlin's brain, but she refused to accept Dubhgall's tormenting. "Get away from me, Dubhgall. Leave me to die in peace."

The voice sighed and was silent for a moment.

Maerlin floated in peace and hoped that the Dark Mage had gone, but then the voice returned. "I know where that pendant came from, Maerlin. Dubhgall doesn't know that. Will that satisfy you?"

"Go away!" Maerlin was too weary to fight any further.

"I gave you that pendant when first we met. It was your mother's. You told me that it was her favourite piece of jewellery. I placed it around your neck before we left High Peaks."

"Nessa?" Maerlin still wondered if this was another one of the Mage's tricks.

"Hush, dear. He'll hear you, and he'll know where I've been hiding all this time."

"How do I know it's really you?" Maerlin demanded, still wary of any further tricks.

"I don't know how to assure you, dear. Listen to my words, and then listen to your heart. It will tell you whether I speak the truth or not."

"Okay," agreed Maerlin reluctantly. "Speak then or leave me be."

"Maerlin, you must block out the pain and get a hold on your fear. They are feeding the Dark Mage. You are making him stronger. Remember the lessons I taught you? Remember the exercise to control your temper? You must use that now and cut off his spell. He needs you to feel pain and fear for his spell to work. You must shut down that part of your brain. You must gain control over your inner-self."

Maerlin considered for a moment and decided that the advice seemed logical. "Nessa, is it really you?"

"Please dear! Don't use my name. It will warn him if he is listening," Nessa warned.

"Where are you? Where have you been?"

"Stop with all the silly questions and focus on your exercises. You're feeding him too much of your power!"

"But why don't you help me?" Maerlin protested. "I'm useless at this sort of thing. Something always goes wrong."

"I can't help you, dear. You must do this yourself. I know what you can do, and you can do this if you follow my directions."

"I can't!"

"YOU MUST! This is your only chance; and the only chance for the others, too. Only you can do this."

Maerlin tried to clear her mind and form the white wall, but the torture was constantly interrupting her concentration. Waves of pain washed through her body as her tormentor broke more of her fingers. "I can't!" she cried. "It hurts too much!"

"Whatever happened to that spirited girl I met in the mountains? Is this the girl who fought off the bullies and stood her ground? Where has that girl gone?" Nessa scorned, goading her to try harder.

Maerlin tried again and managed to get halfway through the exercise before it fell apart.

"Try harder!" Nessa urged.

Maerlin began again. Finally, she found herself in the place of calm at the centre of her being. Sitting there was Nessa MacTire.

"Hush! Don't even think my name," urged Nessa as she silently hugged Maerlin.

"It's so good to see you. I thought you were dead."

"I think I was," murmured Nessa, deciding to leave further explanations for another time. "Now listen carefully for our time is short. If Dubhgall stops chanting, he'll notice that I'm here and I'll be dead for sure."

Nessa instructed her apprentice on what needed to be done.

*****

Cora was startled to hear voices in her head. At first, she put it down to the strange root that Orla had given her, but when the High Priestess called her, she realised that she wasn't hallucinating.

"Ceila?"

"At last, Cora, canst thou hear me?"

"Yes, Ceila, where are you?"

"Listen to me, Cora, we haven't got much time."

Orla glanced over at Cora, startled to hear the novice talking to herself, but her attention was drawn away as a Boarite charged forward, his sword swinging wildly before him.

Orla dropped the reins and charged. Knocking the conscript's sword aside with a sweep of her spear, she spun it quickly around and rammed the blunt end into his face. As his hands rose to protect his head, Orla spun and thrust the spear point into his belly. Another Boarite appeared, yelling at the top of his lungs as he charged forward. He had hoped to frighten Orla, but she had been well trained. Deftly, she yanked her spear free and cast it at the charging soldier. He was knocked onto his back by the impact. The heavy spear had bit through his light armour and pierced his heart, killing him instantly.

Others charged forward and Orla drew her *Tri-crub* in readiness. Crouching, she waited for the first of them to come within range of her wickedly-sharp daggers. Soon, Orla was fighting for her life, and Cora was forgotten.

Cora's horse skittered away across the battlefield, unguided by its rider. The novice was too intent on the conversation in her head, as the High Priestess explained to her the merits of magnesium and its magical attributes in producing bright light.

"Listen!" Cora demanded. "I don't care what's causing the lights. How do we put them out?"

The voices in her head argued amongst themselves, seeking a solution.

"Cora, I'm afraid we don't know. Thou needeth a means of negate it."

"What about fog? Would that do it?"

"Yes, yes. That'd be a possibility!" Ceila agreed, above the babble of other voices in Cora's mind. *"Is there a river nearby or a well?"*

Cora focused her mind and searched for water. Being a Water-sister, she soon found the small brook, which ran down from the ridge. She focused on the water, ignoring the battle around her as she summoned her Wild-magic.

"Come, Spirits of the water. Come to my aid," she urged. When she could feel the Elementals around her, she pictured steam.

"No, Cora. That'll take too long. Try doing it this way, instead." She recognised the voice of her tutor, Madame Muir.

An image filled her mind, an image of mist and fog. It was much clearer than her inexperienced image. She smiled and released the image on the Elementals she had summoned.

The fog descended quickly, thick and blinding; negating the bright light enough to make it a background glare. Although it did not give the Brocians the advantage of darkness, it made it hard for anyone to see as both sides were blinded by the fog. Harsh barking began, as warrior-captains rallied their men for an assault on the Boarite defences.

"I've done it! It's working!" Cora exclaimed, as enthusiasm overcame her.

"Wait, child. Don't get over-confident. This is but the first round. They will try to destroy the mists. Thou must concentrate and hold the mists steady! Move away from the fighting and find someplace safe. Dubhgall won't take long to counter-attack."

Cora did as she was bid, but even as she moved back through the throng of fighters, she could feel the breeze picking up around her, breaking her mists into tatters. Quickly, she urged the horse on, no longer sidestepping the dying and dead at her feet in her hurry to find safer ground.

"Hurry, child. It's breaking up!" Ceila urged, though Cora did not need to be told.

Another voice came to her mind, one of the Air-sisters. It gave her instructions on how to slow the breeze down. She would need to bring a cold front in from the south, to counter the warm air coming down from the ridge. She must summon the Air Elementals from nearer the Broce Woods towards her, and counter the magical wind.

Carefully, for she was not within her own realm of Wild-magic, Cora followed the guided instructions and pulled the air northwards, slowing the breeze that was being forced down from the ridge.

Things stabilized again as the north and south winds met and lost impetus. The mist lessened, but enough of it still remained to diminish the harsh lights. From what little Cora could make out before her, relief filled her heart, as the battle turned once more in the favour of the Brocians.

Although outnumbered by the Boarite conscripts, the warriors of *Clann Na Broce* fought with greater courage and were inflicting fierce damage upon the army of Lord Boare. The Boarites, however, had nowhere to retreat, for behind them stood Dragon's Ridge, and upon its crown sat the ruins of *Dun Dragan*. With no retreat possible, the conscripts were forced to stand their ground. It was becoming a vicious and desperate fight, with neither side yielding. Cora was forced to stand and watch the battle, using her magically enhanced vision to keep track of the combat as the fog settled again over the battle.

350

Suddenly, the wind picked up again, much stronger this time, buffeting at the masking fog and ripping it asunder. One moment, the air had been still, and the next, the wind was screaming loudly across the battlefield.

Cora looked for the source of the breeze, but it lacked any clear direction. It was as if the very air itself was battling against some chaotic force. Something, or someone, was creating a wild vortex of energy. Cora was baffled at the complex lines of energy within the Air Elementals and called out to calm them "Spirits of Air come to my aid!" she urged again and again, but her pleas were ignored. She could feel her control over the Elementals slipping quickly away.

"Try to produce more mist. It's breaking up," urged the voices in her head, though they also sounded confused. She could hear them arguing in the background, as one suggestion after another, intruded on her concentration.

Shutting them out, Cora focused on the water and tried to summon some Elementals, but even her beloved Undines refused to do her bidding.

"What's happening?" Cora asked in panic when even her Water Elementals were ignoring her.

"We don't know, Cora," Ceila replied *"Some powerful magic is being created to the north of the Ridge, but we cannot see what it is. It's hidden from us."*

"Maerlin!" Cora guessed. Grabbing the horse's reins, she kneed the horse into motion *"It must be Maerlin. I'm going to help her."*

"No, Cora! Thou must stay here with the Brocians," Ceila urged *"The others will be with her; if indeed it is her that is causing this. This could be Dubhgall the Black's work. Only he could amass such awesome power."*

Cora ignored the High Priestess's warning and urged her horse into a gallop. She raced northwards, through the mist and into the darkness beyond. As she rode beyond the battlefield, she could see a beacon of bright light ahead and knew that this was the burial mound. Instinct told her that Maerlin was in trouble, and she urged the horse on to even greater speed.

*****

Nessa's instructions had been very specific. She had directed Maerlin to hold the energy within her for as long as possible. Maerlin could feel it building up until she feared that she would burst apart. Every nerve tingled with static charge, and her body twitched with uncontrollable spasms. Nessa had warned her to hold it back for as long as possible, before releasing her pent-up power. This way, she would deny Dubhgall the time he needed to counter her attack. Surprise was her best weapon.

Now Maerlin was ready. Her very spirit sang with the built-up power and her skin had begun to glow. The hairy brute on top of her sensed a change, but initially he ignored it. He presumed that it was all part of the Mage's magic. Maerlin had been lying still and catatonic for some time, and her tormentor had continued his task with enthusiastic gusto. However, as her body glowed brighter and began to heat up, sweat running from her every pore, the soldier paused and looked doubtfully towards the Mage.

Dubhgall was too engrossed in his spell to notice. Only the black-eyed raven gazed back at the soldier with cold, dark eyes. Those eyes searched deep into his soul, as if Macha herself was inspecting a coming harvest. He sensed the raven's antipathy, but dared not strike at the Mage's bird. He did not want to suffer the wrath of the Dark Mage.

Maerlin raised her head and looked at her tormentor, and the eyes that glared into the soldier's were as dark and tempestuous as a winter storm. Summoning a tiny portion of her amassed power, Maerlin released a Salamander. Her bindings burned instantly to cinders as the Salamander rushed to do her bidding. Free at last, Maerlin called to the Fire Elemental and cradled it in her palm. Her hand writhed with flames as she rose up and slapped the soldier across the face. "Burn, you bastard!"

The Boarite screamed piteously. His beard and eyebrows were quickly engulfed in flames. He tried desperately to swat the Salamander away, but the Elemental clung to his face and glowed brightly as it consumed his flesh. Within moments, his eyeballs had exploded, and his brain was melting within his skull. Maerlin cast the soldier's corpse away from her and rose to her feet.

The dying man's scream had broken Dubhgall's concentration. He turned around to look for the cause. To his surprise, he found Maerlin standing naked on the Maiden Stone, looking balefully at him. Her hair had become unravelled from their braids and stood like a wild corona around her head.

352

"You're free!" he gasped in surprise.

"You're going to pay for this, Dubhgall," Maerlin promised as she released some of her pent-up magical rage. The air shuddered as she released the gathered Elementals. They swirled around her in wild abandon, awaiting her command. "Bring on the storm" she growled ominously, her voice rumbling like thunder.

The air cracked loudly overhead, echoing for miles across the plains. The battle to the south stopped as the very ground trembled. The heavens erupted with clash after clash of angry thunder. The first drops of rain fell on the battlefield, and the fighters from both sides looked up in fear at the angry skies.

"That's a pretty little display of pyrotechnics!" Dubhgall sneered. Pointing his hand at Maerlin, he uttered the words of command and prepared to release a spell.

The raven, which had been perched on the edge of the Maiden Stone, shot into the air like an arrow. In the blink of an eye, it launched itself at Dubhgall's face. It struck out with its long razor-sharp beak, pecking furiously at the Mage. Striking with the speed of a viper, it pecked at one of the orbs.

Screaming with pain and surprise, Dubhgall's spell dissipated as his hands came up to protect his face. The raven pulled the eyeball free of the socket and quickly swallowed it, continuing to flap and claw at the Mage's face. It squawked and battered its wings against him in a fury of defiance, as Dubhgall tried to knock it away. "Little Macha! What are you doing?"

Desperately, Dubhgall blasted fire at the raven to knock the enraged bird away.

Maerlin heard a shriek of pain as her mental image of Nessa erupted in flames. She now realised where Nessa had been hiding all this time. "Nessa! No!"

Pure unfettered rage burst forth from within Maerlin, releasing her from any constraints or doubts in her own ability. Her very being seethed with the urge to kill Dubhgall, and the summoned Elementals were eager to do her bidding.

Lightning blasted the ground around Dubhgall's feet. It was all the Mage could do to deflect the worst of the energy away from him. He didn't have time to counter her constant barrage of attacks. The vast quantity of magical energy built up within Maerlin and fuelled by her anger continued to pour forth. Bolt after bright bolt rained from the thunderous sky down upon the Mage. Dubhgall, half blinded and caught off-guard, was unable to deflect them all. One bolt, and then another, struck home, knocking him backwards. His hair singed to powder in an instant, and his rich, dark robes burst into flames as he attempted to ward off the falling streaks of pure energy.

Rage boiled over in Maerlin, and she continued to blast away, forcing him farther back as she struck, again and again. Pulling her depleting energy together, she raised her arms high and sent a final huge blast of lightning towards the Mage's chest.

Seeing the bolt coming, Dubhgall made a vain attempt to divert the blow. As the bolt struck his already-weakened magical shield, it erupted in an explosion of sparks. The mighty blast momentarily blinded and deafened everyone on the mound. The Mage was lifted off his feet by the power of the blow and was hurled backwards off the burial mound. He crashed onto the grassland below, a smouldering heap of burned rags and charred flesh.

Thunder crashed overhead, as if in applause at the Mage's death, or in joy at being given this much freedom. The wind sang Maerlin's praise in haunting howls as it skimmed around the Twelve Warriors and pulled at her wild tresses.

The Boarites turned and fled from the mound. They were terrified of being the next to suffer her deadly attention. Maerlin, however, had other things on her mind. She focused her waning energies on the ropes that bound her friends to the standing stones.

"Release them," she ordered, and Salamanders ate along the ropes. Free at last, Maerlin's companions rushed over. First to her side was the gentle-hearted bard. Quickly, he gathered up a fallen cloak and covered her nakedness, his eyes wet with tears. "I'm sorry, Maerlin. I couldn't stop them."

Maerlin was exhausted, but she managed a weak smile in response. Fighting back the waves of pain from her broken hands, she remembered Nessa's words. "There's a battle being fought on Dragon's Ridge," she managed, as she slid to the ground. *"Clann Na Broce* may need your help. The battle hangs on a knife-edge."

They wondered how Maerlin knew this, as they looked over to the distant glow on the Dragon's Ridge. Vort was the first to act and grabbing his *Tri-crub* from the discarded weaponry, he hurried off to aid his clansmen. Cull quickly followed, taking his own weapons from the pile. Conal's jaw was set in determination as he walked over and picked up his father's sword: *An Fiacail Dragan*. Pulling it from its sheath, the blade glowed brightly in the magical lights as if pulsing with inner life. With a nod to the bard, he set off after the others. Taliesin hung back, not wanting to leave Maerlin alone.

As if reading his mind, she smiled weakly. "Go, Taliesin. A great battle is being fought, and they'll need a bard to record their deeds of valour. Go, and be at the prince's side. I'm in no danger now."

Taliesin hesitated for only a moment longer, still unsure. Finally, with a sigh, he rose, and carrying his harp, he raced after the others.

Maerlin was alone and totally exhausted. Her mind was numb from the magical battle, but she could not lie down and sleep; not yet. Her legs were like rubber as she climbed to her feet, using the Maiden Stone for support. Once upright, she pushed herself away from the stone and headed off.

"Nessa." she called out as she stumbled along. No answer came. "Nessa! Where are you?"

She found the raven at last, lying by one of the dolmen. Smoke drifted up from the charred body.

"Oh Nessa!" Maerlin moaned as she lifted up the raven and cradled it to her bosom. "Don't die on me, Nessa, please don't die."

The bird lay motionless in her hands and fearing the worse, she inspected it. She had only been taught a little of the Healing Arts during her time on the Holy Isle, but one thing she remembered. All living things have an aura about them, which fades quickly after death. It was this aura that she was seeking now, and after a moment, she found it. It was a weak pulsing blue energy, deep within the bird, and it was fading rapidly.

"Oh no, you don't!" Maerlin murmured resolutely as she focused her depleted magical energy. "You'll not get away from me that easy, Nessa *Mac Tire*."

Wiping the tears from her eyes, she poured the last of her magic into the bird, sending healing energy into its failing body. A soft, raspy caw came from the singed body. Cradling the charred bird against her breast to keep it warm, Maerlin collapsed onto the ground. "Praise be to Deanna."

Her mind was completely drained by the ordeal, and she slipped into a deep sleep of utter exhaustion.

Chapter Twenty-Nine: The Shadow of Death

The moon rose over the horizon as Cora galloped recklessly across the plain. Her eyes were focused only on the light in the distance. She murmured again and again "I'm coming, Maerlin. I'm coming."

Her horse suddenly emitted a scream of pain, a loud shriek of protest as a spear struck it in the chest. It stumbled as the second spear pierced its neck, moments later. Cora was flung clear, as the horse fell and thrashed about on the ground in its death throes.

Hands grabbed her as she was struggling to her feet. She managed to scream only once before an armoured fist hammered into her temple, and Cora slipped into unconsciousness.

"Tie her up and gag her," ordered the leader of the unit. "You'd best blindfold her, too. You all saw what that other one was capable of. Let's not take any chances with this one."

"Are you sure that this isn't some Brocian bitch, Captain? She's dark enough to be one of them Pects."

Cora was quickly but thoroughly searched.

"Look ... here's her shell necklace, just like the Mage described."

"We should slit her throat. It'd be safer that way."

"Gebitt, you always were an idiot, do you know that. The Dark Mage told us he wanted her alive."

"Yes, but Dubhgall's dead, Captain. We all saw him blasted to pieces by that witch-girl!"

"I now know why you've been a private for so long, Gebitt. If the Mage thought this witch was valuable, then I'm sure his acolytes will view her of equal value. Dubhgall may be dead, but sorcerers are like rats. When their leader dies, the rest of them will fight over the picking. Eventually, a new leader will emerge. I'm sure we'll be well rewarded by whoever takes over."

"But she could kill us all," protested Gebitt.

"Not if we're careful, she won't. Now, do as I told you and hurry up about it. This place could be crawling with Brocians at any moment. I don't know about you lot but I want to be safely up on the ridge before that happens."

As he said this, a howling echoed across the grassland, coming from the battlefield. It was a dreadful baying that made their blood run cold.

"What, in the Nine Hells, was that?" Gebitt asked nervously.

"I don't know and I don't want find out. Hurry it up, Gebitt."

The baying grew louder as other voices took up the call. Soon, the whole plain was reverberated with the haunting sound. As the soldiers blindfolded Cora, the sound faded as suddenly as it had begun. In its place was total and absolute silence.

"Come on!" the Captain ordered nervously.

Gebitt grunted as he lifted Cora onto his shoulder.

Out of the darkness, a lone figure appeared like an apparition. He fell on the nearest of the Elites with wild ferocity.

"Brocians!" the captain warned, drawing his sword. Vort hurtled forward as if possessed. His triple-bladed *Tri-crub* swirling around him as he danced through the soldiers like a tornado, leaving death in his wake.

Cull emerged from the darkness. Although he didn't fight with the same reckless abandon as the Brocian, he was, nonetheless, a brutally efficient killer.

The captain tried to rally his men, but panic had set in, and many turned and fled into the darkness hoping to escape the razor-sharp teeth of the Brocian's blades and his companion's lethal swordplay.

Gebitt tried to run, dropping Cora as he fled. He only managed to run three paces, however, before another figure emerged from the darkness in front of him. He saw the glowing blade whistle towards him as he struggled to draw his own sword free from its scabbard. The magical blade bit cleanly through his armour and into his chest.

Too shocked to even feel the pain, Gebitt looked down at the legendary sword of the High Kings, still sheathed in his body. His own weapon slipped from his dying hand.

"DRAGAN ABÚ!" Conal yelled the war cry of his ancestors at the top of his lungs. His eyes were ablaze with anger. His mind kept replaying Maerlin's torture at the hands of the Boarite, and this fuelled his rage, as it had for Vort and Cull.

As Gebitt slid to his knees, Conal pulled his blade free, and with a powerful backhand sweep of his arm, he cleaved the soldier's head from his shoulders. It rolled across the ground to where the Boarite captain was standing before his remaining soldiers.

Realising that the fight was lost, the Captain threw down his sword in an attempt to surrender. Vort and the others fell upon them in a berserker-like frenzy. No mercy was given, as the three men sought to banish the horrors they had witnessed earlier in the night.

Within moments, the final Boarite fell, and the night became still. It was only then, as the heat of battle cooled in their veins, that Conal noticed the captive, trussed up nearby. Hurrying forward, he pulled away the blindfold. "Cora!"

Cora had come to, a few moments earlier, and had been shaking with fear at the sounds of battle around her. She blinked a few times, unable to comprehend her rescuers. When the prince removed her gag, she almost wept with relief. "Conal, oh, Conal!" she gasped, and wrapped her arms around him "Thank the goddess you're alive."

Taliesin limped out of the darkness. "What's happening?"

"Taliesin, I thought you'd stayed with Maerlin. What happened to you?" Cull asked.

"Some idiot left a dead horse lying around. I tripped over it in the darkness and twisted my ankle," Taliesin complained.

Cora looked around. "Maerlin, where's Maerlin?"

Taliesin pointed towards the mound.

Conal helped Cora to her feet. "Are you all right?"

"I'm fine. I'm just a bit dazed, that's all. I need to get to Maerlin though. I think she needs me."

"Taliesin will take you to her," advised Cull. "We need to get to the battle."

"It's too late for that now," Vort told them. "The battle's over."

"What do you mean, it's over?" Cull asked.

"Didn't you hear them calling?" Vort explained.

*****

"Orla!" Aiden called again, as he searched the battlefield.

"I'm over here, Father." Orla hurried to his side.

"Where's Cora?" he asked. "I thought you were protecting her."

"I was, but I got ambushed by some Boarites, and by the time I'd managed to break free, she was gone. She was there one moment and gone the next. She disappeared into the mist. I've been looking for her ever since."

"Well, it's too late for that now. We'll need to get out of here."

"We can't leave her. She might be in danger."

"Orla, look ... the moon is rising! We must leave now!"

"But ... what about your son?"

The burden of leadership fell heavily upon the old Brocian's shoulders as he replied "Vort will have to look after himself. The Clan must reach the safety of the woods before first light."

Orla bit her lip, silencing her protest. She knew that Aiden was right.

Aiden raised his cupped his hands to his face and let out a long, mournful bark of command. This, he repeated a number of times until it was taken up by those around them.

Warriors raised their voices in response, a eulogy to their fallen comrades. The sound echoed across the battlefield as the Brocians pulled away from combat and slipped into the darkness. Within moments the battle was over.

The Brocians carried their dead and dying with them as they hurried south, to the safety of their woods. The Boarites refused to follow them into the darkness.

*****

"What calling … you mean that howling? Has your Clan lost? It sounds so haunting."

"No, Cull, they've left the battlefield. They sing to the souls of the fallen before they go. They sing to honour their dead."

"Have the Brocians been defeated?" Conal asked.

"...Only by the moon. They cannot fight an army of Boarites in daylight. The Boare's cavalry would mow them down before they reached the safety of the woods. They left, so that they could live to fight another night."

"That sounds like a good plan. Come on. We'd better get back to Maerlin. If the battle's over, we'll need to find somewhere to hide before sunrise," Cull ordered.

*****

As the moon rose higher to light up the plain, a new army arrived. This army swooped down like wraiths, falling on the dead with raucous cawing. Macha had summoned her ravens to the feast. The goddess of war continued farther, leaving her Dark Angels to harvest the dead on the battlefield. She had other matters to attend to.

Flying beyond the battlefield, she landed on the Maiden Stone and looked around. She inspected the fallen raven closely, sensing the touch of her sister on the bird. It was close to death, clinging to life by the frailest of threads. Flying closer, she readied herself to retrieve the soul within.

"No, Macha ... Stay thy hand. I still have use of this one." Her sister spoke to her from out of the darkness.

"So be it, Deanna-sister," Macha replied "But there is a price to be paid, not only for her life, but also for the form she hides within. She cannot be one of my Dark Angels and serve another."

Summoning her powers, she sent her will towards the disguised priestess of Deanna. The frail-looking bird glowed for a moment as the magical energy pulsed within. Where once a burned raven lay, there now lay the piebald cousin of the carrion bird; the magpie. Although now fully healed and glossy feathered, the bird still remained unconscious.

"Let this be a reminder, Sister-mine. I will grant thee this boon, but she wilt be forever tainted by my blessing. From now on, she must serve two mistresses, both light and dark."

Silence hung in the air, before Deanna reluctantly replied "Agreed."

Macha's gaze fell on the face of the novice. Her eyes read Maerlin's destiny. "Thou hast placed a dreadful burden in such tiny hands, Sister-mine. Art thou sure that she is up to thy task?"

Deanna did not reply. She had already gone.

Macha heard feet approaching and turned to view the newcomers through large ebony eyes.

Vort halted when he noticed the gigantic raven. He whispered a silent prayer to Cernunnos, the god of the hunt, for protection. Cull, who arrived next, had no love of carrion birds and marched boldly forward. He was concerned for Maerlin's safety with the monstrous bird so close.

"Shoo!" he shouted. The goddess ignored him. She had come here for a reason, and she would not be harried by a mere mortal.

"Get away!" Cull brandished his sword, threateningly.

"No, Cull!" Vort warned.

Cull stepped closer, and the huge raven turned and peered deep into his soul. He shivered as fear raced up his spine. His sword arm froze.

"Leave it be, Cull."

Cull shook as he tried to strike the bird, but his arm refused to respond. Sweat trickled down his brow as he fought against the will of a goddess.

"Shoo!" he gasped weakly. The command was hardly audible through his clenched teeth.

"Be still, Mortal, lest I tire of thee and thy prattle. If this was the girl's time, she would already be mine. It is another I seek."

Cull blanched, not believing he could hear her voice in his head.

Macha's eyes turned away, releasing Cull from her hold as she probed beyond, into the darkness. She took to wing, flying to the entrance to the burial mound. There, she found the charred remains that she had been seeking.

"Ah! There thou art, manling!" Macha cawed, letting her voice seep into the faint remaining consciousness inside the burnt-out shell of Dubhgall the Black.

He did not answer. His life was slipping away fast.

"Carrion-eater, hast thou finally given up with thy pathetic lust for life?" she mocked the carcass, taunting the weakened spirit within. There was no answer, but for just a moment she saw his aura blaze brightly. Macha clacked her beak as she laughed at his continued struggle with mortality.

"There's a price for life, mortal," Macha cackled. In one swift motion, her head swooped down and stabbed at his charred face, scooping out the remaining orb. Quickly, the goddess lifted her head, and the glistening eyeball slid from view. *"There is always a price to pay for worshipping me, manling."*

Macha hopped onto the burnt remains of the Mage, and her razor sharp claws bit deep into his charred flesh. Spreading her immense wings, she gripped the carcass and rose into the night sky.

Cull and the others hurried to Maerlin's side, forgetting about the gigantic raven as soon as she had disappeared from their sight.

"Maerlin!" Cora exclaimed, lifting her head gently. "Maerlin!"

Maerlin was catatonic. In the eerie magical light, she looked pale and wraith-like. Cull stepped closer and felt for a pulse. "She still lives."

Her skin was cold and slick to his touch. It was only then that Cull noticed the magpie, cradled in her arms.

"What's this?" Cora asked. She lifted the magpie gently from Maerlin's grasp. "It's alive, but it's as far away from us as Maerlin is."

"Kill it," urged Cull. "Magpies are thieves and pranksters. It bodes ill to have it lying beside Maerlin."

"No, Cull ... wait," Cora insisted. "There's more to this than meets the eye. I sense that the bird is linked to Maerlin in some way. If you harm it, you could harm Maerlin too. I will need to seek Ceila's advice on this."

"We haven't got time for that, now. We need to get away from here," Vort urged, sensing the subtle change in the colour of the darkness. "It'll be dawn soon."

Cull lifted up Maerlin's frail body. "Very well, I'll carry her."

"We can use some of these discarded spears and a cloak to make a stretcher," Vort suggested. Cull nodded agreement.

Cora returned the Magpie to Maerlin's breast and wrapped the cloak about them. Although Cull shuddered with revulsion at the sight of the bird, he refrained from any further objections.

Quickly, they gathered their belongings and headed north, towards the Great Pectish Mountain Range. They hoped to find safety before the mists of dawn cleared. They needed to find a place to hide for the winter.

And so ends Book One of the Storm-Bringer Saga

*****

Other books by the same Author:

The Storm-Bringer Saga-Book One:

The Storm-Bringer Saga-Book Two:

The Storm-Bringer Saga- Book Three:

(Due for release in the summer of 2014)

Learn more on:

https://www.facebook.com/StormbringerSaga

And on my website: www.navlogan.com

Glossary

For a full glossary of the Storm-Bringer Saga go to: -
http://navlogan.wordpress.com/2013/10/16/glossary-of-the-storm-
bringer-saga/

*****

A Final Note from the Author

Thank you very much for taking the time to read this book. I hope that you enjoyed it and that the story has lived up to your expectations.

With my profound thanks.

Nav

About the Author

Many years ago, when I was just a small boy gazing in wonder at his first pubic hair, I decided that I was going to become a tramp. I was going to drop out and go to Strathclyde. Why Strathclyde, many asked? God only knows, but every man must have a goal in life. Being an engineer or a pilot didn't cut it for me. My soul was filled with wanderlust and the need for adventure.

So, after leaving home, I dropped out. I even went to Strathclyde, passing through it in a sleepy haze while being rocked gently to slumber in the passenger seat of an unknown truck.

Since then, I have done many things and seen many places, always following my instincts and trusting in my destiny. I am self taught in many things, a jack of all trades and a master at none, but I've always got by. A strong self belief, confidence, and my stubborn Ulster will, has brought me through many adversities. I try to be the best I can be and often fail, but I continue, nevertheless.

I have been writing since I was that small boy, my mind always wandering. Mainly, it has been poems and the occasional short story. Maerlin's Storm was first written over a decade ago. It wasn't something I planned to do. I didn't wake up and say, I am going to be an author; far from it. Like many things in my life, it all started with a dream. The next morning, I wrote a poem about it. Later, the poem became a story. It grew from a small seed and suddenly became a beanstalk. People read it and enjoyed it, but then life became busy again, and for many years the story sat, collecting dust.

I tried writing a follow up, but it initially petered out due to other commitments. It would have stayed on the shelf, forgotten, but for my wife. She bought me a Kindle. (She may live to regret that moment of madness, but I love her dearly for it).

Made in the USA
Charleston, SC
08 March 2014